SUBVERSION

Ian Sutherland

SUBVERSION

Vindigo
PRESS

First published as Featherstream in 2018
by Vindigo Press Cape Town, South Africa
vindigo.press@gmail.com

First edition 2018
Reprinted 2019
Republished as Subversion
Second edition 2022

ISBN: 978-0-6397-2962-6 (print)
ISBN: 978-0-6397-2963-3 (ebook)

Front cover photographs by Unsplash: Elia Pellegrini and
Amanda Mocci; shutterstock: Claire Slingerland
Back cover photograph by Unsplash: Joshua Earle
Cover design by Monique Cleghorn
Typesetting by Andy Thesen
Set in Stone

Printed and bound by Novus Cape Town

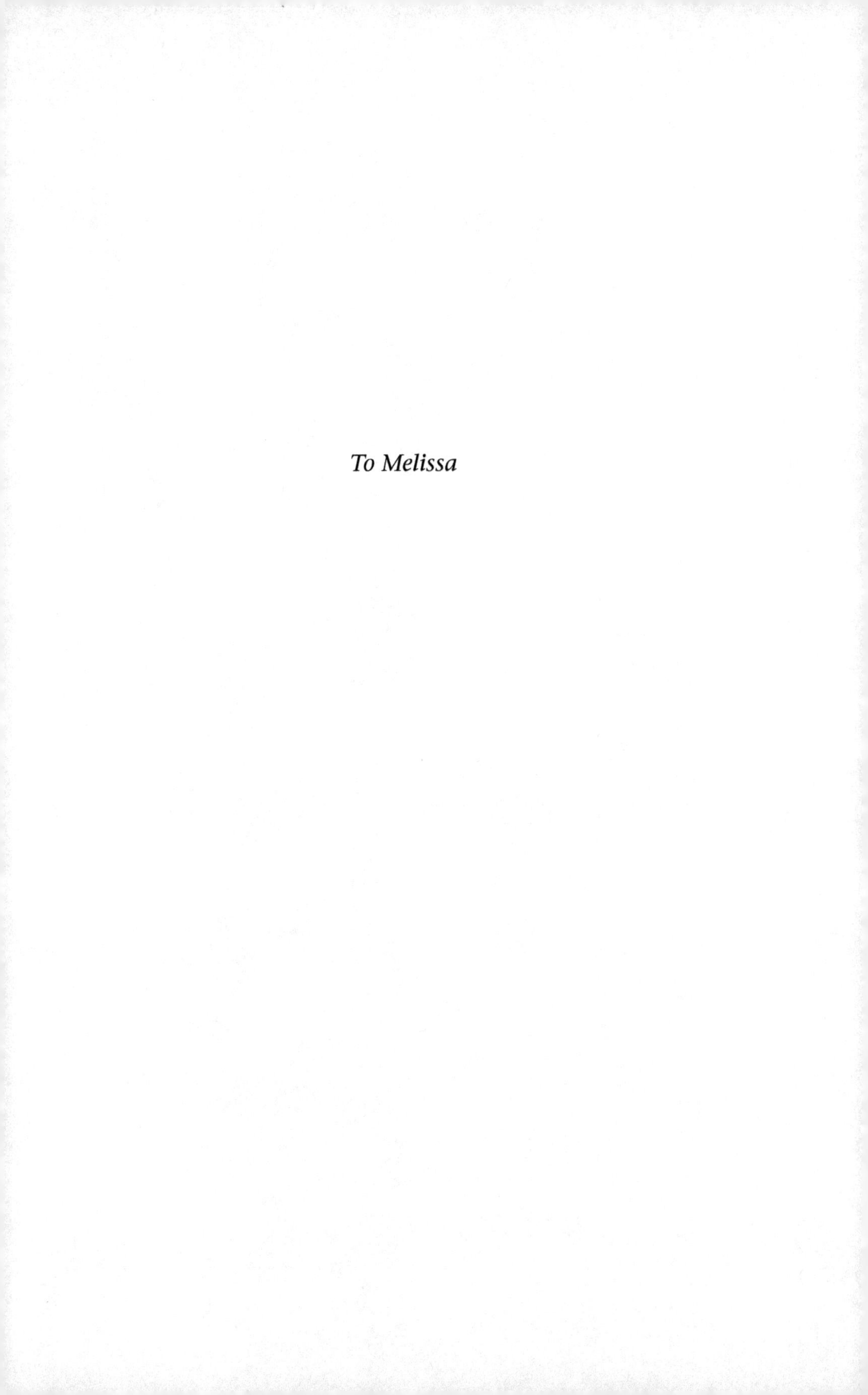

To Melissa

1

RATTLING ALONG THE JEEP track towards the foot of Africa, dread began to displace Anna's joy as the bakkie passed the first signpost to Rietvlei. Five hours had passed since they set out from the ivy walls of her university residence in Cape Town to cross Sir Lowry's Pass and the Overberg's sea of wheat; two since the town of Napier disappeared behind the Akkedisberg.

"I can smell Aasfontein's kelp," Anna said, turning to Kleinjan as they crossed the first firebreak that ran from the slopes of the Soetanysberg across the *fynbos* fields to the coast.

"Ja," he turned his gaze towards her from the penumbra of the bakkie's headlights, cracking a wide smile. His face was barely higher than the dashboard and dark as the sky. "We're making good time."

"Watch out!" she said as a pair of marble eyes glinted ahead.

He braked and they lurched left, straightened, and veered right. There was a thud on the undercarriage and they shuddered to a standstill in a drift of sand.

Anna got out and dropped to her haunches beside a crumple of fur and limbs that a minute earlier had borne the spirit of a Cape hare. "*Siestog.*" She stroked the animal's head, muttered a prayer and looked up sadly.

"Sorry, Miss Anna." Kleinjan took off his cap, dropped his

chin to his chest and stood silent.

"My fault," she said. "I distracted you."

Kleinjan dragged the hare off the track and started to scrape a depression in the sand.

"Ag, keep it for your pot." She wrapped her arms about herself against the chill. "It's dead now."

Kleinjan looked up through the yellow of his eyes. "Thank you," he said. "Hannah will like that." He tossed the body onto the back of the bakkie. "She makes a lekker rabbit *bredie*."

"I've heard." Anna picked the stem of an erica as she climbed back into the bakkie, twirling its head of miniature pantaloons and holding them to her nose. "It would be nice to try it some time."

"I won't tell Papa," she said as they rumbled on toward the spread of the ocean. "He gets so upset about Dries Roux's poaching, he might get the wrong idea."

"Thank you, Miss Anna. Did you hear Dries shot another leopard? Said it took six lambs in a week." He paused. "Sorry, I shouldn't have told you."

"No. That's what I like about you and me, Kleinjan. No secrets."

"Hey, look over there." Something had caught her eye. The water beyond the breakers was smooth and lumpy and shimmered beneath an almost full moon. "Did you see those flashing lights? Stop a moment. Let's see if they come again."

Kleinjan coasted the truck to a halt in a patch of grass to the side of the track. "A ship, maybe?"

"Not likely. Wasn't there talk of dimouts along the coast? At sea at least."

"Ag, I almost forgot. The politicians were arguing about that. Anyway, what's there to bomb out here on the *vlaktes*? Come, Miss Anna. Baas Stefan will be angry if we arrive very late."

"He doesn't even know we're coming tonight, remember."

"That's the problem," said Kleinjan. "He always wants to know what's going on. He'll blame me. He'll ..."

"I'll handle him, I promise."

"It isn't that simple. You know what happens ..."

Anna pulled her shoulders back, her blouse straining across her breasts as she ran her hands through her hair. It was as dark as the shadows and longer than she'd ever worn it. "I've grown up a lot this year, you know. I'll be twenty in March month, can you believe it?"

"*Yoh*. That's still young."

"Not really," she sighed. "Most women my age are married."

"It will happen. Don't worry. Just be careful when Baas Stefan is angry, is all I say. Even your mother …"

"What about her?"

"Nothing." Kleinjan fiddled with the key.

"Say what you have to," Anna said. "Mama's been dead ten years. I'm a big girl now."

The starter motor whined but the engine wouldn't take. He tried again with the same result. "It's just … sometimes … I never saw anything myself. Just the shouting."

On the third attempt, the engine took. The bakkie growled and juddered but went nowhere.

Leaving the engine idling, Kleinjan hopped out, grabbed a spade from behind his seat and cleared sand from the front of each tyre. Then he broke handfuls of thatch from the side of the road and wedged them in front of the wheels. Back in his seat, he rammed the gear lever into first and they wobbled out of the sand, protea branches grating against the side of the bakkie.

After a minute of bumping along, Anna said, "You were saying?"

"I've said enough. My job, Miss …"

"*Jong*. You've worked at Rietvlei for twenty years. Hannah's side for generations. Papa would never send anyone …" She stopped, looked down at her lap.

Neither spoke for several minutes. The bakkie lurched forward, bumped over a rock and sped up.

"Sorry," she said at last.

He didn't respond.

"I miss Willem too."

"I know, Miss Anna, I know."

"We just wanted to stay friends."

"You were always close, *nê*? I still remember when you used to come play by our house after school. Before …"

"I tried to change Papa's mind, but you know what he's like."

The bakkie thudded into a trough, wavered from side to side, found traction and accelerated.

"I got a letter from Willem last week," Anna said. "Tells me our boys up north are holding the Gazala Line. At a place called Sollum."

"That's so. He wrote to me too."

"You must be so proud."

"Ja. But he's only driving a truck."

Suddenly he turned to face her, his eyes wide as if a ghost had run over his grave. "Miss Anna, if anyone hears you and Willem are writing to each other, I'll lose more than my job. The *Brandwag* people, they'll—"

"Don't worry about them. They're just a handful of bullies."

"That's not what I heard after church last week. Our *predikant* has his own wireless, you know. He says that way he gets both sides of the story."

"You mean, Radio Zeesen? Surely you people don't—"

"We're Moravian, remember. Did you know we still have a German missionary with us?"

"Is that right? I'm surprised the government hasn't locked him up."

"In Pretoria no one cares what goes on in Elim," he said. "We're just simple folk."

"You're anything but simple, Kleinjan."

"Maybe. But anyway, about the *Brandwag*, they say people are going to die. And Smuts will only have himself to blame."

"Well, that's all happening in the Transvaal. They won't bother with us here in the Strandveld."

"Hmm. Did you see the photos in the last *Bredasdorp News*? *Jislaaik*, they're like Nazis. Boots, marching, saluting."

"There!" she interrupted. "Slow down. See that flash? It must be half a mile out. South, or maybe south-south-west. Won't you stop again? I want to watch."

As they rolled to a stop she opened her window. The section of track they were on was seventy feet above sea level and at least half a mile from the shoreline, yet the crashing of waves on the rocks was like the rumble of a thousand lions.

"Oh there," he said after a long pause. "Ja. I see it."

The light appeared from the shimmer, winked three times,

stopped. On, off, on again. Anna flicked a strand of hair from her face. On. Off. On-off-on-off, on-off … *"Magtig."* After rummaging in her bag, she pulled out her diary and a pencil.

Kleinjan looked at her with the same patient, seaweed eyes that had seen her take her first steps.

"Yes, I still keep my diary. Not a day goes by I don't write in it."

Kleinjan nodded, his eyebrows raised in half-moons.

"Yes, my prayers too. One minute." She tugged at the door handle. "I need to stretch." She stepped out onto the running board, inhaling the scent of buchu and camphor as she rested her arms on the cabin roof and took in the sweep of the horizon. From the gold stain of Quoin Rock lighthouse on her far right, the coastline saw-toothed a hundred and eighty miles to the smile of Brandfontein Beach and the backside of the southernmost cape of Africa.

There was another flash, this time from the dunes. On-off, on-off. She strained her eyes towards the horizon, scribbling down fragments in her diary, using the roof as a backing. Too fast. There was more flashing, then darkness.

"Everything all right?" Kleinjan called.

"Just getting some air." Anna kept scanning the horizon curiously. Then the light started up from the dunes again. Same sequence. It came from the "Sahara", an expanse of sand dunes covering about five square miles, reaching back from the spring tide mark and ending a stone's throw from Dries Roux's ramshackle homestead. She'd sand surfed there on cardboard in the days when her older brother Frans still deigned to play with his *laatlammetjie* sister. The sequence of dashes and dots played a random dance on the canvas of her mind. Yet the demonstration she'd attended at university was enough to leave her in little doubt that it was Morse code.

2

HALFWAY ACROSS THE FLOOR of the *voorkamer* Anna hesitated. Whispers of pipe smoke carried the muffled voice of her father from the sitting room to her left. Visitors? Why no car outside? Resting her suitcase on the floor, she tried to make out his words over the ticking of the grandfather clock and the distant grumble of the ocean.

She glanced involuntarily at the wall where a photograph of her mother had once hung. A younger male voice was speaking with an air of authority. And then another. Yet she struggled to decipher their words. As the clock chimed half past nine, she suddenly realised why. They were speaking German.

"Who's there?" her father asked, switching to Afrikaans.

Anna shrank at his tone, a little girl again.

"Hannah?" he called. "Leave the wood on the stoep. And close the front door. Make quick."

Anna edged towards the sitting room, trying not to feel like she was approaching the principal's office at Bredasdorp Primary. She peered around the corner before entering.

The three men were seated in a half-moon about the *kaggel*, a *rooikrans* flame purring behind the grating. A fire at Rietvlei in February? Strange. Her father would never volunteer the luxury of a fire, especially in summer, without good reason.

The stranger nearest her father stood up. He was a good six feet tall and lean with a blonde beard. His presence seemed to fill the room.

"Engel. What are you doing here?" Her father, still seated, inspected the rim of his pipe. He'd switched to English for the benefit of his guests.

"I thought I'd surprise you, Papa."

He flicked a leaf of tobacco from the top of his pipe into the fire. "That Kleinjan. Said he was going early for petrol. I'll *bliksem* him."

"It was my idea, Papa." She glanced towards the guests without making eye contact.

"I thought you were staying with your friend Loubser till the day after tomorrow?"

"Lombard," she said. "Elize Lombard."

Her father grunted and continued pressing a palm of tobacco into his pipe. Doubled up in his armchair, with the toes of his size thirteen boots almost reached the *kaggel*. He waved the back of his hand in the direction of his guests. "This is Kurt and Thomas. They're colleagues from Windhoek. On business."

Anna acknowledged them with a nod and turned back to her father. "I thought you'd be glad to see me," she said. "It's been four months."

He glanced up at her without lifting his head, the whites of his eyes reflecting the dance of the flames. "If you missed me so much you'd have stayed on the farm your whole holiday. But you come now only, to grace us for less than a week before you bugger off again."

"But aren't you back in Parliament next week anyway?"

"That's different. It's my job."

Anna smoothed a crinkle from the front of her dress. "Surely you're happy I've made friends at university?"

"Boyfriends, you mean. I bet they're taking you to dance halls. *Vieslik.*"

Anna felt her cheeks burn. When she lifted her eyes from the floor her father was still pressing tobacco into his pipe. The seated stranger had his hands folded, one leg crossed over his knee. His face was soft and flushed, the kind that made a man look younger than his years. Yet there was a brooding, almost sinister presence about him.

"Didn't you get my letter, Papa?" she said.

He raised his left eyebrow. "You wrote to me? I thought you were too busy to indulge your father like that."

"I sent it two weeks ago."

"*Slim* Jannie's censors must have it. You'd think they have bigger fish to fry these days," he said, turning to the guest who was still standing, "like fighting our old enemy's battles."

The man didn't respond but turned to Anna instead. The chevrons about his lips were disarming. He stepped forward and offered his hand. "Thomas."

Anna cast a glance at her father. No response. She accepted the man's hand. "Anna," she said.

"It's a pleasure to meet you." He sounded almost as English as her art history professor, who'd spent three years at Oxford on a Rhodes scholarship and returned more English than King George. People joked that he'd left Cape Town as a Pickford and returned, still unmarried, a Pickford-Dunn.

Her father cleared his throat with a rasp. "Thomas says they've figured a way of importing harvesters from Europe. If only they weren't so expensive."

"Hah," Thomas said. "That's what they all say. Until they start using one."

Her father sighed. "I'd like to believe you. But with Smuts's control boards, I can't see how we'll lay our hands on the stuff. *Daai bliksem.*" He pointed to a *riempie* chair by the far wall as if he was about to invite her to join them, then changed his mind.

Anna turned to the boyish stranger. He stood reluctantly and offered a limp hand. He was slightly shorter than Thomas but equally lean, although plumper at the jowls. His forehead was flat and his eyes so deepset it was impossible to tell if there was life in them.

"My partner, Kurt," Thomas said. "He's the strong, silent type." Without waiting for a response, he turned back to Anna. "Stefan tells me you're studying Fine Art. How delightful."

She glanced at her father. The insolence. How could he allow such a young man to address him by his first name? "And languages," she said.

"I understand Stellenbosch is an excellent university," Thomas continued. "Produced some great statesmen, like Louis Botha, Jan Smuts, and the really smart ones, I believe you said," he turned to Anna's father, "like DF Malan."

"I'm at UCT actually," Anna said. She reached over and tonged a log into the fire. "The University of Cape Town."

"Her mother's request." Anna's father rummaged in his

trouser pocket, pulled out a box of matches. The springbok on its side, the emblem of the Union Defence Force, seemed out of place in their staunchly nationalist home. He struck a match on the side of his chair, cupped its flame over the end of his pipe and puffed at the mouthpiece. Then he spat a wad of tobacco into the fire, where it sizzled for a second before bursting into flame. "I tried to tell Julia the place was a nest of communists, but she wouldn't listen. Never did." He turned to Anna. "She thought I was against it because I hate *rooinekke*."

"But don't you?" she said.

"Ag, you know that's rubbish." Stefan turned to Thomas, then back to his daughter. "Your mother was English. An aristocrat, *nogal*. Why would I marry her if I hate them so much?"

Anna turned to the fire to hide her tears. There hadn't been a day in the ten years since her mother's passing that Anna hadn't ached for her touch.

"I'm sure you're hungry after the long ride," her father said, nodding at the kitchen. "There's still some *bobotie*. And Hannah's bread. Only brown of course." His face darkened as he looked at the seated stranger. "That cowardly Smuts even deprives us wheat farmers of the fruit of our labour. Bloody *hensopper*."

"Ag, Papa," she said, "you always said that without him we'd have lost the second war of independence a year earlier."

"Don't get me started." He waved her towards the kitchen with the back of his hand.

Anna turned back to the three men, looking from one to the other, no longer caring that she'd been crying. "All right, I'll leave you gentlemen to talk." She started towards the kitchen, then turned and fixed on Kurt. "Are you two staying the night?"

The younger stranger's face was a blank. He looked at his colleague.

Thomas cleared his throat and smiled. "Your father is a hard man to refuse. And we're not in any hurry. Our first meeting is only at two o'clock, at the Overberg Co-op."

"Well then," Anna said. "I'll go check on the rooms." She looked at her father. "Do you want them to stay in the cottage or in Frans's bedroom in the main house?"

"The guest quarters will do, Engel. And don't you worry about it; just shout for Hannah." He stood up. "Where is she? *Bliksem*. Gone home already, I bet. We have visitors, for heaven's sake." He turned to his guests, his expression softening. "I'm sorry, our lodgings are basic. But trust me, they're better than the Victoria Hotel."

Anna felt the weight of the men staring at her. The room swayed slightly and the smell of yeast drifting from the kitchen reminded her that she was hungry as well as tired. It was always like that when she first got back to Rietvlei. The world's most irritable father, but also the freshest air, Hannah's fine cooking and a *fynbos*-scented bath.

She headed for the door, pausing briefly to retrieve a couple of loose papers that fluttered from the coffee table as she brushed past. Startled, she struggled to appear calm as she replaced them, but by the time she reached the kitchen she was shaking, her mind in a whirl. She shut the door and sank into a chair. How lightly she had dismissed Kleinjan's concerns barely an hour ago. Yet those papers bore the unmistakable insignia of the *Ossewabrandwag*.

3

ANNA LAY STARING AT the window. The first hint of dawn was just browning the night and the Soetanysberg was no more than a smudge. In the no man's land between dreaming and consciousness, her thoughts hovered over the strangers from the night before. Papa had called them colleagues, yet she had never met them before. Were they members of the *Ossewabrandwag*? Had they tried to recruit Papa? What did it mean?

Oddly, the image that had flickered on her subconscious throughout the night was not the emblem on the letter. It was the eyes of the stranger who had risen to introduce himself. It was his gaze, as intense as a hunter sizing up its prey.

There was a *hoo hoo* from outside, close by under the eaves. Another *hoo hoo*, this time higher pitched. She sank deeper into her bedding. Cape eagle owls, a familiar comfort. Mama used to say that if they roosted by the house in summer the year would be blessed.

Soon an orchestra of sparrows was warming up and a cock began to crow from beyond the workers' cottages. Through the window it was now light enough to make out the rhinoceros head silhouette of the mountain, and the remains of the stone wall built by the Coetzees—the early owners of much of the *vlaktes*—to contain their flock.

Anna got up and opened her closet. The handful of dresses seemed to have faded over the year she'd been at university. She selected the shortest, a knee-length, orange-brown floral. After slipping into it she sat at her triptych mirror and began taming the tangle of hair about her shoulders. In the reflection she could see the ridge of the mountain and above it the remains of the morning star. She thought of the flashes of Morse code coming from out at sea. What were people doing there, off one of the most remote and dangerous parts of the coastline? She'd heard stories about shipwrecks and lost treasure there and had always longed to explore the area. But her father would never hear of it. Perhaps it was time to exert her independence. She was nineteen for heaven's sake. She gathered up her sandals and tiptoed towards the passage. What harm was there in taking a walk on the beach?

The sitting room was almost in daylight. She closed her eyes for a moment, recreating the scene from the previous night. But only the stranger's gaze appeared. She shook it away and opened her eyes. Before her hung a sepia photograph of her grandfather, a gaunt Boer in a veld hat, Mauser across his chest, staring back at her accusingly. She glanced nervously towards the coffee table. The papers were gone.

Outside, the sky was baked in the glow of sunrise. The sparrows were in part two of their symphony, now joined by the finches in the *melkboom* hedge about the *werf*. There was an urgency to their music, as if they knew that by mid-morning the wind would be up, driving all but the hardiest to shelter.

Anna stopped below a branch of the wild fig tree in the centre of the *werf* and surveyed the scene. It was deserted. Papa would be on the lands by now, no doubt hurtling along dirt roads and jeep tracks at this very moment, Kleinjan and the other workers bouncing about on the back of the bakkie. There'd be fences to mend, pipes to lay: there was always work to be done at Rietvlei. Then at nine o'clock sharp, Papa would return in a cloud of dust for breakfast: three eggs sunny side up for the lord of the manor, three rashers of bacon and a pot of bitter black coffee. And God help Hannah if it wasn't ready.

The caw of a peacock above almost made her jump. She moved on past the outbuildings to the reservoir and stopped at the water's edge. The inlet stream trickled from the end of an asbestos pipe, disturbing the surface in concentric rings. She watched her hands sink and distend beneath her reflection.

The water was cold and sweet as it splashed her face, and she shuddered with pleasure as it ran down her neck and spread across her chest.

She stopped at the clearing in the bush that marked the start of the path to the forbidden dune walk. Papa had always frightened her with horror stories of snakes, jagged rocks, and violent, drunken workers who preyed on young girls. But the workers were all busy on the lands, and she was a grown up now. Heavens, she'd already spent a year alone in the big city. Curling her toes over the lip of her sandals, she set out.

The corridor of soft sand was only five hundred yards long, but it seemed longer as she trudged along between the bushes, keeping her eyes focused for a glimpse of ocean ahead. As the track veered sharp right and the cliffs dropped away to the beach, she spotted footprints, and stooped to inspect. Two fresh sets—perhaps three—one slightly deeper and larger.

The tide was almost full, and a head of foam surged up the beach towards the flotsam from the last high tide. Anna stopped at the first cluster of rocks to catch her breath. Months of lectures, assignments and late nights out had taken the edge off her fitness, despite her daily walks. Attempting several miles to the point and back in soft sand would mean missing breakfast. She'd often been that way with her father or brother by bakkie. Maybe it was time to satisfy her curiosity about the coast in the other direction, which was strictly off limits. But she was a university student now, after all. She turned left and headed along the beach towards the rocks beyond the dune path.

"Shouldn't you still be sleeping after your long journey last night?"

Anna spun to her right. Thomas. After a night of imagining, he looked strangely familiar. He was sitting on the scraggly ridge of a dune, twenty yards above the high-water mark. On his lap was a jumbled ball of rope. He picked at a loose end with one hand.

"What are you doing here?"

"Sorry. I didn't mean to scare you."

"A farm girl doesn't frighten that easily," she laughed. "Tell me, your English is very good for a German-speaking South Wester."

Thomas laughed. "You noticed. There's a tradition in our family of sending the boys to public school in England. I had no choice. My forebears were *adel*. Von Eisenheim."

"I have the same burden." Her smile lacked conviction. "Except in this country, aristocracy is an illusion based on race."

Thomas plucked a loose end of the rope. "It's not much different in South West."

"I see." Anna held up her hand to shield her eyes from the sun. "So, where's your friend?"

"Sleeping, I suppose," he said. "Why?"

Anna pointed towards the path. "More than one set of prints."

"I'm impressed. Rather observant for a farm girl." He dropped the rope. "All right. Your father is showing Kurt around the farm. Now they've gone to see the flock. In our business it's best to know your customer intimately."

"Yes of course," Anna said. "You're trying to convince Papa to buy some new equipment we don't need."

"Mechanisation," he said. "It can double a farm's output."

"But why would we want to? We have everything we need here."

"It's happening in every industry. One must keep up. In Europe they ..."

"We're in Africa. We have no shortage of labour."

"The indigenous folk?" He wiped his hand on his thigh. "Your father sees things differently. Says labour in South Africa is only going to get more expensive as the war continues. And there's the threat of unions ..."

"Our workers wouldn't be interested," she said. "They've lived peacefully on our land for generations."

Thomas straightened. His khaki trousers were rolled at the ankles to keep them off the sand. They were at least a size too large. Like they could be her father's. "Excuse me," he said. "I'd better return to the homestead. There's correspondence to catch up on before breakfast." He started for the dune path. "Please. After you."

Anna tried not to blush. There was something about the stranger that excited her. Something edgy and unpredictable beneath his diffidence.

"Come, I insist."

She hesitated. The stirrings of guilt that had discomforted her so often during her year of freedom were back. Her pastor Dominee de Wet's admonition whispered in her ear. The dangers of being alone, unchaperoned, with a man. "Thanks," she said. "But I need some time by myself. You know, lots to think about."

Thomas laughed. "That's fine. I won't take it personally." Then suddenly he tilted his head, looking perplexed, and closed his eyes.

It took her several seconds to hear it. A faint drone, rising from the west but still shielded by the mountain.

"Wait," he said, throwing his head back and tracking the sky from its apogee to the horizon. The sound was easily discernible above the rumble of the waves. "That's a Junkers." He sucked air through his lips and listened again. "Yes. 86Z. German? What is—?"

"Relax," she laughed. "We're not about to be blitzed." The plane was visible now, a fixed wing snake eagle approaching them head on. "It's just the air force's coastal reconnaissance patrol. They're flying almost every day now."

"All the way from Cape Town?" Thomas kept staring at the plane.

"Sometimes. But there's also a landing strip this side of Bredasdorp. I'm not sure about this one."

"What are they looking for?" He was standing arms akimbo, facing her again.

"Looking for? Where've you been?"

He smiled. "South West."

"Of course." Anna laughed, then surveyed the offing. "How could I forget? You know, every other day there's a report in the local papers about someone sighting a German raider. Or a U-boat. The local communities are obsessed. Last month someone even claimed to have spotted a Japanese submarine."

"That is not surprising," he said. "With Pearl Harbour. Now the Malay Peninsula."

"Ja. But how they can tell the difference between a German and Japanese periscope is beyond me."

"The Japanese boats are longer and faster," Thomas said.

"But there's no way they could be operating this far west already ..." He let his arms fall to his sides. "Anyway. That's what I read." He shrugged. "But how would I know?"

A line of white water rolled up the beach past Anna's ankles, bearing a jellyfish leached by a horde of sea snails. "We have a saying in English ..." She watched the snails burrow into the gel. "It says time and tide—"

"Wait for no man." He was exploring her eyes.

"Now *that's* impressive," she laughed. The silence that settled between them felt comfortable, like she'd known him for years. She gazed at the candyfloss mist that still hovered over the water. An oystercatcher cheeped overhead. She didn't want to leave yet knew she must.

"Excuse me," she said at last. "I'm going to try the coast walk today. Change of routine."

He straightened. "Are you sure?"

Anna looked at him, hesitated. His white T-shirt hung loose and had an old-fashioned look, like the type her father wore beneath his long-sleeved shirts in winter. But he wore it well. "Why?" she said. "Is that a problem?"

"Oh. No. It's just that Stefan told me it was dangerous."

"Ha. Let me guess. He said not to go beyond the rocks? Papa's got a rule for everything. It drove me mad growing up. But I guess that was his way of coping as a widower."

"You would know better than me," Thomas said. "But he seems to take the idea of danger very seriously."

"I'll take my chances. Won't you tell Papa I'll be a bit late for breakfast?"

Anna set off down the remainder of the beach toward the rocky outcrop, enjoying the cool morning air and the smell of the sea. Then she scrambled up the slope where the sand turned to bush and paused at the top to take in the view. There was no sign of Thomas against the sand dunes behind her, and ahead were a series of low cliffs interspersed with bush and rock. And then she saw it. Though overgrown in places, it was hard to miss: the other part of the forbidden path, snaking inland and back toward the rocks.

She stopped at the barbed wire fence her father had erected soon after her mother died. The first skirmish in his campaign to extinguish the past. Two wind-bleached signs hung from the top strand of the fence, their writing barely legible. "Danger. *Gevaar*" read one. "Private. Trespassers will be prosecuted" the other. She smiled. "Guidelines" as Frans would say.

Finding the midpoint between posts, she tramped on the second strand, lifted the top wire and crouched, then hesitated, foot shaking. Why had she told the stranger where she was going? Papa would explode. He'd warned her so many times never to stray beyond the wire.

But Anna knew that about a mile from the fence was a cove called Skulpiestrand that her mother used to love. The Dutch East India Company had built a cottage there for shipwreck survivors, she'd said. And Kleinjan had once described how pansy shells lay there by the dozen in the time before the white man came. Beyond that stretched another two miles of rugged coastline to Perlemoen Punt, the nearest beach accessible by public road, where her father had taken her fishing on occasion.

After an hour of clambering and beating a path through the bush, with the roar of the sea out of view to her left, Anna stopped to catch her breath and rub her scratched shins. It occurred to her how few signs of life there had been. Not a francolin, not an oystercatcher, not even a seagull. It was like that silence in a forest after a hunter takes a shot. She looked up at the sun. It was well clear of the Soetanysberg and had heated the air to a shimmer. She swallowed her thirst, remembering how clear the water back at the reservoir had looked.

She was beginning to doubt the existence of Skulpiestrand. Then at last she reached a ledge. She probed the rockface above with her fingers, stuck her right hand into a cleft until her knuckles throbbed. She got one foot up, wedged it in a hole, and gave a final heave, then flopped down on the slab, breathing hard. But within seconds the heat of the rock was unbearable, so she kept moving. Crawling to the edge, she stopped and peered over.

The cove was a three-quarter moon, and the beach ended at a narrow slipway before a promontory. The landward side of the beach was ringed by kelp, then bush. There were no signs of life below. When her breathing returned to normal, she scrambled down the steep slope on all fours. Pausing to brush the sand off her dress, she veered right, crunching over the shells towards the far headland.

Halfway along she stopped, went down on her haunches and rummaged. No signs of pansies. Not even bright colours. Only mussels and perlemoen fragments. When her thighs started aching she stood and looked about. Nearer the water, the gently sloping sand dropped away to form a steeper incline covered in pebbles. Waves kept testing the dividing line. Was this Skulpiestrand? She was about to turn back when she noticed that the sand before the slipway was oddly scuffed, like the ground around a drinking trough. As she drew nearer, the disturbed area began to resemble a rectangle between the shells and the sea. Closer still, it became clear that the marks were from humans. Footprints, even …

Urrrrgh.

Anna spun around at the sound of wood on metal. But there was nothing to see. An echo? She turned again. Crouched at the other side of the slipway, partly concealed by rocks, she could make out a small stone cottage splattered with guano. Why hadn't she noticed it before? Her breathing slowed. She began to wish she'd listened to her father. But her pride held her. She was a grown woman. What was there to be afraid of? Could a fisherman be living here? Curiosity propelled her tentatively forward. The structure had two windows and a low doorway. *Urrrrgh.* The door, weathered beyond its paint, swung open. A breeze tugged at her skirt as she looked inside. It was too dark to make anything out. She felt inside with her hand, caught a splinter in her palm and withdrew it.

There was a rustle from inside. "Who's there?" she called. No response. Behind her a wave gurgled over the watershed and then sucked itself to silence. She picked up a pebble and tossed it through the doorway. Nothing. Then she ducked beneath the lintel and stepped inside, temporarily blinded by the dark.

She waited for her eyes to adjust. In the dimness she could make out a window boarded up. The floor was of pitted aggregate with a scattering of shells. A sudden noise behind made her jump. The door creaked closed, leaving a wireframe of light. Then something struck her face and she was frantically groping at the door, charging into the sunlight, rushing blindly over a crest and then tumbling ...

Anna gradually became conscious of a sandfly hopping along her lip, then her cheek. She tried to wave it away, but her hand was stuck. She yanked. It was wedged between a rock and what felt like a tangle of kelp. She found her other hand and dabbed her cheek. Something felt sticky, like blood. There was a tender lump above her ear.

She opened an eye. The sun was at ten o'clock and angry but the wind was up from the sea. The glare was so strong she had to shield her eyes with her palm. She worked her way to her feet, relieved that she could move both arms.

She felt utterly foolish. She must have disturbed a sleeping bat in the cottage, and her imagination had taken over. With no further appetite for adventure, she picked her way back through the kelp until she found the slipway and followed it away from the ocean towards the spring tide mark, where the concrete disappeared under a layer of buffalo grass and *vygies*. Soon she was in the hardscrabble of *renosterbos*, with no thoughts of scratches or snakes, just the certainty that if she kept going towards the mountain she'd eventually cross the road.

Clunk. Her foot caught on something hard. She stopped and scanned the ground. Nothing. She kicked about in the undergrowth. Something solid. She reached down. An oar, its wood bleached and salted. She scanned the bush. No movement. A chorus of cicadas started up in a port jackson thicket. Then she noticed some *renosterbos* ahead had been flattened. An overgrown jeep track? She stepped into the middle of it and looked back. She was on the outside arc of a ninety-degree curve: the far end connecting with the top of the slipway; the other headed in the direction of the homestead.

Then she heard a diesel engine. Soon the Chevy bounced into view with her father at the wheel, his expression like thunder. Thomas was next to him. Even from twenty yards off his stare looked wild and intense from beneath his fringe.

The truck shuddered to a stop, radiator hissing.

"What the hell are you doing out this side?" her father demanded, towering over her.

"I'm sorry."

"What's this?" He prodded at her dress. "Blood?" He was his full six foot five now, chest puffed and eyes set back by the tilt of his head.

"I tripped." Anna was trembling. It had started in her legs. At first, she thought it must be from all the walking. Soon it was her whole body. She hugged herself.

"How many times did I warn you not to do this walk?" He was in her space now, bunching his right fist. "Bad things have happened there. If you try this again I'll ..."

"Like I told you, Stefan," Thomas said from behind her father, "she was going to do the dune walk. It was me who dared her to give the coast a try." He stepped out from the bigger man's shadow and placed a hand on his wrist.

Anna waited for the inevitable. No one ever touched her father when he was in a rage and got away with it.

Her father let his arm drop to his side. Then he turned his back on the younger man until he was face to face with his daughter. He looked down at the blood stains, and back at her face. "You're lucky it wasn't worse. Don't you ever ..."

Thomas stepped between them. His forehead was level with her father's chin. "It was my fault."

Her father rose on the balls of his feet, head tilted back as if trying to see his nose. His hands by his sides were so large they could have been mistaken for boxing gloves. He was about to say something but stopped. "Come, my girl." He turned. "Let's get back. Hannah's kept you some eggs and bacon."

Thomas waved Anna in beside her father and slid in after her. They bumped along the track to the chug and tick of the diesel motor. Anna felt her eyelids droop, the left falling faster as always. It was a quirk she'd inherited from her mother and her grandmother.

"There were people on the beach," she said, at length.

They rounded a bend in silence.

"Come again?" her father said. The road straightened.

They were passing through a forest of thatch bushes, tall as a man. According to Kleinjan, the previous owners of the farm had attempted to grow it commercially. "People? Back at Brandfontein, I presume. Must have been the fishermen we saw yesterday. Right, Thomas?"

"No," she said. "On the beach at the end of the coast walk. The steep one with all the shells."

"Skulpiestrand?" he said. "That's impossible."

Anna lowered her head. She wiped her hands on her dress then let them rest on her lap. "I never actually *saw* them."

"Hah. There you go."

"But there were footprints everywhere."

"Here." Her father pulled the cork from a cloth-covered bottle and passed it to her. "It's hot as hell. You must be badly dehydrated by now."

"You don't believe me, do you?" she said. The truck trundled on. "I'm telling you." She lifted the bottle to her mouth and drank deeply. When she'd wiped her mouth, she said. "It was like people had been playing rugby on the beach."

"Now you're bordering on the ridiculous."

"Ag, Papa. Why don't you believe me? I'm not a little girl making up stories."

He shrugged. More silence. When the bakkie swerved to avoid a sinkhole, Anna felt Thomas's knee against hers. She shifted to break contact. He glanced her way. Was there a smile? The car surged over a level stretch of firebreak. For a moment they were heading at right angles to the coast and away from it. The bend must have arrived sooner than her father expected because he only started braking in the turn and the three of them were thrust up against each other. When the car straightened Anna had only one thing on her mind. Thomas's leg was still pressing on hers and she didn't want it to stop.

"Your father has a point," he said, not shifting away. "People imagine all sorts of things when they're dehydrated. It's nothing to be embarrassed about. I've seen it happen with hardened men."

Anna withdrew her leg. Resting a hand on the gear lever, she swivelled ninety degrees to look at her father. "Let's go back. Please. You can see for yourselves."

"No good." Her father cocked his head down and squinted out the window. "It's past high tide. Even if there were footprints they'd be gone by now. Which reminds me ..." He fumbled for his fob watch. Balancing it on the base of the steering wheel, he said, "Here now, Thomas, we'd better leave within the hour if we want to get you to your meeting in Bredasdorp." He slapped Anna's thigh. "Relax, my girl," he said. "I'll check it out tomorrow. Promise."

The bush opened around the truck. They were approaching a rocky patch in the road.

"Watch out," Anna yelled. She was pointing at the centre rise of the track. A tortoise, thirty yards ahead, was inching over a stone. It poked its bald head out and back, as if struggling to drag its chequered load. "Ag, isn't he cute?" she said as they approached.

"Hah," her father said. For a second the truck veered to the right until its left wheels ran along the middle section. Then he accelerated.

"Papa ... No!"

The tortoise disappeared under the chassis. She clamped her eyes shut, hoping against hope not to hear the popping.

"Missed," he said as they both glanced back. "*Toe maar, Engel. I was only joking.*"

"Why do you do things like that?" she said, as the truck sunk back into the tracks. "I mean, even pretend. A tortoise never did a man any harm."

"Who says?" her father said. "The buggers bring the rain."

They were between thickets of Port Jackson. A bend, then straight, and the winged face of a windmill appeared above a copse of trees. When they arrived at a gate, Thomas leapt out.

"Leave it to me," he said.

Her father turned to her. "Did I tell you the Prinsloos are coming to dinner tonight? No? Well, good news—Fanus will be there too." He studied her face. "He got back from Stellenbosch this morning."

Thomas was dragging the gate across the sand until it was at right angles to the fence.

"What's wrong," her father said. "I thought you'd be pleased. He's such a well-brought-up boy. Remember how willingly he helped us build that road up the kloof last year? We'd never have cleared all that rock without his expertise."

Thomas waved at them to come through.

"How could I forget? All that blasting kept the birds away for the rest of the summer."

"And did I tell you his father's already making plans to retire? Soon the lad will have both farms to himself. And the quarry."

"He's boring."

As they passed, Thomas tipped his hand to his forehead and bowed. Anna turned to watch him draw the gate closed.

"You haven't given him a proper chance."

"Why should I? He's a fascist."

"Come now."

"It's an open secret that he's an admirer of the *Brandwag*. He's a fanatic."

"*Ag*. Please. You think anyone who doesn't agree with this illegitimate government of ours is a Nazi." He patted her on the leg. "*Foeitog*. You've only been at UCT a year and those *Engelsmanne* have brainwashed you."

"I can think for myself."

Thomas looped the chain over the fence pole, then stooped to align the male and female parts of the padlock.

"Listen," her father said, "you better behave yourself tonight. Do you have any idea how much the Prinsloos contributed to our election campaign in '38?"

"How could I? You never tell me those sorts of details. I'm old enough for you to marry me off but not to be trusted with money matters."

"I've also invited Dominee de Wet," he said. "I know how you two love to talk religion."

Anna inhaled. Her father was a tough man, but he tried. Though he'd lost his faith, he respected her views to the point of encouraging them. It was hard to stay angry with him for long. She looked back. Thomas had the chain in his hand. For a moment their eyes met. "What about your guests?" she said. "You're not going to make them eat at the hotel, are you?"

"Well ..."

Thomas swung into the seat next to Anna.

Her father shoved the gear lever into first. "I've invited them to stay until we return to Cape Town on Sunday," he said. "Isn't that right, Thomas?"

"What was that?"

"You remember we talked about the Prinsloos last night. Got the second biggest herd of merinos this side of the Hottentots Holland. Not to mention the Durbanville farm and quarry. A man in your trade would be mad not to want to meet him."

Thomas stroked his chin. "Of course. It would be my pleasure. But Kurt ..."

The thatched roof of the homestead appeared above the bush. Anna said, "Your colleague isn't very talkative, is he?"

"He's shy, that's all. Especially around the ladies," Thomas laughed. "No. Seriously. He would have loved to attend, but he's been detained in Bredasdorp. Some rich farmer says the shearers we sold him are jamming. You know what it's like. They crack the whip, you jump."

"But we could send Kleinjan to fetch him," Anna said. "Dinner's only at eight."

A moment later they burst out of the bushes and onto the *werf*. The roofs of the outbuildings shimmered above the gravel. Within seconds they had skidded to a halt under the fig tree. After the dust cloud had passed over them, Thomas said, "That is most kind of you to offer ..." He stroked his chin with the tip of his index finger and thumb. It was as though he was waiting for words to catch up with his thoughts. "But he has a meeting. In Cape Town. Tomorrow afternoon. He should stay over at the hotel to catch the first bus in the morning."

4

WHEN ANNA HAD FINISHED placing the silver on the table she withdrew her head to avoid the chandelier and straightened. Her back was stiff from being on her feet all afternoon. First it was rearranging the furniture, then supervising Hannah in the kitchen, then helping her father with the seating arrangements. By the time she'd bathed, dressed and returned to check on Hannah's roast, it was almost seven o'clock.

The dining table was so long there was a legend that her father, after buying it at auction, had to saw it in three to manoeuvre it into the room. Sixteen yellowwood chairs were arranged around the periphery—the one at the far end unused for the ten years since the night her mother died. Anna could still remember the meaty smell of the *frikadelle* she'd been frying on the Aga stove before the doctor called from her mother's bedroom.

"Miss Anna. Miss—"

"What?" As Anna swung about her elbow collided with Hannah's shoulder. "Sorry," she placed her hand on Hannah's forearm. "*Gats*, how did you manage to creep up on me like that? Are you all right?"

"No, everything is good, Miss Anna." Hannah looked towards the *voorkamer*. "The first guests have arrived. In a shiny Bedford."

"That will be the Prinsloos." Anna adjusted her dress, then pointed at the butter dish. "Quick. Fill that. And two more red wines for the table. Then go call Papa. And our guest. Hurry now." When Hannah had left, Anna hastened through to the *voorkamer*. Through the closed door she could hear them on the stoep, Kleinjan's greeting, the Prinsloos complaining about the condition of the roads. She approached the oval mirror on the sideboard, and admired the heave of her corset, the pendant nestled between her breasts and the trace of lipstick. The body of a grown woman but the spirit of a dutiful child.

There was a scraping of shoes on the mat. A presumptuous rap. Anna opened the door and smiled. The first salvo of charm fired in her father's endless battle to retain his seat in Parliament.

"To the country," her father said in affected English, raising his crystal of cabernet sauvignon. On the wall behind him was a painting of the Prodigal Son, his favourite. It had been a confirmation present from his adoptive father in Munich. Rumour had it that it was a Caravaggio, although the canvas was unsigned.

He took pains to meet each guest's eye as they clinked glasses, starting and ending with Hester Prinsloo. As always, the most attractive female guest was seated on his right. She was one of those wealthy Afrikaner women who wear lashings of make-up just because they can, not because they need to.

Her husband, Koos, held up his glass and swirled it in the light of the chandelier, then brought it to his nose and sniffed, one eye on the bottle. "Ah. We have KWV tonight." Though his accent was thick, he spoke passable English. He quaffed the wine. "You're treating us tonight, my friend. I didn't know you had special privileges?"

"I didn't either," her father said, "until last December. As always, it's who you know."

Koos chuckled. "How could I forget? You're a politician."

"And a farmer." Her father swept the room with his glass. "Though sometimes I ask myself why I go to all this trouble to eke a living from this barren Strandveld. It's like pulling teeth."

"So, tell me," Koos said, his furrows deepening, "why toast the country all of a sudden? Wasn't it always the Prime Minister?"

Her father looked like he'd swallowed vinegar. "When it was Hertzog I could still stomach it," he said. "But Smuts … to think he was once our greatest hope."

"Ja." Koos shook his head. "I still can't believe it happened."

"What do you mean?"

"The vote, of course. We depended on you Malan boys to keep us out of the war." His eyes shifted to the opposite wall which was adorned with black and white photographs of parliamentary sittings. He lingered on a close-up of a Purified Nationalist Party caucus. Balding white males, some bespectacled. "Now we're playing Britain's lapdog. Again."

"That was two and a half years ago," her father said. "And we did what we could. Still do. You know that. We just didn't have the numbers."

"Ja, ja," Koos put his glass on the table. "I know. I'm just giving you a hard time. But really, with all that money pouring into the party, you'd have thought—"

"Don't worry," her father said. "We're on the offensive. Daniel's got two new bills up his sleeve for next week's sessions at Parliament. Mixed marriages are soon going to be a thing of the past. Just watch."

There was a shuffling of feet and Hannah bustled into the room carrying a tray with a china bowl and a stack of soup plates. An off-white *doek* covered her hair, and her floral uniform was faded from countless washes. When she'd served the soup to the guests, she waited, tray in hand, at her employer's shoulder.

"Get on with it," he said. Seated, he was still taller than her.

As Hannah placed the plate of soup on the table, Stefan shifted his elbow, enough to catch her forearm. A ring of soup formed between the plate and saucer.

"Ag, no," he said, glaring at her. "Again."

"Leave it, Papa," Anna said. "Hannah's doing her best."

Hannah took the dishcloth from her forearm and wiped the plate.

"Why do you look so *dikbek*?" Her father demanded, his scowl just inches from Hannah. "Smile."

Anna dropped her spoon on her saucer. The clink reverberated about the room. Hannah used the ensuing silence to shuffle out.

"Some things they never learn," her father said. He waited until the footsteps faded down the passage.

"Ja *nee*, absolutely," said Koos. "And worse still, if we don't watch our backs these people will be running the show the day after tomorrow."

Anna's father folded his arms.

"*Toe maar*," said Dominee de Wet. He had one of those fatherly faces that one could never imagine being immature. His hair was white and streaked sideways over his scalp to hide his baldness. "That's a long way off. Tell me, what do you think of that upstart Hofmeyr's motion to extend the coloured franchise?"

"He's as red as a lobster is what I say. And mad." said Stefan.

"That may be so," said Koos. "But he's not stupid. Dangerous, yes. We let him carry on poisoning our young minds, and who knows …"

"That'll never happen while Malan's in Parliament," said the *dominee*. He broke his bread roll on his side plate and took a bite. "He's got the measure of *slim* Jannie and his boys." As he chewed, crumbs fell in a trail down his jacket. "Trust me." He glanced at his wife diagonally opposite him. She had the face of a woman who might once have been pretty before the spread of marriage and childbirth. She affirmed him with a smile. "I know," he continued, "I was at *kweekskool* with him." He looked at Koos. "I tell you, the man's got backbone. Never touched a drop of liquor. But clever as a fox."

"I've no doubt his heart's in the right place," Koos said. He wiped the scum of soup from his moustache and then folded the serviette in his hand. "But he's too much talk. We need a man of action." He swept the room, paused, then said. "Like Van Rensburg. He's our man."

"That's right, Pa," Fanus said, rolling his "r" like a gurgle. He was on Anna's left, furthest from her father and opposite Thomas. His face was soft, even for a part-time farmer. He brushed a crumb from his tie and fell silent.

The host picked up the bottle of KWV and topped up Hester's glass. Only when he'd replaced the bottle did he remember the *dominee*'s wife on his left. "Ag, sorry," he said. "May I pour?" He turned to Koos. "So, what makes you think Van Rensburg's our saviour?"

"Simple. Since he took over as leader, the *Brandwag's* membership has grown to over three hundred thousand. Or four hundred thousand if you read the *Cape Times*. Which of course I don't."

"He's got charisma," her father said, "I'll give you that. But can we trust him? You know whose side he took in the rebellion."

"Come on. Maritz and his boys never stood a chance against the might of the state. You can't hold it against Van Rensburg. His job was on the line. He was young, anyway."

"Yes, but our prime minister?"

"President," Koos said. "We're going to be a republic, remember."

"What?" Anna said. She folded her serviette and placed it on her placemat. "Britain would never allow that."

Her father gave her a look which not long ago would have dispatched her to her bedroom.

"Anna's right, *Oom*," said Fanus. His hair was straight and parted in the middle and a curtain fell just short of his left eye. "They'll never give us our freedom." The other diners looked at him. He paused for effect, then said, "But who says we'll need them to?"

The clock chimed nine from the *voorkamer.* It was that extended lull between starters and main course when guests start wondering whether the host has forgotten the food.

"Would you care to explain?" said Anna.

Fanus looked about the room. He had the self-assurance one could expect of a man about to graduate with a degree in law but who would never have to practise for a living. His eyes rested on Thomas. "Germany will sort her out."

"Really?" Anna said. "They've stalled at Stalingrad. The whole winter campaign's a disaster. Don't you listen to the news?"

"Of course I do." Fanus's neck turned pink. It also had several red marks from shaving. "Which is why I know that Leningrad and Moscow are set to fall. The Panzers can see the spires of the Kremlin. They're just waiting for the thaw."

"That's rubbish," she said. "What news do you listen to?"

The room fell silent. The croaking of frogs drifted in through the open window.

"Ah," she continued. "Zeesen. I should have known. If you believe that propaganda, you'll believe—"

"*Engel,*" her father interrupted, glaring, "this isn't the time."

She held her father's stare. The simmer of a lifetime's humiliation was coming to the boil. She was about to say something but then thought better of it.

Thomas leaned forward over the table, his back straight from his hips. He said, "What I think Anna means to say is that it's important to consider the source of one's information before drawing conclusions."

"But that's not what she said." A shaving splotch on Fanus' Adam's apple looked like it might be about to bleed.

"Leave it," Koos said. "This is what happens when we talk politics or religion. Let's change the subject." He swirled his wine about in the glass and held it up to the light to admire its legs. "Tell me, how's your flock?"

"We carry on," her father said. "You know the story. The bugs are rampant. Bluetongue's hit us particularly hard this year. And then those bleaters balk at taking the dip. Tomorrow we do our first batch of ewes. You?"

"Same," Koos said. "Except we also got maggots. Had to shave half the herd. Talk about a waste."

Anna watched her father catch Thomas's attention. They nodded in what seemed to be some unspoken agreement. Thomas said to Koos, "Pity you didn't meet my colleague here earlier. His equipment would save a shearer at least two hours a day."

"That so?" said Koos. "I'd be interested all right. With half our labourers driving ambulances up north, making the others more efficient wouldn't be a bad thing."

"No!" her father said. "Half? You should have told me you were battling."

"How so?"

"There's a retired general on the Wool Board with me. I've heard nothing's changed on his farm. I'm sure he can help a friend."

"*Ge*," Koos said. He shovelled a piece of bread into his mouth and chewed as if he'd been given a deadline. "That's outrageous."

"Listen now," her father said, sweeping the table with his eyes. "We can carry on talking business after dinner." He turned to his right. "So. Hester. You joining any of those sewing tea parties for the Red Cross?"

"*Jinne!*" Hester blushed. "You think I'm one of those? A King's Afrikaner?" She glanced at her husband and back at Stefan. "You must be joking."

At that moment Hannah arrived with a roasted spur-winged goose on a tray. Anna's father had bagged fifteen in a single shoot at Voëlvlei the previous weekend.

"Can I help carve, *Oom?*" Fanus piped.

"That will be kind," her father said. He waved at Hannah. "Get the carving knife for him."

Fanus set about his task of dismantling the goose with the fervour of a zealot. The conversation at the table had dried up and the guests seemed content to watch as he severed the wings and legs from the carcass.

"You won't believe what I saw today," Anna said to the *dominee*, loud enough for the table to hear.

"Really?" he said. "Tell us."

Her father rolled his eyes till his whites were larger than his pupils. Then he blinked them to normal. Thomas shifted in his chair.

"Footprints on Skulpiestrand," she said.

"That's a small beach on our land," her father explained. "Julia used to go there to collect shells, especially in her last years. None of us have been back since." He glared at Anna. "Not until today."

"There were at least a dozen." Anna got up from the table and joined Fanus at the server. She started dishing meat to the guests. "It was like people had been playing rugby or something. There was even the outline of a field."

"As you can see," her father said, looking at Koos. "My daughter's got a fertile imagination. But I suppose you need that to study Fine Art."

Anna let the fork she was holding clang to the serving dish. She'd never cried in public before and didn't intend to now. Her eyes fixed on her father's. "I can't wait till you leave for Parliament." A glance at Thomas. "Then I'll have all day to explore the coast that was always off limits." She scrunched the serviette. "Now that you've assured me it's untouched by humankind, we know I'll be perfectly safe."

5

ANNA LIFTED HER HEAD from her pillow. She had a vague sense of whispering somewhere nearby. She glanced at her window, not entirely sure if she was awake or dreaming. It could have been the rustle of the bougainvillea against the windowsill. Or nightjars. As she lay half-asleep, the events and conversations of the past day or so began replaying themselves in endless permutations. Flashes at sea, strange men, unexplained footprints. So many questions without answers.

The air in her room was close and the sheet draped over her was moist and clung to her skin. Then she heard a clunk. A door? A box being dropped? Through her open door came the rasp of her father's snoring from down the passage. Nothing else.

Now another sound, outside. A snort and flapping. A mule? Fully awake now, she knew she'd never get back to sleep until she found out what was going on. She dressed, slipped on her walking shoes, and set off down the passage.

The moon was almost full and at its zenith, drenching the *werf* in phosphorescence. She padded across the gravel towards the outbuildings. Through the open window of the first guest cottage she could hear snoring. Fanus or his father. She continued past the second cottage. Thomas. She paused, her breathing shallow. The door was slightly ajar, and all was still. Was he dreaming, even now?

When she reached the shadow of the wild fig tree she stopped. A whoosh passed her face. The eagle owl again. She smiled. Her mother's spirit was with her. She turned an ear to the outbuildings, stopping the other ear with her finger to shut out the grumble of the sea. Whispers like she'd heard earlier were coming from the far side of the shed. Then nothing. She crept up to the entrance. As far as she knew, her father still used the space to store spare parts and old machinery—ploughs, threshers, tractors—but it was years since she'd been inside.

Anticipating blankets of cobwebs and dust, she squeezed through a crack in the sliding door. The smell of flesh and blood was powerful, much stronger than at the butchery in Bredasdorp or the food section of the general dealer. Raw and fresh and animal. As her eyes adjusted she could make out the carcasses, a dozen at least, hanging from improvised hooks on a roof beam. She ran her hand over the closest. It was smooth and moist, the size of a sheep. But why so many? When they needed meat, her father would get the workers to slaughter one, maybe two.

The entire far side of the shed was stacked to head height with crates. She stood on tiptoe to feel inside. One was onions, the other cabbage. The only vegetables Rietvlei's soil could sustain. She stumbled over something. A sack. She ran her hand over the hessian and then pressed her face to it. Grain: the smell of home.

Voices again, this time less muffled. She followed the sound to the half-open window and waited. A snort and stamp of feet. Then a flick of reigns, a chain jangling. She stepped closer to the window. Silence. She pulled back a fraction. When the voices started again she edged forward and allowed her eyes to adjust to the moonlit *werf*. A shape formed, a mule hitched to a cart loaded with a mound of sacks.

Was Rietvlei being robbed? It didn't seem possible. Everyone knew everyone around here, and distances were great.

At the front she could see the hunched outline of two men seated. One shifted. "Is that everything?" The voice was unfamiliar, the Afrikaans pure with none of the cadence of the farmworkers.

She had to wake Papa. But she'd have to explain what she was doing out on the *werf* in the middle of the night.

"Skulpiestrand?" the voice continued.

Anna's mind charged ahead of her heartbeat. Did she

hear him correctly? She couldn't be sure. She really must wake Papa.

She slipped back out of the shed and into the shadows of the cottages. But at the front door of the homestead she hesitated. Could Papa know about this? There were too many strange things going on. Her head was spinning.

The mule brayed, and the driver tried to hush it, then egged it to a start.

Anna vacillated, one hand prising the door open, the other at her dress. She couldn't remember a time she'd been as afraid and confused all at once. She mouthed a prayer.

The cart creaked into motion and headed in the direction of the sea.

Whatever was going on, there was only one way to find out. And no time for wavering. If she let the cart get much further away she might lose track of it.

She waited another moment until the cart was far enough along for the men not to notice her before she ventured from the shadows. In the light of the moon she could make out the tyre treads of the bakkie snaking into the thicket of port jacksons. At first she had to slow her pace to avoid catching up with the clip clop of the cart. But by the time the outline of the homestead roof had dipped below the scrub behind her she was alone, except for a choir of crickets.

When she reached the gate the chain was hanging loose a fraction and the padlock was open. Didn't Papa say only he had a key? For the first time since leaving the *werf* she felt relieved at not waking her father. But what if she was wrong, and he knew nothing? If he found out that she'd ventured out without him, he'd fly into a rage. She hesitated, stood straight, inhaled. There was a time she would have trembled at the thought. Now she felt more revulsion than fear.

As she squeezed through the gap between the gate and fence pole her dress caught on a barb of wire. She stopped, panting. A platanna croaked from a rush of thatch. She felt at her hem. A piece of cloth hung below a tear. Her father didn't miss a thing: she'd have to sew it first thing tomorrow before putting it in the washing. She checked that the gate was closed behind her and stood, dusting her dress.

Anna kept to the *middelmannetjie* of solid ground between the tracks, not daring to look down for the possibility of night adders. The air was cool and clear, but the moon was so bright it had almost drowned the Milky Way. The only two bright stars were the pointers to the Southern Cross. She held her hand up, measured off the distance between them and counted four and a half lengths down the spine of the cross to an imaginary point in the sky. Then she dropped vertically from there until her fingernail hit the rise of the Sandberg, which was as low as a sand dune, just longer and covered in bush. Behind it, she knew, was the Agulhas lighthouse and the endless ocean.

After a while the quarking of frogs here and there in the bushes and the white noise of the ocean lulled her into a state of peace and unthinking as she traipsed the long, unwinding road.

At last a kink in the road broke Anna's reverie. The *middel-mannetjiie* now consisted of patches of *renosterbos* and a bed of *vygies*. The noise of the waves was close and insistent. She shivered, thinking of the scuff marks and the swinging door.

As she rounded another bend, the tongue of a breeze licked her face and she smelled salt and kelp. There was a snort ahead. She stopped, waited. Then she edged forward. She could make out the mule cart standing askance, blocking the road. There were muffled voices.

She took a few steps off the side of the slipway and dropped to her hands and knees. The two men were speaking freely now. Even over the sound of the sea, she could make out the Afrikaans. One was faint, she guessed it belonged to a worker. The other was of a farmer: not the unmistakable drawl of Strandveld but probably somewhere within the wider Overberg. She crept forward until she crested the last rise before the sea and looked out. The path from the slipway towards the water was highlighted by the phosphorescence of the rock's surface. In the shadows alongside the point where the trail disappeared into the water was the outline of the cottage. She stiffened involuntarily.

The voices grew closer, sauntering towards her. Anna crawled behind a bush. As they passed she pressed her body to the ground, overwhelmed by the smell of kelp. Soon the men were close enough to make out faces. No, surely not? Kleinjan!

They had passed before she could see the other's face. He was stocky, his arms swinging wide from his sides.

They reached the cart, and the stocky man hopped onto the back and then flung a tarpaulin to the ground. "Right, we'd better be quick."

The two men took turns lowering the crates and sacks from the cart and then hauling them down the slipway to the cottage. By the time they'd finished, the Southern Cross had dipped below the Sandberg. Dawn wouldn't be long now. Papa would be up shortly before that.

Kleinjan returned to the cart alone and seemed to be feeling beneath his seat. There was a ting of copper as he lifted an object. His hand was fishing about again. Then the slosh from a gallon drum and the shake of matches. He was off the cart in a flash. Instead of joining the other man at the cottage, he turned off the slipway and picked his way up and across a seam of rock that jutted out to sea. At the point he stopped. A scraping. Then a flicker. And a stronger light. Kleinjan was standing now, lantern in one hand. With his free hand he fiddled with a fitting on its side. One flash. Then another. On. Off. On. Off. Then the lantern died.

Anna looked out over the sea to where waves were advancing in haunted whites. Closer to shore was a passage of calm. The mouth of a cove.

Anna wiggled her toes for feeling. It was at least three minutes since Kleinjan had last moved. The other man was still inside the cottage. She should leave. If she jogged she might be back before Papa woke. She was on one knee when she saw the first flash in the ink stain of the ocean beyond the breakers. On. Off. On. Off. A now familiar sequence.

Kleinjan picked up the lantern and made his way off the ledge. His colleague joined him and they scurried back to the cart. There was a scrunch of bush as the cart wheeled about off the narrow track. The mule stamped its feet, shook its head. Kleinjan goaded it and they were off at a trot.

Anna bent to rub her leg awake. The safe thing would be to run after the cart. Or would it? What if her timing was off and

Papa was awake? It would be safer to wait until he set off for the lands. She found a bank of sand at the high-water mark above the slipway and sat. There was a clear view through the mouth of the cove to where she'd seen the flashes.

She shook her head. Again. Her eyes were wide now, every sense on standby. Nothing reached her but the relentless roar of the ocean and the lapping of waves against the shells. Had she fallen asleep? The moon was nowhere and the sky showed a hint of blue.

A distinct splash seemed to come from the direction of the ocean. But there was nothing except splotches of mist hanging over the cove. Then a staccato voice, strained by the rhythm of the waves. Her scalp tingled. Another splash and the clunk of an oar. Then a boat scraped onto the beach and four men jumped into the shallows.

Anna crept backwards over the vygies. Should she run? She had reached the first clump of *renosterbos* when curiosity got the better of her. She lay flat, narrowing her eyes to make out the forms in the darkness.

Two of the men had returned to the boat and were passing crates to the other two in the shallows, who in turn sloshed up the beach with their loads towards the cottage.

A clunk reverberated from the inside of the cottage. Then another. Whatever they were delivering was heavy and hard. Some sort of exchange for the sacks? But why would anyone be interested in food, especially in a farming district?

Her thinking was confirmed when the flow reversed and the men were hauling sacks and crates towards the beach. The whole operation took place in silence. Within minutes they were finished. Then they lined up, two on each side of the boat, and shoved.

"*Scheiße.*"

Anna recoiled, not believing her ears.

An oar clanked on the boat and one of the men kicked at water. "*Stussen,*" he shouted. Together they crouched, then heaved, and the boat grated through the shells until it was afloat.

For a moment it was as though the ocean paused to breathe. The boat was gliding towards the mouth of the cove with an occasional slosh. In the east, the sky was brightening. There wasn't much time now.

As she picked her way back towards the dawn and home, questions kept exploding in her head. Who was the farmer with Kleinjan? Why were they trading provisions with Germans? And most troubling of all, did her father know?

6

STANDING ALONGSIDE THOMAS, ANNA watched Kleinjan tug at the shifting spanner. He'd been awkward in her presence all day, avoiding eye contact, keeping conversation to a minimum. She was beginning to wonder if he knew she'd seen him the night before. But how could that be? By the time she returned to the *werf* there was no sign of life. Regardless, she'd have to confront him. And well before they drove back to Cape Town.

Kleinjan was looking up at the side of the windmill tower. The turbine was spinning in a blur. Apparently satisfied, he slid his free hand up the piston that connected the driveshaft to the pump below. It was sucking up and down. He followed a hose from the base of the structure to the rim of the reservoir where it connected with the asbestos inlet. There was a dribble onto the moss-flaked floor. "It's been a dry summer," he said, raising his head to look at them.

"Cape Town too," Anna said, leaning back against the bonnet of the bakkie. Her legs were crossed at her knees and she held her dress down with both hands to prevent it from billowing. "The reservoirs on Table Mountain are almost empty."

"This doesn't make sense," said Kleinjan, contorting his head in the direction of the windmill. "Everything seems to be working as it should." He stared at the inlet. "Yet there's nothing. I've got to do something soon. If any sheep die, Baas Stefan ..."

Thomas stepped forward. "Here." He held out his hand for the spanner. "Give me that." Kleinjan obliged. Thomas tightened the head of the spanner over a nut on the piston. Then he jammed his heel against the side of the concrete plinth at the base of the tower to steady himself and yanked. Just a creak. His triceps were long and taut. He yanked again. This time a grating of rust on metal. Then a muffled cannon shot from the bowels of the earth. And a gurgle. Soon water gushed in spurts from the outlet pipe.

"*Yoh*," Kleinjan wiped his brow on the sleeve of his overall. "How did you do that?"

"Beginner's luck." Thomas handed the spanner to Kleinjan and ambled back to the bakkie. "And a bit of muscle."

"Not bad for an equipment *smous*," Anna said. "I'm impressed."

Thomas wiped his hand across his thigh, leaving a smudge of grease on his khaki trousers. "I trained as a mechanical engineer. Why do you think your father asked me to come with you to the windmill?"

"And you're in sales now? That's an odd progression."

"Actually not." Thomas centred his buckle and tucked the end of his belt back in the trouser loop. Without looking up, he said, "An engineering degree is a prerequisite for technical sales and support. Where I come from, anyway."

Anna bent down and cocked her head to one side to catch his eyes. "And where's that?" She ran a finger through a stray strand of hair and swept it from her face.

He straightened as if from a stiff back and squinted at the sun. "Enough of me," he said. "I want to hear about you."

Anna held his eyes. They were as clear and blue as the lagoon at Pietie se Punt on a windless day. She swallowed.

"Something wrong?" he said.

She noticed that Kleinjan had wandered over to the far side of the reservoir and was reaching over to clear a nest floating on the rising surface of water. But her eyes were drawn back to Thomas. "Nothing. Well. It's just that no man has ever asked me that before. You know. How I am."

Thomas closed a step between them. "Judging from the cast of characters at the dinner party last night, I'm not surprised."

Anna dropped her eyes to his chest. "Fanus can come across bumptious, obnoxious even, but he's not all bad. You must understand. It's hard with a father like that. The Prinsloos are like royalty in these parts. Imagine the weight of expectation."

"Why don't you go along with it then?"

Anna laughed. She wondered if she was blushing. "What do you mean?"

"I know your father is as ambitious for his daughter as he is in politics or business."

"It's that obvious?"

"Young Fanus is a lucky man," Thomas said. "And I'm not talking about the family fortune."

Anna got up off the bonnet and straightened her dress. She looked across the reservoir. "Hey," she called to Kleinjan, who was scooping animal droppings off the water. "You can finish that tomorrow."

"What now?" said Thomas. "I can't seem to say anything right."

Anna sighed. "It's not you."

"What is it then?

"I'm just irritable. Happens when I'm tired."

"Oh?"

"A little trouble sleeping, that's all. Such a hot and sticky night. We only get a handful of them in a year. Tell me, did the mosquitoes bother you?"

"It was that argument with your father last night, wasn't it? You've been brooding ever since."

"I'm a woman," she said. "Sometimes we're just otherwise. Do you have a wife, Thomas?"

"Fiancée."

She tried not to sound disappointed. "You don't sound enthusiastic."

"You're not the only one with an overbearing parent." Thomas gazed into the distance. It was the time of day when the sky merged with the horizon and the lands were a water-colour of browns and greys. Next to him a sugarbird bobbed up from the shrivelled head of a pincushion protea and chirped into the wind.

Anna withdrew her hands from the bonnet as if suddenly realising it was hot. "Come," she called to Kleinjan. "Pack your tools. I still want to find some flowers on the way to the sheep dip." She stood. "Papa's expecting us at four."

Thomas marched back in the direction of the reservoir. The

toolbox stood three yards from Kleinjan, lid open. "Here, let me help." He reached for the handle. "*Scheiße!*" He flung his arms back. "*Was ist das?*"

Kleinjan grabbed Thomas's wrist and yanked him backwards, then stepped across his path and stared at the ground in front of the toolbox, his free hand in the air. "Wait!"

For a moment no one spoke against the *ee aw* of the windmill.

"*Toe maar,*" Kleinjan said at last. "It's just a puff adder." He edged in a semi-circle about a speckled black and green S that was barely distinguishable from the ground. Carefully he retrieved his toolbox and backed away. "Lazy devil. He won't bother us if we leave him alone."

The wheels spun, sending a fantail of sand behind the bakkie. When they gained traction the vehicle surged forward then stopped. Kleinjan threw the gear lever into reverse and they yawed a three point turn before pulling off.

When they'd reached a constant speed, Anna said, "An overreaction, no?"

"What do you mean?" Thomas's back was half-turned.

"Back there," she said. "Don't you get puff adders in South West?"

Thomas kept his shoulder turned towards her. An ostrich pranced across the road and melted into the bush. "Sure," he said at last. "So many that I developed a childhood phobia. I'm not scared of much. But snakes …"

"Just teasing," she manufactured a laugh. "You're not the only man I know who has a thing about them. Oh, look." An antelope stood knock-kneed at the side of the road. At the sight of the car it startled this way and that, then ducked under a shrub. "You get *duikers*, I take it?"

The engine ticked and revved over a series of potholes. "Sure. Especially in the Caprivi, where it's not so dry." He pointed out the other window. "Hey, weren't you looking for flowers? If I'm not mistaken those are king proteas."

"Yes. Lovely. I'm impressed. You know your *fynbos* better than your snakes."

He smiled. "Maybe I'm just a salesman. But there are advantages to being on the road. I get time to read all sorts of stuff.

For example …" He paused, as if considering his next words. "Did you know Hitler said in a speech that one day he'd be picking proteas in Cape Agulhas?"

"He says lots of stupid things. The man's deluded."

"That's what he likes his enemies to think," Thomas said. "With apparent success."

"Enough," Anna shivered. "Hey, Kleinjan. Stop. Over there."

They climbed from the cab. The South Easter was in full fury about their ears and a tyre tread of cloud streaked the sky.

"How do these look?" Anna held up a clutch of protea cones wrapped in a snowfield of everlastings. Without waiting for an answer she skipped to the next bush. "Here. Even better." Her cheeks were flamingo pink. The world beyond might be in flames, she felt, but here in this place, all was well with her soul. "Aren't they beautiful?"

She watched Thomas bend over and plunge his face into a flower. When he lifted his face he was staring into her eyes. Something stirred in her. No man had ever made her feel such heights of guilt and pleasure without touching. Only when a gust swept a lock of hair over her face did she turn. Kleinjan was nowhere. She swept the hair behind an ear and looked back at him. "So, who *are* you?"

Thomas reached down for another protea and ran his fingers down the wax of its stem until it reached the branch. He looked up at her as though he were weighing something in the balance. Then he broke the stem and said, "That's a question I often ask myself."

"That's not what I mean."

He held the cup of the flower to his nose and inhaled. "So you want to get personal," he said. "All right. But first, tell me about last night."

As always when her sixth sense started flashing red, Anna did nothing.

"I see." His tone made her feel like a cloud had crossed the sun. "It's in order to question my credentials, but as soon as I ask an innocent question, you're speechless."

She glanced at the bakkie. There was no sign of Kleinjan. So much for a chaperone. "We should be going."

Thomas clasped her wrist. She struggled to free it. The grip fastened. His eyes were the colour of the sky reflected off the distant salt pan. "Not before you answer me."

"*Jong*, leave me alone. If Papa hears you've laid a hand on me, he'll ..."

"If you and your Papa are so precious, why didn't you tell him what you saw at the cove?"

Scenes flickered across Anna's mind. The guest room door: it had been ajar. The first tendril of fear tickled her back. No. Stop. She'd learned from her father that attack was the best defence. "Is this how a gentleman repays his host's hospitality, by spying on his daughter? *Sies*, man."

"Spying?" He smiled with half his face. "A deaf man on a galloping horse would have heard you thumping about the yard."

Anna glanced at the bakkie again. "Still, you followed me."

Thomas withdrew his hand. "Only because I was worried about you," he said. "A young woman out on the lands with two workers up to no good. Any man worth his salt would have done the same."

She had to strain to hear his words before the wind swept them over the veld. She watched a fish eagle soar over the outline of the Akkedisberg. She wanted to believe him more than anything. "Did you tell Papa?"

"What you get up to at night is none of my business. But strange men taking fresh supplies to men in rowboats? I had to ask."

Anna considered his response. Would a man so openly discuss a crime if he'd been party to it? "What did he say?"

"At first he claimed ignorance. Until I pointed out that they were his workers using his storeroom on his *werf*."

She tracked the eagle's spiral. More information, all accurate. "And?"

"I'm sorry. He swore me to silence."

"I'm his daughter, for heaven's sake. Besides, I saw it myself."

"Don't make me betray a confidence," he said. "Stefan's more than a customer. He's been good to me."

"Ag, please." Anna paused to inspect the petals of a protea compacta, curled inward about the stamen like a protective circle of flames. "There were lights at sea, men speaking

German. We're at war, for heaven's sake."

"I think you're getting ahead of yourself," Thomas said. "It's not like there aren't German speakers in these parts. I meet one every other day. And the lights—there could be any number of explanations."

"Listen," Anna felt a chill up her neck. "I've had all night to think this through." Her eyes narrowed at the shimmer of the salt pan. "Workers from our farm have been supplying a German vessel. Probably a raider. One of them caused havoc in our waters in '40 and '41. Laid a minefield here off Agulhas. I saw a mine washed up on the beach with my own eyes. Good heavens, that means …" The wind lifted her dress, but she made no effort to straighten it. She was searching his eyes but coming up empty. There was a constriction in her throat as she spoke. "My father's a, a traitor."

"Even if you're right about the boats," Thomas said. "I'm sure Stefan doesn't see it that way. Think about it. The Kaiser welcomed his parents in their hour of need. He told me the whole story the other night, how no one else would have anything to do with renegade Boers. How could he think of them as the enemy?"

"How could he not?" Anna placed her hands on her hips. "He knows what they're doing to the people whose countries their Panzers crush. *Hemel.* My father's a Member of Parliament. He, of all people, should know what's happening on the Eastern Front—not to mention with the Jews."

"Easy now. Calm down. I'm not the one who needs convincing." Then slowly his eyebrows rose, recognition dawning in his eyes. "Ah." He grimaced, chevrons deep. "Because I speak German … you think somehow … I'm involved."

In an instant, Anna felt ashamed. Had the events of the past two days been playing with her mind? She had no solid grounds for doubting him. "No, no," she said. "I never said that. But you could surely forgive me for thinking it a bit of a coincidence. You and Kurt pitching up here the same time all this is happening on the farm." She glanced at the bakkie. "Anyway. Come. We're supposed to be picking flowers."

As they meandered about she pointed out species of *fynbos*, first by their Latin names and then their common ones.

Thomas repeated them after her. When they moved behind a large thicket of bush, he stopped.

"I know this isn't my business," he said. It was quiet in the shelter of the wind. "But your father …" He looked up, watched a cloud scud overhead. "I have a lot of respect for him. Affection even. But I have to say, he's very harsh with you."

She recoiled, dropping the proteas at her feet. "Papa loves me," she said. "He has a strange way of showing it, but he loves me."

Thomas stooped to pick up the flowers. Then he held the bunch out to her. "I can see he hurts you."

"Why do you care?"

"I don't know."

Their eyes danced a tango.

She let him take her hand, this time allowing it to linger. She could see now that he'd trimmed his beard and his skin was paler than she'd first thought. "This isn't right," she said.

"What do you mean? You're here, I'm here, we're surrounded by God's beauty. What could be wrong with that?"

"Everything. *Magtig*. We've only just met."

"How long do you have to know someone to be sure that they've stolen your heart?"

His lips were inches away. She felt a chill cross her chest. Her shoulders were back and her breasts felt hard against the cotton of her dress. She placed a finger on his lips. "Wait," she said. "You still haven't answered my question." She withdrew her finger. "Who are you really?"

This time Thomas drew back. For a moment it looked like he was going to say something. Then a door seemed to slam in his mind. He stooped to pick a porcupine quill off the ground and caress it between his thumb and the tip of his index finger. "I wish it didn't have to come to this."

"What is it?" She took a step backward. A tinder branch cracked. "You look so serious."

He closed the gap between them. The quill twirled between his fingers.

Anna cast her eyes left and right. The bakkie was obscured behind protea branches. Still no sign of Kleinjan. What was she thinking, going out on the lands with a strange man?

Lust. *Dominee* de Wet was right. It was the first course of the devil's feast.

"Ah, there you are." Her father boomed over the bush before his face appeared. It had been years since she'd felt so pleased to hear his voice. "You *skelms*. What the hell's been keeping you? We've already lost an hour."

"Papa." Anna hoped the sunlight would hide her blush. "We just stopped for flowers. Look, aren't the king proteas gorgeous? We just had to—"

"I'm going to give that bugger a *snotklap*." Stefan spun his head ninety degrees towards the bakkie. "He knows damn well we were supposed to start at four."

Thomas stepped between them. "Slow down," he said. "Your daughter has been teaching me about the *fynbos*." He cradled a flower, grinned. "Protea compacta." Using the nail of his other hand's thumb he nudged a bee from its stamen. Then he bent down and inspected a smaller, thinner plant. When he looked up he was grinning. "Leucospermum ..." he glanced at Anna, who mouthed something.

"*Ge*," her father said. "You're sounding like one of those UCT botany professors Julia used to invite to the farm to do research. Spent weeks here, never bothered to shave. I don't know what they did all day. And all we ever saw for our troubles was a tattered copy of a PhD thesis." He trod his size thirteen *veldskoen* on the neck of a protea bush until it snapped. "You'd think they could at least have included a commercial viability study. I had to hear it from Dries Roux how the neighbours are starting to export to Europe. No, man." He stomped over another bush. "Come. The Prinsloos are waiting. We've got a hundred sheep to dunk before dark."

7

THOUGH ANNA HAD WITNESSED a sheep dip dozens of times, she struggled not to gag at the reek of poison as she approached the plunge pool. They were under the partial shade of a bluegum grove, the ground sprinkled with shrivelled bark and twigs. The dip tank was positioned in the corner of a paddock to make it easier to herd the sheep into the chute. Two black and white border collies harassed back and forth, snapping at the ankles of the bewildered animals. A shepherd boy stood by, ready to crack his rawhide whip.

"Afternoon, Anna." It was Dries, tenant farmer and some-time friend of her father. He stood alone on the far side of the chute with his fists on his hips. Koos and Fanus paced a patch of *vlei* grass a dozen yards away, tight in conversation. Dries raised two fingers to doff the edge of his wide-brimmed hat. It was level with his eyebrows, making his nose seem bigger than it was. His checked shirt was faded, the sleeves rolled three inches above his elbows.

"Sorry we're late," she said. "I lose track of time on the lands. You should have started without us."

"Wouldn't dream of it," Fanus said, closing the gap between them at his father's prodding. Without asking he took her hand. His palm felt cold and damp. "You're the main attraction."

"Ag, man." There had been a time, albeit brief, when Anna had been charmed by his flattery. Now it made her feel dirty.

Fanus flicked his head in the direction of the bakkie where Thomas stood, forearm draped over the open passenger door.

For a moment, neither man flinched. Then Fanus turned towards his father, who now stood at the edge of the plunge pool. "Come that side," he said to Anna, tugging her hand. "We'll get a better view." He pointed at a ewe wavering at the edge of the platform. It bleated, then wiggled its stump. "Don't you just love their eyes when they see water?"

Anna's father walked past, tailed by a worker lugging a ten-gallon drum of poison. He took it from the *handlanger* and handed it to Dries. "Here," he said. "Plenty more in the Chevy." He looked up at the others. "Come, men. Let's do it."

Anna pulled her hand free and wiped it on the cotton of her thigh. She looked up at a cloud which halved and then dissolved.

"What is it with you?" Fanus leaned towards her. Even in the wind she could smell his aftershave. "Why such a cold fish?"

"What do you mean?" She swirled around.

"We used to get on so well." With his chest puffed and feet splayed Fanus looked like a jilted penguin. "Remember last Easter? Man, it was less than a year ago."

"Ag, please," she said. "You make it sound like we were *gekys*."

"Weren't we?" He'd deflated somewhat. "All right, I admit it wasn't official. But remember that night after *nagmaal*. We—"

"Stop." Anna rolled back her shoulders and adjusted her bra strap. "I'm a university student now. Don't you realise I've changed?"

"That's normal," he said. "I also went through a rebellious patch in my first year. Just ask Pa." He turned to his father. The older man was out of earshot, watching a worker in overalls prod a ewe up the gangplank to join a half dozen of its fellows on the raised platform. "You'll come around, sooner or later."

"Hurry up," Stefan shouted at the worker. "Dunk her." He looked at Koos then at Dries. "Do something, man. If we bugger around like this we'll never get done by tomorrow. I only got a week's grace from Parliament."

Anna started. It wasn't her father's brusqueness. She was used to that. It was the worker. The man was darker than the local farmworkers. From the eastern part of the province, she guessed. They'd made an appearance before. Migrant workers. Mostly they didn't stay—they couldn't, at least not without a pass. And the local magistrates would see to it that it was temporary at best. There was a familiarity about his stance, something immediate, a menace even. It wasn't the face that bothered her: handsome, with high, rounded cheek bones, and a jawline disfigured by a scar. Rather, it was the expression. Even from a distance, his contempt was obvious.

"What are you looking at, *jong*?" Stefan said. "Get on with it."

The worker kept staring.

"Hey, Dries. Where did you get this uppity piece of work? Sort him out."

Dries strode up to the worker. When he got close he bent down, picked up a dry branch. "Listen here." He drew the stick back and feigned a blow. "Don't make me." Then he lanced the stick through the paling at the hind leg of the nearest ewe. It splayed its legs and scrambled to retreat. Dries shoved. The animal slid on its hooves across the platform and teetered at the edge, lost balance and plunged into the water. On cue, the worker leaned over and held the animal's body under the surface. Every now and again he relaxed his grip to let it up for air.

"Enough," called Dries. "Next."

When the third sheep had been through its paces, Anna strolled back to the bakkie.

"Had enough already?" Thomas said.

"And you? You don't seem very interested, considering you make a living in the agricultural industry." She glanced around. The others were focused on the bleating and splashing of sheep. "Listen," she said. "I may be young, naïve even, by your standards. But I'm no fool."

He rubbed his chin.

"I admit," she said, "you had me. Even an hour ago, you managed to convince me I was imagining things. But the mind works in mysterious ways. They say we think more in our subconscious than our conscious. Though I'm sure you know Freud better than I do—being one of your countrymen."

"What are you talking about?" Thomas took a step closer.

Anna stiffened. "You tried that earlier," she said. "Intimidating me." She looked behind her at the men clumped around the dip. "Things are different now."

"Don't say something you might regret …"

"Regret?" She raised her voice to the wind. "You tell me about regret?"

"Anna. Stop. You don't know what you're getting yourself into." He moved closer, took her hand. She didn't resist. "You've got to trust me."

"I might begin to trust you when you start telling the truth." Her eyes rested on his hand. It felt strangely natural in hers. Like an extension of her body.

"I wish it was as simple as that," he said. "Truth. Falsehood. Good people and bad."

"There you go again, avoiding the question. If you carry on"—she raised her hand to point, but the fight was leaving her—"I'll be forced to tell them."

He drew her closer and placed his other hand over the top of hers. There was a whiff of sweat on khaki. Satisfied he had her full attention now, he said, "I'll explain. I promise. It's just that … now is not the time."

"*Hemel*," she said, looking up at the bluegums. Their branches were bunched like hundreds of connected parachutes straining against the wind. "You can't expect me to wait."

"But you're going to." He glanced at her father who was stroking a sheep dog. "And I believe you know why."

"Oh, so now you're a mind reader? Don't think you know me just because in a weak moment I let you hold my hand. I have a conscience. I'm not going to sit around and watch my country be violated."

Thomas straightened as if with a stiff back. "Do you know what they do with traitors in wartime?"

"Yes. Same as they do with spies."

"I resent that insinuation. But I'll let it go. You're obviously stressed. Anyway, I'm not from these parts. I could be gone tomorrow without a trace." He glanced away and then back to her. "It wouldn't be so easy for Stefan."

Anna pretended to ignore him and gazed instead at her father, who was still ruffling the collie behind its ears. The dog had an expression of delight and adoration. Loyalty was a virtue he'd preached and fought for, bone and marrow; devotion to family and fatherland was his motto. How could she, his own blood …?

"Give me three days," he said. "Stefan wants me to drive with him at first light tomorrow. He says you're to follow with Kleinjan because you don't have a driver's licence yet. We'll meet in Cape Town. I'll explain everything then."

She examined his face for answers. "Why not now?"

"You just have to trust me." He watched her father lob a stick across the veld and the dog bounded after it. "I can't see how you can change any of this."

Her father was walking towards them now, head lowered and eyebrows like miniature horns.

"Let's meet in the Company's Garden," he said. "That's near Parliament. On Tuesday. Noon. You'll be there, won't you?"

Anna tossed the branch into the veld and stared at it long after it had landed. She felt excited, which alarmed her. Goodness knows, she should be angry with him. Scared even. Did he already know that her university residence was just beyond the top gate of the Company's Garden? What else did he know? She had to refuse. "All right," she found herself saying. "The gardens are lovely. I walk there often."

"You do?" His eyes widened. "This is good then. Is there a convenient place to meet?"

Her father was closing in on them, ignoring the dog at his ankles. "Yes, a café. It's just a toasted sandwich dive." She kicked at a rock, which dislodged from the ground, and a nest of ants spread in alarm. "*Magtig*. I don't know why I'm agreeing to this."

"I think you do."

Thomas looked up in the direction of her father and lifted a hand in acknowledgement. Her father slowed and then turned.

With her foot Anna shovelled sand into the hole, trying to stop herself from fitting the last pieces into the awful jigsaw puzzle that loomed in her mind's eye. "Even so, I just don't know if a secret can be kept that long in these parts."

"If you're worried about them," he gestured at the group, "don't bother. They know more than I do."

8

THE MORAVIAN CHURCH WAS the first sight that greeted Anna and Kleinjan as they approached the mission hamlet of Elim from the east. Though bigger than the other buildings in town, its simple thatched structure was a far cry from the Dutch Reformed edifice that dominated Bredasdorp. It was set among a cluster of public buildings that included a mission store, flower shed and watermill. That was as much as Anna knew of the place. She had often passed through with her father on her way to and from Bredasdorp, but only to drop or collect workers. Her Papa wouldn't sanction any fraternising with the locals. They were a cult, he said, inbred. Now she was hoping to find certainty, or at least solace, in their simplicity.

"You've been busy again," Kleinjan said, pointing at the diary on her lap.

Anna pressed it into a fold of her dress. "Ja, I guess. Why?"

He scratched his neck. "You can't fool me, Miss Anna. You only write when you're upset ..." He smiled. "Or ..."

She turned in her seat to face him and prodded him on the shoulder. "What are you trying to say?"

The truck veered off course for a second until he straightened it out. "You can't fool me." He was still smiling. "I know you too well."

Kleinjan was right. No one knew her better, not even her father. She felt herself blushing as she thought of what she'd written in bed on waking. How she couldn't stop thinking of him, of Thomas, a man she'd known for little more than two days. How no boy—not even Willem, or Fanus, the first to kiss her—had ever stirred such feelings.

"Hah," she said. "Don't be silly. We just met."

"I'll say no more." Kleinjan shifted the gear lever as they slowed for a pothole at the outskirts of town. Ahead, a stream of the townsfolk faithful shuffled down Main Road towards the sanctuary.

She looked at her watch. "There," she said, "Quarter to ten. I told you we'd make it. You needn't have fussed so much."

He grabbed the wheel with both hands to steady the bakkie from a blast of wind. "Ai, I know. Worry is a sin. Matthew 6 verse 25." As the gust passed he shifted to a lower gear and used his free hand to align his purple sash to the diagonal of his suit jacket. It had the letters IOTT ELIM CHAPTER stitched into the fabric. Anna had been so self-absorbed since getting into the car that she hadn't noticed his outfit. She struggled to recall what the letters stood for. International Order of the True Templars. Her father had told her how Kleinjan had been an alcoholic in his youth, but after a dramatic prodigal-son return to his religion he'd spent years preaching the perils of liquor.

"Aha, you still care what they think, don't you?"

"*Haai*," he sighed. "It's not that. The *predikant* gets mad when a person is late." Kleinjan slowed to a standstill at the T-junction with Main Road. Opposite was a Coca-Cola sign, heralding the town's general dealer store, and alongside it an easy-to-miss monument to slavery. A hag staggered past the windscreen clinging to the arm of another, her prune face small behind a shroud of black. "We're simple folk," he said. "But I wouldn't want it any other way. It keeps us on the narrow path."

"But thou shalt not keep the Lord's anointed waiting."

Anna wound down her window. The cottages on either side of the street were tiny with thatched roofs and very small windows. Folk of all ages were appearing from doorways: men in dark suits clutching bibles followed by women in head coverings. Even the children were subdued.

Kleinjan jerked the handbrake with a squeak, and nodded recognition at a pair of elderly men as they passed. "What's wrong, Miss Anna. Why are you sarcastic today? It's not like you. Are you angry with me?"

Anna looked past him to the clock above the gable of the

church annex. "Let's talk after the service," she said. "I wouldn't want the community to shun you for being late."

"There again. You're cross with me."

Anna smiled, her anger melting. "You know me too well." She felt an urge to tell him everything. After all, he'd been a listening ear to her when her own father was too preoccupied to care, or worse. But an instinct stopped her. "I just find you change whenever you go back to Elim. Tell me, how long have you been at Rietvlei? Twenty years? Twenty-one? And this community still has such a hold on you."

"You must understand. Even if a man makes a break—like me marrying an Anglican like Hannah—he never really leaves. Not even in death." Kleinjan opened the door. "Remember," he swung his legs out from under the steering wheel, "women use the first entrance." He pointed at her hat on the back seat. "Don't forget that …"

A woman in an all-blue dress with a matching bow on her hat paraded up to the car, beaming as they got out.

"Morning, Joanna," Kleinjan said. "*My jinne*, you look smart today."

"*Haai*," she blushed the shade of her lipstick. "Still the charmer, hey."

He turned. "Miss Anna. Meet Joanna. My cousin."

Joanna offered her glove. "Good day, ma'am," she said to Anna. "Honoured to have you visiting us." Then she turned to Kleinjan. "Would you believe it? We had visitors yesterday too."

"No," Kleinjan said, looking irritated. "Who?"

Joanna lowered her voice. "Also white people. One stayed in the car the whole time. A man. I didn't see his face. The other went with the missionary." Joanna pointed beyond the church roof to the top of a row of trees. "You know how he likes to while away time in Heer-se-Bos. Yesterday he must have been there at least half an hour."

They were interrupted by a clang of bells. Kleinjan looked up at the clock. It was five to ten and the stream of congregants had all entered the church. "Excuse me," he said to Anna. "Men go around the back." He opened the door. "Joanna will show you the way."

The closeness of the air inside the church was a welcome

contrast from the wind and dust of the street, and the thatch above seemed to soften the voices to a stage whisper. At first glance it looked like there wasn't a place to sit, but as Anna made her way up the aisle, a woman in a wide orange hat smiled and shifted her family along the pew to make way.

The *predikant* stood sentinel in the pulpit with both hands resting on the open bible in front of him. His black robe almost touched the platform. He gazed down at an elder who was stepping up to a lectern, evidently relishing the chance to address the congregation. The elder's faded pinstriped suit hung uncomfortably as though he'd inherited it from an over-weight father. He fished a ruffled sheet of paper from his jacket pocket. "Herewith the results of Sunday the first of February," he read, and paused for effect. "First collection: two pounds, fifteen shillings, eleven pence. Second collection"—he looked up at the congregation, unable to suppress a grin—"three pounds, four shillings, six pence."

The *predikant*'s face had softened to foreshadow a smile as he waited for the elder to take his place in the pews. Then he stretched his arms in welcome, raised his head to the balcony, and nodded.

The organ droned the first stanza of "Oh God of Jacob" and the congregation stood. Craning back to glimpse the choir, Anna felt the women's eyes on her. Was it because she had turned, or because she was the only pale face? She ventured a glance across the divide to the rows of men, sombre as stone. Kleinjan was standing beside a pillar. To his right was a slighter man with the same high cheekbones, his face contorted with age. His father? It struck Anna how little she really knew about Rietvlei's foreman. They'd talked often, sometimes at length, but always about what mattered to her: plants, animals, art, politics, even girl problems. How self-centred she'd been.

Anna became agitated as the organ launched into the refrain. She had only a half hour after the service to catch Kleinjan in his home environment. She was hoping he would be more open and at ease here among his own people, before he resumed his duty as her father's driver and clammed up as they continued on to Cape Town. She was going to need all her powers of finesse.

The *predikant* waited for the people to settle in their pews. Then he licked the tip of his index finger, turned a page in the bible, and cleared his throat. When the last whisper at the back of the church had faded, he perched his spectacles on the bridge of his nose and began to read.

"Then a great and powerful wind tore the mountains apart and shattered the rocks before the Lord." He peered over his glasses at the audience. "Our sins won't go unpunished, folks. The Lord sees every wicked thought, every drink taken in secret." His eyes seemed to rest on individuals as if with intent. "The gambling. Even the dancing."

Anna bristled. In her first year at university she'd allowed herself this one indulgence. She swallowed. It didn't seem fair; how could an evening of big band swing be bad? Hadn't the great King David himself danced with abandon before his God?

The preacher glanced down at the page and then up and to one side, as if inspecting a cobweb in the spandrel of an arch. "But the Lord was not in the wind." He straightened his glasses. "After the wind there was an earthquake. But the Lord was not in the earthquake."

As Anna tried hard to focus on the *predikant's* words, an image appeared of Thomas on the beach, calmly picking at the knot, eyes, blue and focused and following her, unblinking. His words carefully chosen in a voice steady and strangely formal. Guiltily she glanced around, sure that the whole congregation was aware of her distraction, reading her irreverent thoughts. Without moving her head, she glanced sidelong at Kleinjan. He had shifted to the far side of the pillar. She turned to confirm. The black-robed man seated beside him wore an expression that brooked no fool, much like the *predikant*, but white. It had to be the missionary. The missionary's gaze drifted in her direction and held hers for a moment. Then he bent his head in prayer.

Anna closed her eyes. Images of Thomas returned, this time among the flowers, close at her side. She could feel his hand on her arm. She opened her bible again and attempted to read. No use. She glanced up at the *predikant*. He was looking straight at her. He seemed to know. He adjusted his robe at the shoulder, waiting a moment too long before dropping his eyes to the text. "After the earthquake came a fire. But the Lord was not in the fire."

Anna tried in vain to shut her ears to the next verse. "After the fire came a gentle whisper." There was no comfort in a God who kept silent. She would rather hear a raging voice than suffer the plague of constant doubt.

"Hear the word of the Lord." The *predikant* closed the bible with a thud.

The service ended and Anna filed out behind Joanna. Eventually they spilled into a clearing behind the church where the congregants began milling about in the shade, exchanging news. The hubbub of voices almost drowned the twittering of the sparrows. In the midst of the assembly stood a rusted diesel pump, and to one side the mission store, a low, elongated structure. Across the clearing, downstream from a catchment pond, was a watermill, the slosh and creak of its wheel just audible above the wind brushing the willows around them.

Anna waited for a pause in conversation to break away from Joanna and made a beeline for Kleinjan. He was standing in a group of men in the shade of a palm, his back to the stoep of the mission store. She took him by the wrist. "Excuse us," she said, smiling at the others. "Kleinjan promised to show me the watermill."

At the double storey thatched structure they stopped. Blocking the path was a narrow bridge carrying water via a trough from the catchment pond to the waterwheel. The bridge was made of stone, packed chest high, and on it was a sign.

"Blessed are the lowly," she read aloud.

Kleinjan chuckled. "They say this is proof that Germans have a sense of humour."

When they reached the wheel, Anna's smile had drained.

"What's wrong, Miss Anna? You look like you saw a ghost."

"You know," she said, "unlike Papa, I've always regarded you as equals: you, Hannah and Willem. I thought we were friends."

Kleinjan glanced over her shoulder in the direction of the church, the chatter of the milling congregants muffled by the splash and groan of the wheel. "But we are," he said, one eye squinting into the sun. "You're like the daughter I never had."

"Then you wouldn't lie to me, would you?"

"Of course not, Miss Anna." He eyed her. "Why do you ask this?"

She watched water cascade off the end of the trough and fall into the rectangular buckets on the circumference of the wheel. "What were you doing the night before last?"

Kleinjan looked at his feet. Above him a dove coo-cooed from the oak tree.

"I saw everything. The meat in the shed, the … Come on, Kleinjan, I'm not stupid."

After several seconds he shook his head. "That you surely aren't."

Anna waited.

"Please. If Baas Stefan knows I spoke to you about this, he'll kill me." He glanced up at her.

Anna nodded, trying to still the turmoil she felt inside. Her worst fears had been confirmed. Her father was involved.

"I didn't want to do it," he said. "I promise. I hate myself for it. But … but …"

"It's all right."

"Don't think badly of me," he said. "He threatened my job. Rietvlei's all I have."

"You have other options. You could go back to thatching, for example."

"At my age?" He straightened his back as if in pain. "Spending months away from home? Hannah's not well, you know."

"I understand what you're saying," she said. "But helping the Germans?"

He looked confused. "Who said anything about Germans?"

"Ag, come on. Enough of this."

He stared at her.

"Skulpiestrand. I was there. Saw everything."

Kleinjan looked across the clearing. The missionary stood at the edge of a group, looking about. "They're not all bad, you know. Take Gustav there. He came out here ten years ago." Kleinjan turned to face her. "Gave up everything." He pointed towards a copse of trees at the end of a path. It was as thick as a broom's brush. "You see down there, past Heer-se-Bos? There's a graveyard. Nineteen headstones, twelve of them for infants." He looked her in the eye. "Two are his."

"Of course there are some good Germans," she said. "But they're governed by Nazis, and we're at war with them. And don't for a minute believe the lies they're telling your people. Elim, Wuppertal, Genadendal … same nonsense everywhere. They won't liberate you, give you back the land."

A gust of wind rustled through the branches above them, causing the dappled sunlight to tap-dance off the droplets falling from the wheel's paddles.

Anna shivered. The lights at sea, the flashes, the row boat. "I knew it," she said, not knowing whether to feel outrage or shame. "It's a raider they're helping, isn't it? Like the one in the newspapers last year. Wasn't a boy from Elim on one of the ships it sank?"

"Ja. His parents were in church this morning. Front pew. Still in black." Kleinjan kicked at the ground. A sheep bleated in the distance. "But it's not another raider."

"What then?"

"It's worse," he said still without looking up. "A U-boat."

Anna thought of her conversation on the beach two days before. "And Thomas?"

Kleinjan hesitated. "He's the commander."

She felt her legs tremble. The waterwheel dissolved before her eyes.

"And the other chap?" she said at last. "Kurt? The silent one."

Kleinjan's lips tightened.

"What's wrong?" she said.

He looked away. "He's … dangerous."

"Why?"

The wind sighed through the willows.

"Tell me," she said. "What are they doing ashore, staying with us? Wouldn't they be safer staying on the U-boat? It's a big chance they're taking isn't it?"

Kleinjan shifted on his feet. He was looking at her now but his eyes were blank. "That's all I know. I only loaded the meat and vegetables."

Anna sensed that the moment had passed, the clam had shut. She looked past Kleinjan towards the pond. The missionary had broken from the group and was wandering down the lane towards Heer-se-Bos. He passed just a dozen yards away without noticing them. In his hand was a sheet of paper and a pencil. Was he also involved? She looked up at the sky beyond the branches and felt a wave of vertigo. Everything she'd always assumed was solid had become a mirage.

Her father, the most fervid of patriots, betraying his own country? It wasn't possible. Granted he admired the Germans, and still corresponded with his foster sister and aunt in Germany. But entertaining Nazi officers in his home? Helping U-boats to sink South African ships? It was beyond comprehension. And yet … Papa, Kleinjan, Thomas, even the church? Was there anyone left she could trust?

9

"THE MOST BEAUTIFUL CAPE in all the world," said the taxi driver as they headed along Victoria Road towards the central business district. But the peaceful scenes drifting past the window of the Pontiac failed to calm Anna's inner tug of war. Her father had insisted she spend her first night back in the city at his Sea Point apartment and join him for lunch the next day. He had made it a condition when she came to university that whenever he was in town she would eat with him—at his discretion, of course. Desperate as she now was for space alone to think, she'd failed to come up with an acceptable excuse. And her fellow lodgers were only due to return today.

Anna wound down the window to escape the smell of Brylcream and leather and stared out. On the common a clutch of women were chatting beneath parasols as their children played cricket. She felt a twinge of envy, even regret. Perhaps her father was right: a woman had no place at university.

A pair of elderly men were skirting the cricket match, heading for a bench. Ahead was the oval of the race track, now empty. In the distance Anna could just make out the finger of the Victoria and Alfred pier stretching into the bay. Beyond it a battleship steamed past the outline of Robben Island. The peace of the day seemed cruelly at odds with her anguish. It wasn't fair. A girl of her age shouldn't have to face such an agonising choice.

Anna's father was making notes in the margins of a document—The Minutes of a Meeting of the Agricultural Board, September 1941. As they rounded Signal Hill to the embrace of

Table Mountain, he stopped to blot his nib on a piece of scrap paper and looked out. "Would you believe these people?" he said, gesturing at a ramshackle area on the lower slopes.

"They're destitute, Papa. Where else are they supposed to live?"

"I don't care. No one asked them to come here." He rested the nib of his pen in the margin of the page and looked up over his reading glasses. "Engel," his scowl softened, "when are you going to tell me what's really going on?" He placed the pen on the page. "I worry about you, you know."

"Really? Since when was that?"

He placed a hand on her leg but then removed it as if self-conscious at the gesture. "You must look after yourself. You're all I've got."

"What about Frans? The golden boy. You must know it's only a matter of time before he tires of the veterinary practice. You'll have all day to farm together. When you're not running the country, that is."

"*Ge.* I'm not so sure. He's got a mind of his own, that child. And that fiancée. What's her name? Lisette. She thinks I'm an ogre."

"It might help if you tried to be nice to them now and again."

"Nice?" He shifted in his seat and grabbed at the ink bottle to stop it from spilling. Do you think I got to where I am by being a pushover? Why can't they understand that?"

Days ago, Anna would have fallen for his self-deprecation and said something reassuring. But now his words catapulted her back into the see-saw of emotions that had tormented her through the night. She felt an urge to lash out, to confront him with the awful truth. "Listen …"

Immediately she checked herself. She knew the right course of action, no matter the consequences to her family. And she had made her decision. But for now, no matter how difficult, sickening even, she must not reveal her thoughts. She must remain the obedient child.

"What's that?" he asked.

"Just be yourself," she said, forcing a laugh. She adjusted his pocket square. "Your better self." She watched the twin plumes of smoke rising from the Dockland Power Station which until recently had marked the shoreline. Now it was surrounded by a wasteland of freshly dumped ground. She swallowed, tasting bile in her saliva. "They'll come around."

"You think so? I have my doubts. Anyway …" He adjusted his tie, flicked a speck of dust off his lapel. "At least we've got each other."

A shaft of sunlight caught his face. The reflection of grey from his skin and his temples made him look older than usual. Vulnerable even. He shuffled the stack of papers and placed them upside down on the seat. "You still haven't told me what the matter is?"

"Why do I feel like I'm in question and answer time?"

He laughed, deep, with phlegm. "Something's troubling you."

Anna shook her head.

"You couldn't sleep last night, hey?"

"Why do you say that?"

"A father knows."

She looked away, not able to bear eye contact. "How?" she said. "You were snoring, even worse than usual."

"Ag, my girl, you're like a ghost." He shifted in his seat to appraise her. "White as a Merino in spring, bags under your eyes … Still as pretty as ever, mind you. The lucky bugger who …"

He turned to the window. She could see, even side on, that his eyes were moist. Why the tenderness, why now? She felt a ripple of anger.

They stopped at a pedestrian crossing. On the right the minaret of a mosque rose above the crumbling houses of the Malay Quarter. A man in a waistcoat and fez stood on the far pavement enjoying the morning sun as he gazed towards the sea. Closer by, an urchin fidgeted beside a vegetable stand. When he saw the Pontiac he grinned and stepped off the pavement with a tomato in each hand.

Anna's father rolled down the window. "Come here," he called. The boy approached the window. His shirt was three sizes too big and his toes hugged the cobbles.

"Wait." Her father scrounged in his pocket. He held the boy's eyes and slowly withdrew his hand and put it behind his back with his other hand. The boy offered a tomato.

Her father produced both hands, bunched and knuckles up. "Guess," he said.

"No, Papa."

"Leave me. There's nothing for nothing." He extended his hands to the boy. "Come on, I won't bite."

The boy's eyes were like those of a barn owl, too large for his head. The taxi revved. He pointed at the right hand. His eyes widened as the hand opened. There was nothing.

"Driver," Anna said, "let's go."

"Wait," her father said. His face softened, as it did on rare occasions, from the eyes. He turned to the boy. "Keep your tomatoes. There, my boy." He opened his left hand. A ten-shilling note unfurled, revealing a portrait of the king.

The boy's eyes widened further. "Mister, that's too much."

"Take it." Her father held his palm out the window. "Buy yourself some shoes."

The boy hesitated. The taxi revved again. Then he grabbed the note and spun on his heels.

"What is it?" Anna said when they were going again. "I've never seen you give a grown man an inch. But with a child, you can be easy on a stranger."

Her father picked up his papers, licked his forefinger and started paging through them. The cloud had descended again. This was how it always ended.

There was already a long line of cars down Parliament Street even with a full hour to go before the first committee meeting. Sunlight filtered through the oak leaves, dappling the black of the cars' roofs. A Mercedes with wide running boards pulled away from the wrought iron palings of the main gate, and another took its place. Then a huddle of reporters converged from nowhere, clutching hats with one hand and cameras in the other. A block of a man stepped out in a top hat and black overcoat. He took two uneasy steps, then turned as if remembering something. His eyes, even from a distance, looked severe beneath rimless glasses. He bowed a fraction and extended a hand to his wife.

"You know who that is, right?" her father said.

A newspaper boy shouted something about Singapore under threat.

"Ag, no," he said. "What have I said wrong now?"

Anna kept silent. Ahead, the man locked his arm in his wife's and guided her towards the steps of Parliament. Eight Doric columns towered beneath the portico, leaving little doubt as to the location of the entrance. Whoever had designed the imposing red brick building had managed to capture both the stolid fortitude of the Transvaal Republic and the grandeur of empire. It exuded power. "You know exactly," she said at last.

Her father pretended not to have heard. Ahead the couple was passing through a tunnel of guards bearing rifles, bayonets to the sky. "Daniel's no oil painting," he said. "But would you believe it, the women say he's got sex appeal."

"He's a dreadful individual."

"Careful. You're talking about the next Prime Minister."

"With twenty-seven seats? Isn't that a stretch, even for you?"

"Don't be fooled by his looks."

"Professor Pickford-Dunn thinks his policies are unworkable, dangerous even."

"Isn't he your art lecturer?"

"Art history. But he also studied law. And knows politics."

"Hah. You think I care what those communists at your ivory tower say? That the hardworking people of this land care? They're just *souties*. One foot in England, the other in Africa, and their *pieletjies* hanging in the water. Happy to let the place go to the dogs and then run off when things get tough."

"Ag, Papa. You said yourself there are English speakers loyal enough to be called Afrikaners. Isn't that what Hertzog said? Your hero? Before you became infatuated with that"—she watched the Malans disappear between the Doric columns—"that grim reaper."

"Liberals will call him names till sheep take swimming lessons, but that doesn't change the facts. The man's a genius. You don't believe me? Read his address to the Assembly." He gazed at the entrance to Parliament where the couple had disappeared. Then he turned to her, eyes bright. "I tell you what. Ask the librarian, Margriet. She'll get you the Hansard. September '39. You've got time before lunch. Trust me, it's poetry."

The taxi pulled up at the gate. Anna got out before her

father. When he met her at the gate she refused his hand. "You planned it, didn't you?"

He paused at the first guard, as if inspecting him, nodded. Then he straightened, puffed his chest. "What do you mean?"

"Making me sit waiting for you in the library while you carry on all busy and important. I could have been working on my portfolio or seeing my friends."

"*Ge,*" he said out of the side of his mouth. He took another couple of steps and repeated his routine with another guard. This time he shook his head. "Is that what you think of me? Always the worst."

They stop-started through the foyer. Her father knew everyone they passed by name, though not all knew his. They were middle-aged or elderly men in ill-fitting suits, bald or short-back-and-sides, leaving trails of aftershave. Some looked familiar, either from previous visits or the newspapers. She ignored a wink, turned from a sideways glance. Though she was used to being a rose among thorns, the leers made her uncomfortable.

They continued to run the gauntlet down the corridor. There was something about Parliament—the opulence perhaps, or the nature of the work that went on within its walls—that seemed to imbue its members with self-importance. It was like a parallel universe where people who were at each other's throats in public became intimates.

She slowed as they passed the entrance to the Assembly. The giant oak throne of the speaker's chair was empty. Draped over the panelling on either side and above it were life-size portraits of the king and queen, as if reminding members by their imperious gazes that whatever they decided upon was subject to higher powers. Men were filing through the doorway in pairs. Others were already seated, chatting. As always, Anna hoped to catch a glimpse of the slender frame of the Prime Minister with his trademark silver goatee, a rare highlight in an otherwise torturous day.

The three-inch thick door to the library swung on its hinges with remarkable ease. Inside, the air felt close and musty. Three levels of wall-to-wall leather-bound books were set between columns of oak. Every dozen feet around the perimeter of the room, a reading lamp hung from a gold chain. The softness of the carpet was in stark contrast to the marble of the corridor.

The librarian seated at the reception counter remained glued to her papers until Anna's father cleared his throat. She was pretty, despite her double chin and ample padding. Her look of delight lasted a few seconds before she swallowed it, but her blush lingered. She glanced at the clock on the panel opposite her. "Stefan, hasn't your portfolio committee meeting started?"

"Two minutes," he said. "You remember my daughter, Anna. She needs a place to rest. We're having lunch in the dining hall at twelve thirty."

Margriet's eyes swept over the oval reading tables and hard-backed chairs towards a plush leather chair in the far corner. A balding gentleman in a pinstripe sat with one leg crossed over the other, the *Cape Times* hiding his face. The headline was bolder than usual: "Japs cross Jahore". She hunched and spoke softly from the line of her two chins. "I'm sorry, Stefan. Your spot has been taken. She dropped to a whisper. "And he's UP."

He laughed. "That's what I love about you. Always looking after my back." He pulled out his fob watch. "Listen. Do me a favour." He blinked one eye, then the other. "No ..." He winked. "I mean, pull Daniel's address to the Assembly of '39. My girl's dying to read it."

Something in Margriet's smile bothered Anna. More than the insincerity. Could it be jealousy? Or simply embarrassment? Somehow, in her childlike innocence, she'd never considered her father with another woman. He flirted of course, in his unique blend of brusqueness and manliness. But he'd never gone as far as bringing a woman home to the farm.

"Of course." Margriet said, her eyes weighing Anna and finding her wanting. "There's space over there, on the other side of the newspaper stands. It's nice and private."

Anna picked up a copy of the *Cape Times* and found a seat by the window where a solitary shaft of sun illuminated a column of dust. After days of bombing Singapore, the yellow horde had crossed the straits. The British were being accused of sacrificing the colony to play for time. A filler article quoted a retired colonel on South Africa's lack of preparedness for invasion from the east.

She replaced the newspaper and sidled up to the bookshelf on the far wall where there was a line of sight to the librarian's desk, picked out a book, and pretended to read.

"Here." Margriet was at her shoulder. "Sorry to take so long." She handed over a hardcover book so heavy Anna almost dropped it.

Anna settled back into her chair. But much as she tried, she couldn't focus. Her thoughts were in disarray. Despite her revulsion for her father's support of the enemy, he was still her father. But how could she dismiss two years of newspaper reports about refugees fleeing Panzers, German bombs destroying villages, ships plunging to the bottom of the ocean? War demanded sacrifice. And courage.

At length a man entered the library, greeted Margriet and asked for a copy of the prior year's no-confidence debate. When Margriet descended to the archives, Anna replaced the book on the table and slipped out. She waited for the library door to suck closed behind her, then made for the ladies' room, which was tucked away out of sight. Then she retraced their route of entry. The hallways were empty except for an orderly pushing a tea trolley, who showed a flicker of recognition. As the woman made to speak, Anna lifted her chin, eyes forward, and strode past.

On the stairs, she looked out over the steel fence palings to the street where the shadows of the branches above criss-crossed the cobbles. She hurried along, pausing only as she approached the gate. There were only two guards now, one on either side. She tugged at her shoulder strap, feeling her breasts firm against her brassiere, then tilted her head at the nearest guard, who looked about her own age. "Lovely day, isn't it?" she said.

"Ma'am." He blushed.

"It would be crime to sit inside all day, wouldn't it?" She held the rim of her hat between her index finger and thumb. "I'm off for a stroll."

Walking down Parliament Street, she forced herself to amble, trying not to think until she was sure she was out of sight. At Church Square, she stopped as always at the statue of Onze Jan. *Is Het Ons Ernst*—the inscription was as grave as the granite it was etched in. The late statesman stared at the barn-like structure of the Groote Kerk across the square. Anna sighed, remembering the tedious sermons and her father's complaints about the cost of reserving a pew for only four months a year.

She continued in the direction of the sea, still raking over her decision. She'd examined her options from every angle. She knew the right thing to do. Still, it gave her no peace.

A young couple at a pavement café were sharing a pot of tea while a flower seller propositioned them with a bunch of roses. The man appeared to protest, then accepted them, reaching into his pocket with the other hand. The lady took the flowers, blushing. Anna's thoughts leapt to Thomas, and she found herself tripping over a loose cobble, clutching a lamp post to steady herself. The Commander of a German U-boat! A killer? And her father a traitor? Oh God, why did it have to be this way?

She continued, ducking as a pigeon swept her face so close that she felt the draught. A car hooted from behind, then sped past the second she stepped aside. She hastened on to the intersection with Darling Street that ran along the length of the Parade grounds. A gust of wind whipped a packet around her ankles, and she stooped to dislodge it, then swept her eyes from the station on the far side of the Parade to the line of palm trees in front of the City Hall to her right. In the distance she could just make out the jumble of District Six at the foot of Devil's Peak.

A double-decker bus rumbled past bearing the slogan "Mother City of South Africa". She bit her lip. Seldom had she felt a greater need for her mother's presence. The *dominee* had been wrong; time was no healer.

Along Darling Street she passed ramshackle stands and eager hawkers. "Luv'ly apricots, ma'am," urged a gap-toothed man. "Peaches, plums ..." She walked past, unseeing.

Near the far end of the Parade she stopped at a ridge of trees through which she could see the tortoiseshell walls of the castle, command headquarters of the Union Defence Force. A Union Jack fluttered over its rampart.

A platoon of soldiers was slow-marching in the direction of the bell-towered entrance. Anna took a deep breath and then fell in behind them, letting them lead her towards the castle. As they approached a bridge across the moat, guarded by a pair of cannons, her steps became more hesitant. The soldiers continued on. Come on, she chided herself.

Tears were welling in her eyes. She sniffed and fumbled in her bag for a tissue. Before she could bring it to her nose a gust of wind yanked it away. She lunged to retrieve it, but her bag tipped and scattered its contents on the pathway. In a blur of tears she squatted and gathered them. When she rose, the soldiers had disappeared. She stared at the arched entrance, trying to gather her will. But her feet had turned to clay. She looked up to an unanswering sky, then turned and stepped from the bridge.

10

ANNA WALKED QUICKLY BACK towards Parliament, her thoughts in turmoil. But as she drew closer, she balked, unable to face the oppressive atmosphere of the library. She veered right off Parliament Street in favour of Government Avenue, the long, shady pedestrian corridor on the opposite side of the Parliament Buildings that led gently uphill from St George's Cathedral at the city end to her university campus on Orange Street, behind which arose the rugged hulk of Table Mountain. Once past St George's Cathedral, a pair of gates to the right opened into the Company's Garden, a green oasis of serenity that extended alongside the avenue, culminating in a rose garden on the border of her campus.

In the gardens she slowed to a stroll, berating herself for her display of cowardice at the castle. How easily she had shrunk from her duty and betrayed her convictions. She wandered aimlessly past the old stone well towards the shade, deep in thought. Water from an open *sloot* gurgled beside her and the traffic was a distant hum. It was a place which she'd often retreat to—an eye of tranquility in the hurricane of the city. But today she could feel no peace. She'd grown up thinking herself a patriot. Imagining that when it came to it, she'd happily sacrifice her narrow interests for the greater good of her people. Now she'd chosen one man, her father, above a nation. How had it come to this?

The boom of the noonday gun startled her from her thoughts, scattering the pigeons around her. Papa would be ready for lunch soon. She quickened her pace and retraced her steps past the old stone well towards the gate. Beyond the ditch on her right, she could see across Government Avenue to the wrought iron fence that demarkated the Parliament grounds. She passed a beggar slumped on a bench. Despite the heat he wore an overcoat with a hat over his face. Papa had always said that the poor became that way through indolence and giving to them only made it worse. But after a year in the city she'd realised that his rigid notion of cause and effect was overly simple.

"Ma'am, spare a penny for a foreigner." She paused in confusion. That voice. She turned.

"Don't mind me," the beggar patted the bench beside him. "Here." He stared ahead like a blind man. "Act like we don't know each other. You're just resting awhile."

She perched as far from him as possible, questions cascaded through her mind. The guilt that had stalked her since leaving the castle had now morphed into fear.

Wordlessly he shoved a slice of bread across the bench, and watched the pigeons gather. As they bobbed closer, he tossed a thumb of bread between them. There was a commotion as they fought for possession, until a large individual on the edge of the group elbowed the others away and pecked the bread off the ground. "Just like people," he said as it flew off, "always fighting for the spoils."

She was suddenly angry. She snatched up the bread, broke off a square and threw it onto the path. "We're supposed to meet tomorrow. *Hemel*, what are you doing here, like this?"

"I'm not sure you'd believe me if I told you."

"You're right. But you may as well try. Why the ambush? Unless you want something from me. Yes. Isn't that what you're all about? Using people. My father. Kleinjan. The missionary. Now me."

"Missionary?"

"Kleinjan and I happened to go to church." A pigeon swooped onto the path and pecked at the crumb. "You're not very careful, Thomas. Or is it Hans, or Herman? For someone in the business of espionage, you leave a trail as wide as an ocean."

"All right." His face was blank. "So, you went to Elim and saw a German missionary at a Moravian station? *Wirklich?*

What else did you see? Or let me rephrase. What else did they see, or tell you they saw?"

"You're denying it? They're honest folk, Thomas. I believe them." She felt a deep sadness. "Unlike …"

"I'm not saying I've never been to see him," he said. "The missionary. But not recently. I promise."

"*Ge.*"

"How many were there, Anna? And when? Please. It's important."

"I'm tired of your games." She kicked at a pigeon, which shook its mother-of-pearl neck and hopped aside. Another took its place at her feet. Why couldn't this fog of confusion clear, at least partially? She knew she had to be strong but her heart was already crying.

Thomas slumped back on the bench and adjusted his hat to cover his face again. "All right," he said. "I'm not a salesman. In fact, I couldn't think of a more depressing way to make a living. But I'm not a spy."

A squirrel scampered along the branch of an Indian rubber tree above them and stopped to sniff the air. Anna wanted to look at Thomas but resisted. "Spare yourself. I already know."

A group of schoolchildren were entering the park, the boys in white shirt sleeves and khaki shorts, the girls in floral dresses with bows in their plaits. A teacher herded them in a wide berth around the bench. "I'm just doing my job," he said. "The navy's all I've known since boarding school."

Anna felt some of her tension drain. Why? At the confirmation of what she knew but had still hoped wasn't true? "A German officer," she mumbled. "Somehow I imagined it differently."

"What. Like an army ant, marching in formation? With a lisp, speaking like zis? Have you ever considered that you've been just as brainwashed as us?"

"If you think you're going to convert me …" Anna made to stand. "I'm not my father."

"Sit down." He opened his hand face up on his lap. A chunk of bread lay in his palm. He waited for a pigeon to swoop down and grab it. "I know you aren't. That's why I'm here."

She looked up at the outline of the sun behind the branches and shivered. "Yes, wasting my time. Telling me things I already know."

Thomas sighed. "All right. So, we can take the gloves off. Aren't you supposed to be in Parliament, waiting like a good girl while Papa attends to affairs of state?"

Anna looked over the paling at the statue of Queen Victoria guarding the façade of Parliament. It reminded her of Fanus's boasting about his student movement's schemes to topple all symbols of British rule. "I know my father can be imperious," she said. "And his enemies say nasty things about him—some deserved—but no one can accuse him of not being a slave for his country."

"I'm sure you're right. But you didn't answer my question. Where've you been? Just now."

Anna gathered her handbag to her lap and stood. "What business is that of yours? Or anyone's? In this country we're free to come and go as we please. It's called democracy."

"I think you protest too much. What did you tell them?"

Anna clicked her bag open, then shut it, and looked beyond the exit gate. A tram clanged up Adderley Street and veered right into Wale, stopping with a screech opposite the cathedral. "I don't know what you're talking about," she said and started towards the park exit.

"The castle's a strange place for a girl to while away the time."

She stopped. How could he have guessed? "You followed me!" she said, turning. "How dare you!"

"Never mind why or how. Just tell me who you spoke to." He made as if to struggle from the bench.

She stared at him. Whether it was his rags, his posture, or even the hint of desperation in his voice, she no longer felt anger or fear. Only pity. He was like a beached dolphin, still glistening but struggling to breathe. "No one," she said, relieved to start with the truth. "I was sightseeing. Fascinating history …"

He put up a hand in protest. She ignored it and continued.

"Built by the VOC—that's the Vereenigde Oost-Indische Compagnie—in 1679. Their second attempt. Did you know

the sea used to lap its walls? That's where the name Strand
Street came from."

He let his hand drop, evaluating her.

"You know," she continued, "Strand, beach. Must be the
same in German."

"This isn't the time for joking." He edged towards her. "What
did you tell them? Please. Lives are at stake. Innocents."

Anna was caught between anger and sympathy. Part of her
wanted to keep him guessing. Goodness knows, he deserved it.
The other wanted to reach out and tell all, hear him reassure
her that everything was going to be all right. She felt teary,
looked at him in a blur.

He dropped his head. "Alright. You had a duty. How could
you do otherwise?"

She was crying now, her face a windowpane in the rain.
"You don't believe me, do you?"

"I don't know."

It was useless, she thought. No amount of denying was
going to convince him. She had sudden longing to wrap her
arms about him and stay there forever.

"Even if I don't tell them," she said, "someone will. The
word 'secret' isn't in the Strandveld's dictionary."

"I know. I know."

"What will you do? The boat. Your men. They could be in
danger."

He glanced down at her chest. It was heaving with every
breath and she felt self-conscious. Then he looked up. "All
right," he said. "We're in this together now. You already know
too much. The men, they will be fine. The boat too."

"But how?"

"My second-in-command has taken her further offshore to
wait on the ocean bed. Don't worry. Even if the South African
Navy drops every depth charge they possess, they won't get
within half a mile."

"But ..." she searched his eyes. "How did you communicate
with them? You've been on the farm all this time. Now here."

"You'll figure it out," he said. "In fact, you already have."

Elim, Anna thought. The two white visitors. The puzzle
pieces were fitting together. But there were plenty still missing.

"The missionary?" There was an edge in her voice.

He nodded. "I don't like it either."

"Sure you don't."

"I'm not religious," he said, standing, "but I regret it when men of the cloth get caught up in things like this."

"How did it happen? Practically, I mean. The communication."

"Simple. He's got a hotline to more than just the Almighty."

"Meaning?"

"He's the only agent this side of Port Elizabeth with a transmitter that actually works."

Anna stepped back. "Agent! Why tell me this? So you can kill me later in good conscience? That's what Nazis do without thinking, isn't it? For *volk* and *vaderland*."

He stepped towards her. Her heels backed against the paling beside the park gate. He held her gaze for a long moment, then looked away. "Those were my orders. From Admiral Dönitz himself. No loose ends."

11

ANNA WIPED HER FACE with her sleeve, bent to dislodge her foot from the gatepost, then shifted around the edge to the outside of the gate. Two steps to freedom. "I thought you were different," she said. "That I could trust you."

There was the clip-clop of a horse coming from Government Avenue beyond a thicket of bamboo. Out of the corner of her eye she confirmed it was a mounted policeman. He was close enough to call. She thought of her father. The implications. Even if his involvement was never proven, the family name could be forever tarnished.

Thomas had stepped back, hunched like a beggar again. "You didn't tell them, did you?" he said. "No. You're in too deep already. I thought so. You can't do it."

"That makes two of us, it seems," she answered. A gentleman led by a poodle brushed past her. She was a body length clear of Thomas. "You must have had a dozen opportunities to kill me once you began to suspect I knew too much. So much for the ruthless Nazi killer."

"My victims are statistics," he said. "Numbers of ships. Tonnage. Shapes glimpsed through a periscope."

"And when you hear the cries of drowning sailors flailing among the wreckage?"

Thomas was staring vacantly at the statue of Queen Victoria. Proof that a woman didn't need beauty to be powerful. "Go," he waved. "Your father is expecting you."

"But what about us?" she said.

"Us?" his left dimple appeared. Then his face stiffened. "You're nothing to me, remember. I'm heartless."

Anna felt a pang of despair. Something elusive was slipping from her grasp. "You said we're in this together. We're going to have to get out the same way."

"Relax yourself," he said. "Soon I'll be gone without a trace. What evidence would there be? Footprints in the sand? If the tides haven't erased them already."

"And Kleinjan?" she said. "He might be forced to talk."

"The authorities would hardly believe the testimony of a coloured farmworker over your father's."

She eyed him. "So why haven't you left?"

He fiddled with his left finger. It was a thick gold band with a lapis lazuli signet.

"I thought you weren't married," she blurted.

He followed her gaze to the ring, then turned it so the signet faced her. "My family crest," he said. "That's an estate in Danzig. It was German for centuries." He looked at her.

The bells of St George Cathedral chimed the half hour. Pigeons fluttered from the pavement. "Are you still here tonight?" she said, surpising herself.

He nodded. "It could be a week until I'm recalled. Why?"

Her surge of courage ebbed. "Nothing, I just thought ..."

"You've given me an idea," he said. "Your father lent me a suit."

"And?" Anna felt her hands shaking. She clasped them at her waist to steady them.

"You like to dance, right?"

She felt her cheeks warm. "And what's that to you?"

Thomas shrugged. "Oh, nothing. I was just wondering ..."

Anna held up her hand to block the sunlight, looked at him out of a half-closed eye. "You're not suggesting ..." For a moment her heart ran away from her words. She wasn't used to having to second guess a man. "A ... a dance hall?" She watched his dimples deepen. "What's so funny?" For the first time she noticed he'd blacked out a tooth. He clearly wasn't the type for half measures.

Thomas laughed. "I don't bite."

"I'm trying hard to believe you," she said, pouting. "But you don't make it easy. Tell me, aren't you supposed to be keeping a low profile?"

"Yes and no. Besides, there's no better place to be invisible than in a crowd." He stuffed his hands in his jacket and pulled out the pocket liners. "This charade was more for your sake. In case you came with your father. By the way, he thinks I'm at the machine shop in Woodstock."

They stood an arm's reach apart, staring into each other's eyes. A couple of ladies with broad hats and parasols linked arms in passing. A seagull cawed overhead. Anna fought back a blink, determined not to interrupt the connection. More than her life, she wanted to stay there forever. Not needing anything or anyone.

"I can see you're a stubborn woman," he said, not breaking the stare.

"What does that make you?" She wiped a ringlet of hair which had blown over her eye.

"I'm trained to stay focused." He made binoculars with his fingers. "Through the periscope, I mean. I flinch, I die."

"You're quite something." Her face was breaking into a smile, but she kept the stare. "The word intense hardly does you justice. Have you always been like this?"

"You mean ..." For a moment he looked sad, then recovered. "Was I ever a child?"

"Yes, I suppose. Don't you ever let your hair down?"

He was still staring at her, but it was obvious he was in another place, another time.

"Did I say something wrong?" she said. "I didn't' mean ..."

"No. No." He snapped to the present. "It's just this war. It changes people. I've seen boys from my high school—from good homes and mother's love—become monsters."

They were still fixed on each other.

"All right," she said, "you win. I think you need some cheering up. I tell you what." An idea was forming as she spoke, her audacity growing. "My friends and I are going to the Mount Nelson tonight. There's a big band, it plays in the ballroom every night."

He lifted his nose. "That sounds terribly posh." Then he looked down, scratched his cheek. "I'm not certain it's my scene. Sorry."

"Oh, no," she laughed. "It's not like that. Really. It's loads of fun." She felt an urgency rising, and, trying to suppress it, she smiled. "Come on. We're meeting inside at ten."

He was smiling now. Like a yoke had lifted.

She giggled. "You're going to make me say it, aren't you, you beastly thing?" She narrowed her eyes at him, trying to look stern. "Please. Ten o'clock sharp. Just be sure to get a makeover first. I wouldn't want my friends to think I'm desperate."

12

RELIEVED TO FIND THE library door ajar, Anna slipped in without announcing herself. Thankfully, Margriet wasn't at her post. Anna made a beeline across the carpet for the newspaper stand. There was no one in sight. Perhaps her absence hadn't been noted, after all. The early edition of the evening paper was already on the rack. Another stunning victory for the Japanese on Singapore Island. Below the headlines was a leader on General Smuts and his wife attending a fundraising event for the Widows and Orphans Relief Fund at the City Hall. When she'd finished reading the article she looked up.

The instant she saw her father sitting alone in the corner of the room, she knew there was trouble.

"Come sit, Engel."

Anna sank into the armchair, clutching her handbag on her lap.

"So." His leg was crossed over the other with *Die Transvaler* folded open on his knee. He tapped it with the end of his fingernail. "A couple of good articles this month. You should try it. Instead of *Die Huisgenoot*. Or the propaganda they feed you at university." He picked up the paper, slap-ironed it. "That Verwoerd guy is still the editor. Now there's a man who knows what this country needs."

"Why are you telling me this, Papa?" She wriggled to stand. Fell back. "Aren't we late for lunch?"

"We wouldn't be if you'd been here when we agreed."

"Ag, you know I wouldn't keep you waiting on purpose. I was in the toilet."

He raised an eyebrow. Then he glanced at the door where the face of a parliamentarian had appeared and retreated. "So long?"

She looked away, shrugged. "Women's business."

"Margriet told me she hadn't seen you for an hour, maybe more."

Anna tried to sit upright but sank back into the chair. She felt like a child who'd stolen the last piece of cookie from the jar and lied about it. Why did he still make her feel that way? It was ridiculous. "You should be pleased I still agree to hang around this … this place …"

"Kleinjan was just here."

She paled. Papa had got to him, she thought. Forced him to confess all. Her knowing. She felt the room turn on its axis below the domed ceiling. Oak panels, books and reading lights swam before her eyes.

"What's wrong?" he said. "You don't look well."

She fought to steady the room, hands clutching the arms of her chair. "I just thought he was with his cousin in District Six. How did he get in here, anyway? I thought servants weren't allowed."

"*Wragtag waar.* You don't know your father by now?" He chuckled. "I long ago organised him a pass to use the deliveries entrance with the bakkie. He's been running me errands for years. When he's in town, of course."

She shrugged and waited. From the corridor came the sound of teacups rattling on a cart.

He shook his head slowly, lips pursing in an expression she knew in her core. Of disappointment when someone failed to live up to his expectations or hadn't listened to a bout of his moralising.

"He's worried about you."

Damn, she thought: what else had Kleinjan said? The servers in the corridor were exchanging gossip in high-pitched vernacular.

He pressed on, "Why didn't you come and talk to me first?"

"Why should I?"

"I'm your father for heaven's sake. I know I can be hard, but when have I ever betrayed your confidence?"

Anna felt her front teeth dig into her tongue. Kleinjan had been Anna's mentor for most of her life. She'd shared many of her deepest hurts and cares, her secrets. Like the time she stole Papa's brandy to learn what it felt like to be drunk. Or smuggled English newspapers from the general dealer in Napier. Her first kiss. No, surely he wouldn't have told her father everything.

"Anna?"

Her eyes skipped from the reception counter to the door and back, buying time.

"Don't worry," he said. "You can speak freely. Margriet's archiving downstairs. The others are at lunch."

She inhaled. Why the tentativeness? If he knew anything of substance he would have thrown it on the table by now. Anna crossed her arms to formulate an attack. She'd had the benefit of a master politician as her role model. "With respect, Papa. You're the one who has something to explain."

He folded *Die Transvaler* and placed it on the side table, breathed out with his shoulders. "*Nee wat.* Imagine if I'd spoken to my foster father like this."

Anna clung to the offensive. "Did you think I wouldn't figure it out?"

He unfolded his legs to a vee. "What do you mean?"

"I may be naïve, Papa. Or I was until recently. But I'm not stupid."

"Of course you aren't. As I always say, you got your mother's brains." His laugh had a timid ring to it. "And my stubbornness."

Anna felt a leap of irritation. He was skirting the issue, trying to find out what she knew before playing his hand. "Couldn't you find some other way? Why Rietvlei? Why endanger us all?"

He leaned forward and then looked at the floor, his jaw shifting, as if ruminating his answer. Then he looked up at her, his voice low. "What is this you're talking about? Really, you've done nothing but attack me all day." His eyes were sad. "Doesn't matter what I say or do. It's like I'm the enemy, some sort of monster. You know I'd do anything and everything in my power ... for you, and for Frans."

She looked at him. How could he swing her emotions in the space of a few sentences? Perhaps he was horribly misguided, but he was being sincere. For the second time in as many hours, Anna felt like letting go, confessing all. If she couldn't trust her own father—the man who'd brought her up single-handedly and provided for all her needs—then who? Instead she pulled back her shoulders. This wasn't the time to fall back into his shadow. "Just tell me why."

He looked away, his eyes lingering on the door. Anna followed, saw what he'd seen. Though it was closing fast, there could be no mistaking. The door had been open.

"Come," he said, standing. "I don't know about you, but I'm not in the mood for the institutional fare they dish us here. Let's go to our favourite." He strode towards the entrance. "We can carry on talking there." He swung the door out into the corridor.

"*Eina!*" A woman's voice, as high pitched as if she'd seen a cockroach.

"What the ..." he said, looking down at Margriet's high-heeled shoes. "I thought you were downstairs sorting."

She placed a hand on his forearm to steady herself and kept it there as she adjusted her heel with the other. Bending had the effect of exaggerating her already substantial bosom. She waited until he'd indulged his view. "Ag, *my lief.* By now you should know how efficient I am. I just thought I'd get some fresh air."

Anna had a chance to study the librarian for the first time. Clearly the war rationing hadn't extended to cosmetics. The result was a face once pretty enough for a fashion model but now severe, lips rimless about a hard mouth. Anna tugged her father's arm from hers, thrust herself forward. "Excuse us," she said. "Papa and I have a date."

Her father's grip tightened on her wrist. She had to almost skip to keep up with him as he strode, pigeon-chested and tall, along the corridor. "So," she said as they passed the entrance to the assembly, "what matters of great national import will you be deciding this afternoon?"

"*Wragtag,*" he said, "since when were you interested? Didn't you fall asleep last time?"

"Is that what they told you?" Anna scoffed. "I was pretending, silly." She elbowed him. "I just couldn't bear all those dirty old men ogling me from down there. To think they're married, some of them with grandchildren. *Sies.*"

Outside, the South Easter was at full strength and the cotton-wool tablecloth was cascading down the face of Table Mountain. Anna tried to distract her father by pointing it out as they approached the young guard at the gate. Instead he stopped in front of the lad, appraised his dress and flicked a speck of dust off his lapel.

The guard shuffled his feet to attention. "Ma'am." It was as though he didn't know where to look. "Did you enjoy your walk?"

"Oh, *comme ci comme ça,*" she smiled, watching a taxi draw to a halt outside the gate.

"What was that all about?" her father said when they'd meandered out of earshot down Parliament Street. "I thought you were in the library. That time of the month, *nê?*"

Anna didn't respond. They turned left and strolled towards the elbow of Wale and Adderley Streets. On the right was the Old Supreme Court building, windowless from its former incarnation as the slave lodge of the Dutch. She glanced down to the bottom of Adderley Street, where the pier had once stood before the land reclamation. The last time she'd been there her mother had treated her to a candy floss from the stash of pounds she kept in her jewellery jar to avoid Papa's rants about wasting money on trifles. The sandstone bell tower of St George's Cathedral appeared now as they turned left into Government Avenue.

"Have you seen Thomas?" her father said.

Anna swallowed. Could he read her mind? She pretended to be distracted by a tram trundling past. "Sorry, what was that?" she said. "You mean the … South Wester? How would I know where he is? Isn't he your friend?"

"Colleague. He was supposed to call my secretary to arrange dinner tonight. Instead he's disappeared."

They were at the gated entrance to the Company's Garden now, skirting the remains of a dropped ice-cream spreading from a squashed cone. Her heart was fluttering, and she was thankful for the group of people between them and the bench she didn't want to see.

"If he makes contact, you must tell me. Promise?"

The bench was empty, save for a pigeon tussling with a bread crust, and Anna breathed out. Her pace increased. She kept her eyes on the path, aware of the crunch of her father's leather on the stones behind her. Though they were in the shade of the fig tree, she felt hot. "Why ever would he?" she said at last. "He's *your* colleague."

His crunching grew louder until it drew level. "I'd say he's smitten, that's why."

They were rounding a bend now. The stone well was ahead and to the left. This time the paving was devoid of pigeons and people. Without looking at her father, she said, "No. You don't mean …"

"*Jong.* The way he looks, asks about you. A father knows these things."

They were beside the well now. An idea struck her. "Is that why Kleinjan came to see you?" She took his forearm. "He thinks I'm going to do something silly? Come on, admit it."

He looked at the sun, held up his hand to block it.

"I'm right, aren't I?" she said. "*Nee wat*! You two are as bad as each other. If you're not trying to keep me away from a man, you're trying to match-make me."

He swallowed. Eyes flitting from one side to the next before focusing on her. "Thomas isn't right for you," he said. "You've got to trust me. Too old for one thing."

"Ag, there you go again. Still trying to run my life." Anna tugged at his arm, steering him across the paving to where the path continued into lush tropical foliage. She was fed up with his patronising. This was the same man who'd torn her childhood friend from her because he was the wrong colour. But she had to appear unruffled. It wasn't the time to lose her temper. "I admit he's nice. And we had some good conversations. But romance? Not a chance."

"Listen here." He cleared his throat. "I don't want you to see him again. You understand?"

She slowed her pace, trying to regulate her fury before putting anything into words. He could say what he liked, but she didn't have to obey. Not at all costs. He could make life difficult, throttle the flow of funds. But in less than two years she'd be independent. She nodded. *"Reg so."*

His eyebrows closed in on one another, his mouth closed and upper lip protruding. It was the look he got when he was pleased with himself.

She dug her fingernails through his shirt sleeve. They were following the path parallel to Government Avenue, separated from it by a spiked paling fence and a ditch. "But only if you tell me the real reason you don't want me to see him."

He jerked his arm from her grip, the whiplash effect toppling her hat. "Look what you've done." She stooped to pick it up, dusted it off.

"Sorry, *lief.* I didn't mean to … It's just … You must be careful what you say."

"Stop trying to justify yourself," she said, hands on hips. In that moment she wanted to reach out and strangle him. "I didn't actually say anything. I just asked a question." A yellowed leaf floated down and settled on the path. Then she noticed his expression. His eyes were flicking to and fro. Like he was unsure, a first in twenty years.

"O hemel," he said, fumbling in his pocket as if he'd just remembered something. As he pulled out his fob watch, a bird flapped its wings from a branch above them. *"Bliksem."* He yanked his hand back. "Can you believe it? The bugger just *kakked* on me?" He stooped down into the ditch. The flow of the stream dammed as he wiped his hands.

As he bent Anna noticed for the first time that the hair on his pate was thinning. It somehow made him seem frailer. He squeezed the water from his handkerchief. "It's cold, hey. Who would have thought? In the middle of the Cape summer, *nogal."*

"Apparently this is from the Platteklip stream, from the mountain."

"Ja, like the spruit at Rietvlei." He folded his handkerchief into a square. Then he checked his watch and looked up at her.

She recognised the expression in a flash. That maddening prelude to obfuscation, the intrusion of something more important. They'd skirted so close to the truth she'd almost felt it. Now it was slipping away. She waited for the inevitable.

"I just remembered," he said. "I'm supposed to meet Daniel

before the session. I really have to be there. *Siestog*, he's having such a hard time. Did I tell you we have a faction? We want to walk out of session tomorrow."

He glanced at her, away, then back at his watch. "That was five minutes ago. Oh, *Engel*. I'm so sorry. Can we make our lunch tomorrow?"

She waited, knowing what would follow.

He pulled out a pound note. Money, his stock-in-trade offering for absolution. "Here. Spoil yourself. He winked. "And don't bother with the change."

13

ANNA STOOD AT THE edge of the dance floor and watched another couple swing-waltz past her towards the band on the far side of the ballroom. A pianist sat, a cigarette smoking on his lips, and caressed his baby grand. He paused just long enough to make eye contact with the lead singer, then continued. To one side of the trio was a row of trumpeters, two saxophonists and a cellist. On the other was a drummer, teasing a cymbal with a drumstick and treading bass. Collin's Dance Orchestra, it read in cursive on the skin of the drum. Anna's eyes settled, yet again, on the wall clock that peeked from a drapery of flags. The Hammer and Sickle took pride of place beside the Stars and Stripes, both flanked by Union Jacks. It was thirty-one minutes past ten and still no sign of Thomas. Her irritation, which had long since boiled to anger, was transforming into worry.

The lead singer coughed into the bulb of the microphone, then he ran his hand through his hair and wiped his fingers on his trouser seam. He was wearing a cream-coloured double-breasted jacket with a black tie, and his face was round and insincere. "This one, ladies and gentlemen,"—he waited for the hubbub to fade—"is dedicated to our Allies across the pond." He nodded to a uniformed man standing like a pillar in the centre of the dance floor. "Oh! Look at me now," he said, and winked at the officer's partner. "By Frank Sinatra. Hope you like it folks."

The lights dimmed. Anna watched Elizabeth and Agnes being led onto the dance floor by partners from a visiting ship arranged by some civic organisation. Rather them than me, she thought. Too wet behind the ears and cocky.

Agnes's partner drew her close, as if needing to whisper in her ear. She giggled, hand on his shoulder.

"Excuse me," a man's voice broke through the music.

Anna ignored it. Six men had already asked her to dance and she'd refused each without explanation.

A hand rested on her shoulder. Still she didn't look. The voice was in her ear now. "Say, ma'am. Would you happen to know where a man can buy a drink?"

Though she'd rehearsed her opening lines a hundred times during the tedium of the afternoon sitting, she could find no words. She listened helplessly as the saxophonists drawled. From the piano came a trickle of notes and a familiar chorus. Still she couldn't move. The hand slid from her shoulder to her side and rested on her waist. The first thing she noticed when she turned was his suit. It was her father's, dark navy, and a little too large.

"Thomas. You scared me."

He pressed the bridge of his wire-framed glasses to his nose. His fringe was coiffed, his beard trimmed to a goatee. He was a carbon copy of Jan Smuts as a young man. The only difference was the smile. "Care to dance?" He offered his hand. The band had slowed. On the dance floor, couples were drawing close.

Anna felt as if she was drifting above the chandeliers. Snowdrops of light sprinkled the hall as the dancers made choreographed twirls.

"I'll understand if you're angry," he said, hand extended. "I also hate it when people are late."

"It's not that." She looked at her feet. A flutter of panic. "It's just … I've hardly ever danced the tango. I'll …"

"Come."

Anna felt him take her hand. It was cool and firm. She found herself following, silent but willing. He stopped at the edge of the dance floor, took her left hand to his side. His other was at her waist, drawing her closer without trying. She leaned towards him, felt his chest hard against her breasts. For several beats they stood rocking an inch from side to side, as though waiting for the music to possess them. They'd moved several feet backwards before she realised they were dancing, certain he was holding her, yet not feeling his hands, as if he was leading more with intuition than force or intent.

"See?" His voice was touching her ear after they'd completed the figure of eight of a backward *ocho*. "You're a natural."

She laughed. "And you're a terrible liar. Goodness, navy man, where did you learn to dance?"

"*Tanzschule,*" he said. "A rite of passage for every German boy." He laughed. "But only for the *adel*, of course." He took her through another figure of eight and paused as if preparing to turn. Her leg folded over his leg, doubled back at the knee. Then they were still, the song over, yet clinging to the embrace.

"Why does this have to end?" she said.

"Quiet now," he said. "There'll be another. We've got all night."

"No." She was squeezing his hand, her breathing fast and shallow. Hoping her voice wouldn't falter. "I mean us. There's no future. It's so cruel."

"Be still," Thomas said. "Forget tomorrow. We're here now. That's all that matters." For several beats he was silent. She could feel his hand, light on the small of her back, hoping he wouldn't notice her perspiration. Next thing his chin brushed the top of her shoulder, and she was swirling. They were in front of the band now. She could see the lead singer's scalp beneath the Brylcreem of his hair and ignored his wink.

There was a pause in the beat. Anna rested her face on Thomas's shoulder. Smelled musty cotton and her father. "Don't go," she whispered. "Don't go."

"Can I tell you a secret?" he said in her ear.

She smiled. "You've been telling me nothing else since we met."

"Funny. But this I didn't know until today." He slid his right leg between hers, first the toe of his shoe then his thigh. She wanted to freeze, instead her balance tilted, leg swinging out. And yet again they were walking the tango. "I've never been in love."

Anna laughed, more from nerves than humour. "Don't play with me, Thomas." She parted an inch. "You're telling me … your fiancée … surely."

He shook his head and led her into a forward *ocho*. When they paused, he said, "I once thought it was love. That is true."

Anna felt his hold tightening. She'd never been as close to a man. Frightened, yet secure.

"I want to see more of you," he said.

"Stop ..." She drew away.

"What is it?"

"Oh, I don't know. I don't know anything any more. It's just ... I can't help thinking what they'll do if they catch you." She felt warm again, in need of fresh air. "Sorry, what am I saying! Oh, Thomas, you're from another world. Think about it. You're older for one thing. Engaged. And German."

He paused to rock forward and backward, his leg brushing her thigh again, gently. "None of that matters. Now we are here, together."

Two steps later they were in a twirl. There was no one else in the room. Only one thing mattered in the stretch of eternity. Anna said, "Tomorrow. The next. You must know it's only a matter of time before they catch you. What are you going to do?"

The tango reached its final, lingering note. Thomas held her body still and slid her foot outward with his own. "Nothing," he whispered at her ear. "Just wait."

Neither seemed willing to be the first to move. Soon the trumpeters were tapping their instruments to drain the condensation and the lead singer mopped his brow. Only when one of the other band members rapped on the microphone to announce an intermission did Thomas relax his hold. Keeping her hand in his, he led her back to the table. Once seated, he hailed a waiter who arrived with a smile in a tuxedo and white gloves. Thomas ordered two Scotch and sodas.

As they waited for their drinks, Anna scanned the hall. She was relieved to see her friends still on the dance floor. Then she rested her elbows on the table and leaned towards him. "What do you think of the band?"

"Not bad. They play with passion."

"They sure do. Did you know they played at the Coronation Ball in '37 here in Cape Town?" The waiter arrived and deposited their Scotches with a flourish. "Maybe that's why the police let coloured musicians play here. In this part of town."

Thomas looked at her for several seconds. "You're shaking."

She looked at her glass. The clear liquid twinkled in the light from the chandelier above them. "I'm sorry." Her eyes darted about the room, behind and to her left. "We shouldn't be here. It's all my fault."

Thomas ran the stirrer around the inside of his glass, chasing ice cubes. The white triangle in his chest pocket appeared to glow.

"When did you take Papa's suit?" she said. "Are you sure he doesn't know? I mean, about you and me being here? If he does, he'll …"

"Say, now." Thomas steadied her glass with his hand. "You see his ghost around every corner. Relax." He smiled a dimple. "Don't worry, I haven't spoken to him since we arrived in Cape Town. I promise. He lent me clothes when I came ashore. Almost a whole wardrobe."

She stared at him, thinking they were the first words she'd heard from him she could be certain were true.

"*Zum Wohl.*" He clinked glasses, sipped his whisky and swirled before he swallowed. "If it's any help, as a submariner I've learned to take it one day at a time. One hour, in fact. You get philosophical lying a hundred and fifty metres down on the ocean bed while a destroyer rains depth charges."

Out of the corner of her eye Anna saw Elizabeth leading her partner from the dance floor towards their table. "But not reckless," she said, "surely. You wouldn't have survived this long."

"True," he said, placing his glass on its coaster. "I know about your conversation, by the way."

"What?" That sinking feeling again.

"With your father. Before lunch." He held up a hand. "Don't ask," he said. "It gets complicated. Just let me say, he doesn't know everything. Even if he thinks he does. And neither do you."

Anna let his words linger. "What are you saying?" She put her glass on the table. "My father's helping to supply a U-boat and you're telling me there's more?"

His face hardened but with the lines he looked more handsome still. "Sorry," he said. "I've said too much already. My orders came through this afternoon. I'm to leave Sunday at sunset. No further contact with anyone. Even our own agents. Now I really have to go to ground."

Anna felt a sinkhole open in her heart. "So, that's it," she said. "You gate-crash my life and steal my heart. And then, then you just …"

Thomas took her hand in his, caressed her fingers. "It may not seem like it now," he said. "But this madness won't last."

"What do you mean?"

"The war." He dropped his voice. "There's no way Hitler can win now. Think of it. Three months ago he declared war on the United States, as if he was just waiting for Pearl Harbour for an excuse. While our forces are already bogged down by the Russians. He's a fool. It's only a matter of time."

"Time?" she drained her glass and thumped it on the table, then stood. "When did love ever just stand still and wait?"

Elizabeth appeared from the crowd, hips swaying. She sat down two empty chairs away. Her partner stayed standing behind her and began to massage her neck. Then Agnes and her sailor boy arrived, giggling.

"Come," Anna said to Thomas. "I'm not feeling well. Let's go."

"So soon?" Elizabeth said, pouting at Thomas. "I was hoping Frank Sinatra here would ask me for a dance before the night was out."

Anna bristled. "I take it you haven't met." She turned. "Thomas, let me introduce you. This is Elizabeth, my flatmate. Her father's also in Parliament."

Elizabeth cocked her head at him. "On the opposite bench, of course," she laughed. "Goodness me, he sure manages to wind old Stefan up. Especially when he raises the Native question."

"Oh, stop," Anna said, irritation rising. "Why do you always have to bring that up?"

"Stefan's crowd thinks they should be suppressed." She ignored Anna's glare. "You know, kept in their tribal lands, the locations, where they belong. That they're no better than—" Her drink rattled and spilled at the force of Anna's nudge. "What is it?" she turned to Anna. "That's what they say isn't it? That ghastly

Malan even has a name for it. Apartheid, or something like that. You'd know." She stirred her drink. "Father says it's a disaster that would put this country back a hundred years. What's wrong …?" she looked at Anna and back at Thomas. "It's God's truth, I tell you. A disaster in the making. A qualified franchise, that's the way to go. Educate them first."

Anna's irritation had given way to anger. "Oh, back off, Elizabeth. How many times do I have to tell you I abhor everything that that Malan creep and his cronies stand for? Father or no father. They're fossils, all of them." She drained her glass and smacked it down on the table. "I'm tired," she said, standing up. "It's been a long day." She took her handbag from the chair and slung it over her shoulder. "Goodnight everyone."

"Anna," Thomas called after her as she disappeared down the stairs. He caught up with her in the driveway. "At least let me walk you home."

She slowed, and they strolled alongside each other down the palm-lined hotel driveway towards Orange Street. The night air was balmy and the stars beyond the fronds were bright in contrast with the blackened city sky. Orange Street was deserted except for a couple of taxis without lights. The sound of their footsteps on the paving rang out above the distant purr of engines.

Beyond the entrance ahead of them loomed the Mount Nelson, where the guard stood erect beside a boom. Across the way was the top gate of the Company's Garden.

"Evening, ma'am," called the guard. "You're home early. Everything in order?"

"Fine thank you, Robert. I've got a chaperone."

At the corner of Hof Street she stopped and gave Thomas a peck on the forehead. "I must go alone from here," she whispered. "Our residence is just there." She pointed beyond the intersection. There was a cypress hedge and behind it an outline of light behind a curtain. "We can't risk a rumour that I brought a man home."

"Where I come from," he said, taking her hand, "we always escort a lady home." He led her around the corner. The moment they were out of sight of the guard he was holding her. This time closer even than during the dance. Her first thought was guilt. It couldn't, shouldn't, be happening. Then anticipation. Was he waiting for her to respond?

She drew back a couple of inches as if to consider. A movement caught her eye from over his shoulder. A truck was speeding towards them, a pickup like they used on the farm. She stepped back just enough to slip from Thomas's embrace. His arms fell limply to his side, like a mannequin turned the wrong way.

"Sorry," he said. "Was I too forward?"

"No. No." She tried not to look behind him at the truck, which had swerved across the road and was pulling up at the entrance to the Company's Gardens. The back was covered by a tarpaulin. She met Thomas's eyes for a second and then was distracted again. The passenger had hopped out of the truck. There was something familiar about him. But in an instant he was lost in the shadows of the foliage. "I'd better be going."

"Forgive me if I made you uncomfortable."

Anna shook her head harder than she'd intended. "No. I've never felt more at ease with a man in my life. Really. It's not that." The truck pulled away and revved off in the direction of the city. "Thomas," she whispered as she refocused on him. "Something's been bothering me. Since Friday. I couldn't put my finger on it until now."

"Yes?"

"What happened to your colleague? The quiet one."

Thomas's eyes narrowed. "You mean Kurt?" He ran the underside of his thumb up his chin. "Interesting you should ask." He was impossible to read in the shadows. "I was wondering the same thing. That boy is like a cat. He walks alone."

"Come on," she pressed. "You don't have a clue where he is? You're on the same side, aren't you?"

Thomas breathed out through his teeth, shook his head. His voice was low and blended with the breeze. "It might surprise you, but the German armed forces don't always see eye to eye."

"What are you saying?"

He hesitated. "Kurt isn't regular navy. Worse, he doesn't even report to me."

Anna wasn't sure what to believe. It had been a day of lies, counter lies and denials. She sighed. "I thought you were the U-boat Commander."

Only his eyes were visible from the outline of his face, reflecting the starlight. "We're a tight-knit lot in this wolf pack. We must be able to trust each other. I didn't want him on the patrol. I tried to stop it."

"Save your lies, Thomas." She put a foot on the first step, spoke over her shoulder. "I really must go."

"Wait." Thomas stepped towards her, reached out a hand to take her sleeve. "I understand why it's hard for you to believe a word I say. It's just—"

She appraised his figure in outline. Despite his oversized jacket, there was something regal in his bearing. She waited for her head to catch up with her heart. "I'm going to have to tell somebody what's going on, you know."

He stepped up the first step towards her. The top two buttons of his shirt were loose and below them the sweat on his collar bone was just visible. Though he'd breached her comfort zone she was determined to hold her ground. How ironic, it seemed, that a man could at once be so attractive and so frustrating.

"I thought we'd been through this," he breathed. A strand of music filtered through from the crack in the doorway.

Anna felt her spirits plunge. She lowered her eyes to his feet. "My thoughts do no end of circles," she said. "But they always return to the inevitable."

"Meaning?"

"I couldn't live with myself if … if I didn't do anything about it, this business. Can you understand that? Put yourself in my skin for a minute. South Africa is more than my country. It's made me who I am."

"And what do you expect me to do now?" He cocked his head to catch her eyes. "You solve your dilemma but create a new one for me."

"No. I think there's another way." She let his hand cup her elbow and stay there. "But you're going to have to trust me."

A sailor in his ice-cream suit and beret stumbled past along the sidewalk, then staggered into the street, crooning the chorus of a love song she didn't know. Anna recognised him from the dance. Soon the air was still again, save for muffled music from beyond the palms.

"I need more to hang onto than a blind assurance," Thomas said. "Please. Otherwise, I'll have to … do something."

"It's not all bad," she said. "I've thought it through carefully these past two days. There's a middle path—one we can both live with. I promise."

She sensed his eyebrows arching.

"Didn't a wise Englishman once say that if it sounds too good to be true, it is?"

"It's my solemn duty"—her hand rested on his shoulder—"to tell the powers that be. But not necessarily right away. And I could start in a roundabout way with the authorities, you'd be forewarned, have enough time to leave the city, the country. There's sure to be some delay between departments. It would give you that little bit of extra time."

"I see." He stroked his chin as if he still had his full beard. "What authorities are you thinking of?"

She hesitated.

"Anna … Give me something to work on. I also have to explain my actions to my people."

A taxi driver drew up nearby and Anna indicated to the driver to wait. "I told you about my art history professor," she said. "Didn't I?"

He held his chin thoughtfully. "Pickford-Dunn?"

"I'm impressed," she said. "You're quite the observer."

"Names, places and times are the currencies by which I live or die."

"Oh, come on," she smiled and pushed him playfully. "Do you always have to be this melodramatic?"

The taxi driver wound down his window, let his hand hang out and drummed his fingers on the metal of his door.

"Just relax," Thomas called, feigning a South African accent. "The lady and I just want to say our goodnights." He turned back to Anna. "You appear to have great admiration for this professor." His face crinkled a smile. "Are you sure it's just his intellect?"

Anna laughed. The angst she'd felt just moments ago had evaporated. "Oh … no, silly. It's just, well, he has connections."

"And what does that mean?"

"I can't tell you more, not now. Give me a chance. I'll speak to him tomorrow. Even if he does break my trust, which I very much doubt, you'll have more than enough time to finish your business and clear out."

He paused, his expression changing from thoughtful to sceptical. "You ask a lot of me, Anna."

"And you of me."

"All right." He straightened, turned his head towards the taxi still idling at the kerb. "One more moment." He turned back to her, shrugged. "Ah, what can I say? I will go." He paused. "But I ask just one thing first."

Anna could no longer see the contours of his face against the light from the street lamp. "Fire away."

"Can I see you tomorrow night?" He smiled. "One last time before I must go."

Anna inhaled. The cool air spread through her lungs and it felt good. A strange sensation rippled down her abdomen, making her thighs tingle. "I don't know," she said. "I really shouldn't. It's not … appropriate, for one thing." She thought of all the times she'd chosen to do what was expected of her, the right thing. Before, what was right had been simple: obey her father, the *dominee*, her conscience. But now everything had blurred. For the first time in her life she was allowing her feelings to override reason. "Let's try Oddfellow's Lodge, down on Hope Street. It's a dance hall." She could sense his half grin in the shadow. "I warn you though," she smiled, "it's not the Mount Nelson."

"What do you mean?"

"Don't look so worried," she laughed. "It's a fun scene. Just … a little different."

14

ANNA DIPPED HER KNIFE into the Marmite jar and spread a wedge of black goo across her toast. Then she spooned the hardboiled egg from its shell and mashed it on top. Leaving it to cool, she padded across the kitchen floor to switch on the wireless. Ghhhh. She tuned the frequency knob. A spike in volume, another ghhhh. After the third attempt she found the BBC World Service. Returning to her seat, she divided her toast diagonally, placed her fork on the plate and listened.

"Our brave men and their loyal counterparts from the dominions are preparing to advance across the desert," the newsreader's Churchill voice droned, "confident that this time the Axis menace of the Desert Fox will be driven back across the Mediterranean for good." Anna sipped her coffee, savouring the warmth and foretaste of caffeine. It had been her fourth night of fitful sleep and the world was losing its lustre. "And now, news from Singapore," the radio hissed. "Our island garrison endured yet another night of indiscriminate bombing by the Japanese horde. But General Wavell has given his assurances that every able-bodied man and weapon is being used to frustrate the advance of enemy forces on the ground." Pause. Another hiss. "Excuse me. Ladies and gentlemen: reports received just minutes ago confirm that British and dominion troops are, as we speak, engaged in a fierce struggle to hold the town of Bukit Timah."

"Turn that down, will you." Elizabeth was leaning against the door in her nightgown, long hair in knots and down to her chest. She eyed Anna for several seconds until her face cracked into a smile. "Quite a catch, hey?"

Anna shrugged, trying to look neutral.

"Coy, are we?" Elizabeth said. "Can't say I blame you." The front of her nightgown had opened enough to show her breasts. She wrapped it closed. "I'd also keep him to myself. Just tell me there are more where he came from."

The BBC newsreader was droning on about the stalemate on the Eastern Front, with Soviet forces preparing for a spring counter-offensive against the Nazis.

Elizabeth swanned towards the table. "What's troubling you, my dear?" She draped a hand over Anna's shoulder. "An attack of conscience? All you did was dance with him for goodness sake. Hush now. It's your second year in the city, big girl."

Anna removed her friend's fingers from her shoulder. "It's not that," she said. "I had a rough night, that's all. Wait ..." She held up her hand to cup her ear. "Listen." The newsreader recounted the latest casualties of the battle for the seas. U-boats had sunk three American cargo ships in the Caribbean, bringing the total loss to tens of thousands of tonnes for the month to date.

There was a rap on the door.

"Expecting someone?" said Elizabeth.

"What if I am?"

"No need to get defensive, my dear." Elizabeth studied the door, then looked back. "Oh, I forgot to tell you last night, a fellow popped around yesterday evening. One of your farming types. Brayed like a donkey."

The only person Anna knew that brayed was Fanus. How had he tracked her down?

"I offered him a drink," Elizabeth continued. "Poor chap looked parched. You don't mind, do you?

"No, I'm just surprised. He isn't normally given to small talk."

"You're telling me," Elizabeth said. "Struggles a bit with English, too, doesn't he?"

Anna laughed. "Not really. It's more a matter of principle. What did he want?"

"You, I'm guessing. No, seriously, he just downed the wine and then asked to use the phone. Next thing, he was gone."

Anna was about to ask something when the rapping started again.

"I'll leave you to do the honours," Elizabeth said. She looked at her reflection in a saucepan, and tussled with a knot in her hair. Then she looked at her slippers. "If it's Anthony, be a dear and tell him to wait outside. I'm in no state for visitors." Then she winked. "Who knows though, maybe it's your Prince Charming bringing flowers."

Anna scowled, dismissed her with a wave.

"Touchy, hey? Just remember our shopping date this afternoon. You promised."

Anna shivered. How did she get talked into going shopping? Her father gave a shoe-string allowance which could barely cover buying a change of underwear every other month. Before Anna got to the door, there was another knock, as if from a slight, yet determined hand. "Who is it?"

"Miss Anna, it's me. Kleinjan."

She opened the door on its latch, and recognised Kleinjan by the sound of his breathing. It was short and laboured. She peeked out. He stood with his hat in both hands. "Why so early?" she said. "Didn't I say half past nine?" She removed the chain, and opened the door, squinting into the daylight.

As always in the city, he was wearing his suit, but his jacket lay over his shoulder. His tie was loose and askew, his top buttons undone, his shirt damp with sweat. Her first thought was that he was the town drunk. But his abstinence was legendary. She took a step back. The sun was clear of the city skyline and already angry.

"*Jong*, what happened?"

"I walked."

"From your cousin's? It's a mile or more."

"It's nothing."

"*Genade*, I asked you to bring the bakkie. That was the whole point."

Kleinjan glanced over his shoulder. "The traffic is almost bumper-to-bumper on Orange Street. The place you asked me to take you is just here alongside. It's quicker to walk. In any case, a person can't leave a vehicle alone on the streets of District Six."

Her shoulders tensed. She'd planned the morning to the minute, but things were taking their own course now. To calm down, she focused on her breathing.

Kleinjan peered past her through the crack in the door. "Can we speak inside?"

She hesitated, hand on the chain lock. "If we have to walk, we haven't got time to chat first, Kleinjan. Really."

He stood, wordless. A face that only a stone heart could shut the door on.

She knocked the chain off its latch and waved him in. "Five minutes." She glanced at the clock. "*Magtig*, we can't even afford that. But all right. Coffee?" Without waiting she filled two mugs and added milk. Then she blew foam to the rim of her mug and looked at him. "So, why did you do it?"

Kleinjan stirred two heaped spoons of sugar into his coffee and watched the island of foam spiral. "Do what?"

"Come on." She leaned forward on her elbows. "Don't beat about the *blombos*." He inspected the side of his mug in silence. "I can't believe I kept trusting you," she continued, "even after seeing your treachery in our own backyard. It's unbelievable." She thumped her mug on the table and coffee pooled about its base. "You really had me there in Elim. I have to give it to you, it was clever. The church service to anaesthetise me; your cap in hand routine at the water wheel." She flicked the back of her index finger at the coffee and foam scudded across the table. "It makes me sick to think of it."

"Please." He looked up. There was no fear, no remorse, only sorrow. "That's not how it is."

"*Ge*. How then?"

He met her eyes without lifting his head, the whites twice the area of his pupils. "I only told your father I was worried about you and Thomas. You were getting too—"

"You told him what?" Anna felt like a train driver that had been hurtling along one track for days only to be flick-switched to another without warning.

"No. No." He was swinging his head from side to side. "You're not understanding me. Baas Stefan caught me out. At Parliament, when I met him there Monday, at the gate.

Normally he gives me a package to deliver or a task. But he started questioning me. First this, then that. About Thomas, about you. *Haai*, you know when he gets going. I had to tell him something."

"But telling him I'm falling for that stranger? That's ridiculous." As she spoke Anna was thinking of the conversation with her father in the library, the one Margriet had cut short. No wonder he'd been suspicious.

Kleinjan stroked the salt-and-pepper stubble on his chin. "It's normal for a father, you know, to worry about his daughter." His smile was wry and deepened the creases of skin on his face. "We were all young once. In any case, he knows you go to dances, that type of thing."

"And what of it? I dance with lots of men. It doesn't mean I'm in love with them."

He lifted his cup with both hands and sipped at his coffee. "That's right." His Adam's apple bobbed. "But just think, it would explain why you haven't been sleeping properly, or thinking straight."

"Oh, come, you sound just like him. That's just male prejudice, pure and simple."

"I know, I know. But it worked Miss Anna, it worked. He told me it all made sense, you going off to Skulpiestrand, the arguments with the Prinsloos. So don't worry. It will be such a relief for him when he hears it's not true. He will forgive you everything." Kleinjan had lost some colour. "But me ..." He swallowed again. "He'll kill me, I tell you. He still thinks I'm your chaperone. He depends on me."

She put a hand on his. "I'm sorry I've given you such a hard time," she said. She dropped her voice. "It's just, there's been so much going on the past few days—so much deceit—I don't know who to trust."

He placed his hand on hers, squeezed lightly. "It will all come right."

She retracted her hand. "Still. Papa now knows that I know. What am I going to do? Just yesterday I told him to his face that he'd put us in danger by allowing Rietvlei to be used ..." She racked her memory, relieved that nothing else stirred. "That's all I said. Thank heavens. It could have been worse."

Kleinjan lifted his hat from the table and ran his forefinger around its perimeter, as if tracing his thoughts. When he looked up he was facing the clock. "We should be going," he said. "Your appointment is at ten, not so?"

"Oh, of course," her shoulders sagged, "especially as we have to walk."

His gaze rested on her. "What's wrong?"

She crossed her arms and rubbed her shoulders. "It's nothing."

"Come, Miss Anna, I know you."

Her eyes shifted to the window. A breeze had sprung up, causing a palm frond to fan the lead-rimmed panes. "It's nothing ..." She shuddered. "Nothing you can help me with, anyway."

Kleinjan struggled to his feet. Standing, he wasn't much taller than her. He edged around the table towards her. "Do you remember the time you came to our cottage? When you didn't know where else to go? When he ..."

She realised her fingers were digging into her shoulders and forced herself to relax.

He shook his head slowly. "*Yoh*. You must have been in Standard Four but it feels like the day before yesterday."

"No. Stop!" Anna couldn't prevent the memory from surfacing. She shivered. It had started without warning, a few months after her mother's death. "Shut up," was all her father had said at first. "Enough of that bawling." Her first reaction had been confusion. He himself had said it was normal to be sad. And though he'd never admitted it, she'd seen him more than once through the bedroom window, doubled over crying with her mother's favourite scarf crumpled to his chest.

"I'm sorry." Kleinjan was at her side, head cocked towards her. "I didn't mean to upset you. I just wanted to remind you how, when you thought the choice you faced was too hard and there was nowhere to turn ... There's always hope, Miss Anna. Always."

"How ...?" She faced him, battling back the tears. "I've hardly seen you for over a year. And I've changed so much. But you still manage to read my thoughts."

He shrugged. A pause. "*Yoh*, but you're upset today. It's about your meeting this morning, isn't it? You don't want to go."

She shook her head, not trusting herself to speak.

"May I ask …?" He adjusted his tie to vertical but its tip was still two inches clear of his buckle. "Who you're going to see? I know people around here, you know. More than you think. Not just family and church. People who can do things. Difficult things."

Anna hesitated. "Ag, it's nothing." She smiled as she absorbed what he'd said. It was a comfort to think he'd be willing to help, even if she didn't accept it. "Just one of my professors. I … I need some advice."

By his expression she could tell he wasn't buying her story.

"In the District?" He put his hat on his head. "*Jislaaik*, that's a strange place for a *plaasmeisie* to find advice." He studied her. "Why not meet him at the university?" He turned to the door. "Michaelis is right across the road, *nê*?"

"I thought the same. But he said he wants me to meet certain people 'from the other side of the political divide'. I don't think he wants to be seen with them. Probably not good for his career."

"I think you're not telling me everything." He tipped his hat forward. "But, *nou* ja, when you get like this I just …" He took his jacket from the back of the chair and folded it over his forearm. "Come. Let's go. It's at least fifteen minutes walk from here."

15

A S ANNA FORGED HER way up Orange Street through the scramble of pedestrians, the gap between her and Kleinjan widened. Her haste was due less to her concern at being late than an unconscious effort to shake the stares and appease her state of mind. She replayed her phone conversation with Pickford-Dunn. She'd given him only generalities, the barest skeleton of her dilemma. "Divided loyalty" was how she'd put it, "just politics". But he'd read more into it, probably from the tension in her voice. His insightfulness as a teacher was what she admired most in him.

She looked up at the rump of Devil's Peak. A lick of wind warmed her face and the sun was high; it felt good to be out in the open again. Approaching the intersection with Buitenkant Street, the unofficial border of respectability that ran from the hem of Table Mountain to the foreshore, she slowed and glanced over her shoulder. Her breathing was shallow and laboured. "What's wrong, Kleinjan? You on a go-slow?"

He stopped and wiped his brow with the back of his hand in a sliding salute, narrowing his eyes to the sun. "*Haai*, have mercy. I'm not a young man any more."

Looking at her one-time mentor, she felt a pang of guilt. What would become of him if she followed through with her intentions? He could end up as a hero or a villain. More likely he'd be caught between two stools. It always seemed to turn out that way for the coloured folk, who had the dubious blessing of being neither light nor dark enough in a land obsessed with contrasts. She kicked a stone standing proud of the cobbles, and watched it plop into the ditch beside the road. Stop, she told herself. This wasn't the time to try to imagine every potential repercussion or to indulge in guilt. She had to focus on the big dilemmas.

"We turn here," he said, pointing left down Buitenkant. "Go on ahead. I'll do my best."

Within a hundred yards, the predictable Victorian manicure of the Gardens area fell away. The cobbled road was strewn with potholes. Piles of rubbish appeared here and there. A couple of blocks further on, Kleinjan drew abreast.

"I can explain the way," he gasped. "Really. It's simple from here."

Anna hesitated. Opposite them stood a barefoot boy, arm around a street pole, a mongrel cringing at his side. An elderly man in suit pants and waistcoat adjusted his fez and nodded a solemn greeting as they passed. "Am I crazy," Anna enquired of Kleinjan when the man was out of earshot, "to be walking through District Six?"

Kleinjan chuckled. "Just because there's coloureds doesn't make it dangerous. Anyway, there's all types here. Blacks, whites, Jews even."

She looked down the sloped canyon of warehouses and shop fronts. With every block it grew more crowded and disorderly. At the far end a sliver of the harbour was visible. She turned to look back. From here the face of the mountain looked jagged and angry. To its right Lion's Head poked up above a sawtooth of facades. "That's not what I meant, silly. You know me better than that, don't you?" She made eye contact again. "But you read every day about things happening, bad people, *skollies.*"

"Ag, that's just newspapers trying to sell. Sure, there's gangsters. The Jesters, the Killers … And *jislaaik*, they can fight. Only with each other, mind you. Stay out of their way and they leave you alone."

"Maybe so. But I'm not going anywhere without you. Anyway, Papa would go mad if he heard you'd left me alone."

"That's no lie. Come, follow me."

In moments they were in a side alley. Strings of washing spanned the gap between windows overhead. Sceptical eyes watched from the shadow of a doorway as they passed.

They turned left again and headed down a gentle gradient

towards the bay. Two blocks later they came to a general dealer store, whose Coca-Cola sign was obscured by a clutter of goods piled high either side of the entrance. On a high-backed chair on the sidewalk sat an old man in a jacket and tie reading the *Cape Times*, seemingly oblivious to the shoe-shine boy crouched at his feet.

Anna skipped to catch Kleinjan. But her mind was two steps behind, trying to absorb the barrage of new impressons. She'd never consciously immunised herself from others. If anything, she'd gone out of her way to mingle. Her love of dancing, for example, had led her to the city's fringe. And she'd made a point of befriending the marginalised, even the so-called disreputable. But this was altogether new, a parallel country, overwhelming in its strangeness, yet comforting in its ordinariness.

"Nothing like the Overberg, hmm?" Kleinjan said.

"I'll give you that." Anna laughed. They passed the former city jail, now derelict, and reached the intersection with Roeland Street. In the distance the ocean shimmered and a tug boat crept towards a British frigate. Huddled below Devil's Peak, ramshackle buildings sprawled southwards towards Woodstock. Pools of stagnant muck lay in the cobbled ditch beside them.

"How much further?"

"Just now, I promise."

Anna felt overwhelmed every time she thought of the task at hand. Pickford-Dunn had been evasive on the phone. Would he be there to make introductions? How much had he already told them? She strode ahead, trying to ward off her doubts. Now they were on Canterbury Street, parallel to Buitenkant and heading towards the sea. The vista of docklands came into focus as they descended the hill and the minaret of a mosque solidified above the haze.

An urchin eyed them from a corner, standing in the yoke of his barrow. "*Aartappels en uie!*" he cried, digging his hands into a crate of vegetables. Then he was in their faces, holding up his wares like an offering to the gods. "*Tamaties* too."

Kleinjan pressed a coin into the boy's hand and waved him away. Then he pointed ahead. "There, Miss Anna. Two blocks."

Anna paused at the kerb, staring ahead. At the bottom of the hill the street made a T-junction with the main artery feeding into District Six. She knew it was Upper Darling Street from its breadth and choke of traffic. Her back tensed.

On the far side of the street, the stone walls of the castle looked somehow more imposing than ever. Even from a hundred yards she felt the shudder of the Union Jack and the orange, white and blue of the Union flag fluttering above the ramparts. She felt just as uncertain as on the day before when she had stood wavering at its entrance.

She bent to relieve the pressure on her spine. A recurring image returned to torture her—drowning sailors flailing in an icy ocean as the cucumber of a U-boat slinks away beneath an oily sea. She steeled her resolve. It was better to sacrifice herself than do nothing while her people suffered at the hands of a ruthless enemy. But to inform on her father? What a ghastly choice. And how pitifully naïve of her to have put all her hope in a middle-aged university professor she barely knew.

Kleinjan stood next to her. "Ag, Anna, I wish you'd tell me what's the matter."

"It's okay." Anna stepped off the kerb. "There's nothing you can do to help me, Kleinjan."

A bus with commuters hanging from its rear rumbled towards the Y-junction of Darling Street and Sir Lowry's Road. The South Easter, growing angry now, whipped dust from the vacant lot opposite.

"One more block." Without waiting, he shambled along the pavement to the next street corner.

He pointed at the house with his head but averted his gaze as he spoke. His face betrayed a blend of disbelief and knowing. She stared at the entrance to a triple storey building on the opposite side of the street. Its pastel blue door and window frames stood out against the run-down street.

"That's the Stakesby Lewis Hostel?"

"Miss Anna is doubting me?" Kleinjan's forehead lines looked deeper. "Ask anyone here." He nodded as a shrivelled woman passed, her face implacable beneath a headscarf. "You know this is where Tabata stays?"

Anna shifted on her feet. "Who?"

Kleinjan glanced at a pair of barefoot boys playing in the gutter with a wire frame car, and lowered his voice. "Your father would call him a communist."

Anna recalled Pickford-Dunn's words. His connections were "of left-wing persuasion". She had assumed he meant liberal-minded, but in truth, she wasn't certain of his political standpoint. On the surface he was as British as the King, a man of the establishment who encouraged his graduates to volunteer for the intelligence service. But there was also something unconventional about him, at ease on the margins of Cape Town society.

Two men in jackets and suit pants stood near the hostel entrance facing the street; another two were seated on narrow wooden benches, hunched over a game of draughts.

"Thank you for guiding me here," she said to Kleinjan. "You can leave me now."

"No way, Miss Anna. These are dangerous people."

A teenage boy in boxer shorts rattled past on a bicycle. "Then wait here, Kleinjan. Please. I have to do this alone. I won't be long."

The two men guarding the entrance didn't blink as Anna approached. Their shoes reflected the morning sunlight and their eyes, barely visible below their hats, were watching. "I'm here to see Professor Pickford-Dunn," she said, feigning confidence.

The one with a pencil moustache eyed her for several moments and then raised a lazy hand to doff his sunglasses. "Afternoon, ma'am." A draughts player slapped down a disc. The other banged the table. Neither looked up. "Up the stairs," the guard pointed. "Left at the end of the passage."

"Hey." The other guard stuck out his foot to bar Kleinjan from the pavement. He stabbed a finger at Kleinjan's chest. "We only know about the lady."

Anna looked at the half-cocked smile of the guard and the uneasy resignation in Kleinjan's eyes. Had she asked too much of him?

Pickford-Dunn had warned her that his friends were "impatient" and "shouldn't be presumed upon". She brushed past the guard. The door lintel was pockmarked, the floor flecked with paint. There was no entrance hall, just a short corridor that smelled of stale beer and ended in a staircase, beneath which was piled an assortment of boxes and an upturned table and chairs. Anna hesitated, swallowed, and then started up the stairs.

The landing was lit only by the weak glow of a single electric bulb dangling from the ceiling. As she edged down the passage the air felt close and stale. She stopped at the last door on the left and knocked three times. No answer. She felt an urge to turn and run. She knocked again.

"Who's that?" It was a male voice but high-pitched.

Anna poked her head around the door. Three men were slouched in easy chairs by an open window, hogging the light. The room smelled of curry and beer. Beyond the window was a hodgepodge of urban decay stretching towards the apron of Table Mountain, in stark contrast to her own view of dappled oak branches and the elegant pink walls of the Mount Nelson.

"*Aitsa,* she's a looker, *nê*? Miss van der Vliet, I suppose."

"Call me Anna. Please."

Oddly, he wore a hat, despite the lack of direct sunlight in the room. His face was boyish, moustached, and his eyes almost shone. He patted his chest. "Mannie. You're a bit late, *nê*? Don't worry. We're happy you're gracing us with your presence, so to speak."

She stole a glance at the others seated beside him. "Where's the professor?"

"*Nee wat,* he didn't explain? Sorry's on me." He pointed at a chair. "Take a seat."

Anna didn't move.

"Pickford-Dunn apologises," Mannie continued. "He's a busy, important man nowadays." He glanced at his friends, smiled. "Plays both sides, you know." He winked. "Must be difficult. But don't worry. We'll get along just fine, you and me ..." He half rose. "Please." He pointed at the chair again. "I insist."

Anna sat. The bottom of the chair seemed to give way as she sank into it. "All right," she said, sinking further. "Why are we here?"

"Sharp attitude, hey," Mannie said to the others. The man

directly opposite fiddled with his cufflinks. The third stubbed his cigarette out in an empty can. "Actually ..." Mannie upended a packet of Commodores, tapped it on his armrest and stooped to gather a cigarette that fell to the floor. "It's more like what can we do for you."

Anna felt her chest constrict in anticipation of the smoke. Instinctively she looked at the window. She wanted nothing more than to get away.

"We understand you have a ..." Mannie stuck a finger between his collar and his neck and ran it around to widen the gap. "What's the clever word you people use?" He clicked his fingers to help him think. "Ah! A co-nun-drum." He glanced proudly at the others. "*Nê?*"

"What did he tell you?" Anna tried to sit upright but after a few seconds she slumped. "Pickford-Dunn, I mean."

"Ag, ma'am, you must relax, really." Mannie cupped the cigarette, lit it and inhaled as if his life depended on it, then let out a stream of smoke from the side of his mouth. "The professor and I go back a long way." He extended his arms to take in his colleagues. "What we talk about here stays here. You have my word."

She couldn't remember meeting anyone who looked less trustworthy. Every instinct recoiled. But she'd thought through her options enough times in the past forty-eight hours, and there was nothing left but to trust the process. "Please," she said, "it's important. What exactly did he tell you?"

Mannie flicked his cigarette with his pinkie and ash drifted to the carpet. "We know about the Germans."

Anna felt her chest tighten, like the room about her. She was sure they would see she was blushing. "But ... he promised ..."

"Relax *mos*, ma'am. We come by our information any number of ways." He coughed. "But if we know, it's only a matter of time before the police know too."

"What else do you claim to know?"

Mannie hacked up some phlegm into his throat, glancing from one colleague to the other and back to Anna. "Excuse us, ma'am, but is this a way to talk to friends? No, no." He stubbed his cigarette, shuffled in his seat as if to rise. "If you like, we can call it quits, right now. No hard feelings."

Anna felt a surge of panic. To face Kleinjan, or even worse, her father, without a plan was unthinkable. Damned if she did, damned if she didn't. She wanted to cry, and was angry with herself for it.

"No, wait," she said. "Please." She looked out the window, dabbing the corner of her eye. "You don't understand how hard this is."

Mannie settled back in his chair, crossed his legs. "Go on."

Anna swallowed. She wished she could think of another way. "I saw them myself. Germans. On the farm. Taking the …" Her chest was closing; she wondered how she would get her next breath. She made another effort to get up, hoisting herself with both hands on the armrests out of the dent in the chair. Then sank again. The men watched, silent.

"All right," she said. "I guess I just have to trust you. It was … only food. Meat, vegetables. Goodness, it would be hard to prove it even came from the farm. Surely that's … not enough for a good man to die?" She choked on the word.

"So …" Mannie was tapping his index fingers together. "It's your father, hmm? You think he's deep in the *kak*? Sorry ma'am"—he grinned at the others.

Anna managed to stand and dusted her dress. "Listen, Mannie. I'm not going to sit around here and let you insult me. You think this is amusing, don't you? You've no interest in helping me. Why would you care about any of this, anyway? I bet all you want is … is money. Tell me I'm wrong."

"Now, now, ma'am, slow down." He pointed his cigarette at his two colleagues in turn, then at her. "All of us here share something else in common, something much more important."

"*Have* something in common." She had one hand on her hip. She looked about the room, coughed. "I can't imagine what you think we have in common."

"How about a po-li-ti-cal con-science?" Mannie was gesticulating with both hands now. "Okay, let me say it nice and simple. We love our country, our people. And I don't mean just you fancy people. No, I mean people like us too, *mos*. Of colour."

Mannie's colleague opposite spoke for the first time. His face was darker than the other two. "Including the workers who slave away on your mines, your factories of war." His voice was deep with a strong isiXhosa accent.

She stared at him. "You're Mister Tabata, aren't you?"

He laughed and fell silent.

"Even if he was, he wouldn't admit it," Mannie interrupted. "The real Tabata's a shadow. Now you see him, now you don't."

Anna kept staring at the man. Something about his manner felt reassuring. A depth of character. It was time to throw caution to the wind. "What if I told you I agree with you?" she said. "About the workers, I mean. It's not right how the government treats them. I do care. Hypothetically, anyway."

Mannie chuckled. "Hy-po-the-ti-cally." He looked at his colleagues. "We're simple people here, ma'am. Let's talk *sommer* or-di-nary English. All right?"

"Gentlemen … please … I don't disagree with your motives. Pickford-Dunn told me all about your organisation. Your trade union roots, even your aims. And it doesn't concern me. Honestly. I wouldn't be here otherwise."

"Good, good." Mannie sat back again. "So … my friends and me, we think there's a way out of your dilemma. With dignity. Where both sides win." Outside a car horn blew and someone shouted. "Where you can do your duty to your country and your father still lives."

Anna swallowed involuntarily, trying to beat down a surge of hope.

"Right, right. I can see this is difficult for the lady." Mannie shifted a cushion behind his back. "Let's stop beating about the bush. If you don't tell the police about the *skelm* business going on at your farm and they find out—and trust me ma'am, they always do—you're both in the *tronk*. If you're that lucky." He ogled her breasts for a second, shifted to her face. "You're over 18, *reg so*?"

She crossed her arms instinctively.

Mannie flicked ash onto the floor. "We know about you and the German."

Anna felt the room contract, squeezing her lungs. "What are you talking about?"

He reached for an envelope at the foot of his chair, slipped out three photographs and held one up. It was a photo of

Anna and Thomas locked in the tango. He passed it to her.

Thomas's face was visible from the side, like the bust of a Nordic god, whispering words in her ear, words that still ricocheted through her.

"You, you ..." she waved the photo, glaring at each of them, "perverts!"

"Easy ma'am. Just think. What would your father say if he saw this business of yours? Or the defence force? I'm sorry, there's nothing anyone can do to help a person caught with the enemy in such a ... such an in-ti-mate pose."

Anna rose on the balls of her feet, inhaling until her chest wanted to burst. "This is blackmail! I thought I was supposed to trust you!"

"Come now," Mannie said. He reached to gather the discarded photographs back into the envelope. "We just need you to pay attention. Please, sit."

Anna felt angry, more with herself than anyone else. "Thank you for your time." She made to turn. "I should never have trusted a bunch of communists."

"Hey," he said, "easy. All my friends want is a free and equitable—"

"Since when do you care about what's free?" She felt a momentary relief in taking the offensive. "Just look at Stalin. Are you people blind? He was in bed with Hitler. Until the devil turned on him. No, you're dictators, pure and simple. The lot of you."

Mannie rose, held out his palm as if in surrender. "This doesn't have to get personal, ma'am. But your father, how is he different? Sticking those laws through Parliament trying to ban workers from striking. But all right. My contacts tell me it's not going to happen, not this year at least. Thank goodness, is what I say."

"I'm not my father," Anna said, lifting her chin.

"That's why we agreed to talk to you, ma'am."

"Well, I still don't understand," Anna said. "Why are you so happy to talk to someone like me?"

"Hah. No flies on the lady," Mannie said. "All right. Let me tell it straight. We think you should tell the authorities. You know, what's going on at your farm."

"And see my father tried as a traitor? There's a death penalty in this country, last time I checked. Tell them yourself."

"We already tried. Through in-ter-me-diaries, of course."

"You what?" Anna felt horror churn her stomach. Were her worst fears about to materialise regardless? She took a step towards the door. "Then what are we doing here? Goodbye Mister ..."

Mannie caught her arm. "Relax."

She stopped. Slapped at his hand. "Don't touch me."

"Let me explain." He took his hand back. "The government wouldn't listen, *mos*. Like I said. They don't see us as humans, even. What, they're going to believe us? They right away think we're just trying to make *kak,* as they say. That's why we need you."

Anna thought for a moment. Something wasn't adding up. "Surely you could get someone else to help you," she said. "I'm not the only white person in this country."

Mannie ground his cigarette into the armrest and tossed it out the window. He tightened his mouth, shook his head. "You'd be shocked, I tell you, if you knew how few white people are prepared to tell on one of their own. Maybe an English liberal, who knows. But your father's a famous man. A conservative. No one's going to believe an Englishman who calls him a traitor." He arched his back, stretching. "But if his own daughter ..."

"Wait a minute," she said. "You said earlier you have a way out of my, my 'dilemma', that would spare him."

"Yes. Easy. I'm getting to that. You'll be clear as a whistle, see? You were in Cape Town *mos*, the whole time, while this thing was going on." He paused, raised his eyebrows. "Right. Thought so. And you found about it when, end of last week? Listen, no one's going to blame you for taking a few days to report the story. I mean, you've been travelling and, who wouldn't agree, it's a *moerse* thing to have to do. That's if you tell them today. Tomorrow latest."

"*Ge.* So far you haven't told me anything new. And what about Papa? There's no way I'm going to save my skin if it means ..."

"Hey. What did I say? Relax. We have some clever lawyers in our organisation, some of the best. Jewish. They say there's ex-ten-u-a-ting circumstances. That they'll get him off on account of him being co-erced."

"And why would the authorities buy that?"

"Because it's true."

"What exactly?"

"Sorry, ma'am. I'm not going into detail. You're just have to trust us. As I see it, you don't have a choice."

Anna felt as though her legs were about to give way. But it wasn't the time to give in. "You expect me to betray my own father to further your nefarious purposes?"

"Nefarious? *Jislaaik*, that's a smart word."

"It means evil."

"Against the law, actually." Mannie drew on his cigarette and let smoke trickle from the side of his mouth. "That's what the word meant originally."

Anna stared.

"Listen here, ma'am. What we're asking isn't as hard as you think. Your father's going to get found out anyway. By jumping the gun you can save him. We'll get him off, don't worry. Our lawyer: man, he's sharp as a razor. And anyway," he scratched behind his ear, "we know you've been about to tell on him yourself."

Anna was shaking now. She felt compromised, dirty, like a pawn in a chess game. Her mind was running in circles, trying to recall faces … the walk to the castle, the fruit sellers on the Parade …?

"Go to hell."

A car hooted far off. Mannie sat back, his face hardened. "Sorry to be blunt," he said, "but if you don't do it, both of you are going to hell."

Anna wanted to run, get away as fast as possible from the awful trio in front of her. But common sense intervened. She stepped towards the door. "There's a lot to consider," she said. "I'll need to get back to you."

Mannie stood, stepped towards her. He was shorter than her, but his presence had a pent-up energy. "Wait," he said. "We need to know today."

She was thinking, but not fast enough. "And if I can't?"

Mannie glanced down at the envelope. "Sorry, ma'am.

Workers' lives are at risk. Millions, on the Russian front, all over the world."

"Russians? *Ge.* So you're doing all this just to help that lot, are you?"

He shifted his eyes to his colleagues. "I told you she was sharp, hey." Turning back to her, he said. "On the money, ma'am." He grimaced. "You see me and my friends ... we've been trying to talk to old man Smuts for years now—about our rights. He listens of course. A real gentleman, he is. But nothing ever happens. He's just kicking a tin can along the road, I tell you. We need something to bargain with."

She shook her head. "Typical."

"What's that supposed to mean?"

"You're going to blackmail him, aren't you?"

Mannie coughed. "Ne-go-tiate. And at least we're doing something for our country. Not like your father, entertaining those fascists in his dining room. Or you ..." he coughed, "doing it with that Nazi."

She felt herself reeling. Her dilemma had just taken on a new dimension. Denial and distance—she'd learned from her father—were safest when floundering. "That bastard," she said, "trying to take advantage of me! Just because I'm naïve enough to believe his sob story, he tries to dance his way into my life."

"Hey," Mannie said, "enough acting. We know you love him. You're a woman, *mos.* You can't help it. Come on, think about our proposal. Just be the go-between. We're not asking more than you were going to do anyway. But we need to know if you're in or out—by tomorrow morning. After that, you and your father are on your own."

Less than twenty-four hours to find another way out. It seemed hopeless. But her mother's voice rose like a whisper. With faith, she used to say, nothing is hopeless. If only, somehow, Anna could summon the simple faith of her mother.

She swallowed. "Give me a day to think about telling on my father. But as for the Nazi," she opened the door, "let him hang."

16

ANNA STRODE AHEAD OF Kleinjan in a silence made stronger by the absence of traffic. On the aptly named Wandel Street, a narrow, winding lane, the industrial grime of the upper district gave way to a gentler residential shabbiness. Here was a drooping branch, there a vine jutting from a break in a wall, or a backyard oak with a tree house. Dreading the lunch date with her father, she was determined not to be late, and had insisted on a shorter but more convoluted back route to save time.

At the T-junction they swung left towards the mountain. Orange Street was only a hundred yards or so ahead, and the familiar palms of the Mount Nelson lifted her spirits. The encounter with Mannie had rattled her. To say he was a rough diamond would be an understatement. Gangster would be closer to the truth. But for some strange reason Anna sensed that his offer was sincere. She just wasn't sure whether or not to pursue it.

"Thank you so much," she said when Kleinjan caught up. "I'll be all right from here. I'm meeting Papa in the Company's Garden." She pointed. "The top gate is just over there."

He nodded, turned.

"Kleinjan," she said. He looked back over his shoulder.

"You know on Sunday, at the watermill, after church?"

"Ja."

"You know that other German? Kurt. You said he was dangerous."

Kleinjan turned reluctantly to face her.

"What did you mean?"

"Hah, Miss Anna. It was just talk."

"No, tell me. It could be important."

He scratched at the crown of his head. "This is just between you and me, right?"

She nodded.

"That farmer I was helping to unload the crates at Skulpiestrand. I overheard him talking to someone in the dark."

Anna waited.

"About a German spy coming ashore. Thomas is the commander, so I assumed ..."

She felt cold. Last night Thomas had said Kurt wasn't regular navy. "Why didn't you tell me before?"

He looked at his feet. "You know young farmers these days, sometimes they just talk big."

"But you said Kurt is dangerous."

He paused. "It's just, the farmer seemed in awe of him. He ..."

"What?"

"I couldn't hear properly. But he said he was going to give Smuts a *snotklap*. Those were his words." He looked down again. "That's all I know, Miss Anna. Could you excuse me please? I should be going."

As she wandered under the shady oaks, she recalled Kurt's brooding, almost sinister presence as he sat with her father.

When she reached Government Avenue her thoughts returned to the conversation with Mannie. She had to think fast. But in the back of her mind an idea was already forming.

When she reached the clearing, her father was standing at the edge of the well with a pigeon perched on his upturned hands, shovelling seeds into its beak. When he saw her he shooed the bird and shook his hands.

She hurried to him, flung her arms about his neck. "You're early, Papa," she laughed. "Some things never change." She pecked him on the cheek. "It's a comfort."

"Ja," he laughed. "But you're late. Again." He reached for his fob watch. "Nearly quarter to one. Where've you been?"

"Ag, you know how I like to walk the city."

He was about to say something but checked himself. "Well, I don't know about you, but I could do with some food."

She pouted, then elbowed him, "How do I know you won't run off again on some government business?"

He laughed. "Listen, *my lief.* I'm sorry about yesterday. Really. Nothing is more important to me than our time together. Let's go for a meander before lunch then."

She locked her arm in his and led him into the shadows of the path. "How did it go, the session?"

"Ag," he shook his head, "if it wasn't bad enough fighting the UP we've got our own Young Turks trying to hijack the agenda."

"Are they still planning a walkout?"

He nodded, pinching his nose. "Ja, can you believe it? This isn't a time for games. We've got to show a united front. Focus on the big issues."

She swung their arms as they walked. "And what may those be?"

"Ja *nee.*" He lifted his chin and surveyed the geometry of the rose garden ahead. "All the things you give me a hard time about. Group areas. Mixed marriages."

She stiffened.

"My child," he said. "Do yourself a favour, take a drive through District Six. You'll see the, the *onsedelikheid* that results when you let nature take its course." She let go of his arm. Did he know, already? "Happening in broad daylight, for heaven's sake. It's like they're showing off. *Skande.*"

No. She forced herself to relax. It wasn't possible.

Soon they were approaching the menagerie. The tops of the cages were visible through the branches. There was a flutter and squawking and then silence. "Before we get to the restaurant," she said, "I've got to ask you again … what I tried to talk to you about yesterday."

He lengthened his stride.

"All right," she said, skipping to catch up. "I can see I'm going to have to spell it out." She drew level and touched him on the forearm. "Did you really think I wouldn't put two and two together?"

"What are you talking about?"

"Of course I knew something was wrong, Papa. From Thursday night already, in the *sitkamer.* For a start, their German wasn't anything like that of the South Westers."

Her father ran the tip of his tongue across his upper lip and withdrew it.

"I know where your sympathies lie," she continued. "Your view on our role in the war effort is hardly a secret. And don't mistake me. It's understandable. Especially for us Afrikaners. Hundreds of thousands think the same way. Not that I agree, of course. But Papa, to help the Germans! Why on earth?"

"It's not what you think."

"Well, what is it then?" She brushed a leaf off her shoulder, looked him in the eye. "I presume you know how serious it is if we're caught aiding the enemy?"

He scanned the shrubbery. Satisfied, he turned back to confront her. He lifted his index finger and wagged it at her. "Don't you lecture me on what I should or shouldn't do. I've got a lot more life under my belt than you have." He scratched a pockmark on his cheek. "You know what it means if Germany loses, don't you?"

Anna held onto a paling. Though she'd known it for days, nothing had prepared her to hear from her father's own lips that he was a traitor.

"No?" His voice rose like a baritone at the end of an aria. "Thought not. Let me tell you then. This is what happens: Britain wins." He turned to check if anyone was approaching along the path, and swung back. "And what's so bad about that, you ask? Mama was English. They're nice to the Jews. Fair enough. I don't like the stories about what the SS are up to any more than you do—even if they're half-true. But think of the alternative. If Britain wins the war, so does Russia." He fastened the centre button of his jacket. "Have you stopped to consider what the communists will do when they take over this country? Think about it. Our civilisation. The church."

Anna felt her spirits plunge. Her religion. The trump card he pulled whenever his arguments faltered.

"Don't look at me like that," he continued. "You think the king won't allow it? Let me tell you something. Even if the Allies win this war, Britain will be bankrupt. Her colonies will be pawns in a global chess game. Trust me. I've seen it at Versailles. No, South Africa will need real friends if we want any chance of restoring the republic."

For a moment Anna felt too helpless to counter the force of his argument. It wasn't by accident that he'd risen from local party organiser for Barry Hertzog's Nationalists to United Party Member of Parliament for Bredasdorp and finally a key figure in the Reunited Nationalists. But she shared his blood and she wasn't going to be lectured any more. "That may all be so. But treason carries the death penalty."

For once he looked uncertain. Or was it fear? "What exactly did Kleinjan tell you?" he said. "That little …" His head seemed to swell and he reddened. "You know what a vivid imagination these simple people have."

"Nobody's told me anything." Anna was amazed at how easily the second untruth followed the first. The lesser of two evils, she consoled herself. "I saw it myself."

They had turned onto a side path, crossed a *sloot*, and reached the intersection with Government Avenue. Her father stumbled on a root and turned to face her. "You saw what?"

"The boats."

"What boats, where?"

"Skulpiestrand," she said. "You didn't think I'd forgotten the footprints in the sand, did you?"

"But Kleinjan—" He stopped himself. "I thought that was your imagination. You weren't feeling well."

"I saw the loading myself."

"*Jinne.*" His jowels wobbled as he shook his head. "You mean at night?" They'd come up against a construction sign. What until recently had been a stately, oak-lined walkway inclining towards the mountain was now a trench flanked every twenty yards with mounds of earth. "*Nee wat,*" he said. "What's this?"

"Air-raid shelters," she said. "You must have heard. It was all over the papers a few months ago."

"Oh, ja. But what difference will these trenches make if a Stuka divebombs the city? Please."

"At least they're trying to give the common people some-where to hide while you parliamentarians scurry down into your bunkers."

They crossed the *sloot*. "What do you know about bunkers?" he said.

"Parliament's basement is riddled with them. It's an open secret, at the university, anyway. You look surprised. The powers that be always underestimate the intelligence of the governed."

A squirrel blocked their path, clutching an acorn, bulging eyes glaring at them. Her father stamped and the squirrel scampered up the oak. She kept her eyes on him. "I can't go on with this until you tell me the truth. What's really going on? And why? I'm your daughter. You owe me that at least."

His pupils widened. For a moment it looked like he was about to answer. Then something changed. He pulled out his watch. "Come. We've only got forty minutes for lunch."

17

AFTER THEIR BRIEF DETOUR they turned back, approaching the statue of the imperialist Cecil John Rhodes, who stood pointing north, hat in hand, above the words "Your hinterland is there". Anna considered her options. She had finally prised a crack in her father's defences, only for him to slam them shut again. Had she missed her one opportunity to level with him? She walked on in uneasy silence.

As they passed the statue he slowed and peered up into the great imperialist's face, as if trying to fathom Rhodes's expression. After a few seconds he looked away. "Yes," he said, "I won't deny it."

She waited, not daring to move or interrupt.

"We gave them meat, vegetables, fruit. Not all from our farm, mind. You'll be surprised how many farmers in the Overberg are rooting for the Axis. The rumours are only half of it, trust me. Some are even spying for them." He straightened his tie. "But we only gave food. And some diesel. Believe me, Engel. I didn't want to. But I had …"

"No *choice*? Goodness, we live in a democracy. For the time being, anyway." She winced at the unintended irony of her words. "At least be honest with me. You *wanted* to help them. *Sies*, man. You're no better than a Nazi."

"*Hemel*," he muttered. The lines about his mouth etched like dongas in the Karoo. "That's quite an accusation. I suggest you take a deep breath and think carefully before insulting your own father like that."

She felt a stab of doubt. How did he always manage to turn her anger around and make her feel guilty? "I'm sorry," she mumbled. "But what else am I supposed to think?"

He sighed. A young boy ran past, bumping him on the elbow. He swung around as if to slap, saw the youngster and relented. He turned back to Anna, his hand fiddling in his pocket. "All right, I didn't want to have to say this." He squinted up at the sun. "They have my foster sister."

Anna was confused for a moment. "Greta? In Düsseldorf?" What did some distant relative from his days of exile in Germany have to do with anything?

He nodded.

"What about her?"

"They've taken her. Against her will."

She stepped closer. "What are you saying?"

"They've got her. Kidnapped."

Anna looked about. Apart from a group of schoolchildren approaching from the direction of the rose garden, there was no one about. She shook her head from side to side. "I don't—"

"Sorry," he said. "German Intelligence. They called her in one day, supposedly to ask a few questions about something or other. It went downhill from there. Now they're calling her a spy. Threatening to hand her over to the Gestapo."

"Greta? A spy?" Anna muttered. "She's more German than Goethe, if I'm thinking of the person you used to tell me about."

"That's just it," he said. "It's complete nonsense. They claim to have intercepted letters that prove she's been passing information to the Allies—through me, can you believe it?"

Anna was struggling to absorb this new twist in the tangled web. She felt a sudden horror at the thought that just an hour ago she'd almost been persuaded to sacrifice her own father. That she'd thought him a willing traitor. She felt an urgent need to sit down. Then she caught a whiff of toast and grilled meat. They were approaching the restaurant. Seldom had she felt less hungry. "But how did they link her with you?" she said, trying to steady her emotions. "You said yourself you haven't had contact for years."

"It's not that hard, you know. The *Abwehr* keeps a file on every person of German extraction in South Africa. Anywhere in the world, for that matter."

Anna's thoughts were clearing. "So, they blackmail you into making Rietvlei a victualing station for their ships rounding the Cape. Clever. Like the Dutch East India Company three centuries ago." The implausibility of it started to dawn on her. Perhaps he'd been forewarned, and just made up this story as a ruse to placate her. She wouldn't put it past him. "And you just sign on the dotted line? Choose your one-time sister over true family?"

"It's not like that. All they asked was for me to turn a blind eye for a few weeks. They promised to be gone by the end of February."

Anna looked up to the sky, where a sheet of high cirrus was advancing from behind the mountain. She appealed to a higher power, her silent anchor in an ocean of change. "And Thomas and that other creature?" She tucked her hair behind her ears. "Another thirty pieces of silver to entertain German officers in our home?"

"*Wragtag*. You really do think the worst of me."

"That's not fair. You have no idea how badly I want to wake up and find out that these last four days were just a terrible dream. That things are normal at Rietvlei. Just you and me. None of this hideous war full of deceit and killing. Persuade me that I've got it all wrong, please."

"It was never supposed to happen," he said. "The agent assured me there'd be no direct contact. Ratings and officers were forbidden to come ashore in Allied territory. Standing orders from Admiral Dönitz. They're building a submarine base in Madagascar, anyway. This was just a temporary measure."

"That's not how it looked on Thursday," she said. "They seemed very much at home."

Her father's shoulders sagged. He shook his head. They were passing the vegetable garden, where waist-high tomato plants swayed above a bed of lettuce. "Thomas just showed up at the front door the night before you arrived. God's own truth. Said his U-boat needed emergency repairs. A fuse box and cylinder re-bore. That's the only reason I agreed to bring him to Cape Town. He said he just needed a day or so to find a machine shop and he'd be gone. He promised to keep me informed." He shook his head once and stopped. "He can be persuasive, hey." His eyebrow hooped. "But I guess you know that."

Anna wasn't going to be so easily drawn. "You could have refused," she said. "Thought of us. The risks."

"Ja." He looked down at his shoes as he crunched over the gravel. "I know. But ... you've met him." Both eyebrows this time. "He's a hard man to refuse. And when he mentioned that his grandfather knew my foster father ..."

Anna felt a tingle of shame. Perhaps she'd been too quick to judge. She was about to apologise when she remembered something. That letter in the *sitkamer*. She was angry again. "You expect me to believe this business about Greta?" she said. "You know how to spin a story for a penny, Papa. I've seen you do it to the press. Don't take me for a fool."

He gave his hurt look, drooped his head a degree or three. "My own daughter calls me a liar?"

She'd had enough now. "Why didn't you tell me you were *Ossewabrandwag*? All this time you've been pretending you're a democrat. Non-violent protest, the primacy of Parliament ... that's what you drilled into me."

His head lifted, his eyes larger than ever. "What are you talking about?"

"I saw it myself," she said. "The papers in the *sitkamer* on Thursday night. You're one of them. You ..."

"No. No." He kicked at the ground. "That was from Koos Prinsloo. He's been threatening to cut our party funding if I don't join. Ask him yourself if you like."

Anna picked up an acorn and hurled it at the trunk of an oak. "So why didn't you join?" She wiped her hand on her skirt. "I mean, you have the same aims."

"Come," he waved at her, "let's keep going." He lifted a low branch from the path to let her pass. "I'll explain on the way."

When they got to the menagerie he stopped, poked a stick through the grating of the cage and allowed a budgie to peck at it. "The party has forbidden any senior colleagues to join the OB," he said. "Sure, we've been staunch allies. That's no secret. But you must have read about the *broedertwis*. They're at each other's throats. Daniel doesn't trust Van Rensburg any more. Thinks he's unstable, a danger to the cause. He's convinced that our best chance of achieving the republic is through the democratic process." He withdrew the stick, causing the budgie to squawk and flutter at the grating, "And you know I've always agreed."

Anna felt light-headed. It was too much information all at once. But she had to finish her questioning before he closed-up again. "What about the other German?"

The tea room was in sight now, French doors flung open to the kitchen, tables and chairs dotted about in the shade. "What's that?"

"Thomas's colleague, Kurt. At Rietvlei on Thursday night."

A waitress was lounging on the patio, unseeing. The proprietor sidled up with an unctuous smile, picked a pair of menus from a pile, and held one out.

Her father took it. "No idea. That was the last I saw of him. Thomas just said he had business in Cape Town." He ran his finger down the price list, muttering about inflation.

Anna stroked a patch of gooseflesh on her forearm. "There was something not right about him."

The proprietor was in her father's face now. His bowtie and dinner jacket looked incongruous with the cheap wood-veneer décor of the restaurant.

"Before we sit," her father said as the proprietor led them to a table. "Can I ask one favour?" He drew a chair for Anna, didn't wait for a reply. "Let's forget this dreadful business. Just for the next half hour, and enjoy a nice meal together."

She sighed, then nodded. How could she change within seconds from wanting to throttle him to this sense of affection?

"*Donderse ding*!" Her father swore, rocking the table back and forth. "Can't they make anything right these days?" He ducked down to wedge his serviette between the nearest foot and the paving below.

A shadow crossed the table from behind her. She turned to find it was a man she didn't recognise. He pointed at her father's back.

"Papa, leave that. There's someone to see you."

"*Bliksem!*" Her father bumped his head on the underside of the table. "What is it now?"

"*Meneer* van der Vliet?" The stranger was thirty-something

and wore a vest under a short-sleeved white shirt. He had a paintbrush moustache and his lips barely moved as he spoke. He waited for her father to get to his feet, then offered his hand. "*Speurder-Sersant* de Villiers. South African Police."

"Ja," her father said, "How can I help?"

"Would you mind if I joined the two of you?" He pulled out a chair regardless. "I have just have one or two questions. It won't take more than five minutes."

Anna's father inflated, eyebrows converging. Then he retracted the chair. "Listen here, *Sersant* … What's it again? De Wit … "

"De Villiers," he said. "*Speurder-Sersant* de Villiers. "Please sir. I'm here under direct orders. Colonel Wessels, Pretoria." He glanced at Anna, nodded a greeting and pulled out the chair again.

"With respect *Sersant* … de Villiers, my daughter and I have lunch a handful of times a year, and I'll be damned if I'll share that pleasure with the likes of you."

De Villiers sat down, picked up a menu and studied it. Then, lifting his eyelids he made eye contact. "I'm sorry, sir," he said. "I'm only doing my job."

Her father inhaled. "I understand your predicament, boy, but it's not my problem." As an afterthought, he drew a card from a silver holder. "If you must, make an appointment with my secretary." He shoved the card across the table. "Now if you'll excuse us, I suggest you take a walk."

De Villiers eased himself further into the chair causing his stomach to fold over the edge of the table. "Just one moment, sir." He pulled a piece of paper from his top pocket. "Have a look at this. Please." He spread it on the table mat and jabbed a finger at a five-cornered emblem. "That's the castle, in case you were wondering. A watermark of the Officer Commanding, Seaward Defence Force, to be precise."

"Ja. And?"

De Villiers jabbed at the letter. "I am vested with the full authority of the state, both civilian and military, to take whatever measures I deem necessary." His lips curled into a smile. "We like to run things by the book. Where we can."

Anna's father waved to catch the waitress's attention. When, on the third attempt, she looked his way, he held up the menu to her. Then he pulled out his watch, flicked it open and laid it on the table between them. *"Reg so. Meneer*—sorry, *Sersant.* I'll give you four minutes."

The detective ogled the waitress as she felt for a pen in her top pocket. "Sir, you must understand. I don't necessarily agree with any of this, but I'm under strict orders to investigate."

"Ja, ja." Her father turned to the waitress, pointed at Anna then himself. "Only the two of us will be eating. Anna?"

Once they'd placed their orders, he turned to the detective. "Get on with it, boy."

"Thank you, sir." De Villiers coughed into his hands. "There have been complaints lodged against you, sir. People from your constituency." His eyes rested on Anna too long for comfort, then looked back to her father.

"People are complaining all the time. Goes with the job."

"Understood. But these are different."

Her father appeared about to say something but didn't.

"They say you're doing more than sheep farming at Rietvlei."

It was subtle, but Anna noticed her father suck in air. "Oh?" he said. "Interesting. Tell me more."

"Our sources say import–export."

"Ah. Is this the sort of brilliance you're paid for, *Sersant*— what was it again?"

"Speurder-Sersant. De Villiers."

"Ja *nee.* Fine Huguenot name. I've got some of that blood myself. Sersant de Villiers, have you ever heard of a farm of over a hundred morgen that doesn't sell some of its produce to foreign markets?"

The detective pulled out a packet of Springbok cigarettes, offered the others and helped himself. "It's my duty to tell you, *Meneer* van der Vliet, that it's a criminal offence to circumvent the regulations of the Agricultural Control Board."

"If you're accusing me of something," he said, rubbing a smudge from the cover of his watch with his handkerchief, "I suggest you get to the point. You've got two minutes left."

De Villiers glanced at Anna, lingered, and returned his attention to her father. "Our sources tell us you're supplying the Germans."

"*Wragtag*. And you'd believe an idle gossip over the word of a Member of Parliament?"

The waitress appeared, placed a cluster of condiments on the table, set two places and scurried off.

"Gossips," De Villiers said. "And I didn't say I believed them." He drew on his cigarette until the end glowed, blew smoke from the side of his mouth, then tapped at the letter in front of him. "But some important people do."

"Rubbish. You know as well as I do, this has nothing to do with facts. It's all politics. You're here because I'm a thorn in the side of your masters. Simple."

"For all I know you may be right, *Meneer* van der Vliet." He flicked cigarette ash onto the side plate. "You know, I'm a big admirer of your party."

"It won't help to flatter me, *Sersant*. I wasn't born yesterday."

"I mean it," he said. "But that's not why I'm here. Just be so kind as to answer a couple of questions. You never have to see me again."

There was silence except for the chattering of other patrons.

"Is it true there's a store full of fresh meat and vegetables on your farm? Enough to feed hundreds. Is that normal, *Meneer* van der Vliet, for just you, and maybe a few workers?"

Her father checked his watch, stood. "Time's up," he said. "And I'll be damned if I'll do your job for you, *mampara*. Rietvlei's only a day's drive. Go see for yourself."

"Our men already did, sir."

Anna exhaled. Throughout the exchange she'd found herself wanting to say something in support of her father, anything. Now she was glad she hadn't.

"Well then," her father said, "you've got nothing, and you know it. This idiocy of yours is wasting our time." He pushed the ashtray towards the detective. "*Vieslik*. These people who smoke during the day. Oh. And I'm going to speak to the Minister of Police. In fact, I'm meeting him tomorrow. My boy, if you show up again without an appointment, you'll have more than your job to lose. I'll make damn sure you're unemployable."

"I'm sorry, sir. I didn't mean to offend." He rolled his khaki sleeve even higher up his arm. "You must understand, I'm only doing what I'm told."

Stefan stared at De Villiers. "So, who's doing the telling?"

"I'm afraid I'm not free to discuss that, sir. But I tell you what …" He pulled a pack of cards from his top pocket and handed one each to Anna and her father. "My office number's there. If you have any information you think might help us, I'd be much obliged."

De Villiers let his cigarette rest on the edge of the ashtray. There was an awkward silence as the smoke curled up and past his ear. "Well, then," he said, rising to his feet. "I'll be going." As if remembering something, he looked at Anna. "Oh, one last thing, miss. He reached into his pocket again, produced a card and slid it across the table. "Is this perhaps yours?"

Her student identity card. Fear gripped her. She remembered her mishap outside the castle the previous day. "Thank you," she muttered, and slid it into her bag.

De Villiers waited for her to make eye contact. "Everything in order?"

"Yes, of course. I'm just grateful someone found it and handed it in." She got up, extended her hand. "If I learn anything of use to you, I'll be sure to return the favour."

They watched in silence as De Villiers left.

"So what was all that about?" her father said.

"What do you mean?"

"That business with your identity card."

"Ag, Papa. Can't we finally just have a meal in peace together without an interrogation? I lost it, all right? It happens."

He held her gaze for a moment, as if weighing things. "Ja. Of course." He looked around. "Ah, here comes our food."

18

ANNA WALKED BESIDE HER father in silence, arms crossed, counting the steps to the junction with Government Avenue where their paths would diverge. The Waldorf salad and bread were sitting heavily in her stomach.

"So … that business with your identity card," he said as they ducked under the beard of a New Zealand Christmas tree hanging over the path. "What really happened?"

"Why?"

"Don't play games with me."

Anna surged forward. "Are you saying it's my fault that fool interrupted us?"

"Of course not. I'm saying that a person doesn't just leave their card lying around." He was level with her now, a dozen yards from the avenue.

Anna shrugged. "I guess I must have dropped it somewhere." It felt like early evening in the gloom of the oaks. "You know, on my city walks."

"Yes, but where? You must know, surely."

"So now you don't believe me?"

"No, no, I mean yes, of course I do. But suppose you dropped it in Adderley Street, where you said you were this morning, and some Good Samaritan found it on the pavement. Wouldn't they hand it in at the police station? Or the post office? How would it get to De Villiers, who happens to be investigating me, on the same day? You telling me it's a coincidence?"

"Search me." Anna shrugged. "But he would have come today anyway. Think about it. If his men have already been to Rietvlei and reported back, it means he's been investigating for at least a week."

"*Ge.* How do we know he wasn't making all that nonsense up? To unsettle us. These plainclothes *manne* are a devious lot."

Anna felt her father's hand clamp on her wrist. The avenue was deserted except for a vagrant slumped fifty yards away. "There's something you're not telling me," he said. "And don't give me that innocent *bokkie* look. This is no time for hide and seek. We've got to come up with a plan."

"No," she said. "Not we. You." She shook her arm free. "You got us into this mess. You get us out."

He studied her eyes for weakness. "You're right. And I will. But first, I need to know everything."

Anna looked at her watch. "Oh dear, it's almost two. My friends are waiting for me." She started walking again.

A couple approached, holding each other close. The woman was slight and dainty as a ballerina, the gentleman barely a grown man. "*Nee wat,*" her father said when they'd swept past. "Not so fast."

"What is it now?" she said. "I really must go."

"You must never see that man again. You know who I'm talking about."

Anna felt her chest tighten. She felt like she was fifteen. The day he found her drinking coffee with Willem in Hannah and Kleinjan's kitchen. A night of lectures. Threats. Another death blow to her innocence. She stood up on her toes, looked down. How could he know? She said, "I'll see who I want to."

"I'm afraid it doesn't work like that."

"So how does it work? I'm nineteen. Second year at university. With respect, Papa, you can't tell me what to do any more."

He coughed, swallowed phlegm. "You're right. If you want to be legalistic about it." His jaw shifted left to right and left again, his eyes sad and avoiding hers. The far-off sound of kids playing floated above the hum of traffic.

"What else is there to it?" she said. "I'm a grown woman now. You said yourself you wanted me to become independent. That it was the normal course of events. Don't you trust my judgement by now, Papa? Surely ..."

"Ja, but ... it's just ..."

She waited.

"Julia said …"

Anna felt a tingle in her spine. "What's Mama got to do with this?" she said.

"I didn't want it to come to this."

"What are you saying?"

"*Engel*," he said, "put yourself in my shoes for a day. I swore an oath to your mother the day before she died. To abide by her wishes." His right cheek broke into a maze of cracks, as if he'd swallowed a shot of lemon juice. "As an Afrikaner, a Boer, son of a *bittereinder*—you have no idea how difficult this has been. First your English tutors. Then the newspapers. Hell, I still want to burn those things when I see them lying about your room. And then," he swallowed, "my own constituents are gossiping. My enemies call me a *volksverraaier* because I let you go to university in Cape Town. It's been nothing but trouble …"

Anna's breathing had almost stopped. She was thinking of another way of interpreting his words. "I still don't see what any of that has to do with me being my own person."

He stepped closer, put a hand on her shoulder. "I promised her I'd look after you."

"But you have. You've done everything." Anna sighed. Looking up into his eyes, she felt a thread of sorrow despite her frustration. He was only trying to protect her. How could she expect him, her father, to see it otherwise? "But …"

"But nothing. You can't be seen with him again. Not ever."

"Seen?" She dropped her shoulder and drew away. "What are you saying?"

"The dance last night. *Sies*, I told you dancing causes promiscuity. You and Thomas acting like you were *gekys*, or worse."

"You followed me, spied on me! How dare you?"

"Ag, come now, Engel. I've got better things to do than spy on my daughter. All I have to do is speak to old loose-lips Douglas. Man, those *souties* from Natal love to talk."

Elizabeth! Anna cursed herself. Did she really think her housemate and so-called friend would keep her promise of confidence? She must have been on the phone to her father first thing in the morning. "You judge me for seeing the very man you introduced me to, encouraged me to entertain on the farm? You hypocrite."

"He's not what I thought he was," he said. "I can't explain now. It's just … he's a danger."

She glanced up the avenue. The beggar was sitting more upright now, turned towards them, face still buried under his hat. She turned back to her father. "And if I told you I'm in love with him? That he makes me happier than I've ever been? Would you still forbid it?"

For a moment he was wordless.

"Don't break my heart again." Anna suddenly felt exhausted. "Thomas isn't Willem. You said it yourself. There are connections. With your foster family. He's an aristocrat. Surely, if you ever would, you'd approve of this."

"Yes, yes, you're right. He's an impressive individual. No one could argue that. And I also like him. But now isn't the right time. The war, I mean. Our world is upside down. You and me, Kleinjan. We could lose everything. Our lives even. Trust me on this. My decision stands. It's him or us."

Anna scrunched her eyes shut. The thought of not seeing Thomas felt like a burden too heavy to bear even for a day, never mind a lifetime; the pain was almost physical. But her father had a point. Besides, no self-respecting Afrikaner girl could openly defy her parent. Not indefinitely, anyway. She sighed and turned to face up the avenue. "You win, Papa," she said. "You always do. Never mind who you bulldoze in the process."

She dragged her feet down the last hundred feet of the oak-arched mile of Government Avenue, regretting her promise to go shopping with Elizabeth. Unlike her new friends, Anna viewed shopping as a means to an end, like the three-hour round trip from the farm to the co-op in Bredasdorp for sheep dip and seed, or the general dealer in Struisbaai for provisions. But for Elizabeth, shopping was clearly a form of entertainment, self-expression even. She imagined Elizabeth in her sleeveless dress with the scalloped hem, milling about the foyer of Stuttafords. How much, apart from fathers in politics, did they really have in common?

"Psst." The hiss startled her from behind.

She spun about. The vagrant now lay prostrate on the bench,

head on chin, clutching a bundle of old clothing. Her spirits soared.

"Sorry," the man struggled upright, face obscured by his hat as his unbuttoned overcoat, fell open to reveal a ragged shirt.

The voice seemed wrong. Anna looked away to avoid eye contact, hope wavering. "Thomas?" she said tentatively, before looking down.

The vagrant lifted his hat lazily, his dark hair tumbling out in a matted knot. "Spare a shilling for the homeless," he said. His front teeth were missing. "There's a good lady."

She reached into her bag, drew out the change from her father's pound the day before.

"God bless," he said, taking the money with a shaky hand.

She turned away, sadness enveloping her like a winter fog.

19

AS ANNA EMERGED FROM the Company's Garden, a man was just rounding the top of Adderley Street in her direction, scattering pigeons as though parting a sea. She recognised his strut immediately, and before she could react he was upon her.

"*Magtig*," she said. "It's you."

Fanus froze, chest out, head back, his clean-shaven cheeks reddening. "Anna! What a nice surprise!" He was recovering fast. "*My jinne*, you're as beautiful as ever."

"Ag," she ran a hand through a wave of stray hair. For all his faults he could be charming. "That's kind."

"Did you get my phone message?"

"When?"

"At your apartment. What's wrong?"

"How did you get my number? Only Papa … goodness, he never learns. When was that?"

"Just after nine. Your friend promised to pass on the message."

"Tch." Anna shook her head. "That Elizabeth."

"Doesn't matter," he said. "I'm seeing you now."

"What was it about?" She immediately regretted having asked.

"Oh, nothing." His shoulder's hunched, and he looked away, back again. "Just … you know … seeing if you want to go out with me this evening."

Anna scrounged for excuses. "I, uh … thought you were on the farm. You said …"

"Ja, that's right." His chest shrank as he exhaled. Though

he was looking at her, his gaze flicked here and there. "I meant the Durbanville place." He turned to look towards the Tygerberg hills. "You wouldn't believe the labour problems we're having at the quarry again. Those people never stop complaining. And fighting each other. If it's not about money, it's because one's stolen another's wife."

She appraised his suit. Three-piece with a waistcoat and tailored too tight as always. His shoes were Italian leather, pointed toes with hard tips. "You sure dress fancy for a farmer, *nê*?"

"I'll take that as a compliment." He looked down and flicked a ball of fluff from his shirt. "You know me, I like to maintain standards, even when I'm on the job."

Anna smiled without meaning it. "Ja. Never one to get your hands dirty."

"What's that supposed to mean?" He adjusted the hang of his jacket on both shoulders. "You mustn't be so cynical. It doesn't suit a lady in your position. Anyway … I was just at the bank".

She sighed. A conversation with Fanus always turned to money. She waited.

"Did I tell you we're getting a new harvester for the Napier farm?

"If you did I wasn't listening."

"Ja. One of those new imported diesel engines will take the place of half a dozen workers, I tell you, and with none of the nonsense."

Anna felt a vague sense of unease.

He coughed into his jacket sleeve. "Oh, I could have sworn … We must speak more often, you and I." He sniffed. "You remember those South Wester *okies* we met at your place the other night, the Germans?"

Anna didn't respond.

He eyed her. "I thought so. *Jinne*, you couldn't take your eyes off that pretty boy. What was his name again, Timothy or something?"

"Thomas." Anna hoped her blush wouldn't betray her. "Way too full of himself. Like … never mind."

Fanus laughed. "Just joking. Anway, the other guy Kurt, he sure knows how to do the hard sell, hey. Came to see me the very next day. On a weekend, *nogal*."

She tightened the cardigan about her shoulders.

"Tell me …" Fanus kept his eyes trained on hers.

It reminded her of one of the reasons she'd stopped going out with him. The way he could make a conversation feel like an interrogation.

"You haven't seen him, have you?"

She tried to stay deadpan. "Who, Kurt?" She forced herself to meet his gaze. "Shouldn't you be the one telling me?"

"No, the pretty boy."

"Thomas? Goodness no. Why?"

"Ag, nothing. It's just they were supposed to revise their quote. *Jinne*, it was expensive. Then they just disappeared."

"That's strange," she said, turning to him. A stream of cars passed, some nearly brushing her. The exhaust fumes made her feel warm and light-headed. Her eyes followed a Chevrolet as it veered into Adderley Street and finally disappeared round the bend onto Wale Street.

Fanus glanced at his watch. "If you're anything like me, you'll be starving by now." His eyes darted left and right, ahead and past her. "Come, let me get you lunch. It's not every day I have the pleasure of bumping into you."

"That's kind," she said, "but I've just eaten. With Papa."

He searched her with his eyes. "Oh …" He glanced up Government Avenue, which trailed towards the distant mountain like a green ocean wake. "Isn't your place in Gardens?"

Anna laughed. "That's where I sleep. I don't have to hang around there all day. Anyway … I'm off to have some fun with friends." She clutched at her bag. "A bit of shopping."

His chest was out again, shoulders back. "*Ge.* I thought you hated the shops. I've always liked that about you, you're not a typical girl." He edged closer. Despite the hour, she could smell his aftershave.

She glanced down at the sensible shoes she'd put on when she realised she'd be walking to District Six and felt a powerful urge to just turn and run. Instead she shrugged. "People change."

"At least join me for tea. For old time's sake." He gestured across the road again. "There's a lekker little place two minutes down St Georges. Come." Ignoring her hesitation, his cold hand took hers, making her shiver as he steered her through a gap in the traffic.

The café was smaller than Anna had hoped and they were the only patrons. Fanus led her to a window table the size of a drain cover with two cast-iron chairs facing each other. He pulled out her chair, slid it under her and sat. They studied the menu in silence. A wiry lady with oversized glasses approached. She looked old enough to have retired a long time ago. "You again," she said in Afrikaans, smiling at Fanus, and then glanced at Anna, her smile turning conspiratorial. "How can I help?"

Despite Anna's protestations, Fanus ordered scones with cream and jam. It annoyed her how he so often did things like that, as if to make a point of her maternal English heritage.

When the old lady presented the tray and retired, Fanus looked out the window and commented on the heat of the day, waiting for Anna to pour the tea. She considered testing his resolve, but it was in her interests to hurry things along.

"Thank you, my love." He spooned two heaped sugars into his tea and stirred. "So." He withdrew his teaspoon, tapped it on the edge of his cup to drain it, then placed it carefully on the saucer. "You sure you haven't seen him? The German."

She bristled. "I already told you, he's not my type." She sipped her tea, then tried to place the cup on the saucer without rattling it. Trepidation was fast turning to anger. "And what's it got to do with you who I see and when?"

"You're right. Excuse me." He stirred his tea again. "It's just that you two looked so comfortable together."

"What's that supposed to mean?"

"You know, cosying up. Like at the windmill."

She glared out of the window, then turned back to Fanus. "You're funny," she said. "A woman has a conversation with a stranger, next thing they're lovers?"

He swallowed a mouthful of tea and grimaced. "I still don't see what you people like about this stuff. Call me a Boer, but I'll take a *moerkoffie* any day." He replaced the cup. "You mustn't put words in my mouth, you know."

She laughed. "I don't have to. Your face says it all. Come on silly, it's been more than a year and you're still jealous as sin."

"Bloody colonials." He glared at the proprietor at the door, who was scouring the pavement for patrons. "They even make a proud Afrikaner woman behave like a *mak Engelse.*"

"Oh, come on. You're not in Bredasdorp."

He straightened. "This is every bit as much my country, I'll—"

She placed a hand on his forearm. "Relax. This isn't the time for a rant."

He pushed his cup and saucer aside. "You're right. Forgive me."

She felt his hand close over hers and she didn't hurry to remove it. Some part of her wanted to relive the feelings she'd once had. They reminded her of simpler times, when her whole world was a thirty-mile radius around the farm. "Fanus," she said, "What are you doing?"

"Give me another chance," he said. "Please. The time before ... we were too young."

"You mean I was," she said. "You were in second year at university, remember." Her hand twitched. His grip tightened.

"We've known each other all our lives." He stroked the top of her hand with his middle finger. "At least it feels like it."

"That's not my fault ..." She stopped. "That came out wrong. You've always been a gentleman to me. Like a brother, really. It's just ..."

The proprietor had appeared at the table, pen in hand again.

"Excuse me?" Fanus turned.

She blushed. "Anything else for you two?"

Fanus declined. When the old woman had left he leaned forward towards Anna. His fringe fell like a stage curtain over his eyebrows. By conventional measures he wasn't a picture postcard, but if she tried, she could make an argument that he was handsome. "It's time to put the past behind us," he said. "Start again. We're older now, wiser." He stroked with his whole hand now. "Just imagine. We'd be perfect."

"You mean you'd be," she said. "It's all about you—your farms, your law degree, your career. All you want me for is to round out the picture. Come on, try to deny it. My only part in your grand scheme would be to look pretty and produce an heir." She withdrew her hand. "That's no life for me, Fanus. I'm not interested."

He withdrew his hand from the table. The proprietor delivered the bill and stood at hand. Fanus signed it without checking, produced a note and told her to keep the change. He watched her bustle into the kitchen, turned back to Anna and said, "You want to be an artist, don't you?"

"A logical assumption about someone studying Fine Art."

"Ag, come on, Anna. There's no need to be sarcastic. Art's always been your passion. *Jong,*" he smiled, "I still remember competing with paintbrushes for your attention." He shifted his chair closer and their feet touched. "Just imagine. You'll have everything. A servant for this and that. You've seen how it is at our place."

Try as she might, in that moment Anna couldn't help entertaining a fantasy of a future without want of money. Not that she'd ever really lacked for anything. As Papa was so fond of saying, they'd always been far better off than many Afrikaners, who'd struggled with severe poverty after the war with the British. Darn your socks, he'd insist. Burn those candles to the ground. Clean the plate. His cautiousness with money came from his years as a refugee before their grandfather established his veterinary practice in Germany. She understood the importance of not wasting, but she was determined never to saddle her own children with the same insecurity.

"That's all very well," she said. "But you've said it yourself." She fiddled with the teapot. "I'm too English. I'd be a liability in your circles."

"Ja, ja." He had that pleased-with-himself look again. "I've thought of that. But it's actually an advantage. When I'm … Let me put it this way. Any politician in this country must deal with the English question. Love them or hate them, we need each other. As they say, Africa isn't for sissies. We have to stick together to survive in this place."

"Stick together against who? *Die 'anderskleuriges'*? You don't need to cotton wool your words with me, Fanus. I know how you see things."

He straightened, puffed out his cheeks. "Oh yes? And how else does a person look at it? Like those disciples of Lenin running that excuse for an educational institution up there." He pointed in the direction of the mountain. "Don't be fooled,

Anna. You may feel sorry for the natives, and with good cause. They haven't always been treated right. Even I understand that. But at the end of the day it's not about wages, working conditions, economic opportunities … It's a power struggle, plain and simple."

Anna pulled a tissue from her sleeve and dabbed her nose, then replaced it. "I don't care. There's no excuse for what you people are planning."

"You people?" His cheeks grew even rosier than usual. "Let me remind you whose party is leading the charge for separate development."

She made to stand. "How dare you bring my father into this?"

"Well, I mean, if anyone's a racist it's—"

Anna stood. The table rocked on its feet, rattling the tea set. "That's enough."

Fanus was up in a flash, blocking her path to the door. "Wait," he said. "I didn't mean to offend, promise. You know how I admire your father, his ideals. Even if we don't agree on the means."

They stood beside their table. There was now an elderly couple seated at the far wall, though they appeared not to have heard anything.

"I know how close you are to each other." Fanus's cheeks sagged and had lost some colour. "But he won't always be there to dote on you, you know."

"Papa's not going anywhere."

"He's a man, Anna. You can't expect him to stay unmarried forever."

"Who said I did? I keep encouraging him to go out."

"A person sees what they want to."

Anna thought of Margriet, the blushing, the touches.

"Come now." Fanus was close to her now, his aftershave like roses and ice.

"Think what a couple we'd make." His shoulders were back. It looked like he'd won the jackpot at the races. "I'm going to be a powerful man," he said, glancing about, voice softer now. "Sooner than you think. Believe me. The farms will be the least of it."

Anna paused before responding. Something bothered her. "I'm not following your logic."

Fanus glanced about. The proprietor had retreated to her cash register and was hammering at the keys. He leaned forward. "You know I'm an activist," he said. "All through my time at Stellenbosch. I've never kept that from you." His eyes were focused and large, like seen through a magnifying glass.

She swallowed, waited.

"I can't explain now." He looked out the window. An old lady with white hair in a bun nudged past. "But, as God is my witness." He turned to Anna. "We'll have our republic. Believe me."

She felt the room moving.

"And when it happens, I'm going to be a leading light. Trust me on this one, my love. We'll make your father proud."

Anna took her bag.

"All right. I can see all this is still hard for you." Fanus fished into his inside jacket pocket and pulled out a business card. "It's understandable. The harvest doesn't ripen in a day."

She raised her eyebrow, trying not to think what he was about to suggest.

"Let's do something fun together for a change. No heavy talking. No pressure. How about the bioscope tonight? Lectures haven't started yet, am I right?"

"Oh," Anna struggled to think of an excuse. "I've … my friends want me to …"

He handed her his card. "Come on, it will be fun. You choose the flick. Hey, there's one with Cary Grant, just came out. Called *Suspicion*, something like that. You love that *oke*, don't you? Fontaine doesn't look half bad in that red dress, either. You should see the posters."

"I'm sure. Ag, it's sweet of you to ask me, but …" At a loss for what to say, Anna resorted to the truth. "I need an early night tonight. All the travelling—I only moved back into my lodgings the night before last. And you know how I always battle to sleep at first."

"Fine. I understand. Tomorrow?"

"Oh. Just us? But, what about—"

He put a hand up to stop her. His chest was out. "Don't worry," he said. "I've spoken with your father. He's fine with us being alone, even here in the city. He trusts me, remember."

"That may be," she said, "But I don't need his permission any more. I'm nineteen for heaven's sake. I'm my own woman here in Cape Town."

"Ja. But you know me. Come Anna. Just this once. Is that too much to ask of a friend?"

"I'm sorry," she said. "I can't commit. Not now."

He offered her the card. "That's my number at the quarry. If you change your mind …"

She slipped the card into her handbag. "Thanks for the tea," she said, looking at her watch. "My friends will be wondering where I am."

"Think about it at least," he called after her. "Think of all the fun we used to have."

20

O N THE TERRACE OF her university campus cafeteria, Anna sat in the dappled shade of an oak, her slingbag of art supplies and personal effects at her feet. She was running Detective de Villiers' business card between her fingers. She was still mulling the decision she'd made during a restless night. How she envied the carefree manner of the students passing her table. Despite the dreadful short-term consequences, the force of Mannie's logic was overwhelming. Reporting to the authorities right away and pleading clemency was her best hope of saving her father's life.

The students criss-crossing the plaza were mostly men. She wondered how many had registered to avoid the embarrassment of not volunteering. Coming down the driveway was a classmate from her drama course, blonde hair bouncing and a spring in her step. Unlike Anna, she seemed to know everyone already. She was from one of those private schools in Natal where they spoke the Queen's English, and Anna wondered if her *platteland* accent was the reason she was still struggling to fit in. Or was she just socially awkward?

Only once in her life had she felt as alone—three weeks before she turned nine. Her mother's body was already cold by the time she was allowed into the room. Yet strangely, she had looked more alive then than during the previous months, her fingers clasped above the crocheted spread. It had been hard watching her mother suffer, but Anna was thankful for the time together the illness gave them, the lazy hours of reminiscing, jigsaw puzzles, tea on the stoep as the sun broke through to dazzle the fresh puddles on the veld. All that rainwater had reminded her mother of holidays in the Lake District as a child, and of her parent's tears when she told them she was eloping to Africa.

"There you are." Her father was approaching, not quite arm-in-arm with Margriet, but brushing hips as they walked in step. "Say, Engel." He pulled out a chair, settled Margriet and removed his jacket. He was out of breath and there was sweat staining his shirt. "Sorry we're late. So much to do. Margriet also had to pull some newspaper articles for Daniel." He glanced across at the clock on the façade of the medical school building. "*Jong*, this afternoon's session is going to be critical."

Anna tried not to notice their exchange of glances. "Goodness, Papa," she said, poking him in the ribs. "You're out of shape, hey. What's the walk here? Half a mile, three-quarters?"

He laughed. "Feels a lot longer when you have to march." He swirled around, hand up to flag a waiter.

"Papa, it's my treat. Please. Relax."

"Ja, but you didn't count on Margriet joining us, I'm sure. It's all right I hope?" Not waiting for an answer, he picked up the menu board. "Right. We'd better order. Margriet, what are you having?"

Margriet this. Margriet that. Anna's stomach was suddenly queasy. "The tart is good."

"Mmh." Her father strained to read the price, then turned to Margriet. "What do you think, *my lief*?"

Lief. Anna wrinkled her nose.

"Oh, no thank you," Margriet said. "I'm going to have the salad."

Anna kept studying the menu. "Ag, Papa, go ahead and have the fish and chips. I know that's what you really want."

He laughed.

"It's self-service," Anna said, slipping the business card into her purse. Rising from her chair, she forced herself to look at Margriet. Floral dress to the ankles, clingy, with a pearl necklace. Why must this woman dress up every day like the Prime Minister's wife at the opening of Parliament?

Her father's forehead furrowed. He glanced at the queue at the counter. "Really, Anna, I told you we should have eaten at

Parliament. You know how I hate waiting for food."

"You hate waiting for anything." She dropped the menu board onto the table. "Can't you just relax for once and let me spoil you? Why must it always be your agenda? Really. Sometimes I don't know why I try."

"Ag, Engel," he placed a hand on her forearm. "I'm sorry."

They waited until the queue had shortened a little and then got up. Her father towered above the two of them and the other students. He was silent throughout the three-minute wait, but it was clear he was trying hard to contain himself.

They returned to the table, set the trays down and unpacked their food and drinks. "So," he said when they'd settled. "How did lectures go today?"

"I told you," Anna said, bracing herself. "They start on Monday."

"What?" He lowered his fork, chewing his pastry with his mouth half-open. "You arty people are still buggering around while these serious *okes*"—he pointed at a student bustling past in a white coat—"are busy working their backsides off already?" He sat back, adjusting his serviette.

"Just because we deal in the abstract doesn't mean an artist is any less serious than … a doctor, say."

A drama student with a rucksack loped past, probably on his way to the two o'clock rehearsal at the Little Theatre. "*Magtig*," her father muttered, "that character could be a girl. *Sies*."

Anna was cross with herself for even thinking that another lunch with her father could make things any clearer. Especially with this floozy on his arm. And the last thing she wanted to hear was another diatribe on the declining morality of the youth.

"Tell me," he said. "What exactly were you doing with Kleinjan yesterday," he said.

Anna stopped chewing. "What do you mean? I was with you."

He eyed her. "In the morning."

She put her fork down. How did he know, and what? "Ag, we just went for a walk. I wanted to get some exercise and, you know, some parts of the city still make me a bit nervous." She watched his face soften. "I hope you don't mind," she pressed her advantage. "Kleinjan said you didn't need him for anything."

"Didn't need him," he chuckled. Then he continued chewing, swallowed and took a sip of water. "Is that what he told you? Little *skelm*."

"Ag, Papa. You mustn't be cross with him. It was my—"

"*Toe maar*," he said, dismissing it with a raised palm. "Just a last-minute errand I needed him to run. But I found someone else." He glanced at Margriet. "Anyway, I'd rather you were safe and sound."

Anna felt a resurgence of the guilt she'd been fending off. For all her father's faults, there was no denying he cared for her. She fervently hoped her plan was not a reckless gamble.

A seagull swooped under the eaves, touched down beside their table and stepped towards her father. He kicked at it, and the bird fluttered out of reach with a squawk.

"How was your walk?" he said.

Anna picked at her pastry and tossed a crumb to the seagull.

"I was asking you something."

"Sorry?"

"How was your walk? See something interesting?"

She took a bite, chewed, taking time to swallow. "Ag, I just went to a few shops. Those smaller ones that sell arts and crafts, necklaces, bracelets. The kind of place you can't stand. Remember how Mama used to love them ..." She turned her head quickly and stared hard at the Mount Nelson's palms and the table top of the mountain, trying to control her emotions.

She heard Margriet push her plate away, although she hadn't eaten much. By the time Anna was able to turn back, Margriet had fished out a lipstick and a mirror and was touching up her lips. Anna couldn't bear to watch.

Margriet snapped the lid on her lipstick, then stood, straightening her dress. "I think it's better if I leave you two alone. Thank you for the lunch, Anna," she said icily, then turned. "I'll see you back in the library, Stefan."

Anna's father made an attempt to stand and called out to her, but Margriet was marching down the path to the plaza and around the corner. He turned to glare at his daughter.

"Listen," he half-cocked his index finger in front of her. "What did you do that for? Margriet might not be up to your lofty standard of virtue, but she's … good for me." He scowled as a spike of sunlight pierced his eye. "It's been ten years, my girl, since your mother died. When are you going to get over her?"

Anna let her fork clatter to her plate, unmoved as the students at the next table swiveled to look. She tried to stand and caught the underside of the table, spilling her drink.

"Get *over* her?" she said. She didn't care if her tears were showing. "I'm done with you saying this, with your putdowns, your shouting." She grabbed her bag, pulled out a tissue and dabbed her eyes. "Yes. Papa. I'm crying. Just like all those nights you sent me to my room without supper for daring to say her name. *Crying.*"

"That's enough." He glanced about. The conversation at the nearby tables had stopped. "Sit. Please."

Anna closed her bag. Her shoulders pulled back, as if by themselves. She felt a strength she hadn't known, as if her fury had burst the dam that had been filling for a decade. "One of the wonderful things about leaving home last year," she said, "was not having to endure your … your abuse."

"Now, now, *Engel.*" He rose, put a hand on her forearm. "There's no need to make such a scene."

"A *scene?*" Her voice went up another notch. "That's all that matters?" She glared at the group at the next table, then turned back. "All you care about is your bloody public image."

"Ag, Anna. It's not ladylike to swear. Sit." He patted her forearm. "*Asseblieftog.* Let's just be friends—like we've always been. *Kom nou.*"

"Friends?" Anna removed a strand of hair from her face, but still couldn't see clearly. "Since when have we been friends? When I obey your every command, maybe, play the helpless little girl. Well, things have changed. And if you think you can wipe out the memory of the only person who ever truly cared for me in favour of that, that tramp, well, you're wrong. And if you don't flinch at betraying the memory of your own wife like that, why shouldn't I …" Shaking, she yanked her hand free and slung her bag over her shoulder, hitching her thumb under the strap to steady it.

"Ja?" he said. "What were you going to say?"

"What do you mean?"

"You were going to say something. Like why shouldn't you do something or other."

"Why should I carry on as if everything's all right when it isn't?"

His eyebrow was raised again. "Come on, I'm not stupid."

His tone, the way he made her feel, was the last straw. Anna pushed her chair in. "Papa, it's best we don't see each other any more. For a while at least."

"Engel, what are you talking about? You can't just get up and leave like this. I won't have it, I—"

She turned to leave. "It will be better for both of us."

21

EVERY STEP ANNA TRUDGED down Strand Street along the edge of the Parade felt heavier. The intermittent shade of the palms offered scant relief from the three o'clock sun and her dress was damp at the arms and the small of her back. Several times during the mile-long walk from campus, she'd taken De Villiers' business card out of her pocket, as if reading it enough times would answer the question that haunted her.

She stopped opposite the entrance to City Hall and studied, yet again, the address on the back of the card. Why was his office here, not at the police headquarters? The document he'd shown them earlier had the watermark of the castle. She conjured up his face. The brush moustache, short back and sides, fastidious manner. How could a man so obviously steeped in the bureaucracy of government be trusted? No, she'd made the right call.

She pressed on towards the castle, passing the statue of Edward VII with his cap in hand and flowing cape. She thought of Fanus and his Stellenbosch friends ranting against the empire. At the time she'd dismissed them as blind fanatics. But they did have a point. What right did this distant monarch have to lord it over them? She continued, keeping to the intersecting circles of shade from the palms. Beyond the castle she could see the junction she'd approached the day before. She thought of Mannie and his colleagues and shuddered. They were so near yet so far—the Parade was like a no man's land between the two halves of the city.

She came to another statue, this time of a khaki soldier supporting an Afrikaner girl in distress. Unusual for Cape

Town, it was an Anglo-Boer War Memorial, its inscription written by the victors. "Never a king had such loyal subjects", it read. What nonsense. Afrikaners loyal to an English king?

At a stone's throw from the castle she stopped. A platoon of soldiers was marching past the lion busts and across the moat, buying her a bit more time. But with Mannie blackmailing her, she didn't have much choice. There could be no backing out. It was only a matter of time before she lost the moral high ground and any chance to plead for clemency.

The soldiers halted before the guard. The drill sergeant's salute made her think of Thomas. His certainty, the way he led her on the dance floor. What was it about him? Somehow he could keep a conversation flowing with no fear of silence. And the way he made her feel. The constant promise of a kiss. How could she be forced to betray the two men she loved most in all the world? Why was life so cruel?

She waited until the platoon had disappeared under the arch. The guard stiffened as she approached, pretending not to notice her. She could see past him through the entrance to a line of men snaking along the grass of the courtyard. The guard shifted on his feet, squishing the gravel. There was still a chance to turn. Why not stew on it a little more? Go back to the farm perhaps. Things always seemed clearer there, with more time and space to think.

"Yes, ma'am?" the guard asked. "Is your boyfriend here?"

She looked past him. The men in the queue were in civilian dress, a score or more, chatting. Some sucked cigarettes. Others chewed. There was a sense of excitement, like kids waiting for a ride at a funfair.

"Ma'am?"

"Sorry?" Anna turned back, as if waking from a daydream.

"Who have you come to see?"

"Oh." She adjusted her hat. "The officer in command."

The guard braced as if preparing to have his height measured. The branch of a bougainvillea rustled over his helmet. "That won't be possible, ma'am. A prior appointment must be made."

Anna dropped her chin, crestfallen.

"May I help?"

She lifted her chin an inch. The orange flash on the soldier's shoulder gave her an idea. "Actually, I'm here to volunteer. Woman's Auxiliary Defence."

The guard raised an eyebrow without budging his head. Then he shifted the rifle across his chest. "You old enough?"

Anna took a step towards him. "Are you questioning my age? I've been driving a tractor and cooking for a household since you were in nappies. "

His face was still like the stone behind him.

"Listen." Her nose was almost touching his. "I'm sure you don't want me to tell your colonel how you leered at a lady."

"No, ma'am." He patted his rifle.

She reached into her bag for her purse, pulled out her student card and waved it across his face. "Professor Pickford-Dunn sent me. A graduate recruit."

As Anna sailed across the lawn the men grew quiet. Some grinned, others stared. From the anonymity of the end of the queue she surveyed the scene. Inside, the castle seemed smaller and less intimidating. The star-shaped layout of the perimeter was intersected by a residential building with an entrance designed to impress. To one side was a simpler doorway.

Just then an elderly soldier draped in medals appeared. He made as if to assess the weather and retired. Anna turned to the nearest recruit. "Say, who's that?

"I don't know." The man clenched his cigarette between his teeth and adjusted his cap. He looked around at the others. "We're like you. Green as the fields of England. But if I had to guess, I'd say he's the OC." He extended a hand. "Patrick."

Anna brushed his hand as she passed. "Thanks. Good luck up north."

No one tried to stop her from entering the building. Out of the sunlight she struggled to make out the layout of the hallway. There were two open doors. Through the nearest she could see a woman hunched over a typewriter. Anna tiptoed to the second door and knocked.

"Yes."

She entered. An officer was seated at his desk.

"Excuse me, sir," she curtsied, removed her hat. "Terribly sorry to disturb, but …"

"What is it?" He placed his pen on the pad and looked up. "Do you have an appointment, young lady?"

"No, but—"

"Janet," he called. "Here."

"Wait." Anna stepped up to his desk. "I need to speak to you in private. It's—"

The officer stared at her. "My dear," he said. "If I had to stop what I was doing for every passer-by who popped in for a chat I'd never get anything done. There's a war on, for heaven's sake." He glared at the door. "Janet. I said now."

Anna turned to the door. There was a rustling of papers and heels on concrete. She turned back. "If I told you I know of a U-boat harboured on our coast, would you spare me five minutes?"

The officer stroked his moustache and eyed her. There were more steps in the hallway. "It's all right, Janet," he said. "I'll take this one. Close that door will you."

He straightened the papers on his desk and motioned for Anna to sit. "Go on. My next appointment is due in … three minutes."

Anna shifted.

"I'm waiting."

She looked down, rotated her hat on her lap. "I'm sorry," she sniffed. "I can't do this."

"What's the matter?" The officer leaned forward. "Why are you crying?"

Anna rummaged in her handbag, pulled out a tissue. A stash of papers and a pen followed. "He's my father," she said, gathering them. "How could I?"

"I can only help you if you open up. What you say will stay in this room. You have my word."

She looked up. Her first impression had been that he was an honest man. But now there was a hollowness behind the eyes. Like he wasn't quite human. She wiped her eyes. Come on, she chided herself. It's too late now for second thoughts. She looked down again, said, "The farm." She tugged at a tissue in her sleeve. "They've been supplying a German submarine."

Anna could hear the men outside laughing. A pigeon coo-cooed. The officer peered at her. "You saw it yourself?"

"No, but ..."

The officer straightened. "My dear, if I received a medal for every rumour of a U-boat sighting along our coast I'd be a field marshal." A chuckle of relief. "Let me guess. You saw lights winking in the dark? Heard voices?"

Anna gripped her hat on her lap with both hands. "How can you not believe me? You haven't even ..."

"What's your name?" he said, picking up his pen. "I'll take down your particulars. Get our men to look into it."

Anna stood and placed her hat on her head. "I can't believe it. I'm telling you there's an opportunity to intercept an enemy operation in our waters and you're dismissing me as a gossip?"

He studied her. "Hang on. Haven't I seen your face before? Yes. In the papers, the parliamentarian's girl, that's it."

From outside there was a knocking and then voices.

"Sounds like our time is up." Anna dusted her dress. "It was a pleasure meeting you, sir."

She barely noticed the khaki-clad man talking to the secretary. Felt a momentary lightness upon bursting into the sunlight of the courtyard. Although technically she'd stopped at the Rubicon, she felt a certain relief. It was as though by the simple act of examining her fears, they'd shrunk. And, more importantly, she'd lanced the boil, made a call, even if it was wrong.

22

THE TAXI DREW UP alongside the dance hall and stopped, its fan belt whining. The wail of a saxophone was audible in the warm night air. A bouncer in a shiny suit and hat stood impassive at the entrance. Anna remained in the back seat, as if pinned down by the weight of guilt. The scene at the castle was still tormenting her. Despite her best efforts to distract herself with household chores, she'd thought of little else all afternoon. Having recognised her, the commander was bound to investigate her claim, especially if he had any dealings with Detective de Villiers. And then it was only a matter of time before they pieced things together. Mannie's claim that they would be granted clemency seemed little more than wishful thinking now. She had not only betrayed her own father, but signed the death warrant of the only man she'd ever loved.

"Oddfellows on Hope Street, ma'am," the driver said, adjusting his cap. "As you asked, right?" He met her eyes. "Ma'am?"

"Oh, yes, of course." She scratched for the fare, as if buying time. How did she have the audacity to see Thomas again, after her revelation at the castle—and her promise to her father? And what if they were discovered together by the authorities? It was reckless in the extreme. But at least here on the margin of the city they were less likely to encounter any public officials.

Anna recognised the angle of his shadow, slouched against the sandstone wall, cigarette in hand. She felt a rush of excitement mingled with fear, as if poised on a ledge above a rock pool, frightened but determined to jump. She opened the car door enough to be visible, and waited.

Thomas extinguished his cigarette against the plaster and

turned. "Ah. You made it."

She swung her legs into the opening.

"I was starting to think you'd changed your mind."

Anna hesitated, then stepped onto the pavement. "Why would I?"

Thomas kissed past her left cheek. As he turned for the right one they bumped noses.

"My fault," he said. "I forget I am not in Europe."

She looked at her watch. Fourteen minutes past nine. She smiled to cover her awkwardness. "Don't you people still do the *Akademische Viertel*?"

"You know about that? I'm impressed."

She laughed. "Papa uses it as his excuse for being late. Which is often, you'd be surprised to hear. It used to drive Mama mad. You'd have sworn *she* was the honorary German."

Anna craned her neck to peer past the bouncer through the entrance. It was difficult to make out how many people were on the dance floor but it clearly wasn't full. Which raised the odds of being recognised. "Come," she said, squeezing Thomas's upper arm. "Let's get a drink first. Things don't really get going here before ten."

"*Jawohl*," he said as she slid her arm under his. "Just tell me one thing. Are all South African women such strong characters?"

Anna laughed, poked him in the ribs. She led him to the next street corner, feeling lighter than she had in years, despite the dark shadow in her heart. It was crazy how he could evoke such polar emotions simultaneously.

The café had about a dozen tables, mostly for twos and fours, spilling out onto the pavement. Each table had a candle buried in an orange vase. The flames refracting through the glass were almost perfectly vertical. A pianist sat at an upright near the entrance and pawed out a jazz tune.

Anna chose a table away from the others. "So," she said. "What have you been up to all day?"

"This and that."

She cupped her hands about the vase. The flame was short and fat and ate into the candle. "I've missed you, you know." She put the vase down suddenly. "Goodness, what's wrong with me?" She felt her cheeks warm. "I can't believe I just said that."

"It's in order." He placed the menu board face down and looked at her. "Really."

"No, I shouldn't say things like that. It's just that all this is new to me. My word, I've never missed anyone after one day. Except my mother ..." She withdrew her hands and put them on her lap. The flame hissed for a moment, as if it was about to go out, and then flared to life again. A silence hung in the air.

"You were very close to her, weren't you?" Thomas said.

His face was somehow different. More human than before. It was as though he actually cared about her response.

"I wasn't even ten. Doesn't every little girl hang onto her mother's apron?"

"I suppose so," he said, also staring at the candle. She noticed a faint scar the size of a keyhole at his hairline which hadn't been visible before. "But I've never been a girl, so I wouldn't know, right?"

"Oh, come now." Anna chided. "Didn't you have a sister?"

He held his finger an inch above the flame. Only when a patch of black appeared did he withdraw it. "Didn't I tell you I was an only child?"

"There's a lot you haven't told me. Make that everything." She could have sworn there was a tremor in his hand. "What's wrong?"

"There's a reason I don't talk about ..." He gazed across the street. A couple sauntered along in the direction of Oddfellows, the man dark-skinned with straight black hair, his arm resting self-consciously on her exposed shoulder. Thomas swung back to face Anna. "All right. I suppose it makes no difference now ..." He picked up the menu again without looking at it. "My mother was a beautiful woman. Glamorous, the newspapers said of her. There wasn't a social function of consequence in Heidelberg you wouldn't find her at. Father was the same." He closed his eyes and grimaced. "People called them the golden couple."

"But?"

"*Macht nichts.*" Thomas looked up and about for a waiter.

"It's just, she never really wanted to be a mother—that's what I thought growing up, anyway."

Anna placed her hand on his forearm and felt him tense.

"She was thirty-five when I was born," he said. "Is that even possible?"

"Ag, Thomas, you mustn't think just because—"

"No." He withdrew his hand. "She even told me once. That I was a—a mistake."

"But that's terrible."

"Not really." He straightened a fraction. "I told you, I had everything I needed, I—"

"No, I mean … what you just said about being a mistake. It's awful you think that."

"It's in order. Really. I had everything a boy could want. *Mein Gott*, our house was almost as big as the *Schloss*. The finest gymnasiums, even boarding school abroad. It's not normal in Germany. Not even for the *adel*."

They fell silent. There was just the hubbub of the other tables and the whoosh of a car cruising past. Then Thomas flung himself backward on his chair as if to seal the interlude of intimacy, and grinned. "Hey, I turned out well, didn't I?"

She appraised him from several angles, smiled. "I'd say."

He tapped a cigarette from his pack and put it to his lips. "Oh, sorry," he said, proffering her the pack. "You don't mind if I indulge?"

She eyed the crowned emblem. With the green and gold packaging it was a stylish proposition. "Ag, it's all right."

"You sure? It's not good for a man to smoke alone. What's wrong?"

"Oh, nothing. The *dominee* says it makes a girl look cheap."

Thomas leaned back, laughed. "That's funny." He swept his hand. "So you think all these ladies smoking here are … cheap?" He tossed his head back, exhaled. "*Wahnsinn*. How old are you again?"

"Don't be silly. I wouldn't be here alone …" she scanned the room, "if I wasn't my own person."

He offered the packet again. "Go ahead. I can keep a secret."

Anna laughed. "That you can." She picked up the box and tugged at the wrapping. "Elizabeth's been on my case for months. Says it makes a woman look sophisticated. I don't know. Do you agree?"

"Me? I think you should do what pleases you. I've spent too much of my life listening to others."

She helped herself to a cigarette and brought it to her lips.

Thomas struck a match and held it up to the tip. "What, you look sceptical?"

Anna sucked on the cigarette until the end glowed, then quickly removed it from her mouth. Her lips felt dry and there was a burning at the back of her throat so she coughed. "Yuck." She pulled a face at the smoke escaping from her mouth and dropped the cigarette. "So, this is the way you rebel, is it? Incognito in a colonial backwater like Cape Town. Playing spy."

Thomas laughed, leaned back to light his own cigarette. When he'd blown smoke he signalled a waiter. After ordering two Martinis he looked out across the road in the direction of the dance hall. A taxi had rolled up to the entrance and a couple tumbled out. Even from a distance they were conspicuous. Both were men. One wore a sleeveless sequined dress draped in pearls, his face paler than it should have been and his eyebrows fixed in paint. The other wore a woman's wig, red lipstick and denim shorts below a blouse cropped at the waist. Both wore high heels.

"I see what you mean about this place being different," Thomas whispered. "How often did you say you come here?"

"Oh, stop, silly. Probably three times the whole of last year." She watched the couple disappear into the hall. "People don't have issues here about race, language."

"I can see the attraction. Really," he eyed her. "Plus, you're not likely to run into your father."

She laughed and they slipped into easy conversation. After finishing their drinks, they wandered back to the entrance to Oddfellows.

As they approached, the bouncer straightened. He was half a head taller than Thomas and twice his girth. In spite of the dark outside, he wore sunglasses that covered half his face. "Ma'am," he tipped his hat as they passed, "where are your friends tonight?"

"Ag, can you believe it? They went to the bioscope." She glanced at Thomas. "I'd rather boogie till my feet blister. So who's the band tonight?"

"Ah." His face came alive. "Who else, sister. All the way from Joburg, *nogal*."

"No, not Sonny's Jazz Revellers?" She turned to Thomas. "You'll love them." She elbowed him. "Hey, don't look so worried. A dancer like you'll get the hang of the *vastrap* in no time. It's as easy as one, two, three, literally."

The bouncer appraised Thomas through his sunglasses. "Relax, *my bra*," he chuckled. "They also do the quickstep and a waltz."

Thomas smiled, nodded. "Thank you," he said and kept walking. "You must excuse me. I'm from the north."

Anna squeezed his arm as they stepped into the foyer, leaned in to his ear. "Why did you do that? Talk about up north. That could have all sorts of connotations. Not just upcountry."

He slowed. "Just having some fun."

Inside, it was like a school hall, warm and dimly lit. There were so many people it was impossible to move without squeezing between bodies. The ceiling was highest at the centre, with four-cornered arches ending at a plaster parapet that circumscribed the walls. Above and behind them was a balcony, in front was a semi-moon stage. The band was arrayed below the platform: a drummer in a tuxedo and an assortment of brass instruments, but no violin.

Anna felt herself perspiring before they reached the dance floor, her breath short. It annoyed her that the excitement of being out alone with a strange man would trump her confidence as a dancer. She looked at her feet. How often she'd prayed for them to stop growing, exasperated by the taunts of her class-mates. Her growth spurt had been mercifully short-lived, but there were still times she felt clumsy. She was almost relieved when she felt him pulling back. For a moment she considered suggesting another drink to calm her nerves. Instead she tugged at his hand, smiled. "Say, where do you think you're going?"

As he shrugged, the neck of his jacket crumpled. "Maybe some fresh air before we start? I don't know this music."

She laughed, feeling more at ease. "Hey, you can't do that.

Last night you had me in knots with the tango. Now it's your turn. Here ..." Anna took his hand. "It's easy, really." They were facing each other, their chests almost touching. She waited as he appraised the stance of a couple dancing past, then shivered as his hand settled in the small of her back. "That's it," she said, raising his leading hand to shoulder height. "Now, just follow my lead." She giggled. "This time at least. If you can bear it. Step, step ..." They still hadn't moved. "Quick one, two," she could feel his hand through her dress as if her back were naked, "three, and away you go ..."

"What was that?" he said. "Step, step, quick one ..." They were moving with the beat now, their feet in perfect sync.

"Two, three," she continued, "and away we go ..." When they had completed a circuit she turned her head to face him. On her toes her eyes were level with his, their noses almost touching. "Is there anything you can't do, mystery man?" They continued past the band. "Talk about a natural," she said at the next pause in the music. "I've been doing a variation of this since I could walk and you just about put me to shame."

Thomas laughed. "You're too modest. I think you don't tell me everything. Who taught you to dance like an expert?"

Anna went quiet for two twirls.

"Ja?"

"Relax," she said as the music slowed. "It was a friend. Willem." As Thomas reversed the direction of the turn they pressed up hard against each other at the waist. Her lips were just below his ear. "We haven't seen each other for ages."

Thomas looked up at the band as he danced, moving to the rhythm without thinking. He steered her closer to the centre of the dance floor and stalled to let another couple pass. "Why is that?"

"He went up north. To fight." Her eyes glittered. "Or, rather, to drive a white man's truck. He's Kleinjan's son."

He leaned closer. Another couple whirled by. "I am sorry for this war," he said. The song reached its crescendo and faded out. "You may not believe me, but truly I am. There was no need for any of this madness."

"Shh," she said. Their cheeks brushed. The music had paused, but it felt like the entire universe was holding its breath. "It wasn't just the war that tore us apart." The band struck up a waltz. It sounded like a Strauss but she couldn't be sure.

He shifted his hand up her back and adjusted the angle of their arms lower. "What then?"

They were taking small steps through the crowd now, their feet gliding in tandem. She couldn't remember dancing as close to a man before, and though it scared her, it felt wonderful, and she didn't want it to end.

"He volunteered. One of the first in the Cape."

"You must be proud of him."

The music had slowed and she was leaning into him. "Ja, but it wasn't his choice."

"How so?"

"Papa made him."

"Why?" He tensed and pulled back a fraction to search her eyes.

"That's how it works on a South African farm."

The waltz ended and the band leader grabbed the microphone to rasp an apology for the lapse into sentimentality, promising a more upbeat set after the break. Then he introduced the band members, from the saxophonist to the trumpeters. Each stood, lifted his instrument in salute and bowed at the couples drifting back towards the tables.

Thomas and Anna stayed in their embrace.

"Tell me," he said, lowering his lips to her ear, "why did you come tonight?"

She drew back, felt his hand firm on her back. "What sort of question is that?"

"I'm sorry," he said, "Only that I didn't expect you to follow through. It must have been a risk for you, no?"

She pulled away further. The pianist had struck up a tune and the trumpeters were draining their instruments. Soon the dance floor was empty but for a couple of stragglers on the far end. "Do I strike you as someone who would stand a man up? Really?"

He cleared his throat. "It's just, your father. We're not seeing eye-to-eye at the moment."

Anna tried to look surprised. "Oh?"

He shifted his hand at her back, not relaxing his grip. "He's ignoring me. It makes me think he's about to turn on me."

"But that's—"

"No. It's in order. I would do the same." He studied her eyes. "*Also*," he coughed, "I suppose it's *verboten*, you and me, no?"

Anna held onto him, not wanting to move. They were alone on the dance floor. People were sitting at tables, ordering drinks. Some were looking at them. "I don't care what he says any more." She let her face press against his neck. His aftershave smelled like sea mist.

"Is something the matter?"

"You want to know why I came tonight?"

He nodded.

She tried to steady the tremble in her legs but couldn't. "Sorry," she said, looking down. When their eyes met again she drew back. "To say goodbye."

"Steady now." He shifted closer. Their legs were intertwined now. The pianist was trailing off a high scale over the hubbub in the hall.

"And you?" she said. "Why did you come? You must know we have no future. Or are you just like every other man. Taking advantage of a girl while you can." It felt like there were tears in her throat but she was too distressed to cry.

"Shh. Anna, I can't change the way you feel about my kind. What they've done to you. The anger. I can't even promise I'm not going to hurt you. How can anyone promise that? And in war ..."

"But. This thing between us. It must end."

"Nothing is forever."

"What about death?"

"Even that will pass," he said. "At least for the living."

Anna clung to him, not caring about the stares. "It's ten years since my mother died. Yes, the memory of her face is fading. But pass? I don't know. Sometimes I think it gets worse with the years. Or maybe it's this war making us all more aware of death. How long can it go on, Thomas, how long?"

"A war never lasts for ever. Especially this one," he said. "I know it's hard to believe it when the world is in chaos and every small man prophesies doom."

"That's easy to say." She felt the heat of their bodies touching.

"Anna, we talked about this last night. My country has taken on too much."

"Perhaps. But that … little monster. He'll drag us through Armageddon before we're done."

Thomas scanned his surrounds and then his eyes fixed on hers. He ran his tongue along his upper lip. "Let me just say, not everyone in Germany supports him. I would be surprised if he lasts to the end of summer. And then the generals, they'll sue for peace. This bad dream will soon be over. Trust me."

"And what if you're wrong?"

"All right, maybe it takes longer. But it will happen. It's inevitable."

"And where does that leave us? You'll go back to sea. It's in your blood, I can see it. It's what you do."

He straightened and they pressed together. "Ja. I suppose."

"I've read of the risks, Thomas. The *Cape Times* published something the other day, specifically about submariners. Two thirds of submariners in the German navy don't make it." She felt his trouser stiffen against her as he shifted his lips to her other ear. They could whisper now; the sounds around them didn't matter. "Tell me I'm wrong."

"I think it was Freud who said that everyone is defined by an event in their adolescence. You are proof of this, with your mother. Me?" He averted her eyes for a moment. "When I was ten they discovered I had polio. That meant staying home. No physical contact. Even my parents kept their distance." He ran his fingers through her hair, lifted a few strands and let them fall. "Do you know what that feels like? To be an island?" He brush-kissed her on the cheek, then on the neck. "For eight months. A lifetime at that age." He ran his eyes down her neck until they stopped at her bosom. "Back in the village there were stories that I'd lost both my legs and my arms—a monster, they called me, crippled for life. When I got back even my teachers wouldn't go near me."

"That's awful."

"It's in order." He looked at his legs. "The only mark of this is that my left leg is half an inch shorter than my right. And even that I have compensated for, no?"

She smiled. "I'd say."

"So why do I tell you this?"

She sighed. "Why do you need a reason for everything?"

"*Nun gut.* I will tell you anyway. I survived, that is what. And I have been surviving ever since. My men say I'm charmed. Except, as you say, sometimes the burden of the living can seem heavier than the relief of death."

Anna realised her eyes were wet now, despite her attempts to dam her distress.

"My dear …" He held her by her upper arms. "I can call you that, can't I? Just this once. Anna, look at me. Standing here with you, I am happier than I've ever been. No woman has ever …"

Anna thought of her grandmother's warnings. The shallowness of a man's passion. Empty pledges. Lies. She felt the smoke burning her lungs and her breathing was shallow and sharp. "Come," she said, relaxing her grip. "Let's get some air."

"If you prefer," he said.

They passed the first empty table. "Can I buy you a drink?"

She declined and continued towards the door. The hall had thinned somewhat, away from the bar. Couples and foursomes sat at tables and chairs about the perimeter of the dance floor with drinks, joking and teasing. Most of the men wore jackets and ties, but there was little evidence of the three-piece suits of the Mount Nelson. It was an altogether more colourful crowd.

Outside, the bouncer was helping a drunk from the pavement. He handed him to a friend and watched them stagger off over the cobbles. When he saw Anna he tipped his bowler hat and resumed his post at the entrance.

"Where are you going?" Thomas called after her. "It's still early, surely …"

She turned, pointed to the dance floor. "What's the point of this? Us being here. Together. It's just going to make the pain last longer."

He caught up, placed a hand on her shoulder to stop her. "Do not talk like that. Please. We still have time."

"Time?" Her chest was rising and falling and she felt her lungs wheeze. "You say we have time? I'm not the sort of girl that can just eat, drink and make merry, when I know it's all about to come crashing down." She nodded toward the entrance at a gaggle of women smoking on the pavement. "But if you're looking for one, I'm sure there'll be no shortage of takers."

He followed her onto the street.

She ignored him and held up a hand at an approaching taxi. The driver wasn't visible as it slid past and around the corner. "Come, Anna, give me credit. I'm more than that."

She looked at him. For the first time she imagined his one hip being higher than the other. The thought made him seem more vulnerable. "I'm sorry," she said. "It's all been too much for one day."

He took her hand, making no attempt to close the gap between them. "You know"—far off a bottle shattered on stone followed by a shout, then the blast of a fog horn—"every goodbye we say to anyone could be the last. War just makes it clearer."

Looking at him her tears welled until he was just a blur against the lamplight. "You may have been charmed, as your crew put it, until you met *me*."

He stepped closer. "Now, now. What are you saying?"

"It's true." Her voice was cracked and thin. "A week ago you were in command of a U-boat, about to complete yet another successful mission. Who knows, another decoration, a promotion." She looked him up and down. His oversized trousers gave a shabby look to him. "Now you're a renegade."

He shifted closer again until there was barely an inch between them. He still held her hand at his thigh. "Renegade? What do you mean?"

Anna felt cold now. There was a breath of wind from the slope, and the smell of the ocean carried a hint of kelp. "There was a detective yesterday," she said, "at lunch."

"Yes?" He tightened his grip on her arm.

Anna glanced around. The girls had drifted back in to the dance hall and the pavement was empty, with no sign of the bouncer.

"Yes?" He turned her away from the entrance. They looked down past the now-deserted café to where the lights of a tugboat inched through the harbour.

"Promise not to tell anyone you heard this from me."

He nodded.

"A nasty detective called De Villiers barged in on Papa and me." She thought of the business card in her handbag. "I think he operates from the castle. What does that mean?"

The lines about his mouth were pronounced in the half light. "And?"

"They know, Thomas. About the supplies."

His face was a wall.

"They've even been to Rietvlei to investigate."

His eyes narrowed as though he was blowing smoke. "Continue."

Fragments of the exchange at the restaurant ran through her mind. Her student card being returned. Perhaps she was overthinking the situation. There had been nothing from De Villiers since. "Papa told me afterwards not to worry, they have nothing."

His eyes narrowed further. "You don't agree?"

"I don't know. But what if there was a crate left behind or something, a loose end. No one's perfect."

His eyes relaxed to oval. "How did it end?"

"Ag," she smiled, "Papa threatened to destroy his career, that's all."

Thomas chuckled. "Sounds like Stefan."

They fell silent. Inside the hall the band had struck up again. "Doesn't it worry you?" she said. "That they went to the trouble of driving all the way out to Agulhas. They must know something, surely."

Thomas paused. A couple stumbled out of the hall and shouted at a passing taxi. After they'd bundled into the car, he said, "Never credit a bureaucrat with too much intelligence."

"But it's not only De Villiers."

He let her hand go. Stroked his chin with two fingers. "What do you mean?"

"Others know about you," she said. "That's what I came to tell you. That and goodbye." She threw her arms about him, put her face against his chest. "You must go," she said. "Disappear. Back to your boat, whatever it takes." She drew him closer. "My darling … Sorry. It's silly to call you that when we've only known each other a few days." For once she didn't try to disguise her trembling. "We can't see each other again. Not tomorrow. Not ever. Please promise."

"Stop." He ran a finger down through her hair and rested it on her shoulder. "What is this now that you are saying?"

She shuddered his hand free. "Please. Don't … It's too dangerous. You and I, we …" Anna drew back. "*O, magtig.*" She slipped from his grasp. "No. I can't bear this, I …" A taxi appeared from a side street. She waved at it and then willed it to a standstill in front of her. "Goodbye, Thomas." She grabbed at the door handle. At first it wouldn't open. Why did it feel like she was running, taking the easy way out yet again? Only when she was seated did she dare to make eye contact. "Godspeed," she whispered, and blew a kiss.

23

ANNA HOVERED FORLORNLY AT the intersection of Hof and Orange Streets, long after the tail lights of the taxi had faded around the bend, as if to prolong her precious last evening with Thomas, clinging to the image of his face, his breath on her ear, his warm touch on her back. If she ever heard of him again, it would surely be a report of his capture or death.

Above the pineapple tops of the palm trees, the moon was bulging over the mane of Lion's Head. She sighed, thinking of the hours she'd spent at the edge of the *vlei*, watching the moon rise above the melkbos, wondering if somewhere in the world a man, destined specially for her, was watching it too. And now, just when she'd found him, she had been forced to say goodbye to him forever.

Slowly, reluctantly, she walked towards her residence. As she approached the entrance she glanced up, noticed a light on in their apartment, and hesitated. An interrogation from Elizabeth was more than she could bear at this moment. She walked around the side. Through the hedge she could just see the outline of the kitchen window. There was no way to tell for sure if her friend was home. She waited, straining for signs of movement.

A flicker of headlights streaked the leaves and she heard the familiar putter of a diesel motor approaching. She stepped back into the shadow of the vegetation. A farm truck stopped almost diagonally opposite her, beside the entrance to the Company's Garden. Two men hopped out—one slight, the other a block— and the truck shuddered off again. Anna pressed herself against the hedge. The men stood still on the pavement until the purring of the truck had faded. The slighter man turned to scan the road. The streetlight gave him a sepia hue which made his eyes look more sunken, but there was no doubting. It was Kurt.

The two figures melted into the shadows of the gardens, leaving the length of Orange Street deserted again. All was quiet, but for a shiver of wind in the pine tops above her.

From behind the hedge came the muffled rattle of a chain and a door opening. "Who is it?" Elizabeth's voice was uncharacteristically cautious. A dog barked a few houses up the street. "Anna? Is that you?"

Anna waited, pressed against the leaves of the eugenia bush, the smell of its resin pungent. She re-imagined the man's face.

The dog bayed, stopped, bayed again. Elizabeth shouted for it to be quiet. Then the door clapped shut.

Anna felt the branches of the eugenia shaking at her knee and tried to steady it. What was Kurt—a Nazi spy, maybe even SS—doing disappearing into the Company's Garden the night before last, presumably, and now? He was clearly up to something, and by all accounts, he was dangerous.

She hesitated. She should call the police. But what good would come of it? They would probably dismiss her at once. But if they didn't, she would only be increasing the danger her father and Thomas were in. She had to leave Thomas enough time to rendezvous with his boat. But she needed to find out what Kurt was up to.

She waited for a pair of cars to pass, then stepped out from the hedge, and crossed Orange Street. The entrance to the Company's Gardens was locked at night, barred by a gate. Finding a narrow gap between the gate and the fence, she tested the wire before slipping through. Anxiously she stared towards the row of oaks on each side of Government Avenue, their boughs forming a tunnel as black as pitch. Would anyone hear if she screamed? The fence shivered at her touch. As she edged forward over the cobbles her eyes began to adjust. She could just make out the shapes of treetops and buildings and the hump of Lion's Head.

Her leg brushed something solid. She felt with her hands. Hard and cold. The leg of a bench. She thought of the vagrants.

Where did they sleep? Were they, too, afraid of the dark? Gradually she was better able to discern form and depth, and moved more easily down the avenue. She was so conscious of the shadows that she barely noticed the sleeping lions at the entrance to her campus and the arch of the Little Theatre.

A rustle in the agapanthus made her freeze. Summoning her courage, she kicked at the bush, and the rustle grew fainter and was gone. The branches above had grown thinner. Looking back, she could just make out the slab of Table Mountain. Tonight it seemed more a menace than a comfort.

The pillars of the National Gallery appeared, rising like ghosts against the base of Devil's Peak. Then the trees closed to re-form the tunnel. Hemmed in now by a wrought iron fence on either side, the place seemed darker than before. Her anxiety grew with every step deeper into the park.

Noticing a faint flicker of light far ahead on the left of the avenue she felt her way along the fence paling, stopping only when it came up against a post. Somewhere a dove cooed and a song of crickets started. There was no need to read the embossed sign on the gate to know she was entering the rose garden. Inside, the trees gave way and the clearing was luminous with roses, and gently scented. Anna followed the path parallel to the avenue until it plunged again into the darkness of vegetation.

She paused for her eyes to readjust. Soon she could make out the stand of palm stalks to one side and the bamboo thicket on the other. The air was cooler now, and damp. After a couple of minutes she emerged from the jungle into another clearing. Beyond the fence to her right she could make out Tuynhuys with its Victorian balcony and lead-paned windows. She imagined the Governor General, sleepless in his study, striving to hold his country together under the increasing tensions of war.

Just then Anna picked up the distinct sound of voices. Her heart turned to ice. Cautiously she stop-started forward, conscious of every crushed leaf and twig snapping underfoot. Then she was among the jungle of cycads, bananas and drooping branches.

The flickering of light was more insistent now, through the leaves of a hedge. She stepped off the path and onto the lawn, shuffling towards a New Zealand Christmas tree whose bearded trunk ran low, and parallel to the ground for several yards before rising through the shrubbery. Soon only a waist-high hydrangea hedge stood between her and the light. She crept the last few feet on her knees. She could hear the thumping of her heart, the wheeze of her chest.

Through the greenery, in a clearing, she could see the stone wall of the well. Behind it, the trunk of an Indian rubber tree stood like a mangle of organ pipes in the moonlight.

The voices came again, faint, but growing clearer. Then a scuffle and its echo. She dared not move. The forms of the two men appeared from behind the rubber tree. Their faces were indistinguishable.

"*Jissis, maar die goet is swaar,*" the larger man said, straining. Then there was a thud as a crate dropped to the ground.

"*Pass auf,*" the other said. "This is dangerous."

The larger man sat on the crate and patted his top pocket. He stuffed a cigarette in his mouth and struck a match. The end of his smoke glowed red.

The German stepped forward and snatched the cigarette. "This is not permitted. You want to kill us both?"

The giant sprang up, grabbing the German by his shirt collar. "*Luister hier, doos.* Don't think you can stand there giving orders while I do all the work."

"Put me down immediately. *Schweinhund.*"

Anna held her breath. No one insulted an Afrikaner man's pride like that without a fight.

Kurt hadn't flinched. "You know what we do in Germany with people who disobey our orders?"

The giant spat. "We're in South Africa, *doos.* We don't take orders from anyone."

Kurt laughed, high pitched and brief. "That will change."

Anna felt the slime of a snail on her ankle but tried to ignore it. In the distance a car hooted, then there was silence. The giant let go of Kurt's collar, stooped for the remains of his cigarette and returned it to his pocket. "Okay, sorry. I'm just *gatvol* of carrying everything myself. Where's Von Eisenheim?"

The words gave her an electric shock.

"He doesn't know about this," Kurt said. "Keep it so, understand?"

The giant looked over the edge of the well. Kurt stood an arm's length from him.

"But where is he?" The giant reached for the crate as if testing its weight again. "He left Agulhas for Cape Town. We know that."

Kurt watched as the giant shifted the crate to the well. "He had to get spare parts, and do engine repairs. But he hasn't reported to central command since Sunday."

"So what are you going to do? Doesn't your escape plan depend on the U-boat?"

"I'll think about it."

There was silence. Anna felt a scratch growing in her throat, and swallowed desperately, fighting the urge to cough. Crickets started up from the bamboo thicket and she looked up at the stars. The pointers to the Southern Cross were subsumed by moonlight. It seemed like an eternity to crouch without moving.

"*Achtung,*" Kurt stepped over to the well and looked down. "It does not matter." He lifted a ladder and rattle-tested it. Then he walked back to the crate and tugged. "Come. Help me."

The giant leaned his weight to move the crate.

Kurt pointed at the ladder and waited as the giant lowered himself into the well to waist height. "The repairs were not serious. The U-boat still operates. And … If our mission is successful there will be no need for escape."

"Ja, but you said it must look like the Afrikaners are working alone."

"This is true. But do not worry. I will find Von Eisenheim. You just—"

"And if you don't?"

Kurt shoved at the crate. It scraped over the stone ledge until it began to tilt. He guided it to the giant's waiting hands. "I have communication with his deputy. He is an able commander. And *his* loyalties are in the right place. By the time anything happens I'll be half-way to Lourenco Marques, sipping schnapps in the wardroom."

"Coward." The giant leaned on the wall and waited.

"What is wrong?"

"Nothing. I need a rest. And I was thinking …"

"That is good. I did not think you did much of that kind of thing."

"*Fok jou*!" The giant spat on the ground.

"Be quiet." Kurt looked at the sky. "We must go faster. There are three more."

Anna watched the Afrikaner sink below the wall, followed by Kurt. She waited, her heart pounding, considering what to do.

At length a cloud passed overhead, shutting out the starlight. She crawled out of the hedge, ducked under the beard of the Christmas tree and crossed the clearing to the well. Reaching over the rim, she ran her hand around the inside wall. The stone bricks were smooth and damp. The ladder was still there. She braved a peek over the edge and recoiled from the reek of urine. Hastily she removed her shoes, hitched her dress, and stepped onto the ledge, then turned and lowered herself rung by rung. The stench of rot and urine was nauseating.

The moment her head dropped below the ledge she heard sloshing below her, clearly audible above the gurgle of the stream. Then a light flickered against the slate. Anna clambered frantically upwards, skipping rungs, and threw her body over the wall. The stones on the clearing were smooth and her only thought was not to slip as it changed to grass underfoot. Then she remembered her shoes and bag, and retrieved them, fumbling with the straps as the giant's voice echoed from the well. Soon she was scrambling through the hedge, branches cracking, barely aware of thorns scratching her arms as she dashed away.

Only when she reached the rose garden did she slow down slightly, her breath rasping against her rib cage. She kept her ears pricked, listening, praying that they hadn't heard her above the sloshing in the well. But had they noticed her footprints in the flowerbed? She probably had a few minutes at most. On the avenue now, everything seemed lighter than before. She was only a few hundred feet from the gate. She strode as fast as she could, listening intently for pursuers.

At Orange Street she hugged the shadows so that Robert, the guard, wouldn't see her from his post at the Mount Nelson. The lights were out in her apartment when she tiptoed in. But her heart still thumped.

24

ANNA LAY TOSSING AND turning, tormented by a shapeless forboding she couldn't fully identify. She turned on her bedside light and tried to calm herself by reading, but her swirling thoughts would not allow it. What did it all mean? One thing was clear—Thomas was in danger from his own people. She had to warn him. But how? They'd parted without any thought of seeing one another again. Her visit to the castle had only endangered him further, not to mention her father. Guilt and regret engulfed her.

And they were not the only ones at risk, it seemed. Whatever Kurt and his accomplice were up to at the well, their motives were sinister. Something dreadful was going on, serious enough for a U-boat commander to be expendable. She had to call the police. But she couldn't possibly take the risk of making things worse for Thomas. She had no idea what to do.

Around five o'clock she could not lie in bed a moment longer. She dressed and, in a daze, wandered to the kitchen, put some coffee on the stove and leaned her elbows on the window sill. It was almost light enough to read a newspaper outside, and the swallows were chirping full throttle. She stared through the fronds to the rock sandwich of Table Mountain, aglow from the yet-to-rise sun.

The pot began to hiss and liquid bubbled down the enamel, leaving a wake of chicory flecks. She dipped the ladle into the brew, lifted it and blew steam. The aroma of Rietvlei's kitchen filled her lungs. She closed her eyes and sipped. It was bitter coffee, but a comfort.

"I'll be damned if it isn't Princess Anna herself."

Anna swallowed, felt the liquid scald her throat. "Ag …" She took a cloth and dabbed at the coffee stain on the front of her dress. "You know me, early to bed, early to rise."

"Oh, we'll get the farm girl out of you yet."

"Sorry, I tried to be quiet." She pointed at the radio. "At least I've resisted that temptation. Until now, anyway. Won't you …"

"Woah, mercy, girl." Elizabeth wagged her finger like a windscreen wiper. "Some of us had a drink or two last night." She was in her nightdress, a smear of lipstick still visible on the side of her mouth. She dipped her pinkie in the coffee and withdrew it. "So, we missed you. What happened?"

"Oh, I just didn't feel up to it. You wouldn't believe how far I walked yesterday." She picked up the pot and poured the steaming black liquid into a mug. "Care for some?"

Elizabeth soured her face. "That witch's brew? What do you call it again?"

"*Moerkoffie.*"

She took a mug off the shelf and placed a tea strainer on it. "Before I forget, your father was looking for you yesterday." She kept her eyes on Anna.

Anna placed her mug on the table, reached for the sugar bowl. She scraped the teaspoon around, first clockwise, then the other way. "What did he want?"

"Didn't say. But he sounded agitated. Like he really wanted to speak to you."

"No message?"

"No." Elizabeth twirled a loose strand of hair at her shoulder. "Oh, hang on. The second time he said to join him at breakfast. Half past eight. You'd know the place."

Anna clenched her lips, then relaxed them. Since yesterday's lunch she had been determined never to see him again. But her heart always seemed to win. It was infuriating.

Elizabeth plucked the teabag from her mug and pointed at the pot. "I've changed my mind. Could do with a kicker to get going."

Anna hesitated. "I thought you'd want to go back to sleep." There was a pause. "It looks like you need it."

"Ooh," Elizabeth drew back. "Catty today, are we? Something happen last night?" Her eyes narrowed. "A lover's tiff?"

Anna brushed past her to switch on the wireless. It crackled as she adjusted the tuning. An advertising ditty began playing, about a new device to wash clothes.

"You saw him again, didn't you?" The corners of Elizabeth's mouth twitched a fraction.

Anna continued to fiddle with the dial until she found the BBC World Service. She stooped to listen.

"Nothing to be ashamed of, my dear." Elizabeth filled her mug. "He's gorgeous."

"Leave it."

Elizabeth laughed. "Okay. Just tell me one thing and I'll stop." She put her mug down, eyed Anna. "Did you do it?"

"What do you mean? You know I don't …"

"Heavens no, of course not. Not our Anna, waiting for Prince Charming to arrive so that they can live happily ever after. I meant, did you kiss him, silly."

Anna felt her cheeks warm.

"Oh lordy," Elizabeth said, "you don't say." She clutched her nightgown at her chest. "If you're not going to make a move, for goodness sake, give me a chance."

Just the act of talking about Thomas engulfed Anna in powerful emotions. She wanted nothing else but to hold him again, feel his chest against her, hear the calm strength in his voice. The tear forming at the corner of her eye only intensified her self-reproach. How pathetic she was, feeling sorry for herself when so many others were risking their lives. She dabbed her eye with the back of her hand.

"Lord, I'm sorry, I didn't mean to …" Elizabeth put an arm about her. "I was just teasing. You know me …"

Anna sniffed, her head cradled against her friend.

"Oh, my dear, you can talk to me anytime. Trust me, I know what it's like to have your heart broken. Men. Really."

Anna shook her head, averted her eyes, desperate to unburden herself in that moment, even if just in part. "I've made a terrible mistake," she said. "I'm a dreadful …"

"Now, now, my dear. Don't blame yourself. That's what we girls always do. It's not right."

"No. It's not that." Anna looked at her, not caring about the tears. "Elizabeth, what would you do if you thought the man you love was in great danger and you've done nothing to help him? Nothing except cut him off." She let her face fall on her friend's neck. "I told him never to contact me again. Can you believe it? And I tell myself I love him. That doesn't make sense, does it? Besides, I've never come close to truly loving a man." She turned to the window. "I felt so wonderful when I was with him. We talked and talked and never seemed to run out of things ... And when he held me ... I don't know ... Something happened."

"It's all right. It's all right." Elizabeth placed her hands on Anna's shoulders, insisting on eye contact. "Listen up, girl. You'll get over him. You've got to believe me."

Anna shook her head. "No. It's not that. He's in danger. His own people! There's no way he can ..."

"What are you talking about?" Elizabeth looked confused.

Anna looked at her feet, appalled at what she had nearly confided to her friend.

"My dear, how am I going to help you if you don't tell me anything? Don't you trust me? I was just joking earlier. I wouldn't dare try to take him from you. Wouldn't stand a chance, anyhow. I mean, look at you." She wrapped her nightgown tightly around her. "I'm not even in the same league. Really."

"Oh, you're just saying that." Anna smiled and it felt a small comfort.

Elizabeth stood staring at her, hands on her hips, fingers pressing into a fold of flesh beneath her gown. "My dear girl. I have no idea what you're talking about. But if you think people are in danger, you've got to do the right thing. You really—"

"It's not so simple. I can't explain. But it's dreadful."

Elizabeth pulled the cord about her waist. The hourglass effect was flattering. She said, "Well, I've said my say. I think—"

"Shh," Anna stooped to the wireless. A newsreader was delivering a monologue. The Japanese advancing across Singapore Island, heavy bombing, and then a despatch from the front lines. A rant along the lines of the future of the empire depended on repulsing the Japs. The imperative to fight to the end.

Anna felt a surge of guilt. She thought of the island garrison, the rubble, bodies left to decompose in Asian streets for fear of bombs. Of men suffering in the jungle, at sea, or on the frozen steppe, staring death in the face daily. And here she was vacillating, crumpling at the slightest setback. She was pitiful. She flicked the wireless off in mid-sentence.

"Excuse me," she said, straightening. "I'm going for a walk."

"As you like." Elizabeth stepped back.

Anna went to her room and put on a pair of takkies and grabbed a torch and a rain jacket.

Elizabeth looked quizzically as she passed. "What's that for?"

"Oh, you know Cape Town. You can never be sure."

Anna let herself out. The air felt fresh and clean. There was no traffic yet on Orange Street as she crossed to the gardens, where the gate was still locked. Government Avenue appeared deserted as she started under the tunnel of branches hugging the side of the path, her stomach fluttering as vivid images of the previous night returned.

The roses were still drenched in dew, and clumps of mist lingered in the clearings as she retraced the path she'd taken just hours before. She could make out the red and white brickwork of Parliament flickering through the vegetation on the other side of the Avenue. She followed the path through the jungle where banana trees and date palms leaned over the lawns, and soon the menagerie appeared, then the white-washed arch of the slave bell. The birds were not yet visible, but for a few budgies clawing at the mesh.

Her heart skipped a beat as the well came into view. Whatever Kurt and his accomplice were hiding underground, she was going to try to find out. She'd read that the early Dutch settlers had built a whole network of canals to bring water from the mountain to the Company's Garden and the castle, turning Cape Town into "a little Amsterdam" before the British took over and covered them all over. Who knows what might be down there now?

The area was deserted, Anna looked around anxiously, feeling exposed in the clearing. If she got caught … she'd heard what the Germans did to their enemies. She leaned over the lip, shivering at the cold of the stone against her dress.

The ladder was gone! She cast around. Nothing. What to do? Leaning over again, she peered into the gloom, and turned on the torch. The grating was back in place but covered in fallen leaves. She looked at her watch. Quarter past six. Assuming it would take an hour and a half to go back, change and return for breakfast by half past eight, she had less than an hour to spare. It was risky but there was no shrinking now. She tucked the torch under her chin and worked herself over the ledge.

Standing on the grating below, Anna could just see above the rim of the well. No one was about. She crouched in the half-dark, gagging at the stench and widened her stance. Reaching down between her feet, she brushed aside the leaves and grasped the grating with both hands. The metal was cold and moist. She tugged. No movement. She shifted her grip. Another tug. Nothing. At her fourth yank there was a grate of iron on iron and it shifted aside. She shone the torch into the hole. Water pooled into the well from the side closest to the mountain, clear and fast flowing.

She tucked her skirt into her underwear and slithered down into the hole, bracing her shoes on the sides of the well to help support her weight, while clinging to the edge of the grating.

Then voices from above! They had to be close if she could hear them above the swirling water. She guessed they were approaching from the same direction she had. She ducked her head, switched off the torch and lowered the grating over her. She waited apprehensively, poised, barely daring to breathe.

"Where's the bloody ladder now?"

It was the giant from the night before. Water was dribbling onto her left shoe, and she felt a creeping chill.

"You should not be asking this question. The instructions were clear."

"Ja, but nobody was going to find it last night. Only two hobos sleep in the garden, up at the top. We checked. And they're always drunk. I told you before, *doos.*"

Anna stared up at the circle of sky and leaves above, terrified at the thought of descending into the claustrophobic cesspit below.

"*Wat die donder ...*" The voice sounded directly overhead.

She shrank further down into the tunnel, feet splayed, using the ridges between stones as footholds. The stream gurgled below her in the dark.

"Only the gardeners could have been here last night. They've probably stacked it somewhere. I'll—"

"Shut up." The German's voice rang around the well. "And look down there."

Anna's thighs were quivering.

"Some newspaper. So what?"

"Look more carefully."

"All right. You tell me, clever bastard."

"The grating, you idiot."

"What about it?"

"No leaves on it. This is not possible."

"Ag, I haven't got time for this *kak*. See the water coming out the pipe there? It washes things away."

"I talk about what is above the grate, stupid. Last night I covered it for camouflage. Now there is nothing."

"You people are a pain in the arse! You imagine things. Let's go. I need breakfast."

"*Überhaupt keine Chance*. These are my orders."

"You can stick your orders up your German arse."

"Also, it is not necessary to insult my people like this. We are helping you, no?"

The giant spat into the stream just inches from Anna's nose. "Then I'd better keep my mouth shut."

"*Nun gut*. You stay here at this well. If there is someone down there, they will have to come out. Then you will know what to do, *oder nicht*?"

Anna gingerly lowered herself, one foot, one hand at a time.

"And you? Where are you buggering off to while I sit here like a *mampara*?"

"I will go to the other entrance. Do not move until I return. This is an order."

There were other voices now, getting louder. Kurt exchanged pleasantries with someone and then silence.

Anna's feet had reached the bottom and were now submerged in the flow of water. She was finding it hard to think clearly. Returning up the well now would be suicide.

She stared into the darkness. There must be more than one underground river down here, perhaps a series of tunnels. If there was another entrance, maybe there were more. But how to find her way in the wet and dark? What if she got lost? Or stuck. Fighting a surge of panic, she slumped to the floor, heedless of the chilly water.

Come on, she urged herself, remembering why she was there. A huge man had made his way through the tunnel dragging a crate, for goodness sake. How hard could it be?

Still with the torch off, she shuffled a few feet downstream in a crouch. A cobweb brushed her face and she paused to pick it off with her fingers. Desperate to straighten, she ran her palm along the slime of the arch. There was no let up. She switched on the torch and panned the brick of the tunnel. A cockroach scurried over the funnel of light, sweeping circles with its antennae. Anna shifted her focus to the floor. The water was clear and looked about eight inches deep. She stepped forward following the stream.

Straightening her shoulders, she began to establish a rhythm of sloshing and squatting. Soon the light from the well had faded and her only guides were the crescents of torchlight wiper-blading ahead. How much further before she reached a storm-water drain? And what if there weren't any? From what she'd read of the *grachts*, this tunnel would once have been the Heerengracht, Adderley Street's earlier name. Like the others, it must eventually drain into the harbour. But with the reclamation of the foreshore underway, there was no guessing how far that would be. She felt a wave of nausea. Could she last that long?

Just then the brick on the right side of the tunnel melted to black and she paused. The air about her was warmer now and close. Even in the damp of the tunnel, she was sweating. She glanced back down the tunnel. From the gradual curve and the light of the well in the distance, she guessed she was somewhere below the Wale Street entrance to the Company's Garden, with the nearest drain at the top of Adderley Street at least a hundred yards ahead.

The torch probed the void. It was a side tunnel, this one rectangular and dry, no doubt crossing beneath Government

Avenue within a sling's shot. Another opportunity for escape, perhaps? She thought back to her school outings to De Mond's caves, the warnings about taking a tributary underground. She looked back and forth. Where to for guidance? It was hard to imagine a higher power in such a godforsaken place.

Hedging her bets, she picked a stone from the stream and scratched an arrow on the wall. Then she stepped into the void of the side tunnel. Relief. It was high enough for her to straighten. She waited for the water to drain from her shoes and then started walking. After twenty paces there was a trickle of light from above. A shaft topped by a grating. The shadow of a pedestrian passed, then another. She groped about for something to stand on. But there was nothing except water and silt.

Then she crouched to inspect something on the floor—a series of striations that looked recently made. She followed the dashes that disappeared beyond the range of torchlight. After thirty-two steps she intersected another tunnel. The marks continued across it. There was a strangely sweet smell in the tunnel now, which grew stronger with every step. It reminded her of something, but she struggled to name it. Another twenty steps since the cross tunnel. Or was it thirty? The buildings of Parliament must be overhead now. What chance was there of an exit?

Ahead in the shadows she heard a rustle. She killed the light. At first the dark made it impossible to see her hand. Then more rustling, closer and on the floor. She flicked the torch on again and stabbed it towards each sound, first right then left. There was a rectangular opening in the wall, but no telling, at first, how deep it was. She took a step forwad, then another.

A squeal at her feet startled her, and the torch fell with a crack, its light fading away. She stooped, fumbling. The floor was smooth, almost oily. She found the torch flush with the wall, grasping it with a shaking hand. There was no response to the switch. She banged it from behind with her palm and tried again. It came to life, illuminating a pair of eyes, bulging and insolent. The rat stared back, poised on its haunches.

Anna stamped. It held its ground, whiskers quivering. She stepped closer, stamped again. The rat slunk into the shadows.

The opening formed a room as wide and long as Rietvlei's storeroom, but with a lower ceiling. The air was dank but cooler than in the tunnel, the sickly odour stronger, like overripe bananas. There'd been a whiff of it last night in the gardens, but she'd assumed it was from the wild banana trees.

Anna ran the light along the apex of the ceiling's arch. At the far end were squiggles of graffiti. Going closer, she could decipher "Johannes. Dirk. 1801". Prisoners? Then she saw stairs leading to the rectangular outline of a trapdoor set in a flat section of the ceiling. She ran her palms across the underside of wood and iron ribbing.

A shuffling sound. From where? She cast around frantically. Had someone followed her? Should she try for the trapdoor?

A muffled echo. Then it became a voice.

Her fingers located a padlock. She pried at it without success, closing her eyes as flakes of rust threatened to blind her. She placed both palms on the underside of the trapdoor and shoved. It lifted a fraction. Peering through the crack she could see what looked like filing cabinets. The archives of the Parliament Library? Maybe even the basement of the General Assembly? She positioned her shoulder blades against the wood and tried to straighten. The door lifted a fraction further but jolted at the padlock. After three attempts she wiped her face. There was no escape.

The voices were louder now, but unidentifiable. Could it be the German? "I will go to the other entrance," he'd said earlier. If not him, who would be traipsing about under the city? The room felt smaller with every passing second.

"That's a hundred and twenty."

Anna stopped breathing. Fanus! Impossible. She flashed the light around in desperation. It picked out a step in the far wall, waist-high and running end-to-end. She tiptoed over and felt the top surface. It was a tarpaulin.

"A moment please ..."

Anna exhaled through her teeth. The German had found her.

"According to my calculations it is one hundred and

twenty-seven." The voices were near the entrance. There was a clunk on the stone, and the distant trickle of a stream.

"Ag, you bureaucrat. It's a hundred and twenty. I can't help it you have such short legs."

"Our orders are to be precise. It will not help to insult me."

"*Hoor hier.* Stick to what you do best—like covering your arse. I'll deal with the fireworks."

Anna felt the weight of the city pressing down on her, the room shrinking. She lifted the edge of the tarpaulin, squeezed underneath and lay lengthways, her back against a row of crates. The air was warm and the smell of bananas strong now, tinged with oil.

"Here," Fanus said. "Hold this."

From the footsteps Anna was sure he was in the room, approaching. The tarpaulin flattened her nose and drooped over her mouth. The stale, oily air made her want to vomit.

"And pass me the end … No, other one."

"This is enough." There was a click of a heel on stone. "You will speak to me with respect."

Anna felt an itch in her nose and fought to suppress it.

"Respect is earned. Like trust."

"You forget we are not obliged to help your organisation. This place is no longer so important to Germany."

"Nonsense. Just ask the British why they sent almost their whole army here for the *Vryheidsoorlog*. And the Dutch before them. *Jissis*, even the Portuguese …"

Dust was gathering at the back of Anna's throat. The oxygen under the tarpaulin was depleting.

"You forget one thing, *oder*."

"And what's that, smart arse?"

"Japan is with us now. The Cape is no longer so important for Germany."

"Really? I'd have thought the opposite. Getting cosy with the Japs means more trade, not less. And with Rommel stuck up north, the Suez won't open for you any time soon."

"I did not say the Cape was unimportant. But it will no longer be Germany's responsibility alone."

Anna could hear Fanus breathing. It always got heavy when he was angry. "Are you telling me you're going to throw us to the yellow dogs?" He was almost shouting. "Why the hell are you here, then?"

"Germany is loyal to her friends."

"*Ge*. Tell that to Stalin."

"That was different. It was—"

Anna choked back a sneeze.

"Hey." Fanus' voice was close and clear. His breathing was louder. Then a scuffing of a shoe sole on the tarpaulin. "What was that?"

The only sound for several seconds was a sloshing far off. Then scratching on stone and another pause.

"So," the German said at length. "You scare for a mouse."

"*Luister hier*." Fanus's voice reverberated. Then there was a scuffle, more breathing. "You calling me a coward?"

"Put me down immediately."

"And if I don't?"

"I report you to your high command."

"That's funny," Fanus said, "considering I am the high command."

The German cleared his throat. "Perhaps. But if I put in a bad report when this operation is finished, it will be different. You are aware of this, I know. Now let me go." There were shoes on stone. Then a padding on cloth. "That is better. Now. Continue."

For a moment there was only Fanus's breathing. Then the whine of a reel and a rustle approaching along the floor. It was quiet again, then another scuff.

"Right, we're done here. Let's go."

"*Ein moment*. We must connect this?"

"Listen, I'm the expert. In fact, you'd better show me a bit of respect: I'm all you've got."

"Incorrect. We have Thomas."

"Really? I heard he got lost."

Anna was desperate to shift. She'd been still so long she couldn't feel her extremeties. She worried that the thumping of her heart was audible.

"Who gave you that information?"

Silence. Anna noticed the sound of dripping for the first time.

"That's my business. Where do you think he's got to, anyway?"

"He is making repairs for the U-boat."

"*Jinne*, I thought you people were so good at organising things. You telling me you don't even know which machine shop he went to?"

Anna felt a tinge of excitement, closed her eyes and strained to listen.

"Of course. Paschen Engineering."

"So you know? Why don't you check with them?"

"I am not stupid." Kurt sniffled. "He has not been there yet. Paschen will tell him to telephone us when he arrives."

"And you still trust him? Thomas?"

"Ja, *sicher*. He is one of our most decorated U-boat commanders. You must not be concerned." Kurt cleared his throat. "We will find him, we—"

"Suppose you don't?"

There was a pause.

Anna stopped breathing. Her shoulders were in knots.

"That is not your business."

"*Ge*. I say we do something about him now."

"*Nein*. This assignment is bigger than one person." His shoe scraped the ground and clicked closer. "In any case, your people will win the vote tomorrow. *Nicht so*?"

"Fat chance. Malan's a dreamer."

"That is not what the girl's father said."

"You mean van der Vliet? Don't believe him. You know he was married to an English woman, hey? Fence sitter."

"This is strange? He gives his farm—?"

"Ja, ja. I'm not saying his heart isn't in the right place. It's just his methods. He thinks this … this Parliament is the answer for everything." There was a little thud of spittle against the tarpaulin.

"Come. We're wasting time."

Anna waited as the footsteps were swallowed by the echoes in the tunnel. Then she rolled out from under the tarpaulin and stood, sucking air. After lifting the canvas, she switched on the torch. There were two rows of crates, stacked three high. She felt the nearest latch. There was no lock, so she lifted it.

The banana smell that hit her was pungent. Then she remembered where she'd smelled it before. When Papa and Kleinjan were blasting a road through the kloof. With Fanus directing.

She trained the torch light to its source. Inside, the box was stacked with oversized cigars. She ran her hand over the top row. It felt oily and soft. Her heart was throbbing at her neck. Dynamite.

Reeling in horror, her only thought now was to get back out. As she headed for the exit her foot caught on a piece of string and sent her sprawling. She scrambled to her feet. Now she was in the passage, turning left for no clear reason, right then left again. Thinking only that she couldn't return the way she had come, she chose left. She ran blindly down the passage, away, as fast as possible. At last, out of breath, she slowed. There was a half-moon of light ahead. Craning her neck, she could make out a manhole, way above at the end of a shaft. And a ladder, out of reach. Then the manhole cover was shifting. There was a grating on iron. Then a call.

She ran, not thinking about direction. Suddenly she stumbled and the torch flew from her hand. Then she was sinking. The tunnel floor had given way to a pool. She flailed on the surface until her feet settled on a bed of pebbles. Gasping, she waited for her eyes to adjust to the dark.

She heaved herself out of the depression and onto her haunches. Her dress was soaked and clung to her, but she felt warm. She tested the water in the pool. It was sweet and cool. Lowering her face to the surface, she drank with abandon.

The incessant gurgling of the stream was oppressive now, her thoughts only of escape. Downstream or back? There seemed to be no right or wrong in this dungeon, just endless gloom, so she waded on.

At length the tunnel grew wider and she could stand up. The air was fresher now, flowing onto her face from downstream. Then, as she rounded a gradual bend, she felt a waft of air on her neck. She looked up and ahead. There was a riser in the tunnel ceiling, and the light from it was diffused. At chest height she noticed the first rung of a ladder. Not daring to hope, she climbed. The ladder ended at a shelf. Beyond was a vertical manhole cover. She put her backside against it, wedged her feet behind the ladder and heaved.

The cover fell outwards with a clang, and air and light flooded suddenly into the tunnel. She wiggled through the opening on her hands and knees and found herself on a patch of grass and weeds. The sun was directly ahead, well proud of the skyline, and though blinding, a blessed relief. She stood, staring at the railway line, beyond it the rubble of the foreshore. Before her was Strand Street. A few cars were criss-crossing but the nearest pedestrians were a hundred feet away. She closed the manhole and stepped away.

The relief of her escape was eclipsed by the sheer horror of what she had discovered in the tunnels. She had expected weapons, yes. But dynamite? Crates and crates of it, packed together below … the Houses of Parliament? She reeled from the enormity of it. The lives of countless of her country's leaders were at stake, even the country itself. She had to do something to prevent it, and fast. But what? She sensed the wall of the castle towering behind her and shivered. Surely, this time, she had no choice but to follow through and tell the authorities.

25

STARING UP AT THE ramparts of the castle from up close, they seemed higher and more solid to Anna. The Union Jack above was a sliver in the calm. She pressed herself against the stones which were already lit by the morning sun, soaking up what scant warmth they offered. She looked down at her dress, soggy and splotched, clinging to her legs and brushed it with her hands, glad for its busy floral pattern that helped to camouflage the damp and the marks. She'd barely begun to think through the implications of what she was about to do and her resolve was wavering. If she told the authorities anything specific, like the provisioning of the U-boats, her father faced certain imprisonment, if not hanging. Also, Thomas, would no doubt be branded an enemy spy and killed. Even though—if the conversation she'd overheard in the tunnels was to be believed—he wasn't involved in the plot. She shivered. The thought of losing the two men she loved most in the world was unimaginable.

Anna glanced at the sun. Papa would be waiting at the restaurant by now. A grumpy, tortured soul, to be sure and sometimes cruel—but her flesh and blood. Besides, for all his faults, he was worldly-wise. Surely, she could trust him enough to confide all? She felt terrible about the dilemma it was bound to cause him—deciding between the interest of the country and that of family and his foster sister. But he'd know what to do. Besides, what choice did she have?

Resolved, she set out towards Church Square. Outside the Sailor's Eye restaurant, its signage obscured by the wrought iron curlicues of an external balcony, she paused to smooth her dress.

It was still damp. Glancing about, relieved there was no one around, she considered how best to approach her father. She would hear him out first, she decided. When he was placated, he would be more open to what she had to say.

Inside, the dark wooden-panelling oozed masculinity. Her father sat in a booth, staring out of the window, a cigarette and coffee in his left hand and a pen in the other. He saw her reflection and turned, his eyes widening, then glaring at her over his reading glasses. He placed his pen across a sheaf of papers.

"What the hell happened to you?"

She tousled her hair. "Just showered, that's all."

"And the mud? You look like you've been playing with the boys again."

"Ag …" she laughed to disguise her anger, then clutched her knee, "just a bit of *eina*. They're digging that ditch along the avenue. I slipped in the dew."

"Please." He pointed at the seat opposite, picked up his pen and flattened the bottom of his page. "I just have to sign this motion."

"Attending to matters of national importance at breakfast?" She forced a smile. "Do you never rest?"

"Sorry." He put the pen down, shoved the papers to one side. "Always so much to do. And never enough time. Don't you feel like that sometimes?"

"Not really."

"Listen, Engel. I was meaning to apologise for yesterday. You know, Margriet and me. Maybe I shouldn't have invited her along. It must be difficult for you. It's all … so new."

Anna stood. She wasn't ready for this conversation now.

"Go on, sit," he said, pointing at the seat again. "You're making me nervous."

Anna sat down again. "So," she tried to sound airy, "what's going down in the halls of power today?"

"Quiet day, thank the Lord. Just some debates on terms of trade, that sort of thing."

She pointed at the document. "So why the haste."

"I like to be prepared." His dimples deepened in lieu of a smile. "Tomorrow's a big day."

"Oh, why so?"

He leaned forward, his voice husky. "This is strictly confidential. Right?"

Anna tensed. She had come planning to confide in him not the other way around. But why not hear him out first? She picked up a menu. "I may disagree with your views, but I'm no *skinderbek*."

"I know, I know." He waved at a waiter. "Come, let's order first."

The waiter smiled a fraction longer than was necessary. Anna looked away, then pointed at the scrambled-egg-on-toast-and-coffee special on the menu. Her father asked for three poached eggs on white toast, and sausage. His usual.

When the waiter was out of earshot he said, "You know the detention-without-trial provisions?"

"I've read some stuff in the papers."

"The government has been using them to round up our leaders. Two more just yesterday. Taken from their homes in the middle of the night and sent to Koffiefontein. It's terrible."

"Perhaps they deserved it," she said.

He leaned back in his chair, took a deep breath.

Anna wondered if he knew he was in danger of being arrested himself. Surely, now was the time to tell him …

"Don't start this nonsense again, please."

Anna glared, completely forgetting her resolve. "I'm allowed to have an opinion. Different from yours, that is."

He took his glasses off. "Come on, Anna, let's not fight again."

She watched a man totter past outside in a black coat and bowler hat, umbrella under his arm. He could have been in London. A sea mist had settled in the square and only those passing right against the window were visible. "That would be nice."

He sighed. "It's not like I don't try, you know. But whatever I say, you take it the wrong way. It's like walking on eggshells."

"Well …" She looked away. "It would help if you accepted that I'm my own person. Just because I grew up under the same roof doesn't make me a carbon copy of you."

He twirled his pen and they both stared out at the mist. After a minute he said. "Anyway, as I was going to say, Smuts will defend his proposed amendments tomorrow afternoon. History is going to be made. You must come along."

"Urr ..." She fished for an excuse. "I'm not sure. Elizabeth—"

He threw his head back. "There you go again. Elizabeth will be there, all right. Her father will make sure she is."

Anna was relieved to see the waiter approaching. He was of the generation that still regarded his job as a profession. He bowed their plates on to their placemats and melted away. She watched her father pour a pond of tomato sauce onto his side plate, then tip the salt cellar over his egg. Nothing. He cursed under his breath and tapped it on the table. "*Jong*," he said, "I don't know why I still come to this place. Nothing works." He knocked the cellar's base with the flat of his hand and there was a sprinkling of salt.

"Why's the amendment so important?" she said, reaching for the pepper shaker. "I know these special powers for the police have a bitter taste for you, but it's been a while now."

"Ja, you're right." He sawed off a piece of sausage and shovelled it into his mouth.

"So what is it then?"

He chewed several times, swallowed and wiped his lips with his serviette. Satisfied that no one was listening he said, "This is confidential, *hoor*."

"You've said that already."

He leaned forward. "This time we're going to abstain."

"But why? That would hand it to them on a platter. That's not your style."

A smile teased the corner of his mouth. "Then we're going to table a motion of no confidence in Smuts."

Anna swallowed a bite of egg. It was greasy and the yoke broke before it reached her mouth. She missed Hannah's cooking. "How does that work?"

"It says we don't believe he's fit to govern."

She blew steam off her coffee and brought it to her lips. "But doesn't the government still have the votes? What's the point?"

He was unable to contain his smile. "Not everyone in the United Party caucus supports the bearded devil." He took a chunk of bread in his fingers and used it to clean the yolk from his plate. "The rest is a long story."

She leaned back. The coffee and a full stomach was comforting. "I've got time."

He glanced at his fob watch. "I wish I could say the same." He slurped at his coffee. "Anyway, mark my words, it's going to be historic. Remember, the Assembly will be packed. And the media ..."

Anna felt her appetite drain. *All of this should not be necessary if they vote correctly tomorrow.* She placed her knife and fork on her plate, tried not to let him see that she was shaking. "And if you lose the vote?"

He dabbed yolk from the sides of his mouth and tacked the serviette back into his shirt. "It's all right. It will still be a propaganda coup."

"Then why don't you look happier?"

He closed his eyes. When he opened them his expression made him look older by a decade. "Our own people ... Just when we need to be united. Would you believe it?"

She placed a hand on his. "What is it? Are they still planning to walk out? Even with this motion?"

He nodded. "It's worse. They're threatening to boycott the whole session."

Anna swallowed. An idea was forming. If her father didn't attend Parliament tomorrow, he would be safe. Then, perhaps with Thomas' help, she could figure a way of preventing the crisis without having to confide in him. That way, he'd be spared the dilemna of having to choose between his own life and the good of the country.

"Shocking, isn't it?" he said.

"Yes. But maybe you need to reconsider things. Why not join them? You've already got a reputation as a hardliner. People would expect it."

"Yes, but how could I just change my path like that? What about Daniel. *Jislaaik*, it's hard."

"So what will you do?"

"Well ..." He took a bite of toast, chewed. "I'm in two minds."

"Ha." She leaned back. "That will be a windless summer at Rietvlei. My father is undecided."

He eyed her. "What do you think I should do?"

She had to go easy, try to lead him to make the decision himself. "I don't know. You must do what your political conscience tells you. For better or worse. Isn't that what you've always told me?"

He scanned the restaurant again. Only one other booth was occupied, three away from theirs, by two serious balding businessmen who had just finished their breakfast. "Ja *nee*. It's not that simple."

Anna felt desperate. Perhaps it was time to finally lay down her cards. Or was there another way?

She leaned forward. "Don't go to tomorrow's session," she said. "Promise me you won't."

He stared at her, eyebrows raised in a question. "Why on earth not? It's my job."

Anna glanced around for inspiration. "I can't explain," she said at last. "Not now, at least. Just do this one thing, Papa." She slowly closed and opened her eyes. "Promise you'll stay away. For my sake. Please."

Though still taller than her, even seated, her father seemed to have shrunk. "I don't understand." His expression was sad and lonely. "But for your sake," he sighed, "I'll think about it."

She felt close to tears with relief.

He downed the remainder of his coffee, plonked the cup on the table. "Ag, no man. I can't let Daniel down like that. Shame."

She felt a resurgence of alarm but masked it with irritation. "He doesn't look like someone you need to feel sorry for."

"*Reg so*. But I wonder how he handles all the infighting. Not to mention his battle with the establishment. I wouldn't want his job in a hundred years."

"You expect me to believe that? Come on, I know how ambitious you are."

"You may not believe this, but I know my limitations."

"That's funny."

"Listen," he placed his hand on hers, "there's no way. Think about it. I'd have to move to Pretoria for half the year." He looked her in the eye. "No way in hell I'm leaving you like that. Or the farm."

She wanted to withdraw her hand but it wouldn't obey her. "Since when did family considerations stop you getting what you want? Anyway, I'm in Cape Town now. I've got friends, a place to stay."

"I know, I know. It's not just that." He glanced out at the fog, then snapped back, looking right through her now, lost in a parallel world.

"You mean Margriet. You've fallen for her."

He laughed, reddening about his neck. "She's all right. Good for a laugh. But she's not a shadow of … you know."

In the background a tune crackled to life on the gramophone, a recording of Vera Lynn. *I may be right*, she warbled against the saxophonist, *I may be wrong; but I'm perfectly willing to swear …* Anna didn't trust herself to speak without crying, so she listened … *that when you turned and smiled at me, a nightingale sang in Berkeley Square.*

"Sorry, Engel. I didn't mean … We'll always have each other." He straightened his knife and fork on his plate and glanced about for the waiter. "As far as I'm concerned, anyway."

"What's that supposed to mean?"

"Just … I see the way men look at you these days. And you at them."

She laughed. "Come on. That's normal."

His face grew serious, leaned forward. "Tell me you haven't been seeing him again?"

Anna felt her cheeks warm. A cocktail of caution and sorrow. She didn't trust herself to respond.

"Ah, I knew it."

Anna withdrew her hand, looked down to fold her serviette.

"I warned you," he pressed. "He's trouble."

As Anna glared at him she experienced a moment of clarity that both shocked and thrilled her. Her father, love him as she did, was no longer the most important man in her life. "I don't have to sit here and be cross-examined like this."

"Wait." He pointed at the chair. "Don't you run off like that again. It's rude."

"Call it what you like. I won't stand for it any longer. I'm a grown woman now. When are you going to accept that?"

He ripped his serviette from his shirt and threw it on the table. "*Luister hier.*" At the far wall, the waiter straightened. "Don't try me, my girl. You see that man again and there'll be consequences."

"Consequences? You might have scared me with that when we were on the farm. Now … I just don't care."

"Right." He stood, his head just shy of the ceiling fan. "That's enough …" He glared at the waiter, who had bent to adjust a place setting. "You so much as talk to that man again without telling me and your days at Michaelis are finished."

"How dare you? I've already registered. I'm—"

"That's meaningless. I could make irrelevant any so-called agreement you may have entered into."

"No you can't."

"You're not twenty-one, Anna. You have no rights. Believe me. If there's one thing I know more about than you, it's the law."

A pensioner shuffled to the closest booth, took a seat and buried his face in the menu. Something inside Anna had snapped. "Do as you please," she said. "And for your information, I had no intention of seeing that German again."

He looked chastened, regretful. Then his eyes narrowed again. "Had?"

"Yes." She wanted him to remember her stare. "And now the same applies to you."

"Ag, Engel …"

"Stop '*agging*' me. I'm done with your patronising. No, you're worse. You're a bully. You bully the farmworkers. Your staff. I don't even want to think what you did to Mama. Now me."

Though she'd come with the intention of confiding all, Anna just wanted to get away from him and stay away. He was a twisted man. Prejudiced in the extreme. Women; coloured people; Jews; no one was good enough for him; no one worthy of his respect. It was time to make her own way in the world. Fight her own battles. Or, at least find another ally. She turned, composed herself, and strode out.

26

THE SEA MIST WAS surprisingly cold for summer and droplets tickled Anna's face as she marched across the guano-stained paving in the direction of the mountain. She was shaking with anger, their slanging match reverberating through her. Yet the image burnt into her mind as she stared at him had left her hollow. Her once all-powerful Papa had appeared stooped and shrunken, radiating defeat. As determined as she was to escape his domination, she hadn't expected such a sudden reversal of roles. For the first time in her life, she felt a responsibility to protect him. But that didn't mean she had to see him again. Or listen to his nonsense. In fact, she'd do the exact opposite. She'd contact Thomas. He was a military man: he'd know about explosives and how to disarm them. Besides, she desperately wanted to see him, even if just one last time.

Halfway across the square, a pair of pigeons flapped from the ground in front of her and settled on Onze Jan's head. She stopped, breath billowing, and looked up. The statesman's brow was wide and furrowed; it was hard to imagine so severe a man being adored by a nation. A car appeared from the grey and passed. It stayed ahead of Anna as she passed the Old Slave Lodge and the Groote Kerk towards the city but then disappeared ahead of her. At Adderley Street the mist had thinned and splotches of blue were showing above the buildings. A breeze had sprung from nowhere and the red, white and blue of the Union Jack was tugging at the flagpole above the Supreme Court. With relief she spotted the proud red phone booth on the opposite street corner, exactly where she'd remembered it.

It was even colder inside and cramped. She opened the dirty phone book dangling from a chain bolted through its spine and thumbed to the business pages. Paschen Engineering was listed in bold with two numbers. The tickey rattled on metal as she fumbled for the slot. Then she braced her back against the glass and dialled.

"Hallo," a male voice, thickly accented, answered after several rings.

Anna tried to speak but couldn't.

"Yes. Who is this?"

"Sir. Good morning. I was hoping you—"

"Wait a minute, Miss?"

"Van der Vliet." There was a crackle on the end of the line.

"I see. And what can I do for you?"

"A customer of yours: Thomas von Eisenheim. I was wondering if you know where I can find him. He's a friend of mine."

The man rasped a cough. "Thomas, you say? I am sorry, you must understand, we have hundreds of customers, I—"

"He's German."

"Miss van der Vliet … The name of our firm is Paschen, ja? Most of my customers are of German origin."

"He was at your factory yesterday. For engine repairs."

"Ah, I was not in the works yesterday. You are not to worry. I will speak with the foreman. Your number, Miss van der Vliet?"

"Sir." Anna sensed the conversation was running away from her. "Please. He's of medium build; light brown hair, blue eyes that are hard to forget."

There was the sound of shifting furniture in the background. A pause.

"Mister Paschen? Are you still there?"

"Ja, ja. Sorry, I am not able to help. Goodbye, Miss—"

"No, wait." The time for timidity was over. "Listen, please. He's in danger."

The line went quiet. When Paschen's voice returned it had lowered an octave.

"I will see what can be done. Is there a message you wish to leave?"

Anna drew in air. The future would hang on her next sentence. "Yes …" She stalled to choose her words. "Tell him … things are not as they seem."

There was a click, then a dullness on the line that was more than silence. Then Paschen was back. "One moment."

The air in the booth had warmed to stale and the window was misted. Anna could just see the outline of a man standing at the edge of the opposite pavement. He had an overcoat with a newspaper tucked under his arm. Something about him was familiar.

"Anna?" Hearing Thomas's voice, she began hyperventilating, leaning back against the booth to stop from falling.

"Anna, is that you?"

She opened the door a crack. The air that flooded in was cold and welcome. The man was in focus now, side on. There was something stolid in his posture, something vaguely familiar. Not taking her eyes off him she pressed the handset to her ear and spoke. "Thomas. I knew you would be there. I just knew. I—"

"Shh. Slow down. How did you know to contact me here?"

"Oh, my darling, I …" The line beeped and paused and beeped again. Anna scratched in her purse. There was only one coin left and she pushed it into the slot. "My darling, there's so much to say but we're about to be cut off. I need to speak in person. Today."

"I understood we were never to see each other again."

"I can't explain now. Everything's changed. Please."

"All right. I'll come. Where are you?"

Anna looked outside. A double-decker bus rumbled past and then the stranger was there again, his form still partially obscured by the misting. She swallowed. "Corner of Wale. Outside the bank."

"Good. Stay where you are. Give me twenty minutes."

Anna rubbed the window. The stranger was facing her now. There was a tingle in her spine. "No. Wait. Not here. Oh, Thomas, they're here, they're—"

"One moment. What is the matter? Who is there?"

There was a beep down the receiver.

"There's no time to explain. Just tell me where I can meet

you." There was another beep. She wanted to shout.

"All right. I tell you what. If you like, you can come with me …" The beeping was more insistent. Another click. Then his voice again, softer. "Are you wearing closed shoes today?"

She looked down at her damp, soiled takkies. "Yes, why?"

"Good. Meet me at the lower cable station. I will—"

"Cable station? There's no time, Thomas, in twenty-four hours …"

"I will explain. It will make sense. I …" The beeping changed to a drone. Anna replaced the receiver. It felt like the booth was moving, or was it the buildings outside? The man was still standing there. She picked up her bag. Her only hope, slim as it was, was surprise. Before fear got the better of her, she forced the door open.

"Inspector de Villiers." She'd only recognised him when she was almost upon him. "To what do I owe the pleasure?"

The newspaper dislodged from his armpit and he stooped to regather it. When he looked up his face was reddened and more lined than she'd remembered, his sideburns litmus ends of silver. "*Jissis*," he blurted. "If it isn't Miss van der Vliet."

"Oh please. Don't pretend this was an accident, Inspector. I may look young but I'm not stupid."

"I didn't think you were," he ironed her with his eyes, "stupid, that is."

Anna resisted the temptation to look down, conscious of the splotches on her dress. "Why have you been following me?"

He twitched his moustache like a mouse its whiskers and glanced back in the direction of Church Square. "Who says it's you I'm interested in?"

"I hope that's not a play on words, Inspector."

His ears reddened. "Tell me something," he said. "You're close to your father, aren't you?"

Anna tensed, bracing her mind with the acrimony of their parting. "Where is this leading?"

De Villiers knitted his brow. "He's in a lot of trouble." He stroked the hair at his Adam's apple. "But I think you know that already."

Anna considered him. Another man who couldn't be trusted. "I had breakfast with him ten minutes ago. But I guess you know that already. He seemed fit and strong as a horse to me."

"Ma'am, do you know what the punishment is for treason?"

She forced her face to stay deadpan to mask her panic.

He fished in his trouser pocket. "Let me remind you. It's death, death by hanging. Not a nice way to go. Trust me, I've seen it myself."

"It's never happened in South Africa. A civilian, for treason. I've grown up in a political home, you know."

"But we've never had a situation like this. And there's a war on. Our Prime Minister answers to a higher power."

"He always has."

"Miss van der Vliet. I can see I'm going to have to spell this out. Again." He twisted his mouth and sniffled. "Your father has been instrumental in supplying enemy ships. For three months now at least. Our navy boys always wondered how that raider last year could bugger around in our waters for so long, sinking so many Allied ships."

She searched him with her eyes. "If you have any evidence, why plead with his daughter for help?"

A bus hissed to a stop beyond the next robot, and De Villiers watched a woman in heels with a handbag step out. Ignoring his ogling, she walked towards the bank and into the revolving door. "Because we'd prefer it if this problem went away quietly."

"Excuse me?"

"Let me just say, we don't want this to come out wrong in the news. Someone with your father's credentials would be a martyr. A cause to rally the … conservative elements of the *volk*."

"But?"

"Ja *nee*. You're right. There's always a catch." He cleared his throat. "My bosses need a good story. Something to counter the criticism their political enemies—the lefties—will throw at them."

Anna waited.

"There's nothing like a patriot to stir the emotions of the masses," he continued. "Especially if it's a woman. A daughter choosing her country above her blood."

"Mister de Villiers." She straightened. "If you think I'm going to …" She clutched her bag under her arm. "You're wasting my time." She glanced across the street at the clock on the court building. "Now, if you'll excuse me ..."

He extended his arm. "Meeting someone?" When he'd stopped her he took a handkerchief and dabbed his nose.

"What if I am?"

"Well, that depends who it is."

"Mister de Villiers ..."

"Inspector."

"As far as I understand, we still live in a free society. Who I socialise with is my concern."

He stuffed the handkerchief in his pants pocket and eyed her. "Not if that person is a foreign national from an enemy state. And is wanted for questioning."

Anna's stomach muscles tensed, causing her shoulders to hunch. She drew herself upright. "I'm confused. You said it's my father you're worried about. Now you're accusing me of, of what?"

He shook his head several times. When he looked up she saw the steeliness that doubtless made him good at his job.

"Miss van der Vliet." He scratched behind his ear and flakes of dandruff sprinkled on his shoulder. "We have reason to believe you have been consorting with Commander von Eisenheim. *Kriegsmarine.*"

Anna felt her cheeks burning.

"Everything all right, ma'am? Yes? Good. Now, tell me if I'm on the right path with his. And remember, lying to a commissioned officer of the South African Police is a criminal offence."

Anna looked up. The mist had cleared enough to make out the mountain beyond the tree tops opposite. The cable was visible but no car going up or down. What if she were late and Thomas gave up on her? There was only one place she wanted to be now and that was in his arms. But she mustn't look desperate to leave. She said. "Listen to all the juicy hearsay you like, but I'm not biting."

He stared at her. "He's not telling you everything, you know."

"What do you mean?"

"Von Eisenheim. You think he's a good German, don't you? Not one of Hitler's lot. I'll bet he's even given you the story of being in the *Widerstand*. Makes for good drama, I admit."

Anna felt like she was falling backwards in slow motion, with nothing and no one to catch her.

"Part of me understands why you'd fall for him. Your lover boy's a charmer, if nothing else."

"Lover? He's nothing of the sort."

"So then, you admit you know him."

"Don't put words in my mouth, Inspector."

He tutted, shook his head. "It seems there's a lot you don't know about this Von Eisenheim character."

Anna felt an uneasiness but tried not to show it.

"Have you wondered why your friend is paddling his U-boat around our sleepy shores when America is where the real slaughter fest is? No? I'm told the Southern Ocean is where Admiral Dönitz sends his misfits. And rogues. Those that do things like shoot survivors of a sunken ship. Yes, we're told the Admiral is a stickler for international conventions. That good German we were talking about. If such a thing exists."

"Even in the hell of war, I like to believe there's not one of us that's all good or all bad."

"Said as someone who's seen the hell of war ..."

"You don't have to be on the front to know. Listen, Inspector, you must be desperate to make up nonsense like shooting survivors. A commander could be assigned here for any number of reasons and you know it."

"With respect ma'am, I don't have to try and convince you of anything. Except that if you don't cooperate things could get ugly.

"I'm not scared of your threats."

"And if I told you what we think he's doing sniffing about here in Cape Town?"

"Look. I'm not interested, all right?

He signed and dusted a flake from his lapel. "*Hoor hier*, I'm only going to say one thing more. It's going to look bad for you if this business gets out. Think about it. Who's going to have any sympathy for a tart who sleeps with the enemy?"

Anna rose on the balls of her feet. "That's enough. I'm going."

"One last thing," he said as she passed.

Anna slowed.

"What I proposed earlier—making good with your father—will not be on offer after close of business today."

She stopped.

"In fact, you're lucky I haven't taken both of you in already. It took a lot to convince the commandant to give you till tonight."

Anna thought about it. The temptation to give in and confess was suddenly overwhelming. The bomb plot would be stopped, that was certain. Many lives saved. Important lives. The tide of history turned. But she'd be condemning her father, her own flesh and blood, not to mention her chance at love. No, there was still time to solve it another way. Tell Thomas, for one thing, what she'd seen and heard in the sewers. Maybe he'd have a solution. And if not, at least she would have warned him before she went to the authorities. It would be easier to live with herself afterwards.

She turned to face De Viliers. "Good to see you again, Inspector. I'll call you if something comes up."

27

D ETERMINED TO IGNORE DE Villiers, Anna walked on up Adderley Street. Only where it turned into Wale Street did she pause and glance back. The detective had disappeared.

She quickened around the bend, the cathedral opposite her. Approaching the next intersection, she became aware of a car keeping pace behind her and turned to look. It was a taxi. She skipped ahead towards the pedestrian crossing. The car accelerated past her and then slowed. The back door flew open. Only the boots and long socks of a passenger were visible.

"Get in," a familiar voice said.

Anna stooped to peer inside, not daring to believe. "Thomas?" He was in khaki shorts and a floppy hat. "Was that you passing back there?"

"Sorry, I wasn't so interested to meet your policeman friend."

"Good sense. But I thought we were meeting at the cable station."

"I was worried about you."

"Oh, Thomas, don't be so ..."

"Quick, get in before your detective sees us."

She hesitated. "You're not thinking of going up the mountain, are you?"

He grinned. "I mentioned the cable station, didn't I?"

"Yes, but really. Do you know how long it takes to get up there and back? It's crazy. There's way too much at stake to be messing around—"

"Slow down ..." He grew serious. "You wanted to meet with me, didn't you? Well, here I am. And I needed to be up the mountain. So why not combine the two? Also, we can have lunch: I have some provisions. Trust me, there's no other way. Come." He patted the seat. "I'll explain on the way."

She glanced over the palms to the mountain, where the overhead sun cast the stone ledges in stark relief. This hardly seemed the moment for a jaunt up the mountain, but it was probably as safe a place as any to speak with Thomas.

"It's all right," he said. "It will only take a couple of hours. There's something I want to share with you. You won't be sorry. I promise."

She didn't know what to think. On the one hand, something in Thomas's manner was calming. He seemed to know what he was doing. Already, she felt better about her decision to confide in him. But going up the mountain was a delay she hadn't anticipated. And what if the weather changed and the cable car stopped running? Worse, what if Thomas reacted the wrong way? How could she be a hundred per cent sure he wasn't involved with Kurt? He was a German officer, after all. Surely the left hand of their armed forces would know what the right was doing?

He reached out for her hand. She held hers steady, afraid of him suddenly. But when she felt his skin on hers and the surge of desire through her body, she changed tack. A picnic with the man of her dreams: what could possibly be wrong with that? It was a time of war. Who knows if either of them would have another chance of such happiness on this earth? She slid into the seat beside him and closed the door.

"So. Bunking lectures, are we?"

"This isn't the time for silly jokes."

"No? I think a sense of humour helps in any situation."

"Talking of which: what exactly is our situation? Why it so important we go up the mountain, now of all times?"

"Ssh. Have some faith." He pointed to the driver. "You'll find out soon enough."

They kept holding hands as the taxi veered right, ran a stop street, indicated left and turned into Buitengracht. The driver waited for a nanny to push a pram across the road, then accelerated. Anna's eyes strayed to a wine bottle between the heels of Thomas' boots. It was wrapped in a khaki shirt and drenched. The top of Kloof Nek was approaching, and the umbrella top of a pine on the Camps Bay side rose above the road. They were in the roundabout for a heartbeat before peeling left up Tafelberg Road. Both silent as the road narrowed. They were gaining altitude in broad curves now and the traffic had thinned. The city lay behind them and the mountain loomed ahead.

"Fantastic view, no?" Thomas said.

"Listen. There's no time to loll about admiring the sights. I told you—"

"Slow down." His other hand was over hers, stroking. "There's purpose in this madness. You have to believe me."

The taxi's engine started to groan as they entered the first switchback. As they progressed up the slope the pressure built on the inside of Anna's ears and she had to yawn for relief. She wound down the window and the scent of *fynbos* flooded the car. On the uphill side the road had steep clay banks with exposed pine tree roots in places. At last the road straightened and ran horizontally on a contour line, with the full face of the mountain on their right. She could see the cable car sliding down the rock face. As it approached the stone and concrete cube of the lower station it slowed to a crawl. She looked at the sun and guessed that it was eleven o'clock or thereabouts. The taxi pulled up at the pedestrian crossing outside the station, engine running. Without prompting, the driver opened the boot. Thomas climbed out of the car and when he reappeared, he had a rucksack slung across his shoulder. He slipped the driver a note and, without waiting for Anna, headed for the ticket counter.

The cashier was a woman with a girth that swallowed her chair. She ignored them, reading a Mills & Boon romance on her lap. When Thomas coughed she looked up indolently and pointed to the pricing on the board above her. He slid the money towards her and waited, rapping his fingertips on the counter.

Her eyes shifted from the money to his fingers and paused. "On honeymoon?" she said without taking her focus from his signet ring.

Thomas nodded. The tapping had stopped. He coughed. "We—"

"Tommy's treating me to a picnic," Anna interjected. She prodded the rucksack, giggled. "I can't wait to see what he's got in there."

"Well," she pushed two tickets across the counter, "you're not only lucky in love."

"How so?" Anna said, taking the tickets.

The cashier's breath was laboured as her arm rose to point behind her. "Not a breath of wind up there today. Let's hope it holds." There was a whirr and clunk from beyond a door. "There you are." She winked at Thomas. "Looks like you've got her to yourself."

The woman was only half-right. Seconds after the door of the cable car shuddered open, a youngster with shaggy hair and an overbite stepped out. When he saw Anna he beamed and held out his palm. She handed him the tickets and took Thomas's hand. After studying their receipts for several seconds longer than necessary the boy waved them on board. Then he pointed to the clock and stood, arms folded, and waited. Only when the minute hand ticked the top of the hour did he step back inside and slide the door shut. He rattled off a welcome and safety routine, and a few seconds after he finished, the winch motor began whining again until the cable clunked stiff.

The car inched forward, and the slab of the station dropped away to reveal the veld below. The conductor had been gushing nonsense since the end of his spiel and it became clear that he was simple, in protected employment. The car gathered pace, rocked back and forth, and suddenly they were airborne. Anna pressed her face against the window glass and stared ahead. The skirt of the mountain was a hessian of *fynbos* strewn with boulders that might have been hacked from the cliff and hurled down by an ogre. The front face of the mountain was sheer and harsh, broken only by the womb of Platteklip Gorge.

Thomas leaned over and whispered into her ear. "Are you all right?"

"Why wouldn't I be? I'm with you."

"You're about to damage my hand, that's all."

"I've got a bit of a thing about heights."

"Ah. I was beginning to think nothing scared you."

"Ja. When you grow up on a farm surrounded by men, you

don't have much choice but to play the tomboy. Actually, I love mountains. Just not the sheer cliffs."

The car had reached top speed now and the cable station was shrinking as the smile of Table Bay and the heights of Tygerberg rose to centre stage. The city had for the most part revealed itself and the sun had consigned the mist to a few wisps about the docklands. Anna pointed midway along the belt of green that started at the down-slope from the reservoir and ended at the narrow rectangle of the Company's Garden. "Can you spot my place?

"How could I? You've never invited me there."

She pinched him with her forefinger.

"Ouch. What are you doing?"

"Never mind." Anna glanced at the simpleton through the corner of her eye. He was staring at them, his mouth like a fish. She turned and glared at him until he looked at his feet. Hoping that he was too stupid to put two and two together and wonder why her fiancé had never been to her home. Then again, maybe he hadn't overheard the converstation with the cashier. Either way, it was pointless worrying. She squeezed Thomas's hand, released it and looked away. The cliffs of the table were hurtling towards them and she had to swallow to pop the pressure from her ears. Though she'd done the cableway half a dozen times, the view of the peninsula took her breath away. To her right was the knob of Lion's Head, its rump petering out to Signal Hill and the fringe of Sea Point's apartments. Beyond that the shimmer of the ocean grew larger until Robben Island appeared on the offing.

"You might want to make a note of that," she whispered, pointing to a cargo ship steaming past the island under escort of a frigate. "Keep your handlers happy."

"I see that you wish to spoil a perfect day."

"Well, it's the truth, isn't it?"

Thomas ignored her and turned to the conductor, who was looking at his feet, lips moving but without voice. There was only the creaking of the cable outside.

Directly below them was the outline of a path on a traverse between two rock faces. The ridge couldn't have been wider than a few feet, with a plunge of hundreds of feet on either side. There were two climbers below them, one of whom was waving. Anna, amazed, returned the greeting. But soon her vision blurred and the car's floor seemed to spin about her. When she looked up she was sure they would crash against the slab of rock hurtling towards them, but soon the cable stiffened and they glided into the receptacle of the station.

When the car stopped, the conductor started blabbering again about safety and closing times and the need to have a good time on the mountain. Thomas smiled at Anna, shrugged and hooked a thumb under his shoulder strap. The instant the door clanked open he was pushing past the conductor into the tunnel. Anna felt a tinge of fear and regret. All alone on the mountain with a strange man, and an enemy combatant at that? Her grandmother would turn in her grave.

The conducter was staring at her. His tongue rested on his teeth. It gave her an idea. Her eyes followed the cable's droop to the lower station. "Are you going straight back down now?"

He nodded. His mouth hung open. "Next one's at quarter past twelve, ma'am. Every hour, at quarter past the hour. Last one is at quarter past six."

Anna corralled her feelings. She'd thought the matter through. Regardless of her fear, there was no backing down now. She touched his wrist. "Can you do me one small favour?"

He blushed. "Ma'am?"

"I'm just a little worried we may get lost. My fiancée, you know, he's a proud man. Not good with maps."

His overbite lengthened in anticipation.

"Listen, if we're not back here for the quarter past two car, will you call my father? I'll give you his details."

He pulled a pencil from behind his ear and made to write on the stub of their tickets.

"His name is Stefan van der Vliet," she continued. "He's an MP. That's a Member of Parliament. Van der Vliet is spelled V-l-i-e-t. Here let me help." She wrote her father's name and number. Then she touched him on the wrist. His face lit up. "I'm depending on you."

But she had barely exited the car when she had regrets. What if the conductor called her father right away and he interrupted them? The last chance at figuring a way out of her dilemna without confessing all to him would be lost. And her pride couldn't allow that. She was still considering returning to the car to reemphasise the timing with the fool when she bumped into Thomas.

"Having second thoughts?" he said.

"No. Just enjoying the view. Isn't Lion's Head lovely from up here?"

"Ah, but much better from the sea."

"Very funny."

He grinned and took her hand and together they exited the building to a deck with viewing points about its perimeter. The sky was wide and clear, meringue-whisked with cirrus. He stopped at a telescope and took his rucksack off. It slumped to the ground.

"You got a load of bricks in there?"

"*Scheiße* … No, I mean, this needs a coin." He stooped to sight his eye to the horizon. Then he tapped the scope. Far below, the ocean shimmered like an unevenly iced cake. A flotilla of ships appeared stationary and the sun on the water formed a column of light.

"Don't be so impatient. We'll just have to enjoy the view the old-fashioned way. Hey, look: another frigate for you to report on."

"Ha," he grimaced. "Was it necessary to say that?"

"I'm done with turning a blind eye to your spying, Thomas."

"Having spied," he said. "I believe that is how you describe it in the past tense. How could I continue after I've known you?"

She elbowed him. "Go on, you think I'm so naïve as to believe you'd choose me over your country? A charmer like you? Goodness, you must break a heart in every port."

He stared through and then past her. "Look!"

She turned to see what had caught his attention. Far below the palm-fronds of Camps Bay beach grinned at them. There was a glint from a car moving parallel to the beachfront, then another. He stepped closer and pointed to a white smudge in the nose of the bay. As her eyes focused, she could make out a rock with waves crashing about it. She followed his finger to a stripe of foam extending a handbreadth from the rock across the offing.

"Do you see the shape of the feather?" he said.

"Mmm. No. Too straight."

"I don't mean of a bird."

"What then?"

"It's a naval term. For the wake of a periscope. Like this." He held the nail of his index finger at his nose and ran it forward through the air.

"Feather. That's lovely."

"Yes, but when you see one, it means a submarine is under way below the surface."

She felt his hand at her back now, pressing. She momentarily forgot her fears and misgivings about being up the mountain with him. Holding her hand as if to salute the sun, she narrowed her eyes in the glare. "Do you miss it? The boat. Your crew?"

"I would be lying if I said I long for them." He stared out to sea, then left along the peaks of the Twelve Apostles to the south-east. His dimples smiled but he looked sad. "After weeks or often months together in a cigar of tin, wondering if the next ping on your radar means the end, they become part of you." He picked up the rucksack and heaved the strap over his shoulder. Then he started across the platform in the direction of the city, veering onto a path of stone-speckled concrete.

"Where are you going?" Anna called. "There's a bench, right here."

He strode on.

Every instinct warned her to stay close enough to the cable station to call for help if she needed it. What if Thomas turned on her? On the other hand, if she didn't get to talk to him before her father arrived, the consequences were too ghastly to contemplate. No, she had to take her chances. Reluctantly, she set off after him.

A few feet to the left of the path the ground fell away to nothingness and beyond it the fan of the city and Table Bay. Apart from a band of cirrus there was only the last haze of morning mist between them and the concertina of the Hottentots Holland Mountains beyond False Bay. The path was worn smooth, with occasional ponds of rainwater or dew that had somehow defied the day and the heat. Though the ground was level, Anna had to take care not to trip as she skipped to keep up. Soon they were passing through a garden of moulded cheese granites. Bonsai-like trees clung to the rocks, their gnarled trunks twisting from crevices in the fight to survive. After a while the path petered out and she had to pause to make out Thomas in the distance hopping from stone to stone.

She had arrived at a ledge that dropped several feet to another, and soon the pimple of the cable station had disappeared behind them. Once again, she hesitated. Surely, it wasn't wise to be in an isolated part of the mountain with a man she didn't know? But she'd come too far to back out. Besides, by now she was curious to know what he had in the rucksack and why he so badly needed to be up the mountain.

She scrambled down, using her hands to steady herself and found him standing on a ledge, his back to her. He held a map in his hand but when he saw her he quickly tucked it into his pocket. She dropped onto her haunches and inched forward to join him on the ledge. A spitting distance from them the rock plunged to a wooded kloof. Perhaps two hundred feet across the chasm, the opposite wall of rock rose a similar height, its face banded in greens and greys. To the right was the apex of the canyon; to the left the undulating folds of the cliff opened to the saddle of Devil's Peak and the sandy flats stretching to False Bay. They were alone, and the air reverberated with the stillness of noon.

"*Liewe vader!*" she exclaimed, momentarily forgetting her fear of heights and misgivings. "I had no idea Platteklip would be so dramatic from this angle. It's lovely. How did you know about it? I'm supposed to be the local."

He patted his trouser pocket. "It is my custom to know the field of battle, better even than my enemies."

"So, I'm the enemy now?"

"You tell me." He delved into his rucksack and held up a bottle wrapped in a khaki shirt. Drops of condensate garlanded its neck. He peeled the shirt away to expose the Constantia label.

"Not one for half measures, are you?

He smiled. "Good vintage, 1939, no?"

Anna shivered. The start of the war. Was that simply a coincidence? She looked across the gorge. It was so still she could make out a hum from the city below. But the peace she'd just felt had been stolen. She was in the tunnels again, the reek of bananas overpowering her as she lifted the crate's lid. "Put that away," she said. "Please."

"And now?" He drew the bottle to his chest. "*Was ist?*"

"I'm sorry, Thomas, but this is wrong. Don't look at me like that, all sweet and smiling as if I'm putty in your hands. No. If you think you're going to make up for your duplicity by plying me with favours, you've got the wrong girl." She glanced down the gorge and felt dizzy, as though the enormity of the nothingness below was tilting her towards it. She looked down to secure her footing in a crevice. "I deserve answers, Thomas."

His face darkened but he didn't respond. Instead he felt in the rucksack and produced a pair of glasses from a dishcloth. Then there was a knife in his hand and he was cutting the bottle's seal. He shuffled towards her on the ledge. His muscles were thin and sinewy but stood proud of his arm.

Anna felt a stab of fear. What business had she fraternising with an enemy officer? How easy it would be for him to topple her. The sun had merged with a cloud and she felt a momentary chill. She considered running. Though out of earshot now, she could make visual contact with the cable station in minutes.

Thomas tossed the collar of lead into the abyss. Still not looking at her, he flipped the knife closed and flicked up a corkscrew. "Thinking of going somewhere?"

Anna dared not respond.

"Don't worry. If I needed to kill you, I'd have done it already. All right, I admit, I have a liking of the dramatic, a sense of occasion …" His arm swept the view. "But here, like this? Why spoil the view?"

"That's not funny."

"Thinking me a murderer is less so."

"Why are we here, Thomas?"

"You are the one who called me, as I remember it."

"I mean why are we up the mountain."

His eyes followed a speck of black gliding across the opposite cliff. "What's wrong? You don't like this?"

"Oh, stop it. A man as meticulous as you doesn't lug a bag of rocks and a *plaasmeisie* up a mountain in the heat of the day for no reason."

"I'll explain now, I promise. First, we drink." He twisted down on the corkscrew, the bottle between his legs.

Just then a brown creature appeared from under the opposite ledge. It was furry and round, like a rabbit crossed with a squirrel and the colour of the stone.

"Isn't it cute?"

Thomas shifted away. "What is it?"

"Only a dassie, silly. And just watch, where there's one there's a dozen."

He shooed it but the animal held its ground, eyes angry glass and whiskers twitching in synch with a ruffle of its coat.

"Technically, it's a rodent."

"Whatever it is, I'll kill it if it comes any closer."

"*Foeitog*, man. How can you say that?"

"Sometimes I think you love the natural world more than the human."

"At least animals don't lie."

"They don't love either. Here …" Without taking his eyes off the dassie, he pulled at the cork. It *thloeped* from the bottle. Then he inspected it and poured a finger of wine into his glass. He held the glass to the sun to inspect it and then quaffed. Satisfied, he filled both glasses and offered her one.

She hesitated. An instinct told her there would be no turning back from here.

"Come on. It's not poison."

He was right, she reasoned: if he'd meant to harm her, he would have done so already. Anyway, he was her last hope at foiling the plot, so why antagonise him?

"You're a difficult man to refuse," she said, reaching for the glass.

He laughed. "I'm sure my men would agree. Except for different reasons."

Her hand was shaking as she accepted the glass, causing wine to spool out and onto the rock. Was it fear or excitement?

"*Zum Wohl*." He held her eyes as their glasses clinked. "To us."

Anna held the glass at her lips to steady it. She wanted to ask him what he'd meant by "us". Instead she sipped. The wine was oak and caramel and cool in her throat. Just then a cry rang from the gorge. The speck gliding opposite had grown wings and was black against the rock. Then Anna noticed a movement along the ledge. A large bird. And another. One flapped and took to the air, the second in close pursuit. Once clear of the face it caught a thermal and soared.

"Verreaux's eagles," Anna said, "watch." Their wings were level now, like inverted parentheses in silhouette. The closest one tilted left, then banked suddenly right and plummeted. After a second of free fall it pirouetted twice and straightened to another glide. The other bird followed a second behind, twisting in the opposite direction.

"*Wünderbar*. The Lüftwaffe could learn from this."

"Ja. Lovely. Like tango in the sky."

"Or ballet."

Anna watched as the eagles chased each other in loops towards the apex of the gorge. In the distance a lone kestrel winked and dived, winked and dived and then flew off. From somewhere far below a voice called out, echoed and died—but she was too busy fighting back the tears to think much of it. Another pair of eagles had taken to the sky. Their movements seemed choreographed with the first two.

Thomas shifted closer and their arms touched. "Did I say something to upset you?"

She sipped at the wine. A lone bird whooshed overhead and dropped beneath the ledge. His hand was on her leg now; it felt like it belonged there. "I'm just reminded of my mother, that's all. She was a dancer with the Royal Ballet School. Before she met Papa ..."

"You say that as if it was a bad thing. You certaintly have a tortured relationship with him, don't you? So much anger."

"They may have been in love once. Tender to each other. But all I remember is the way they fought. Or, shall I say, the way he ... I think it was almost a relief for Mama when she fell ill. Only then did he appreciate what he was about to lose. Of course, I was too young to know for sure, but I remember she was so much calmer than before. Isn't that terrible?"

She felt his fingers touch her thigh and shivered. She didn't trust herself to speak and instead watched as a pair of eagles corkscrewed into the gorge. Another one was approaching the ledge, talons poised at its chest like the landing gear of a Spitfire. The sun and the heat seemed to have silenced the day except for the flap-braking of the eagle against the thermal like a kite.

Thomas turned and was staring into her eyes with an intensity that both frightened and excited her. "It's the human condition not to see the beauty before us until it is gone," he said. "But there's more that troubles you than this: am I correct? The reason you called."

She turned to face him. It was now or never. To confide in him or not? The result could alter the course of history. But in a sense, just by being here, she'd already decided. She tipped her glass, watched the liquid run down the rock and trickle into the void. When it had disappeared she shuddered, as if breaking a trance and said, "People are going to die tomorrow, Thomas. Important people, maybe even one I love more than anyone."

He put his glass down. "Die? Tomorrow?"

She studied his eyes, his posture. His face was bronzed from the sun and there were beads of sweat on his brow. The shadow of an eagle swooped towards her, banked and disappeared behind her. "You really don't know, do you?"

"Maybe, maybe not. Go on."

She cleared her throat. "Remember the other day we talked about Kurt?"

"Streicher, you mean?"

She nodded. "You said he's not regular navy."

"*Sicherheitsdienst* probably, or *Abwehr*, it isn't clear. They're both part of our intelligence services."

"And you don't know why he's here?"

"I have my theories."

"Oh, come on, with him on board your boat? Surely." She glanced towards the ridge and up at the sun. "Time is short. Don't play with me. There's a lot at stake."

"Anna. You must stop thinking me a liar. All my superiors told me was that he was on a matter of national importance, that I must accommodate *Obersturmführer* Streicher and afford him every courtesy. Beyond that, you don't question the SD."

"When last did you see him?"

He looked out towards the Cape flats. "I suppose at your farm."

"And that doesn't bother you? That an intelligence officer is going about without you knowing the first thing about his movements?"

"I can speculate, but it's not my business."

"The hell it isn't." Anna heaved herself up, careful to stand back from the edge. Though angry, she was now certain he was telling the truth. At least enough of it. She scraped granite particles from her hands and straightened her skirt. Then she riveted him with her eyes. "All right, there's no easy way to say this. There's a plot to blow up Parliament. Tomorrow."

"What? *Mein Gott*. This is impossible. Our orders for this mission to South Africa are clear. Reconnaissance only."

"Well, your *Sicherheits*, whatever they call themselves, obviously see things differently." She swallowed. "With some help from the likes of my, uhm, ex-boyfriend."

He stared at her.

"Yes, Fanus. He's with the *Ossewabrandwag*. I take it you've heard of them. Afrikaner fascists. They take their cue from your lot."

Thomas ignored her jibe.

"He's on the Grand Council," she continued.

"And he told you all this?"

She shook her head, looked at her takkies. Her feet still had pins and needles from sitting. "I was in the tunnels this morning, I …"

"Go on."

"There are dozens of them beneath the city. Streams from the mountain. Look, there isn't time to explain. But they've got dynamite down there, loads of it. *Magtig*, I felt it with my own hands."

Thomas gazed over the gorge, thumb on chin.

"I can't be sure," she continued. "But I think they're planning to blow up the House of Assembly. Tomorrow." She was unsteady now, the weight of the void seeming to want to topple her. "Papa is supposed to be there too." She felt his hands on her shoulders, steady. The smell of aftershave and the earth. "You seem so … calm, I thought you'd be shocked."

He was quiet. Another voice echoed from the gorge below, still indistinct. Perhaps it was just a trick of nature. Or a baboon. "Parliament," he muttered, "*Mein Gott.* I'm a fool."

She waited.

"I'd be lying if I said I didn't have my suspicions. But after the Leibbrandt affair, High Command gave up on attempts at changing governments. In Southern Africa at least. It's too far from the main theatres of war."

"Well, it seems things have changed. Unless my eyes and ears are deceiving me. And my hands. There's a room full of the stuff just below the House of Assembly. And it makes sense. Tomorrow there's a special sitting. Smuts, most of his cabinet, my … Oh, goodness, I don't even know why I'm …" She was shaking and felt her eyes moisten. "It's not fair me telling you this; you're a soldier; you have a duty to your country; oh, Thomas, my darling, I don't know where else to turn."

He put his arm around her. "You've done the right thing. You mustn't worry. We'll defuse it."

"You mean you're not going to …? But—that would be—treason. They'll."

"No. This … plot: It's … how do you say … mischievous. It's my duty to stop it."

Anna stared at him. It hadn't been the reaction she'd expected. Too good, perhaps, to be true. But she was with the man she loved, in a place of unimaginable beauty, and he was telling her all would be well. How could she not be happy? And even if, somehow, he couldn't or wouldn't stop the plot, there was a good chance she'd managed to pursuade her father not to attend.

"Well …" Thomas reached for his rucksack. "I suppose this is a good time to explain why I insisted on coming up the mountain." He unzipped the lower and middle compartments and pulled out a rectangular contraption with holes and dials and then another, similar in shape but smaller, and a battery—and laid them side by side on the ledge.

"A radio?" she said.

He raised his eyebrows.

"Don't look so surprised. The Special Signals Corp gave us a demonstration at the end of last year. The castle is on a drive to recruit graduates. Specifically girls, now that the cream of the men are away. Can you believe it? We're good enough in war but not in peace."

"What has made you so cynical about men? We aren't so bad when you get to know us better."

"Ha. That's the problem. I've been surrounded by you lot all my life."

"And then there was … me." He flashed a grin. "So, didn't you take it? The job."

"It was tempting. The thought of my own salary, independence."

"But you chose to keep studying art. A lot of money in that, no?"

"I believe there are two types of people in this world, Thomas. The man of commerce—and I include the warrior here—and the man of letters, the artist. The latter way is narrow and seldom understood."

"I believe this is an oversimplification. But all right, if it makes sense of the world for you, then it's a good thing."

"Oh, don't you patronise me too!"

He raised a hand. "One moment. Please. I have to concentrate on this first." He connected the first two blocks to each other with a tube, and the next two with a cable. Then he pulled out another, two-pronged device labelled Kristall 6.18' and connected it to the others. After adjusting the nearest dial to 5–8 MHz, he flicked the switch and turned another dial, first one notch, then another. Finally, he sat back. "So, there was more to it than the love of art, no? Such a good opportunity, this signals business."

"You're not being serious, are you?"

"I'm German. We're always serious."

"Papa would have killed me."

"Papa this, Papa that. Why do you care so much what he thinks?"

Her eyes dropped. "It's not just that. I want to finish my

degree. You have no idea how badly. It's like I have something to prove. I'm the first woman in our family to go to university."

He coughed. "Don't be angry with me for this, but what about marriage?" His eyes scanned her. "A girl like you could have her pick of husbands."

"Why can't I have both?"

"Touché."

"Ja. In my dreams. Unfortunately, every man I'd be interested in is up north. And who knows for how long, what with all the see-sawing with your Rommel. I may as well improve myself in the meantime." She fell silent, looking out over the sliver of False Bay in the distance. Imagining the point of Hangklip and many miles beyond, the farm. "Tell me something," she said. "On the way home last Thursday, I saw a light flashing from the sea just off the coast by Rietvlei. That was your crew communicating with the farmers, right?"

The lines of his face were deeper than usual but unmoved.

"Don't ask me exactly what was being said," she continued. "But I got a word here and there. Enough."

He didn't flinch.

"I did a class on Morse; most of us did; it was offered at no cost."

"And your question is?"

"Why Morse? If every other first year university student is learning it."

"Ah, you wonder why we communicate in a language our enemy is familiar with? But you see, our messages are encrypted. You may recognise a word. But when you string them together they make no sense." He followed a wire until his index finger rested on a key at the top left corner of the transmitter. He tapped once, and again, and a bulb flickered. Then he twisted yet another dial until the flickering brightened. "Also, there are situations where we want the enemy to understand."

"I was right: you really are a spy."

Thomas laughed but was then distracted by a Verreaux that had appeared behind them, hovering on a thermal. It was close enough to see the hook of its beak and the zebra pattern under its wings. After a few seconds in suspense, it banked and disappeared. Then Thomas reached into the bag again, pulled out a set of earphones and set them on the rock. "So. How long have we known each other now?"

"Feels like a lifetime."

"That can be taken two ways." He smiled. "Seriously ..." He counted on his fingers. "Less than a week. And yet you trust me with your life. Unbelievable." He placed the earphones over his head and waited, his finger ready at the key. After a brief pause, he started tapping. In response, the light flashed on and off in sync.

Anna felt a chill. Had she been wrong about him, after all? She risked a glance at the ridge behind him. A dassie twitched but otherwise it was still. She was on her own. "I don't understand, Thomas. Why this whole charade when all along you intended to betray me to your handlers? It's cruel. What happened to the man I've fallen in love with?"

He looked at her, expression blank. "You don't—how do you say—beat around the bush, do you?"

"How else? There's no time. God only knows. Tomorrow we could both be dead. Today."

"Relax." He wrapped both hands over the earphones and looked towards Devil's Peak and the opposing cliff. "It's not Berlin I'm speaking to."

Confused, Anna followed his eyes. An icing of cloud had accumulated over the Hottentots Hollands range. The hunter moon of False Bay beside it. "Your boat?"

He nodded, tapped again, and waited. In the air over the gorge there must have been a dozen eagles now. One glided towards them, talons extended. Its tail feathers were fluttering like a yacht sail in a storm. "Still nothing," he said and tapped the same sequence.

Anna ransacked her memory of dots and dashes. The light was flashing fast now but she could make out individual words. "But that's straight German?" she said, confused. "Don't you encrypt your messages?

"No time to use a cipher: anyway, we think the enemy has decoded them. My men and I, we have our own codes. Your Signals Corp will have to relay this to the British and in, say, three days, they'll crack them. Another before they react. By then we'll be gone."

Anna felt a jolt, then a hollowness. For a second she'd imagined his "we" to mean the two of them. But obviously he meant his men.

As if reading her mind, he said. "I am arranging a rendezvous."

"Not in Cape Town, surely? That would be suicide."

"Don't be so sure." He felt in his back pocket. "Here is a photograph my colleague took of the city not so long ago. Do you recognise this? Yes, the lights off Seapoint before the dimouts. A beautiful sight, no?"

The photograph was yellowed and its edges frayed, but the outline of Table Mountain from the Atlantic shore was unmistakable. "Unbelievable: who would have thought? While we slept soundly … It couldn't happen now, of course."

"Why so?"

"There's radar for one thing. A whole section of the castle was turned into a receiving station. Trust me, I was there for interviews. In the harbour, you'd be like ducks on Zoetendalsvlei."

"Ja, ja, we know that."

"Well, where then?"

He tapped at the transmitter. *"So, du verstehst Deutsch?"*
"Ein bißchen."

He pulled in his chin. "With an honorary German as a father? I think you're too modest."

"Okay. Let's give it a try."

He tapped another sequence and then they waited in silence. Then his palm shot up. After an exchange of signals, he removed the earphones and placed them on the rock. "Did you get any of that?"

"Sure," she smiled. "I translated your keystrokes from Morse to German to English. Just tell me your plan, silly. I'll try my best to believe you."

"You don't let up on this spy business, do you? What do I have to do to show I'm telling the truth?" He reached into his rucksack and withdrew a loaf of bread, a hunk of cheese and a knife. He cut two slices of each and gave her one. "Eat.

We're going to need it."

"Meaning?"

"That detective bothering you, the plain-clothes fellow ..."

"De Villiers? What about him?"

Thomas worked his food to the side of his mouth. "You said his men had been to *Rietvlei* and found nothing, am I right?"

She bit into the cheese, nodded. "Mmm, this is ripe. Where did you get it?"

"In Kloof Street. A man can get anything there. A *Bäckerei*, *Metzger*, it's just like a Bavarian village."

"Ja, Papa's taken me there many times. De Villiers said his men were at Rietvlei, that's it. Papa thinks it means they didn't find anything."

"De Villiers was correct." He drained his glass and set it on the rock. "There's nothing to find."

Anna felt her back tense. "You're not thinking of going back to Skulpiestrand?" She felt the sun burning her neck and put her hand up as a shield. "Even if you were mad enough to go back there, why tell me? Wouldn't it be top secret?" She searched him with her eyes. "Unless this is one of those communiques you wouldn't mind if the enemy understood."

"I give you my word." He stroked her forearm. "That's where we'll meet them. On the beach. I believe you call it Perlemoen Punt—although it's not marked on the map. Sunday after sunset."

Her eyes dilated and stared straight into his. "What did you just say?"

"The beach. There's a road leading to it, yes?"

"You said '*We'll* meet them'?"

He tossed the crust of his sandwich over the ledge, took her one hand, then the other, as if to steady her. "I want you to come with me."

The city to her left was rotating clockwise, as if the emptiness of the gorge had magnified gravity. "But Thomas, wouldn't that be a huge risk? To go all the way there to say goodbye?"

"No, I mean come, come to sea with me."

"You can't be serious."

"Look at me, Anna. Am I laughing?"

"Stop it. Don't tease me like this." But her words lacked conviction. She was being drawn to him without his pulling. Sensing his presence before his touch. "You know I have feelings for you. It isn't fair."

"I never tease." His voice was at her ear now, stubble on her cheek. His fingers massaged her shoulder blades.

"But … I've never even been on a boat. Other than a fishing trip from Struisbaai. Oh, what am I saying? This is madness."

Thomas was distracted by another eagle that slowed to a landing close by and started preening. When he turned back to her his eyes seemed deeper set than usual, yet stronger. "Come away with me, Anna."

She looked at him, afraid that if she blinked the moment would be lost. "In the U-boat?"

His nod was barely noticeable.

"That's, that's ridiculous."

"Do I look like a clown?"

"But, for one thing, I'm English."

"You know German. You don't have to say much at first. Trust me. I've thought it through."

"You seem to have forgotten I'm a woman."

"Impossible." He grinned. "Don't worry. I have a spare uniform to cover the curves." He tousled her hair. "We will need to give this a trim though. Seriously, if you keep to yourself, we'll be well underway to Madagascar before the crew realises who you are."

She felt herself swaying. Either that or a breeze had sprung up. "And then?"

"My men have served with me for eighteen months. I'm like a father to them."

"Maybe, but we'd get to one of your bases, sooner or later."

"The first one's Lourenco Marques. We'll go ashore before that. It's Portuguese, neutral territory. Much of the coastline is uncharted. No one will find us."

"So, we sit on the beach and drink coconut milk for the rest of our lives?"

The first eagle had shuffled clear of the bush. Its head was half-cocked, as if enquiring. Thomas stepped close to her, held her shoulders again. "I am as serious as I have ever been, Anna. You can see I am not a superstitious person. But it is clear we were supposed to be together."

She let her cheek rest on his and where their skin touched it felt warmer than the day. A finger ran down her neck and lingered at her arm. "We shouldn't be here," she breathed. "Like this. I can't bear it." She didn't move as his finger continued down her neck and stopped at her cleavage.

"Quiet now," he said. "Don't care for the past. What was right, what was wrong then. Or the future. We're here, aren't we, just us? The world be damned." His hand was on her breast now, first flat, then cupping its weight.

"What are you doing?" she said, looking in his eyes now. His mouth was close and she could feel his breath on her lips. Then his other hand was at her back, drawing her closer, and they were kissing. Tentatively as first but then full-mouthed. Past his ear she could see the sheer cliffs and the plunge of the gorge but for once she wasn't afraid of anything, no height, no depth, not any power. Every man and woman in the world could be watching, she could be dying—it didn't matter, for once she was happy.

28

FAINT ECHOES DRIFTED UP from the hollow of the kloof, like the far-off bark of baboons, or stones falling from the cliff. Only at a squawk from the ridge behind them did Anna break their dream-like kiss. She didn't move at first. Thomas was in front of her and behind, an enveloping presence, his hand still pressed against her back, as if it were bare despite her skirt.

"It's only a bird, I'm sure," he said.

"Yes, but what disturbed it?"

"A tourist, perhaps?"

She looked past him to study the skyline.

"Not likely. The fellow at the cableway told me it's a blue moon when anyone strays further than two hundred yards from the telescopes or the tea room."

"Perhaps, but he did not look like a person to rely on for information."

A thought was gnawing at Anna's memory. "What's the time?"

He firmed his hold. "*Was ist*? This is good, you and I here like this. We should forget about time."

"Darn. I shouldn't have … Oh, Thomas, I'm sorry, I'm so sorry."

He relaxed his grip, drew back a fraction. "What are you talking about?"

"I told him to call Papa if we didn't make the quarter past two cable car." She couldn't bring herself to make eye contact. Her focus jumped from rock to bush, as if not sure what she was looking for, then to the sun. "What if the fool got the message muddled up? Like thinking quarter past one for quarter past two . Please, don't look at me like that. I wasn't sure of … your intentions."

"And you are now?" Thomas grinned.

"Shh. Listen."

"If he did call after quarter past one: that's half an hour ago. Surely your father would not have worried right away? It would take him hours, no?"

"Ha! You think you know him. If there was time now I'd tell you things that would make your hair stand straight up. Like the time my friends and I had a *braai* at Brandfontein. We were finished with school for goodness' sake, supposed to be adults. But no, there he was tearing through the dunes with his bakkie, dog on the back. It wasn't even sunset."

Thomas laughed. "I can imagine the scene."

"It wasn't funny." Anna stood apart by now, angry with herself. The contentment she'd savoured in Thomas's arms had long-since fled. "I'm my own person now," she said. "I'll be damned if I'm going let him keep controlling my life. Let him breathe fire. I don't care."

The echoes sounded again: it was hard to tell if they were closer.

"Sounds like someone's coming up Platteklip." She peered over the ledge. "Why not use the cableway?"

"Maybe they're coming from there too." Thomas was on his haunches, gathering the remains of the picnic into the bag. Then he pulled the cords from the radio. "Except then it would be the authorities, not your father. Which is unlikely."

They were trapped. She felt panicky. "What do we do then?"

He drew the map from his pocket and tapped it. Then he motioned towards the opposite cliff.

At first she thought he was being funny. But he was right: they couldn't go back to the cable station. She followed him up the ledge as it rose to reveal the tip of Maclear's Beacon, the highest point on the mountain. "You're not thinking of going down via Skeleton Gorge, are you? It's miles." She pointed at the radio. "Especially lugging that."

"Exactly." He lifted the transmitter above his head, ready to hurl. "It is time to shed ballast."

Anna almost lost her footing as she reached forward to stop him, but in vain. For several seconds there was nothing, then a clack and its echo zigzagging up the kloof. Before she could say anything Thomas had ditched the receiver and battery unit.

"What did you do that for?" she said as the crash of the landing ricocheted.

"This equipment must not fall to the enemy—sorry—into British hands. Also, it will be a useful distraction for whoever is coming up there. They'll think we are this side."

Within a minute they were clambering over cheese granite and lichen towards the ridge. They veered ninety degrees, then crested and followed the path parallel to the edge of the gorge. As if they needed reminding, there were signs at intervals to warn them from straying from the path. The ground was uneven, the stones smooth and the going was slow. Out of breath, they were sliding down a rock face, finding the path again, then at a crossroads. A sign pointed right for Kasteelspoort, left for Platteklip. As they studied it, another call came from the gorge. Closer this time, and more human.

In an instant Thomas was off, Anna following him up a path of loose stone to the top of the next ridge. The landscape flattened to an expanse of bush and reed, then dropped off to undulating rock and an ocean iced with cloud. He was in full stride now, one hand clutching the map and the other hitched under the shoulder strap of the rucksack. For a stretch the path was of sandstone and wound through the veld, before sinking into a corridor of shoulder-height reeds. Beside them a gurgling stream hosted an orchestra of frogs. Ferns covered the ground in a carpet and beneath that it was sponge. Moments later they were through the corridor and the view opened again, showing wrinkles of swell on the ocean.

Anna caught up with him and came alongside. "How do you know they won't be waiting for us down Skeleton?"

"I don't. But my guess is it's your father and Kleinjan. Why would he have informed the authorities, especially if he knows I'm here with you? It compromises him."

She mulled it over. He had a point. Papa and Kleinjan would be way too thinly stretched to cover the cable station, Kasteelspoort, Platteklip and Skeleton. And investigating the smashed radio would take up a chunk of their time. She began to relax into her stride and they walked in silence.

"You do much hiking?" she said at last.

"I used to. You can't walk far in Heidelberg without meeting a hill. These days the only exercise I get is climbing the conning tower. And you?"

"On the farm I walk everywhere. Helps me think. *In ambulare solvare.* But it's mostly flat there. The Soetanysberg is hardly an alp. But *jong,*" she stroked the front of her thigh. "I've done enough climbing to know we're going to suffer today—downhill is the worst." She broke off a stick of thatch and bent it double. Somehow, mindless actions like that were a balm. "Tell me about Heidelberg."

"There's a university. That's about it." He quickened his pace, powering around a clump of proteas and out of sight.

She found him waiting, back to her with both his hands hitched in the straps. "Did I say something wrong?"

"Nothing. Something personal. It's not important."

"Tell me. The good and the bad."

"I should still be there."

"Oh?"

"My grandfather, father, every generation has produced an academic." He kicked a stone from the way and strode on, the crunch of their footsteps the only sound in the heat. Only when he got to a stick figure of shade from a dead tree did he pause. "In 1938 I was enrolled for the winter semester, the classics. In the beginning it was *wünderbar.* I hired a house with friends above the Alte Brucke, the same side as the Philosophenweg. There was a perfect view of the *Schloß.*"

She waited.

"Kristallnacht. November '38. It is impossible to forget. Everything changed." His face grew lines. "But it actually started long before then. The SS was infiltrating student organisations for years, leading smear campaigns against academics who were not Aryan enough. It was mostly propaganda, no violence. But that night they burned two synagogues. In Heidelberg of all places. *Wahnsinn.*" His eyes were trained on his shoes, as though his mind was elsewhere and he was merely speaking through the motions. The path rose towards a ledge.

His breathing was audible between sentences.

"How terrible."

"I would be lying if I said it upset me at the time. I just wanted to get on with my studies, maybe have a good time on the way. What was happening with the Jews, the Communists, it was not my business." He slowed, trod over a boulder and pressed on. "Then the Wehrmacht started to recruit. In the beginning I was excused as a student. But later the pressure was too much. I got into the navy. My father has connections. We thought it would be safer." He chuckled. "We forgot about the U-boats."

"You'd have made a marvellous scholar. I can tell it's your passion, thinking things through."

"This is true." He held up his palms. "But I'm practical too, *oder*?"

She shoved him playfully. "A renaissance man, hey."

He laughed. "Like Goethe. Ah, I wish for that. He was in the grounds of the *Schloß* once. They say his spirit still wanders about when there is mist in autumn. If you come there one day, you'll see why they say this. The place is beautiful enough to believe that a great intellect would choose to haunt it."

"Goethe this, Goethe that. You're just like my father. I can't tell you how often he would quote him. It used to drive me mad. I don't even agree with the chap's philosophy."

He turned. "How so?"

"Oh, I don't know enough really. Most of what he says flies over my head. I just remember some business about man becoming part of nature. It's hocus-pocus to me."

Thomas laughed. "*Gemüt*, you mean? That is a long discussion. What is it you object to?"

"To me it's simple." She spread her arms. "God created all this. When you look up there—the sun and the moon and the stars—and there, the flowers and the ants, can there be any other explanation that makes sense?"

They'd arrived at the cairn of rocks piled above eye-height with a beacon atop that marked the high point of the mountain.

Thomas stroked a rock. "Can you believe they used this to calculate the curvature of the earth for the first time?"

"If you say so." She scanned the horizon, first the table top they'd come from and then the saddle of Devil's Peak below.

There was no sign of their being followed but still she felt uneasy.

"We should be going. It's too exposed up here," he said.

The path wound downwards ever steeper, and they had to concentrate to avoid slipping on the loose stones as they descended. Although the sun was well past its apogee, the day was getting hotter with every mile. Anna had to swallow often to suppress her thirst. The mountain seemed tiered like a wedding cake, each layer progressively shallower and wider, revealing more of Constantia's vineyards and Muizenberg Beach beyond. They had to stop at an exposed rock face. Below was a secluded dale of *fynbos* heather and fern, with a lean-to of granite. Thomas slithered down ahead and offered his hand. Out of pride she refused, edging across the ledge instead, and then slid, feet first.

Then his hands were at her waist. At first she was self-conscious about her sweat-drenched blouse, but the feeling soon gave way to excitement and she held her ground in his arms.

"You know what I am coming to love about Africa?" he said in her ear.

"Me?"

"That, of course," he laughed. "But I was meaning the open spaces. That a man can walk for hours on end and not see another person or building is a freedom I can't describe. In Germany, it's impossible. Every few miles there is another village. Civilisation, or so it's called."

"And in the mountains? I thought you had tons of them?"

"True. But even in Bavaria, if you climb an alp on any day of the week you can expect to meet someone, or a rescue hut, even a hotel."

"I wouldn't be upset if I saw a restaurant now."

"But then there'd be people." He tightened his grip on her waist.

She wanted to stay there forever.

"And not this moment of peace together." He'd hardly said it and the buzz of an aeroplane came from behind the ridge.

"Keep still," he said. "Down." They crouched together against the ledge. The buzzing grew louder but just as Anna was convinced it would be directly overhead and see them, it started to fade.

"What was that?"

"Reconnaissance. Probably a routine flight."

But his pace was faster than before and within minutes they reached the base of the valley, where a stream crossed the path. The water was stained brown but clear enough to see the algae-coated stones beneath. Thomas hesitated at the bank.

"Go on, silly. It's good for you." Anna dropped to her haunches and cupped her hands under the surface. She drank. Despite its colour, the water tasted sweet and it was cold and lovelier with every mouthful. Satisfied, she splashed her face and neck and stood. "And?" She became self-conscious again, more so when she realised her blouse was soaked. It was the first time she could remember being thrilled at the thought of a man looking at her in that way.

"I'm sorry if this sounds like a cliché," he said, looking in her eyes. "But I have never seen a woman as beautiful."

Anna wrapped her arms around herself. "Don't lie. I know my limitations; I'm just a *plaasmeisie*, for heaven's sake." A breeze wafted from upstream, ruffling the pond and causing a dragonfly to rise, languorous. She shivered. It was happening too fast, and there was no telling where it could take her if left unchecked. She turned her face to the path. "What are we going to do? When we get down, I mean. The day's almost over, and tomorrow ..."

As if he hadn't heard, Thomas stooped to drink. After several handfuls he rose, dripping. "I said it earlier. I will frustrate their plans." He squeezed water from the hem of his shirt. "That is all."

"You make it sound so easy."

"If it's only dynamite and a fuse down there, as you report, it will be a simple matter. I must only be careful they are not alerted. They must expect to succeed until the very last moment. That way they will be trapped."

She processed his words. "I don't understand." she said at length, "Why would you want one of your own men to be caught? This is a war, after all. And you're soldiers."

"Ja, *bestimmt*, war has become my trade, this killing. But there are reasons for the conflict. A just cause, I believe you would call it."

"Ah, that's what they all say. But really, the Blitzkrieg? A just cause? What nonsense you people are fed. Read one of Churchill's speeches, or Smuts if you'd find that easier to stomach."

"I have." His face was impassive. "Both, their speeches and writings. And if you paid attention to the transcripts of Smuts during the Versailles conference you would have heard him warning the Allies not to be so harsh with the vanquished. Germany's land taken, the debts … Do you know the suffering that caused? We were fortunate, my family, but I am old enough to remember the desperation." He fell silent and the only sounds were the trickle of the stream on the other side of the path and air sighing through reeds.

"I understand," she nodded. "At least I'm trying to. But isn't Kurt one of yours? In intelligence, perhaps, but a soldier nevertheless."

It was as though a cloud had passed overhead and his face was in shadow. His expression frightened her. "That bastard is no soldier." He kicked at the sand. "The SD, Brownshirts, these are constructs of that, that painter's twisted imagination."

"Don't expect me to understand you people." She plucked the front of her blouse away from her breasts and felt the air cool her skin. It caused her to shiver. "But I can't stand by and let that happen to Fanus. He can be idealistic, bombastic even. But he's not a bad person. If he was caught he'd be hanged. I couldn't bear it."

"He's intelligent enough to understand the risk."

"Yes, but there must be a way." She shuffled a pebble from her shoe and tossed it into the pond. A tadpole surfaced and ducked back in the water. An idea was forming in her mind, but for now it was good just to stand and feel the breeze cool her face. "Ah, I know," she said to herself as she stepped back onto the path.

"What was that?" he said, taking her by the wrist as she passed.

"Nothing."

"I don't believe you."

"That's rich coming from you. Mr Truth himself."

"Anna. I told you I'll take care of things."

She yanked her wrist free, glared at him. "You expect me

to sit around like a hapless *hausfrau* waiting for you to 'fix' everything? Well, I'm sorry to disappoint you, but you've got the wrong girl." She stomped down the path.

Only when she'd crested the next ridge did she pause. Where she stood was the apex of Skeleton Gorge, which was covered with dense vegetation. Far off, the Cape Flats were obscured by a haze made orange by the sun's fading.

"At least tell me what you're thinking of doing?" he said when he'd caught up.

"He's still in love with me."

"I can't say I blame him. But don't tell me you're considering what I think you are."

"He'll listen to me, Thomas, I know he will. I'll make something up, tell him the police know—it doesn't matter. He's an Afrikaner, remember, I know how it goes. For all our bravado, we're pragmatists."

"No. This is madness. We're dealing with fanatics."

"I owe it to myself to give it a try."

He smelled the air, lips pressed together. He shook his head, slowly.

Just then they heard another airplane engine only a deeper drone this time, coming from the direction of Maclear's Beacon and growing louder by the second. Anna scanned the sky above the ridge. "You still think it's just Papa after us?"

"But ... I don't understand. Maybe someone else ... Come."

Fortunately, the dense foliage was only a stone's throw away and they were in it before the plane crested the ridge behind them. For a few anxious moments they stooped beneath a tree and waited for it to pass, and then hurried on. The path plunged, switchbacking into the kloof, their shoes skidding here and there on loose gravel. Soon they were under an even denser canopy of yellowwood and cape beech trees in a golden smattering of sun. The ground became hard clay, veined with roots worn smooth by a thousand shoes and the air darker, the twittering of birds everywhere and nowhere. Then they were in a dry riverbed among boulders adorned with moss and fern. They had to shimmy, feet first, down a series of ladders. The plane passed twice more overhead and then must have given up the search. After the ladders the path resumed, steep at first and then flattening. The light faded as the roof of the forest thickened. Anna trudged several paces behind Thomas, the heaviness of her thoughts adding to her exhaustion. The more the stick figure of her plan grew flesh, the more worried she became. The two airplanes meant it was probably the military after Thomas—not her father. Ironically, she reflected, this was a good thing—they probably didn't expect her to be with him, which gave her a certain amount of room to manoeuvre. But the flip side was that more depended on her.

It was a relief when they finally intersected a jeep track and could follow its winding left. The world opened up again and Anna's mood lifted. Although the sun had left the valley, the sky was still light. Then the road gave way to a lawn that fanned out like a delta to banks of tidy flower beds and silver trees. They stood side by side to take in the view. "Could be England, hey?" she said. "Tame as a shrew."

"Or Germany. And now: *quo vadis*?"

"Downhill. Even a seaman couldn't go wrong." Then she was running, fast as her tired legs would allow, the grass soft and welcoming. The path narrowed between ericas and protea bushes mulched at their stems. Now and again a plant had a label at its stem or pegged in the ground. Then they were on a steeper stone path between ancient cycads, which soon gave way to stinkwoods and yellowwoods, beside a stream that gurgled down to a bird-shaped pond where they paused.

It was a secluded space, almost dark, with branches sagging to the surface of the water. As good a place as any to catch their breath and consider what to do next. Taking off her shoes and socks and hitching her skirt, Anna stepped into the pool. The water was clear, and even in the gloom her toes looked white and swollen. Then she splashed water on her thighs and ran her hands down her quivering legs.

"Lady Anne Barnard's bath," she said.

"Yes, although the name is technically incorrect." He removed his shoes and stepped in beside her. "She left the Cape with her husband before it was constructed."

"How do you know all this?"

"I read a book once. They lived at the castle. With a dining room for ninety-nine guests. *Wahnsinn.*"

"Ja, the army commandeered that very room for their radar listening room. And a barracks for the girls. To think: I'd be working there now if I'd joined Signals. Yuk. So narrow and crowded."

"Sounds like life on a U-boat." He splashed his face and let the water run down to his already sweat-soaked shirt. It was quiet by the pool except for the trickle from the inlet. Somewhere far off a child shouted.

"I've been thinking," she said. "About what you told me up there. Your plan, as you called it."

"And?" He was watching his toes twitch on the cement floor of the pond.

"It's madness. We'd be outcasts."

"We already are."

"No. You are."

A frog quarked from the far side of the pool. There was a plop and it went quiet. Thomas plucked the end of a branch from above him and tossed it beyond the water's edge. "Do you seriously think the authorities aren't aware of your dealings with me?"

"Dealings? Is that what this is?"

"You know what I mean. Why would that De Villiers character investigate you if he had no witnesses?"

"Investigations, witnesses. *Magtig*, can a woman not go for a picnic with a man she finds interesting? It may get tongues wagging, but it's not a crime."

"It's only a question of time before they decode my communique, Anna. What then?"

"You didn't mention me by name, did you?"

"I didn't have to—they'll join up the dots. If you will excuse the pun."

The child was calling again; this time from closer.

She felt his eyes stray to her breasts. They were damp again and her nipples were hard against her blouse, but she felt no shame. There was nothing in the world she wanted more than to abandon herself to him, agree to his scheme, and the consequences be damned. But some ingrained proprietary restrained her and she scrambled for resolve. "We're not even engaged. How can we go off together? It's wrong, it's …"

He moved closer, embracing her and his knee pressed intothe folds of her skirt. Above them the tapestry of branches filtered a hundred splinters of afternoon light. "Normally, I would not want to make you do anything faster than you are comfortable with," he said, lifting a strand of hair from her cheek and tucking it behind her ear. "But in this time, nothing is as it should be." His voice was low and his breath tickled her forehead. "Even my own people, the most civilised and educated of Europe, are looting and killing like in the dark ages. *Mein Gott*, this world is upside down."

"That's no exaggeration." She straightened a crook in his collar. His top button was undone and she could see his chest, smooth and hairless with a sheen of moisture. "But that doesn't mean we should just ... abandon our values, our beliefs." She was forcing words she wasn't sure in that moment she still believed. She could feel him against her now, firming as his kisses trailed from her forehead to her neck, where they paused.

"Beliefs? How can anyone not believe in love?"

From the thicket behind, the squeal of children drew nearer, a reminder of the fragility of their seclusion. She drew back just enough to meet his eyes. Her breathing was shallow. "Did you just use the word love?"

He grinned. "I believe I did. Is this in order?"

"It's nothing to joke about, Thomas. I'm not some floozy you can bandy that word about with. How can we be in love? It's been less than a week."

"It's how deeply we feel that matters," he said, edging closer, "not for how long."

Reason was urging her to break the dream, to run, but her body refused. She leaned into him, cheek on cheek. Below, a tadpole darted between her toes. "Why would you love me?" she found herself saying. "I know I'm not unattractive, but a brunette, brown eyes ... hardly the ideal *hübsches mädchen*."

He felt for her hand, intertwined his fingers through hers. "Look at me." He was begging with his eyes. "I'm about to give everything up. Command of my vessel. My career. Who knows, perhaps my life. This is so much more than superficial. Love. Love. I love you, Anna van der Vliet."

She looked down. Her legs were shaking beneath her skirt, as much from the chill as the descent. "I'm sure you say that to all the girls you seduce."

"Here." He drew her closer. His voice was touching her ear and she felt her arms around him and their bodies as one. "I have never felt anything like this. Not even close. Just being with you is enough. Like this." Their lips met, uncertain at first, and then they were kissing again.

"What is the matter?" he said, pausing to look into her eyes. "Why are you so sad?"

She sniffed. "I don't want us to end." Then they were embracing again, melting into the dappled shade. "Why can't we just stay here, Thomas? Be normal, like other people, marry. You can reinvent yourself, go to ground. Others have done it. Goodness, there's enough sympathy among the *volk*. Even Papa will come round when he knows your intentions are honourable."

"Impossible. You must know that. Our countries are at war."

"Our countries maybe, but not our people. Not all of them, anyway." She held him tighter; it felt like there wasn't a part of their bodies that wasn't touching. Thinking, what harm would it do to go all the way, just this once, a first for her but he'd guide her, surely. It wasn't strictly right, but she loved him and he her and tomorrow there might not be another chance. "Don't leave me, Thomas," she cried. "Please." She was holding him so tightly her fingers were digging into his back. "I'll do anything. I mean, anything." She plunged into a kiss again, probing, left and right and wrapping her legs about him closer still and he seemed to be responding which excited her even more.

Just then a woman's voice warbled from beyond the bushes— a girl's name, again and again. Then a child broke into the clearing, a girl no older than six with knee-length socks. When she saw them in the pond she was owl-eyed and gaped.

"Oh ..." Anna gasped as she drew back. Thinking in the heat of the moment how cruel, how terribly, terribly cruel life can be—not how the interruption could have saved an embarrassment far worse or the guilt—that came later. "Never mind us," she was conscious of how wet and crinkled her skirt was, "we were just on our way." She motioned towards the pool. "The water's lovely. You should try it."

Thomas took her hand and shuffled past the girl, then her mother, and hurried along the slate path, passing the thatched tea house and finally reached the taxi rank on Rhodes Drive. He led her to the line of taxis. "Now," he lifted a hand, "we'll go separately. I'll take the next." The driver acknowledged the call, and his engine spluttered to life. "And Anna ..."

She tensed at the knowledge of what he would say next. The taxi rolled closer.

"I will defuse it. I am trained in explosives."

"You're going to thwart a plot sponsored by Germany itself? That will make you a traitor. They won't even bother to give you a proper trial, will they? You can't, Thomas, they'll ..."

"There is no need to worry. Think about it. If I am successful, no one will need to know. I will escape via another tunnel and be out of the city centre before anyone tries to look. And the U-boat ... we have a secret rendezvous on Sunday."

"But what about your deputy? Kurt is in communication with him."

"Fischer? Thomas dismissed her with a wave. "Our families go back three generations. He would never betray me."

"And if you're wrong?"

"Listen to me, Anna. It's too dangerous. You mustn't attempt anything."

Something in his manner more than his words reminded her of her father. The put downs, the condescension. "You expect me to stay home and wait for your call?" She thought of her father, the threat to Parliament, her country. "Not a chance."

The taxi door swung open and Thomas held it. The sudden hardness in his face chilled her. "I think I know you well enough now not to try to persuade you. But let it be on record that I warned you." Then his face softened and he kissed her forehead. "Please," he whispered, "wait. You must trust me."

It felt like a punch to her stomach. She was about to express her thoughts but stopped. "Goodness, this is so difficult, what must I say? Be careful, and remember that, that I love you. It feels so right to say that now. Why, I don't know. These few days with you have been the hardest but most wonderful in my life, and I don't want them to end, not ever." She closed the door and wound down the window, not caring if he saw her tears. "Watch out for yourself," she blew him a kiss, in defiance of her guilt and the taxi pulled away. "And don't leave a message when you phone. Elizabeth's totally unreliable."

As the taxi wound along Rhodes Avenue, she clung to her last image of him, standing on the kerb, expressionless and unwaving. Tears rolled freely down her cheeks—not so much from the agony of having to choose, but from the implications of the choice she'd already made. By now she was convinced she'd never see him again—that, even if he did foil the plot, he'd be caught or killed afterwards. And this wasn't all: her father was in mortal danger, and with him the entire Union cabinet. She exhaled. The prospect of her country and its naval bases falling into Nazi hands was beyond contemplation. It could even turn the tide of the war. No, she couldn't leave all this in the hands of one man, until recently, a sworn enemy. She had no choice but to act.

29

WHEN ANNA STEPPED OUT of the taxi at the corner of Hof and Orange, the sun had long since sunk behind the nek, and dusk was settling over the city. She walked to her apartment, half expecting her father to be camped on the doorstep. If he'd got her message from the cable car operator, he'd be fuming.

Rounding the hedge, she was relieved to find the way clear. Had he gone up the cable car to look for her himself? She felt a wave of guilt. Beneath his infuriating overprotectiveness was an ocean of care.

The first thing she noticed was the tidiness of the kitchen. Elizabeth must have been out all day. The table was clear except for a scrap of paper wedged under the pepper grinder. Two messages in Elizabeth's handwriting. Both from Anna's father, demanding that she call him.

She had to make the phone call right away or she'd lose the courage, so she delved into her bag. The business card shook so violently in her hand that she could barely read the detective's number through her tears. She glanced at the front door, wishing she'd bolted it from within. It would be terrible if Elizabeth walked in now. With the index finger of her other hand she felt for the digit on the receiver's dial, flicked it clockwise and released. Then she held her hand over the microphone and waited for the exchange to answer.

"Number please," said the operator.

Anna read out the digits from the card, keeping her voice low to disguise its tremble.

"Just a moment, my dear."

She flipped the card to occupy herself as she waited. Outside the kitchen window the garden was still in the afterglow of sunset, the flat top of the mountain silhouetted against the western sky. She imagined herself on the ledge, eagles circling, the back of his hand brushing her cheek. Elope on a U-boat? Thomas' proposition, though ridiculous, resonated in her heart. But there was more to life than flights of fancy. Duty, for one thing, and the love of blood and country.

Her daydream was interrupted by a tone on the line.

"De Villiers *wat praat.*"

Hearing Afrikaans was somehow reassuring. Anna's mouth opened but no words came out.

The detective coughed and switched to English. "Hello, who's there?" A pause. "Listen here, can I help you?"

"It's Anna."

"Ah." The line went quiet. Then a scratching. Silent again. "The elusive Van der Vliet girl. You have come to your senses at last. Good."

"I need to speak with you," she said. "It's urgent."

A pause and a click on the line. "I'm listening."

"In person, detective. Today still."

"I'd like nothing more, ma'am. You can be sure." He rasped another cough. "But I'm afraid it won't be possible to meet this evening. I have an engagement now, with my boss and his boss. But perhaps we can meet for dinner. Or later, when I'm off duty."

"And when would that be?"

"That's the trouble. You can never tell how long these bleddy meetings go on for. I can guess half past eight, maybe nine."

Anna berated herself for not role playing the possible inter-sections of the two halves of her hasty plan. "Please, sir, can we make it earlier?" She cast around in vain for inspiration. "I have a date tonight that I can't change. I've already messed him around once. Please, sir. It's extremely important."

There was another scratch, and a sound like a coin flipping on the back of a hand. "Are you in any imminent danger tonight, Miss van der Vliet. Yourself, that is?"

"Uh, no."

"Then I am sorry, it will have to wait until tomorrow." The line crackled. "I tell you what, how about breakfast? I know a place on Parliament Square. On the corner. Oh, of course, you were there yourself this morning."

"Detective, what I need to tell you is far too important to wait for your bacon and eggs."

"With respect, ma'am, I will be the judge of that." There was a sound on the line like the shifting of a chair. "If only you will trust me. Come on, tell me what the story is. What do you have to lose?"

Anna despaired. She should have known it would come to this. Laying herself bare on the airwaves. Not having grown up with a telephone on the farm, she was far more comfortable conversing face to face. Now there was no choice. She inhaled to steady herself, said, "I can blow the operation wide open for you, Detective de Villiers. Names, dates, places."

"Did you say operation? Can you elaborate please? I need to know we are singing the same tune."

"Listen, you know perfectly well. You asked me to call if I had—"

He coughed to interrupt her. "Forgive me, but when I interviewed you at lunch the other day, you and your father, you were still as a mouse. This afternoon you are up the mountain cavorting with an enemy agent, disappear, and now, like magic, you want to tell me everything you know."

"Please, sir." She felt like putting the receiver down; she was hyperventilating. "You must know how hard this is for me."

"That's just the problem. How am I supposed to believe you're ready to give up your own father?" There was a pause. "I'm right, aren't I? That's what you're proposing."

She closed her eyes. "I have no intention of throwing my father to the wolves. Yes, that's what you people are. Before I tell you a word of what I know, you have to promise me he won't be charged."

His laugh was the chug of a steam train. "Put yourself in my boots, Miss van der Vliet. Why would I do something like that? Your father is a traitor, and you know it. He deserves to spend the rest of his days behind bars—if he's that lucky—and I intend to make sure he does, so help me God. No ma'am. Me and my men have spent ten hours a day for weeks building this case. There's no way I'm going to chuck that down the drain."

Anna felt a glimmer of hope. He had taken the bait. All she had to do was reel him in. "I understand," she said. "I'd feel the same in your shoes." She paused. "You've got your man, so why not make an example of him. It could deter all the other German and Japanese sympathisers. Especially those in your own ranks."

"I knew you were a smart girl."

"Woman, Inspector. I'm nineteen. If I call you by your rank, please be courteous enough to address me as an adult."

"Ma'am."

"Thank you. Now, suppose I told you that my father's alleged involvement is just the periscope of the submarine, so to speak. That I can show you what's really going on."

There was more crackle on the line. Then the strike of a match and a pause. "I'm listening."

"All right. I'll tell you everything you need to know, but only in person."

"Fine, but it will have to be tomorrow."

"If you insist. But no later than half past eight."

"Very well. My office then. I'll make coffee. Boere style."

"Detective …" Anna was distracted by the gate squeaking outside. She hoped against hope it wasn't Elizabeth. "Before I come in, there's something you have to promise me."

"I'm a policeman, ma'am, not a priest."

"Well, then you're just going to have to change your uniform."

"I'll stick with the one I have, ma'am."

"Then I suggest you take a photograph of yourself in it. Because if you don't take the opportunity I'm offering by its horns, there won't be much of a career for you in the force."

"Tough talk for a lady."

"Why don't you just say, 'tough talk'? Why the patronising?"

"I'll try harder next time."

For once Anna felt good being angry. It steeled her for what she had to say next. "Listen, I have all the evidence you need."

He scoffed. "I've got enough to put your father away for life. If he's lucky."

The gate outside squealed shut. A familiar whistle outside torpedoed any hope that it wasn't Elizabeth. "I'm about to have company," she said. "Let me put it this way: whatever you're accusing my father of is child's play compared with what I have. It will be the case of the decade, maybe the century. National, even international fame for you. Not bad for an uneducated *boereseun* from Pretoria."

"What is it you want me to promise?"

"Something you should find easy." There was a dangling of keys on the other side of the front door. "I want you to arrest my father."

"Excuse me?"

"You heard." A key scratched to find its hole. "Tonight, straight after this call. Take him to safe custody and hold him just for twenty-four hours."

Silence. Elizabeth swore through the crack in the door, more key scratching.

"You there, detective?"

"Ja, ja. I'm trying to understand you. First you say we mustn't charge your father. Then we must arrest him. I think you've had too much sun."

"I said arrest and hold, not charge him. And only you and I are to know about this. Hear me?"

"Hold on a minute."

"We can talk as adults. We're equals, in a manner of speaking."

"I can't simply arrest someone without reason. We're a civilised—"

"Nonsense. You know as well as I do that you can lock someone up on a whim for days, weeks even, without trial."

"But a prominent politician? It would be a scandal."

Elizabeth shoved at the door. It shuddered but didn't open. She swore.

Anna said, "Better that than being forever known as the law enforcement officer who turned down the chance to save his government."

"Government? What are you talking about?"

"I'll explain over coffee."

"Phew. I don't know what your game plan is, lady, but it worries me."

"That's the first time I've heard a man admit he's worried.

So, are we singing from the same sheet?"

"Ha. You're protecting your father, aren't you? He's got mixed up in something much bigger, and now you're trying to—"

"Would you prefer that I find someone else to tell?"

Static consumed the line and then faded. "Detective?"

"Ja, ja. I'll see what I can do."

"That isn't good enough. I need your word."

"And if I can't give it?"

The door flew open with a gust of the South Easter. Elizabeth stood at the threshold, a paper shopping bag under each arm, and a puzzled expression.

"Well then," she turned to the window, keeping Elizabeth at the periphery of her vision, "it's goodbye and good luck."

"*Eina*," he said after a pause too long. "They breed them tough on the *platteland*. All right, I'll do it."

Anna turned from her friend, spoke towards the wall. "He's at 425 Victoria Road, Seapoint, flat 213."

"Good. I'll have confirmation tomorrow. My office, half past eight. The address is on the back of my card."

Elizabeth stepped in and the door slammed shut in the wind. "What's all this about?" she said, dropping her bags on the table, which were so full they stood on their own merit. She whisked a strand of hair from her face. "You haven't been talking to Prince Charming again, have you? I don't think he's good for you."

Anna backed towards the stove. "You're right. But it's like I keep going back for more."

Elizabeth applied lipstick to her pout. "It's the story of my life." She looked for a mirror. "Listen, if he's too much to handle, I'll happily take him off your hands."

Anna smiled inside. Elizabeth's shallowness was almost endearing. The tonic of a polar opposite. "Trust me," she said, "this one's way too complicated. But I'll spare you the temptation." She scrounged for matches. "Sorry Beth. I love you. Some tea?"

Elizabeth shifted her attention from her own reflection to the clock above the mantelpiece. The hour hand called seven. One of her shopping bags toppled to reveal an assortment of blouses. "I need a Scotch after that."

"Help yourself," Anna said, "it's too early for me." She dropped tea leaves in the pot. "You sure?"

"Not for me, thanks." Elizabeth picked up her bags. "I'm going to try these on again." Then she stopped. She pointed to the messages on the table. "I take it you read those. I've never heard your father so agitated. Even in Parliament."

"Ja. He worries too much. I was just on the mountain again. Sorry, I should have told you. It was spontaneous. Such a beautiful day."

"Yes, that's why I went shopping."

"Funny. Listen, do me a favour, please, call Papa for me. Tell him I'm safe and sound."

"Anna, what is it? He's your father."

"I know, it's just that we've been arguing. Please. Just this once."

Elizabeth nodded. "Oh, and before I forget." She reached into her handbag and waved a pair of movie tickets at Anna. "That cocky chap dropped by again earlier. The one with the thick Afrikaans accent. Said he'd changed to the late show, hoped you'd reconsider."

"Fanus?" Anna's first response was irritation. But then relief. She plucked the tickets from Elizabeth's hand and studied them. They were for the quarter to nine showing of *Suspicion*. She closed her eyes and smiled in thankfulness. Things were going her way at last, helping her to execute the plan she'd thought up earlier. Fanus was still in love with her, that much was obvious. It would be easy now. She could pretend to fall for him and when they got close she could convince him to abandon the whole thing. At the very least she could get him to talk about the plot and pass that on to Thomas or De Villiers.

"That's his number in pencil on the back," Elizabeth said. "Two admirers at one time, hey. You really are the flavour of the month."

"It's not what you think."

"Oh yes?"

Anna put the kettle on the stove. "He's an old boyfriend, in a manner of speaking. Goodness, I hardly kissed him."

"Still." Elizabeth adjusted her bra strap. "You've got options, while the rest of us can only wait for this bloody war to end. Don't tell me there aren't advantages to growing up a Boer."

"That isn't fair." Anna kicked a chair further under the kitchen table. "Almost half our volunteers are Afrikaans. Not to mention the coloureds. You English are too quick to believe your own propaganda."

"Hang on now," Elizabeth poured a splash of Bells in a tumbler. "Didn't you say you were English yourself?" She added a thumb of water. "Half, anyway."

Anna opened the lid of the kettle and watched bubbles form on the bottom and rise to the surface, one after another. Suddenly she was overcome with melancholy. "Truth be told, I don't know what I am."

"What's the matter, my dear? Your mind is somewhere else again."

Anna's shoulder's drooped. "I'd be lying if I denied it."

Elizabeth put an arm about her shoulders. "You really have fallen for the handsome officer, haven't you? I told you he was a heartbreaker. Poor girl. Come, let me help you with that." She poured the water into the teapot and stirred. "I thought his ship had sailed?"

Anna shook her head. "Soon." She added a dash of milk to her cup and passed it to Elizabeth, waiting for her friend to pour. "But it doesn't matter. It's over."

"Drink up," Elizabeth said. "That's better. I know you don't think so now, but you'll get over it. Believe me, I've been there. Remember that Welsh fellow last semester? My God, he was perfect. I thought my heart was going to break."

Anna sipped and allowed the tea to comfort her throat. "It's not just that he's leaving." She sniffed.

"What then?" Elizabeth's hand was on her shoulder again.

"I can't tell you," Another tear ran down the length of her cheek. "That's the worst of it."

"For heaven's sake," she said. "What can possibly be so heavy you can't share it with a friend?"

Anna pulled a tissue from her sleeve and dabbed her nose. "It's too terrible," she said. "What's been happening on the farm, what's about to happen. And I'm, I'm …"

"Slow now." Elizabeth pulled out a chair. "Why don't you sit down? We'll get through this together. Promise."

They sat, chairs a foot apart. Anna looked at Elizabeth through a blur. She felt a twinge of guilt at her friend's compassion. It was a side she hadn't noticed before.

"Tell me about the farm," Elizabeth said.

"No." Anna felt calm return. "I can't burden you with this. Not now. It wouldn't be fair."

"Well, all right then. If that's the way you want it. Shame, you really have had it rough lately. A love that got away. Fighting with your father." She pointed at the tickets. "At least somebody still loves you. What did you say his name was?"

Anna sat upright. "You're right. It's time I stopped feeling sorry for myself." She looked at the tickets. Back row, centre. "Fanus. Fanus Prinsloo."

"Prinsloo? You telling me the fellow who dropped by for you was Fanus Prinsloo? Of Prinsloo Granite? Mercy, even I've heard of them. Listen," she shifted her chair closer, caught Anna's eyes. "He's no oil painting. That much I'll give you. And that accent, it would grate the most patient. But a Prinsloo? You'd be set for life, my girl. What are you thinking?"

Anna stood. "You know, Elizabeth, you're right. Thank you." She straightened the tickets. "Fanus might not be a patch on my officer friend, but he's solid. How could I not at least give it a chance?" She studied the tickets again. "Besides, I do love Cary Grant. Don't you?"

30

THE PAVEMENT IN FRONT of the bioscope was awash with light. Above was a giant poster framed in neon, featuring Joan Fontaine in a swoon with Cary Grant against a backdrop of red. "Each time they kissed there was the thrill of love … the threat of murder!" ran the tagline. Fanus was in the foyer reading a poster. His hands were clasped behind his back, the buttons of his suit jacket straining. Anna paused at the entrance. The idea of getting close to him had seemed such a simple idea just a couple of hours ago but the moment she'd put the phone down she'd been wracked by guilt. She hated any kind of deception, especially leading men on. And then there was the risk of being exposed.

Just then Fanus turned and saw her. He smiled, not with surprise or affection, but with pride. Then he bowed his head enough to expose his middle parting.

"*Vaderland*, but you look beautiful," he said, and kissed her on the lips.

"Thanks." Anna reached for her shoulder, forgetting she was in a strapless dress. Her gaze was diverted to the glint of his shoes. "You're smart for the cinema. What's the occasion?"

"Does there have to be?" he said. "I'm just pleased you're here."

Three old ladies brushed past, leaving a trail of perfume and mothballs. One looked up at a poster with the expression of a teenage girl with a crush. Another gave Fanus a dirty look and confided in her friend.

"You're nothing if not persistent," Anna said as they trailed the threesome through the entrance. The ruby carpet was soft underfoot and the walls were adorned with posters advertising coming attractions. Fanus led her to the back of the queue for the snack bar. Ahead, a youngster in a cropped waistcoat and bow tie was plunging a trowel into a stash of popcorn.

"I was surprised when you returned my call," he said.

"How so?" Anna avoided his eyes and smiled at the server. The lad blushed and asked the couple in front of them for their order.

"You've hardly been forthcoming lately."

"Ag, you know." Anna opened her purse and closed it. She tried to force a blush. "A girl can't resist a man like you forever." She smiled with innocence. "I can't fault you for effort."

Without asking her, Fanus ordered two large popcorns and Coca-Colas. Then turned to her. "That's what you like, hey?"

Anna shrugged. "The consummate lawyer. Always knows the answer before asking the witness a question." She shook salt on her popcorn and scooped up her drink. There was something comforting in the familiarity of holding them to her chest and the smell of seasoning and butter.

The usher behind the cordon looked cadaverous, old enough to be a great-grandfather. As Anna and Fanus approached he pointed to a notice board and tapped his watch.

They paused under the poster for *Suspicion*. "I heard it's based on a book," Fanus said. "*Before the Fact*. No doubt you've read it."

Anna elbowed him. "You think I lie around all day consuming novels, don't you?"

"Not all day."

"Fine Art is harder than you think," she said. "Try three creative projects simultaneously. And that's not counting the theory. Art is work, you know, just like the law. A mistress every bit as demanding as the High Court. Except there's no judge telling you when to adjourn."

"A mistress, hey." The residue of his smirk lingered in the curl of his lips. "If only she paid you for your troubles."

Anna dug her fingers into the popcorn. "The reward is in the doing."

"I like that. Sounds like one of those quotes you get in a Christmas cracker."

"I'm being serious," she said. "When you're busy with a sculpture, same thing for a painting, every faculty is engaged and it's as if all the brokenness of this world never existed, and everything makes sense. How can you put a price on that? Okay, don't worry. I don't expect you to understand."

He looked hurt. "I might be a man of commerce but that doesn't mean I don't have an appreciation of the arts."

"Consuming beauty is different from creating it."

His lips suggested a smile. "That's what I love about you. You're so different; you keep me honest."

She lowered her eyes, not trusting her reaction. Her first instinct was to challenge. Call his patronising what it was. Instead she said, "You're not such a bad sort, yourself, you know."

He took the popcorn and Coke from her and put them aside. Then he took her hands in his. "I was being serious earlier, you know."

She still couldn't bring herself to face him.

"We were made for each other, Anna. I've known it from the time you passed me the note in class in Standard Five. 'I think you're cute' you wrote. Remember? Always spoke your mind. It's a pity I was so shy in those days. We could have been going out since then. Think about it."

Anna focused on the backs of his hands. They were slender and freckled with tufts of blonde hair—the hands of an intelligent man, more lawyer than farmer. She tried to imagine waking up to them every morning of her life, and to his lack of humour. But every compromise had a price. Besides, the idea wasn't entirely unbearable. He had his strengths. Though narrow in his views, he felt deeply. A patriot, albeit flawed. And rich.

"Oh," he dropped her hands, checked his watch. "I clean forgot."

She could face him now. "What is it?"

"Forgive me, I'm going to have to leave you." He glanced at the programme board. "Just for a minute, promise. A phone call."

She tried to feel upset. "But we were having such fun, chatting like this. Like old times." At the bioscope entrance the cadaver was unhooking a rope from a stanchion. "The show's about to start," Anna said. "What can possibly be so urgent?"

He patted his jacket, fished a coin from a pocket. "Ag man, we had a terrible accident this morning, a rock blast gone to hell." He winced. "One of our workers died, poor bugger; the other's in hospital."

"Oh, I'm so sorry." She waved towards the door. "Go. Cary Grant can wait."

Relief broke on Fanus's face and he marched to the exit. To pass the time Anna wandered over to a couch near the snack bar and picked up a dog-eared movie guide and started to leaf through tit. As she skimmed the captions her mind reviewed her performance. Fanus appeared to have taken her at face value. She was off to a good start.

When she turned the last page of the magazine she felt the first pang of worry. How long could it take to pay respects to the wounded? Besides, it was out of character for Fanus to be so concerned about the welfare of his staff. She picked up another magazine. It was the *Horse and Hound* with a cover photograph of a fox hunt. She replaced it and got up for a visit to the bathroom instead.

His voice at her ear jolted her. "I'm so sorry."

"Fanus." She swirled about. "That was quick."

"Told you. I hate to miss the start of a film. Especially a thriller."

"How is he?"

"Who? Oh, yes, of course, he's fine. Just slurring his words. But you never know. These guys are hard to understand at the best of times."

"Will he make it?

Fanus chuckled. "Cracked ribs, pelvis, leg snapped in two. It's a wonder he's still breathing. But he'll live. They always do."

"Oh, stop it."

"There you go again. Always taking their side. A man would swear you loved them more than your own people."

"People are people."

A hubbub of voices distracted them. Moments later people began emerging from the cinema door. The usher swung the cordon clear and patrons fanned out across the foyer towards the exit. Without exception they were couples, mostly elderly. When the last had either detoured to the bathrooms or passed, the usher replaced the cordon and stood sentry.

"How did it happen?" she said.

"What was that again?"

"The accident. You said it was a blast gone wrong."

"That's right."

"Well, isn't it just a question of sticking a piece of dynamite in a hole and lighting a fuse? How is it possible to get stuck under falling rock?"

"You ask me." He laughed. "These guys are capable of anything. You'd swear they had a death wish." When she didn't laugh, he added, "Actually it's a lot more complicated than some Tom and Jerry cartoon where the person stands back and watches the fuse burn. Any number of things can go wrong. A break in the fuse, the angle of lie, a wet patch. It takes years of training to get it right, and even then, accidents happen. Why do you think every farmer and his dog hasn't opened a quarry? *Bliksem*, enough of them have mountain acreage."

"And the dynamite? Do you use the same stuff you gave Papa that time to blast the kloof road?

He eyed her. "Why are you suddenly so interested?"

Only a handful of stragglers hovered about the foyer, waiting for their partners to return from the cloakrooms.

"Ag, I was just thinking, we'd better be careful next time we try it on the farm. Papa wants to expand the road up near the dam. You know how proud he is, he wouldn't dream of calling in a professional."

Fanus laughed. "Just lets the workers take the risk."

"That's not funny. A life's not worth a penny to you if it doesn't have a pale skin or blue eyes, does it? Shame on you." She prayed he wouldn't make a move. Hold her hand or worse. How had she ever found him attractive? Perhaps it was his views more than his person that repelled her now. Had he grown more bigoted or she more enlightened? In any case, she'd come this far, she'd have to go through with the pretence.

"Come now, Anna. What's all this concern about working conditions? Next thing it'll be pay. Why bother yourself?"

"Common decency, Fanus. Remember that concept?"

"You're way too soft on them. Trust me, they won't return the favour. Look how they're threatening to strike, just when our government can least afford it. Not that I care for the government in this case. They deserve it."

The cadaver swapped cordons and prepared the way for the next lot of patrons to enter. The three old ladies wandered past again, averting their gaze.

"That's a distortion," she said. "Don't you read the news? The Communist Party's a hundred per cent behind the war effort."

The usher took the tickets from the last of the entrants.

"*Ge.* Only because Hitler invaded Russia. The two-faced jackals. The day before they were marching in protest."

"I can't disagree on that one," she said. "But not every worker's a communist. You know that."

"Ha, just give them a chance. Union bastards. If they come near our business I'll kick their arses to Cairo." Fanus handed the tickets to the usher. "I'm sorry, we shouldn't be arguing about something so silly. Can we agree to disagree? Just for tonight."

She wanted to slap him. Instead, she swallowed, said. "Sure."

The carpet inside seemed even thicker than in the foyer. The theatre was empty but for a handful of scattered patrons. Fanus whispered to an usher, who led them down the ramp. They stopped now and again to read the row numbers glowing on the floor. To Anna's dismay, they continued to the back row which was darker and unoccupied. There they sank into their seats with the popcorn and Cokes between them.

First came the silent advertisements, flipping like a slow-motion slide show. One showed a car battery with a cartoon mechanic shrugging and holding both ends of a jumper lead; in another a glamourous woman blew smoke while clutching a carton of cigarettes. A handful of trailers followed, and then the cinema darkened. Whispering broke out as the patrons waited while the projector room whirred behind them. Once the reels had been changed, the screen flickered to life and an aerial pan of the Hollywood sign appeared, followed by the start of the feature.

"Makes me think of you," Fanus whispered when Joan Fontaine made an appearance. "Quite the lady."

"Stuck up, you mean? Thanks."

"*Nee wat*, you'll see."

Anna kept her arms to her sides, conscious of his slightest movement. Expecting him to make a move at any time, she was happy for the reprieve. Finally, when Grant and Fontaine had eloped and come unstuck, his hand settled on her thigh. "Why is it," he said, leaning into her ear, "that a beautiful woman always falls for a cad?"

Anna stiffened. Fanus was telling her something. She berated herself for being taken by surprise; nothing he did was without intent. In her mind she ran through the plot of the film: prim and proper McLaidlaw falls for a rascal in spite of her parents' warnings, and after an attempted suicide has a sticky end in prison. It was no coincidence that they were watching *Suspicion*. Fanus had intended it as a parody of her and Thomas, and a warning. "Ag, it only happens in the movies," she said, trying a giggle. "We're far more pragmatic in real life."

"You sure of that?"

"How can we be sure of anything?"

"No need to get deep on me again—I was asking a question at face value."

"Oh, come on," she nudged him. "What do you want me to say? Anyway, how would I be able to answer—the men in my life so far have been difficult characters, but decent."

"*Ge.*" His hands were on his lap again, attention on the credits rolling down the screen.

"What's that supposed to mean?"

"I shouldn't have to spell it out."

"Listen." She poked him in the ribs. "Jealousy doesn't suit you. You're a bigger man than that." She wiggled in her seat. "Of course I've gone out with other people since we broke up. Was I supposed to pine away like a princess in a turret until you rode back into my life?"

"Yes, but a foreigner?"

"All right. If you must know. Yes, there was something between Thomas and me. But so what? I find many men attractive. I'm in the prime of my life—it's natural. And guess what, if we'd been married twenty years it would still happen. It doesn't mean anything comes of it." She sensed it was time to shift gear, put her hand on his knee. "What we have is way stronger than a childish flutter."

Anna's assurances appeared successful and Fanus settled back in his seat. They held hands but didn't speak again until the film ended. She rose while the credits were rolling, and they filed out with the dozen or so other patrons into the light of the foyer.

The snack bar was deserted and there was no sign of the popcorn server. Feeling panicky, she excused herself to the restroom. There, after washing her hands, she stood in front of the mirror and stared at herself. Shrinking isn't an option, she repeated to herself. There's too much at stake.

When she returned Fanus was waiting for her at the couch.

"I've arranged a car to fetch us," he said. "Five minutes. We may as well relax so long."

Anna sat at the far end of the couch, legs crossed. Fanus sat half way along it, facing her with his arm along the back rest. He waited for the last of the couples to pass and said, "Have you thought further about what I proposed this morning?"

"Huh?"

"You know, you and I, giving it a go?"

Anna inhaled sharply. Waited. A great deal would depend on how she responded. Though she'd rehearsed her words a dozen times on the way to the bioscope, she still felt naked and frozen in the moment.

"Well, have you?"

"Do we have to talk about this now?" The first lines carried the biggest risk and had to be nuanced. She could almost hear her heart thumping. "Can't we just enjoy each other's company? Take it one day at a time ..."

"Under normal circumstances, I would agree." His eyes were sunken and seemed too close together for comfort. "But times are far too strange for that. In fact," he looked away, "they're about to get completely mad. For a while, anyway."

His palm on hers felt cold for summer and too smooth for a farmer. She needed to reel him in slowly. "What do you mean?"

"I can't tell you exactly. You just have to trust me."

Anna stifled a retort but couldn't stop her wince. A couple appeared from the theatre exit and wandered past. Fanus waited for them to drift out to the street. Then he said, "I need to know you're with me, by my side."

Things were going too fast. "How do you mean?"

"The war is at a turning point," he said. "In so many places. Take Singapore. The garrison is going to surrender any day now. The Japanese will take India in months, I promise. You don't have to be a prophet to know what will be next. Already they have submarines off Mozambique."

"South Africa?" Anna feigned surprise. "That's preposterous. The sea lanes are way too important. The Allies will never let that happen."

"That's what they said about Manchuria and the Philippines. That lying bastard Churchill is still saying it about Singapore." He shuddered. "Sorry, my *skattie*, I didn't want to go on about politics. Something far more important is at stake for us." He took her free hand and stepped closer till his suit jacket touched her dress.

"What are you doing?"

He dug into his pocket. Then he was opening a box, then a cloth.

"I love you Anna. You have no idea how much." He drew the ring out between his thumb and index finger. Held it up as if for payment. "Will you marry me?"

Anna felt her stomach turn. She'd meant to tease him, encourage his devotion. Now he was diving straight in and asking her to marry him. She shifted the strap of her handbag further up her shoulder and looked to the usher for salvation. He was still nowhere to be seen so she stared at her feet. "You honour me. I'm …" She paused to buy time. The thought of living the rest of her life with Fanus may have appealed to her in her early teenage years of fantasy, but now it was awful. But in terms of her plan to infiltrate the conspiracy, it was perfect. She could demand a full explanation. And what better time than now?

"So, you accept?" His Adam's apple bobbed.

"No … What I mean to say is, have you spoken to Papa?"

"Many times. He's a hundred per cent in agreement."

"One moment," she said, withdrawing her hand. "This is such a big question." She allowed an appropriate pause.

"And before I even try to answer, I need you to promise me something."

"*My lief,*" he said, "anything."

The foyer was empty. Outside, an urchin had his face pressed up to the glass of the window. Anna leaned towards Fanus, her lips almost brushing his cheek. "I know what you're planning," she whispered.

"What?" He straightened. "What are you talking about?

"The plot," she said. Confidence was all important now. There was no retreat. "To blow up Parliament."

Fanus looked shaken. "I, I don't, that's the strangest thing I've ever heard."

"Don't play dumb," she said. "I've been in the tunnels, seen the dynamite."

"Tunnels? Now, now, slow down."

"That's why you were there, wasn't it? Prinsloo Granite's explosives. I saw them myself."

His lips moved before his words. "I don't understand." He looked her up and down. "You mean you were there, crawling about. How could you?"

"How could a woman, you mean?" He looked momentarily out of sorts.

"I'm not your average *poppie*, Fanus. If you're going to marry me you'd better come to terms with it."

"I don't understand." He was recovering his composure. "When we met for tea yesterday, you must have known. Why didn't you say anything?"

"Hang on," she said. "It's you who owes me an explanation."

"How so?"

"Did you expect me to agree to marry you and then discover you're a rebel?"

"A patriot."

She felt a rush of anger. He really did believe his own propaganda. "What's the difference in this case? People die when you blow up buildings. Innocent people."

"Every cause worth fighting for involves sacrifice."

"Words are cheap. Though I suppose for a lawyer that isn't strictly true."

"That's funny," he said without laughing. "No, the

time for talking is past. Where has Malan's blabbering in Parliament got us? Nowhere. Worse, we're pouring ever more resources into helping our sworn enemy. Pure-blood Afrikaners are dropping in the desert like the flies that lick them."

"Many more will die if your scheme goes ahead. My father, for one."

He held her shoulders. "*My liefling*, our men have been moving mountains to persuade him to boycott the session. Every day another angle. He's a stubborn man."

"So you wash your hands? Just like that? The end justifies the means." Anna shuddered. "Since I heard your voice down there, I've tried so hard to persuade myself otherwise." She shook her head. "You really are a fascist. If not a Nazi."

"That's unfair," he said. "All we want is a country our people can call their own. Civilised values. The church."

"You're dreaming," she said. "Van Rensburg, the Great Council, the lot of you, thinking you can bring back Kruger's Republic. Are we all supposed to ride around on horseback again, in wagons? Women in *kappies*? You're dinosaurs, young but obsolete." Anna watched his face redden and his chest expand. It was gratifying for a moment, until she remembered her mission. "Look, I'm sorry." She closed the gap between them until they were almost touching. "I didn't mean this to become a slinging match. We don't have to agree on politics." She felt him tense. "There's so much more to a successful union, isn't there?"

"You mean that?" His eyebrows rose. "You mean you'll …?"

She made the faintest of contact, breathed in and out so that her breasts lifted and fell beneath her dress. "Ag, Fanus, how can I put this?" She shifted her eyes to one side and then down. "You've been good to me. I know that. And despite everything I might have said in the past year, I'm still fond of you, more so now …" She looked at him wide-eyed. "But I'd be lying if I said I can be sure I love you. Not yet, anyway."

He recoiled.

"Hear me out," she continued. "What is love, really? Sometimes I think deep down it's more a curse than the blessing it's wrapped in." She edged closer until his chest pressed against hers. "You know, I'm starting to believe you may be right." She felt his hope swell. "Perhaps we could have a future together. If only …"

"What is it?" He took her hand. "Come, these people need to close up. Let's talk outside."

She felt herself shaking. She wished she'd thought things through properly. She'd never expected things to come to a head so quickly. But perhaps it was just as well. The plot was imminent. If she didn't act fast, it would be too late. It was time to throw the kitchen sink at the situation. She said, "I've told them."

Fanus stopped pulling her. They were in the entrance way. There were life-size posters in lit frames on either side of them with show times listed on black and white plugboards. He said, "What did you just say?"

"I've told the authorities."

"Told what? What are you talking about?"

She tried to read his thoughts through his eyes. "The plot against Parliament."

His reaction was calmer than she'd expected, more matter of fact, an absence of denial. "What authorities?"

"Special branch, Pretoria."

Though expressionless, his face looked pale against the backdrop of the street light. "Why?"

"Because I care for you." She waited for the half-truth to settle. A car rumbled past, then another.

"And you prove it by trying to destroy my life?"

"I didn't mention names," she said. "Just time and place."

"I don't believe you," he said. "Why would you be here with me like this if you'd ratted on us? No, you've never been a good liar, Anna. You're way too much of an open book."

"I'll take that as a compliment." She shrugged. "Abandon it, Fanus. There's still time."

"Impossible." He scanned the street, fixing on a pair of headlights approaching from around the bend. An unmarked Ford pulled up to the kerb and the rear door swung open. "Here it is, our company car. Let's go somewhere we can talk some more … I tell you what …"

Anna waited as he put his head inside. He was obviously conferring with the driver, but she couldn't hear anything.

Finished, he held the door for her again, said, "Come on, let's go to Signal Hill. It's such a romantic view from up there. And quiet."

"That would have been lovely," she said, clinging to a lamp-post. "But Elizabeth is expecting me. I'll walk for the fresh air. It's barely ten minutes."

"Come on," he said, holding the door open and showing her inside. "It's been a big evening, such a lot to talk about. We can't leave things in suspense like this, can we?"

The back seat was empty. Her better judgement urged her to stay away, but her mission was unfinished. Fanus was not yet persuaded. De Villiers had been too non-committal for her to be sure her father was safe. She needed to stay close to Fanus, if only to learn more.

Inside, the driver mumbled a greeting in English without turning. He wore a chauffeur's uniform with a peaked hat. His hairstyle was short back and sides. Without waiting for instructions, he slipped the clutch and steered them away from the kerb. Behind them, a taxi switched on its lights and pulled into the road. Was it following them? Unlikely. Anna dismissed it as a coincidence and stared ahead.

31

THE LIGHTS OF THE city faded and the mountain appeared darker and heavier as they snaked up Kloof Nek Road, so different from the same ride twelve hours earlier. Anna strained to make out the lower cable car station, recalling the splendour of the eagles' tango, the shattering radio, Thomas's proposal … He'd trusted her implicitly. And warned her.

She tensed as Fanus's shoulder pressed against hers as the car banked around the circle, passing the turnoffs to the cableway, Camps Bay and the Rotunda, then hugging left at the shoulder of Lion's Head. From there the road ascended again, dark and steep through pine boughs and starlight. Through the open window came wafts of pine and *fynbos* resin as the road straightened and then levelled. After a mile or so the city reappeared on their right and they passed a sign to the Kramat, a sacred site of the Cape's Muslims, then accelerated along the spine of the lion before slowing and banking around its rump at Signal Hill.

The car slowed to a crawl as the road widened into a parking lot. On the mountain side beside the steel lattice of the radar tower stood a Bedford truck without lights. Ahead and to their right a low wall enclosed the parking lot, forming a sweeping lookout beyond which lay a band of partly suppressed lights and dark blotches, and then the ocean. There wasn't a breath of wind, and a sliver of moon had risen, casting a dress train of glimmer over the sea.

"Here is fine," Fanus said, tapping the driver on the shoulder. They drew to a halt in front of the wall. "Let's stretch our legs."

Anna hesitated. Something didn't feel right.

"Come now," he said, taking her hand. "I don't bite."

Anna couldn't think of a good enough excuse to refuse, so, after glancing about uneasily, she allowed him to lead her across the parking lot to a low wall, where they sat, legs dangling over the front. For a while neither spoke and Anna found herself absorbed in the spread of the bay beneath them and the growl of distant waves.

"So what happens next?" he said after a long silence.

"That's a strange question."

"Well, I mean it. What do we do next?"

"You just asked me to marry you. Shouldn't you be taking the lead?"

"That would be right," he said, "if you were a normal sort of girl. Waiting on your man, I mean."

She didn't dare say anything.

He inhaled till his chest was puffed, said. "Why did you have to speak to De Villiers?"

A breeze began to ease down the slope, and Anna hugged herself to rub the goosebumps from her arms. "I said I had spoken to the Special Branch." Her voice was tenuous. "Who said anything about a De Villiers?"

His legs stopped swinging. "I have a little confession to make," he said. "My men convinced me they needed to tap your phone line."

"You what?" She thought of the conversation with De Villiers. The crackle on the line. "But how ...?" Elizabeth, of course. She'd invited him in.

"Your friend is something else, hey," Fanus smiled, apparently at the memory. "Do you know she propositioned me before I'd even finished my tea? Don't look so worried. We never did anything, no more than a kiss and a cuddle, is all. It was a necessary evil."

Anna struggled to swallow. "How could you, you ..."

"The real question is, how could we not? Imagine you blowing our plans out of the water like that. We'd be finished, man. In prison or hanging. I felt bad giving permission for the tap, I admit. But now? Hell, no. If anything, I was too trusting."

Anna felt an urge to get away. Like a claustrophobia, except in the open air. She tried to recall the conversation with De Villiers. How much had she told him? Either way, she had to try and bluff. "Give it up, Fanus. They know too much already. Going ahead now would be suicide, and you know it."

"If he knew so much, what were you so eager to tell him over breakfast tomorrow?"

For a moment she didn't have an answer.

"Come on, there's a better way than this fighting," he said, edging closer until their legs touched. "I understand why you wanted to do it. Sell us out, that is."

"Ag, don't say something like that. De Villiers has a file on every one of you. If you'd listened properly to our phone conversation, you'd know."

"*Ge*. Don't worry, *liefling*, I understand why you did it. To protect your father. It's all right. Any *opregte* Afrikaner would have done the same. Family before anything, except maybe God. I'm proud of you." He took her hand. "I meant what I said earlier. You're the only woman I've ever loved. Be my wife, Anna van der Vliet. Together we can achieve greatness."

Anna didn't know what to think. Was he being serious? Still wanting to marry the woman who's betrayed him and his mission? Impossible. Either he was deluded or trying to trap her.

She ripped her hand away. Sprang up from the wall. "I couldn't think of a worse fate," she said, starting towards the car. "Bye, I'm going."

"Stop acting like a child, I beg you," he called after her. "Be reasonable. It doesn't have to be like this, we have a future …"

The car shook as she jumped into the back seat and slammed the door shut. "To the bioscope," she ordered the driver. "I'll pay you whatever you want. Just hurry."

The driver adjusted his cap but stayed put.

"Go," she shouted.

He didn't budge. Anna hammered her fist on the seat back. "Move, damn it. What's wrong with you?"

Fanus appeared at the front passenger window and tapped on the glass. The driver leaned across and wound down the window and said, "Plan B, I suppose."

Anna froze in horror at the accent. "Kurt?"

"We meet again," he said as Fanus slipped into the seat beside him. "I am sorry it is not under more favourable circumstances." Then he fired the ignition and reversed the car.

As they approached a clump of trees at the far end of the lot, a stationary car revealed itself from the shadow. Anna's fingernails dug into the seat. It had an interior light on, albeit dim. She formed a scream in her mind.

"Looks like your sidekick is having a sleep," Kurt said to Fanus. "I thought you said he was dependable."

Anna leaned forward.

"Why do you think the worst of people?" Fanus asked. "PJ's back at the bunker. He's a good man. You'll see."

Anna felt quietly for the door handle, squeezed her fingers about the metal. She watched the bushes passing the window, imagining her thigh striking the asphalt.

The car thudded off the edge of the car park and they were off the tarmac and onto a dirt road, gaining speed with every bounce. To their left an intermittent fringe of pines was silhouetted on the lion's back. Opposite was a hedge of *fynbos* and before them openveld.

"There is nowhere to go," Kurt said, reading her mind. "You are not to attempt escape."

"Escape?" She leaned forward, pulling on the seat back. "Am I a prisoner now?"

He coughed.

"Fanus," she cried, feeling panicky. "Tell me that's not true."

He kept staring out the window. The wind had strengthened, and the tops of the trees bent away from the mountain.

"This is nonsense," she said, ripping at the door handle. With her foot she managed to open the door a few inches, but it was pushed back by the wind. "Let me out!"

Kurt turned to Fanus. "Your friend is a difficult one, *nicht so*?"

"That's enough," Fanus snapped. "Every courtesy, remember, even with Plan B." The car was bumping down a slope, getting steeper. Below in the distance was the overbite of the Sea Point promenade and a panorama of ocean.

The car braked in fits as a thicket of port jackson approached. Kurt switched off the ignition and killed the lights. The engine sighed and they waited. Ahead and below, a rectangular structure materialised from the dark, with a concrete slab for a roof and a steel door. After a minute or two the door opened a crack, followed by a torchlight flashing, then closed again.

"Wait here." Kurt got out and strode towards the bunker.

The door swung open and the figure of a man with a long beard filled the doorway. A rifle was slung diagonally across his chest. He shifted on his feet as Kurt approached. Without bothering to shake hands they proceeded to confer in hushed tones. Every so often they glanced back at the car.

Fanus tapped Anna on the knee. "That's Pieter-Johannes. My hostel roommate at Stellenbosch. Except he dropped out and joined the police. He's a good man."

"How can any of this be good? Murdering innocent people."

Fanus sighed. "Come on, it's war. There's a difference. War is all hell."

"William Tecumseh Sherman."

He stared at her. "How did you know?"

"I don't just read novels, believe it or not. You surprise me: quoting a Yankee general. I'd have thought you'd be more impressed with Stonewall Jackson."

"Yes, but he lost."

"Funny."

Just then there was a rap on the window and Kurt's face appeared, ghost-like in the moon-silvered light. "*Alles ist in ordnung.*"

Fanus stepped out and opened her door. "Come, *my lief.*"

"Don't you dare call me that."

"Come on," he said, "we really have to be going inside."

"Listen." Anna felt at her dress, damp and sticking to the seat. "There's something I want to clear up."

His hand went limp but remained extended. "What is that?"

"Back there. Kurt talked about Plan B. Were you always planning to lock me up if I didn't agree to marry you, and go along with your madness?"

"You must understand," he implored. "I don't act alone. There are dozens, no hundreds, not to mention the *volk*, who depend on the success of this operation." He took her hand. "There's still time. I promise, you won't regret it. There's a great future for us. You must believe me. Just give me your word and all this will go away."

"*Raus!*" Kurt had appeared behind them. "*Und macht schnell.*"

Fanus rose to face him. "That's enough German. You're in South Africa."

Anna pressed herself against the far seatback. Waited for the close-set eyes to peer into the car. "Don't touch me," she said, slapping his hand as it reached in.

"*Scheiße.*" Kurt withdrew it in a flash. "Here, Fanus, you sort your girl out. Remember, there is not much time."

Fanus's face appeared again, pleading. "Just come, now," he said. "You'll understand everything tomorrow. I'll give you another chance, promise."

"To hell with your promises," she said, shaking off his hand. "I'm not going anywhere."

The ground crunched outside. "Enough," Kurt called out. "You know where you have to be now, Fanus. PJ, *kommt hier.*"

There was harder crunching and the bearded giant's face appeared. His breath smelled of meat and garlic and his grip brooked no resistance. Anna felt a bolt of pain up her shoulder and in an instant she was out of the car with her wrists behind her back. "You'll never get away with this," she shouted as they approached the steps to the building. The door was of corrugated iron, braced by angle irons and heavy on its hinges and through a crack she could see a single bed. Alongside it was a table with a lit candle. "They know everything."

Behind her, PJ laughed. His breath was warm and foul.

The car revved and then was gone.

"Ask Fanus. It's true. You don't have a chance. I told the police everything."

She wriggled to free herself, but the giant's grip was unyielding.

"Don't be fooled," he said. "Our people are everywhere."

As the giant's hands shoved her onto the steps and towards the doorway Anna felt a wave of regret. Why had she taken De Villiers at his word? It was common knowledge that many in the police force were sympathetic to the *Ossewabrandwag*, if not active members.

Another push and a grunt from behind and she was stumbling inside. The stench of urine and charcoal was appalling.

Without warning she was shoved and fell on the bed. Her face pressed into a blanket that scratched and smelled of dust. She rolled over hastily and sat up.

The giant wasn't to be seen but Kurt stood in the doorway, his smile cold and brief. "You mustn't be so hard on Fanus," he said. "He really does love you. He just loves his country more."

"*Ge.*" Anna shook her head.

He straightened, stepped back. Behind him and outside, the giant stood erect, facing away.

"If you are thinking of escape," Kurt said, feeling for the door behind him. "Do not waste your time. I am told this bunker was designed to stop the *Kriegsmarine*. There is no chance a girl like you can do better. And just in case …" He had a smirk. "PJ will be spending the night on the stairs."

The door clanged shut, and after it came the click of a padlock. His footsteps trailed off and then the only sound was the wind teasing the doorway. Anna felt the walls closing in on her, pressing her down on the bed. To distract herself she bounced gently, testing. The bed was firmly sprung. On the table stood a jug of water and a glass. She filled the glass, sniffed it and drank. Then she stood. The low concrete roof felt oppressive, and she traced the soot ring cast by the candle. The room was only just longer than the bed and three-quarters as wide. A couple of feet from the door was a rectangle in the wall meshed with steel. It looked like it had once been a window but now it was bricked. She stood in front of the door, hammering her fists on the steel, her spirits sinking with every blow. When it felt like they were bleeding she stopped. Kurt had been right. There was no escape.

As she was about to lie down, there was the sound of the car sputtering to life. Then its headlights seeped in around the door for a second, brightened and faded with a scrunch of tyres. It was still again. She stood up and began pacing, trying to think.

"Pieter-Johannes," she ventured.

There was silence, then the flicker of a match.

"I know you're there." She switched to Afrikaans. "Answer me."

"I'm sorry," he said. "I am under instructions not to talk to you."

"I need to go to the bathroom."

"There was a pause. "There's a bucket. On the other side of the bed. And paper."

"*Sies.* You'd let a lady go through that? Come, you're a better man than that."

There was a shifting of feet on gravel and the wind.

"Listen," she said. "I know you think you're just doing your duty."

The wind whistled under the door.

She waited for what felt like a minute. "You're a patriot, aren't you? Just like my father."

The wind sucked and went silent.

"You know him, don't you? Van der Vliet. MP for Bredasdorp."

There was a scent of tobacco, rich and sweet, but no response.

"Why do you want to go down with these people," she said. "You must know the plot can't succeed. The government has infiltrated every cell of your movement, even the Great Council itself. They know everything."

"You are lying," he said, voice as rough as bark.

"I was there myself," she continued. "In Parliament, this week. General Smuts said himself they have the OB in the hollow of their hand. All the names. The army is waiting for an excuse to round them up. You have a sweetheart, PJ? Children? Think of them before you throw it all away." There was no response. In the silence Anna hoped against hope. The smell of tobacco grew stronger and then waned.

"I'm sorry," he said at last. "I can't help you."

Anna stretched out on the bed and lay staring at the slab. She'd thrown her last hook and it had come up empty. Her thoughts turned into a hailstorm of regret and self-condemnation. Her father's warnings, Fanus, even Thomas. What vanity to go it alone, to think that she, a mere girl, could defy them. She was overcome by the hopelessness of the situation. Eventually, a great weariness weighed her into a fitful sleep.

<h1 style="text-align:center">32</h1>

SHE MISTOOK THE FLICKER of light around the door frame for a dream. Only when it brightened did she realise she was awake. Up from her bed in a flash, she pressed her eye to the crack between the door and its frame. It wasn't possible to see clearly but from the crunch of gravel and purring she could tell a car had arrived. A door opened and closed with muted clunks, followed by soft and cautious footsteps. She froze in fear. Was it Kurt? No, he'd be more confident, surely. Likewise, PJ. In fact, where had he disappeared to? She could only think it was an accomplice. And who's to say he wouldn't be more of a menace than PJ? As quietly as she could, she shifted away from the door and withdrew to the far side of the bed. The outside lock jingled and there was a tug at the door. She sank down on the floor. It wouldn't entirely hide her but perhaps it would be enough. There was a shove and another and then it was silent. She held her breath.

"Miss Anna?" a familiar voice whispered.

No, it can't be, she thought. What are the odds? She waited. Outside, the wind held its breath.

"Are you all right?" the voice whispered.

"K-Kleinjan?" she stammered. What on earth was he doing here?

"It's a long story," he said, seeming to read her mind. "I followed you to the cinema."

The wind had died. Then boots scrunched closer on the gravel.

It had to be PJ, she thought, terrified. "Go!" she urged.

"What's the problem ..." There was a muffled shout and a scuffle, then all went quiet.

Anna lay for a few seconds listening to her heart beating. What had just happened? She could only think that PJ must have returned. She jumped up and ran to the door. "Hey," she shouted. "What's happening?" The lock wiggled, and she backed away hastily as the door swung open.

Standing in the entrance was the hulking figure of PJ. He had Kleinjan, whose head was slumped forward, in a bear hug. He ignored Anna, hoisted the lifeless body a little further off the ground and manhandled it into the centre of the room. There, he let it slump to the floor.

Anna dropped down beside Kleinjan's body. Put her ear to his chest. The lack of obvious breathing confirmed her worst fears. She turned to face PJ. "What have you done to him?" she cried.

"The bastard deserved a good beating," PJ growled. "He bit me." He shoved the toe of his shoe under the body and rolled it half over. "What kind of person would do such a thing?" Then he turned and stomped out, slamming the door shut behind him.

Anna was devastated. What had she done? How idiotic to think she could seduce the ringleader of a rebellion and turn him to her cause without consequences. Outside, the lock clicked shut and the footsteps faded. She turned her attention to Kleinjan again, feeling at his neck. Was that a pulse or was she imagining it? "Ag, Kleinjan, what have they done to you?" she cried. "I'm so sorry: its all my fault. Don't leave me, please, I couldn't bear it."

For an age she sat, alternately stroking his forehead and feeling for his pulse. She was about to give up hope when she noticed one of his eyelids flicker. She shook him lightly. Please, she prayed, let it be what I think it is. Then the other eyelid flickered and then both opened. His eyes were glazed over but from his pupils she knew he was alive.

"*Magtig jong*," she said. "You gave me such a fright."

He struggled but eventually managed to turn on his side.

She held the candle up to see him better. "Here," she said. "What's this? Oh dear: you're bleeding."

He ran his hands down his cheeks, patted his sides. "Don't worry," he said. "I'll be fine."

Anna studied the contours of his face in the candlelight. His cheekbones were high and shining, his mouth shrivelled. "So, it was you in the taxi from the theatre?"

He nodded.

"But why?"

His face dropped, the scar from an old knife wound on his forehead reflecting white in the candlelight. "I'm not supposed to say."

"It's Papa that told you to follow me, isn't it?"

"Ja. He said you've been acting strange."

"What else did he say about me?"

Kleinjan glanced nervously at the door. "I've already said too much."

"Ag, come on," she cried. "The two of us are locked away in a prison of sorts below Lion's Head while out there some thugs are planning to blow up Parliament and all you're worried about is your job? No man, if we don't do something, there'll be no Rietvlei to farm, never mind a foreman."

He looked away and stared at the semblance of a window. Then rubbed the peppercorn stubble on his chin. "You're right," he said at length. "You always saw things more clearly than others, even as a little girl."

"Don't be. It was you who taught me how to think, anyway. What did Papa say?"

Kleinjan paused. "*Yoh*. Baas Stefan. I've never seen him so angry. He was literally shouting."

"Go on. It's important you tell me everything he said as close as possible to the actual words. It could help us find a way out of this mess."

He looked at the candle with rheumy eyes. "*Haai*, you know how I am, I can't even remember Hannah's birthday."

"Come on, try."

"Let me think. He said you were …"

"What?"

"It isn't right, Miss Anna. I can't say it."

"Come on, this isn't the time to be shy. What did he say?"

"He called you a lying whore. For running off with 'that

German'. He said he warned you. That he's going to ..." He fell silent.

"I'm a grownup. I can take the truth."

"All right. But don't make a judgement before you've heard me out. You know your father sometimes says things he doesn't mean."

"That's no exaggeration. But go on."

Kleinjan looked her in the eyes. "He's ... stopping your university."

Anna stared at him in disbelief. "He's what?" she shouted. "That's impossible." She kicked the bed. "He's got no right ..." She inhaled, took the two paces to the far wall and spun about. "And when is all this supposed to happen?"

Kleinjan lifted himself onto the bed. "Tomorrow. I'm to collect you and your belongings and drive you to Rietvlei, same day."

"What?" She roared. "The cheek of it. He can go to hell before I give up my studies!"

Kleinjan's face fell and he was silent. Anna immediately regretted her outburst. She paced up and down the room several times and eventually sat down next to him on the bed. "I'm sorry. I'm so, so sorry. It's not your fault. I'm shooting the messenger. Will you forgive me?"

"Of course, Miss Anna, of course. After what you've been through I'm surprised you're so controlled." They sat for a long time, listening to the wind complaining fitfully at the door. At length, Kleinjan spoke. "What did you mean just now, that tomorrow was the end of things as we know it. My job. Rietvlei?"

Anna hesitated. How much should she tell him? Papa, Fanus, Thomas—every man she'd trusted in the past week had betrayed her.

"*Haai*, Miss Anna, you told me yourself this isn't the time to be shy. I told you everything."

She looked at him. He looked older than usual and vulnerable. Oh, how she loved him. More like a father or a grandfather, than a mentor. They'd been through so much together. And it wasn't right to put him in a basket with the others just because he was a man. "*Magtig*," she began slowly. "Where to start ... Do you remember last week on the way to the farm, we were talking about the OB, the nonsense they're up to, the bombings?"

He nodded.

"And you know that Robey Leibbrandt business at the end of last year?"

"The Nazi Boer? Wasn't he that policeman boxer who stayed in Germany after the Olympics?"

"Ja. Then they dropped him on the Namaqualand coast to help the OB organise a rebellion."

"But it fizzled out, didn't it?"

"Ja, they say he was betrayed by Van Rensburg himself. Now he's been convicted of treason—although Papa says he'll get the pardon. Apparently his father rode commando with Smuts in the *Vryheidsoorlog*."

Kleinjan frowned. "Excuse me, Miss Anna, but why is this important?"

"This Leibbrandt business was just the fin of the shark. There's a much more serious threat to our country. And we're right in the middle of it."

"You mean the U-boat business at Rietvlei?"

She nodded.

"*Haai*." He whistled. "I never should have—"

"Shh. I don't blame you. Anyone in your position would have done the same. But there's more to it than meat and vegetables."

The lines on his forehead deepened.

"You know that … that ogre out there?" she glanced at the door. "He's OB, with Fanus or maybe some splinter group. They've planted dynamite underneath the Parliament building, can you believe that? They're planning to blow it up tomorrow, *nogal*. It's hard to believe, but it's true. I saw the dynamite with my own eyes."

He stared at her.

"I was down in the tunnels. Felt it in my hands. There was at least three times as much as you used for the road at Rietvlei. And you can guess who's behind them. The Germans."

"Thomas?" He looked at her with mountain pool eyes.

"No. He swears he doesn't know the first thing about it. I believe him. Ag, it's complicated, but like you said, Kurt is the dangerous one. German Intelligence."

"*Yoh*. Does Baas Stefan know about this?"

"I don't think so." Anna's breath cut short. Something was troubling her, a barb from her conversation with De Villiers. "Tell me," she said. "When did you last see him?"

"Let me think." Kleinjan counted on his fingers. "I think ten o'clock. Or maybe half past nine. Why?"

She worked back through the sequence of events to the phone call. De Villiers had mentioned a meeting with his boss. That would account for him not having arrested her father yet. Still, something niggled. "Where was he when you spoke to him?"

Kleinjan's eyes fell to his feet.

"Come on, *jong*, its important."

"I know you don't approve of her. You know, the library lady."

"Margriet!" Anna almost shouted. She forced her voice lower. "Tell me I'm not hearing this. You're saying he's at her house? For how long? All night?"

He nodded, still staring at his feet. "I know it's hard for you, Miss Anna, but your father, he's been alone so long. This is good for him."

"It's not that. Sure I don't like her. She's a gold digger. But it's much worse than that. Papa had to be at home tonight, or he'll be in Parliament tomorrow! We have to stop him, please …" She was fighting back tears. "What are we going to do?"

Kleinjan put his hand on her shoulder and then withdrew it. "Don't worry, Miss Anna. With God, there's always hope."

"I used to be so sure of that. But now I don't know."

"Now, now. Has he ever let you down? No. That isn't possible. And he won't today. Be strong and very courageous."

Anna looked at him through a blur. "Why does he always seem so far away? Especially when you're hurting? It's as though he doesn't care, like he's the headmaster of Bredasdorp Primary, just waiting for a person to fail."

"I know, I know. It can feel like that. But there is something you must remember. A person's view of God comes from their own father."

Something broke inside of her and Anna burst into gasping sobs. Kleinjan kept his arm about her shoulders but said nothing until her crying had stopped. "Baas Stefan is a hard man. And I know you can't believe it now, especially with him threatening you like now, but he loves you. You're the apple of his eye. Really."

"That's the problem," she said. "I don't want to be his bird, an object of his affection." She wiped her face on her sleeve and turned towards him, still heaving. "I need him to take me seriously!"

They sat next to each other, staring at the door. The wind rose to a crescendo, blew fragments of leaf through the gap, subsided, then worked itself up again.

At last Kleinjan spoke. "You mustn't take it to heart. Sometimes I think the only person he regards highly is himself. It's not that he means to talk down on a person, he just does."

Anna hadn't thought about it that way before. But it made sense. Perhaps he was more unable than unwilling to give her what she'd always craved from him. Had she misunderstood him so badly all these years?

Just then there was a violent gust from outside and something blew up against her feet. It was a feather, broken at the stem. She picked it up and ran it softly under her nose. Then she stared at it and closed her eyes. She was back on the flat mountaintop, gazing at a line in the sea, with the first man she had ever loved beside her. The memory was raw and caused her to burst into tears again. This time there was no consoling her and she lay face down sobbing. When at last she tired of it, she stood. "We have to get out of here," she cried, "Now." She grabbed at the window mesh and, with all her strength, tried to shake it loose. "But there's no way out. Except if we …" She stepped to the door and put her ear to the metal. Footsteps shuffled some way off, and all was still. "Damn, I thought we could at least try one more time to persuade PJ to switch sides. Now there's nobody there."

Kleinjan began to inspect every square inch of their prison—walls, floor, roof, but, given their lack of tools, the only possible exit was the door—and that had been heavily padlocked from outside. "I'm afraid there's only one thing left to do and that is to wait and hope they come for us in the morning."

"We could shout," Anna said.

"Yes, but do you know how isolated we are? I don't even think the hiking trail passes closer than a hundred feet from here. And that's if someone's mad enough to be hiking at this hour. No, in this wind, all we'd be doing is showing our captors our last card. Let's rather wait until the morning."

Anna paced up and down, kicked at the bed. "I hate this."

"And I wish I could change it." Kleinjan took a blanket off the bed, folded it in half and lay it down on the floor. Then he stretched himself out on his back. "But I can't. So let's at least get some rest. Tomorrow's another day."

"I suppose you're right." Reluctantly, she stretched out on the bed. But rather than sleep, she lay, wracking her brain. Surely, there was a way to escape. She'd read the adventure books: a literary hero somehow always finds a way. Perhaps if she tore the mattress apart they could use the bed springs … But it was hopeless: she just went around in circles, getting more and more agitated until the candle became a lump of wax on the base of the saucer and the rings of light on the ceiling faded.

"You should be sleeping," Kleinjan said at last. "You're going to need the energy."

"Speak for yourself."

"You're thinking of Thomas, aren't you?"

"I can't help myself."

"It's normal. You're in love."

"It's not just that. I'm worried. He says he'll try to frustrate the plot. But what if they catch him? How could we live with ourselves if we'd sat here doing nothing, knowing the fate of our country is in the hands of … an enemy soldier?"

"I don't know. But remember, it's not man who holds the fate of nations."

"Ja, I know, I know. But still, surely God uses people, simple people sometimes, like us, to achieve his purposes. I mean, how else does it work?"

"Miss Anna is right, he will give us what we need and when. We must just have faith."

She sighed. "Don't you sometimes wish it was simpler? That there'd be a sign showing us which way? Or a booming voice? I miss the old days, you know, running about the *werf* with Willem and the boys, knowing there were other people to make the decisions. Do you think that's what happens when a girl gets married? That there's someone to carry her burdens?"

"*Ja nee*. There are always things a woman must bear alone. I think of Hannah before we met."

"But why?" Anna cried. "Why does it have to end like this? Why does it have to end at all? We love each other. You know how long I've waited for this love. It's so unfair."

At first Kleinjan didn't respond. His breathing was slow and rhythmical. "*Ai*, it's hard, I won't lie." He sighed. "I'm going to tell you something I tell nobody … I also lost my first love. Permanently, I mean. A car accident. *My jinne*, it was terrible. The pain. Like I was going to die myself."

"But it's so cruel," she said. "We're made for each other. We think alike, laugh at the same things. It's like we read each other's minds."

"Ja. That's what it's like."

"Yes, but why did it have to stop, just like that? No time to even say a proper goodbye. It's so awful. And this war. *Magtig*, when will it be over?"

He blew through his teeth. "I don't know. That's why we must try to look for the beautiful things in this life. Take now, we're talking again. Properly, I mean. Like the old times, when you and Willem used to shoot *kettie*. *Aitsa*, you were a tomboy then. And look at you now. Like a beauty queen. The men falling for you left, right and centre."

"Hey," she teased. "There's still the charmer in you, *nê*?"

They laughed and fell silent and, as Anna lay listening to the wind's tone change from a whine to a moan, an idea came to her. Kleinjan had joked about her effect on men. What if she exploited that on her captors? In a way it was repulsive—using her sexuality to deceive. But, as she watched the moonlight spread about the doorframe, she couldn't escape the conclusion that in this case the end justified the means. She even started to feel hopeful. And, at least now, there was the semblance of a plan.

33

SLEEP CAME IN WAVES in the end, and she was half in it and half out through the night until the stirring of birds outside welcomed the dawn. For a long while after waking she lay there, ruminating on the kernel of a plan she'd formed in the night. Then, when it was clear in her mind, she sprang out of bed, stepped over Kleinjan and tip-toed across the floor to the door. There, she pressed her eye to the crack about the doorframe. At lock height it was a quarter inch wide and she could see the orange light of dawn flooding the horizon outside but no sign of anyone else. She put her ear to the opening. Nothing but the birds at first, not even wind, but then she heard a snore.

She retracted her ear and returned to Kleinjan. "Hey," she whispered. "Wake up."

"I'm here, Miss Anna."

"Shhhh. I've got an idea."

He stared at her.

"Okay: listen: when PJ wakes up I'm going tell him I need the bathroom and if he lets me out I'm going to distract him. It'll only last a minute or two. You must slip away."

"*Sho.*" His eyes widened. "That's dangerous. Did you see how far it is to the nearest bush? Hasn't he got a gun?"

"It's a risk. I'm not going to lie. But what choice do we have?"

"You're right. I've been thinking about it all night. We can't depend on the German. There's something fishy about his story. And we can't think about our own safety when there's a threat to the whole Parliament. Not to mention, Baas Stefan. But … how will you create the gap—for me to leave?"

"Don't worry." She stood, fluffing her hair with her fingers. "I know his type. More muscle than brain."

"And if he doesn't fall for it?"

"Then we both die. At least we tried, though. Listen, I've thought it through. First, you must run for the clump of proteas across the way. From what I can make out through the door, it's about seventy feet. Then crawl to the top of the ridge. He won't see you from that angle."

Kleinjan looked sceptical.

"I know it's risky. But once you're on the road you should be fine. Just *bundu* bash across the spine of the lion, through those pine trees we see on the horizon from town. There's a single row, maybe double. If I'm not mistaken, you back left towards Signal Hill parking lot after you get to the tar road. There's a service road somewhere, going down to the Bo-Kaap."

Kleinjan nodded. "I know my way from there."

"You must find De Villiers. He's our best chance. Tell him everything."

"But what if he's one of them? You even said there's a chance he's OB."

"True," she said. "But something tells me he can be trusted. Rough, but a rose bush at heart."

"But if this works and I get there, why would he believe me?"

"Why ever not?"

He coughed. "Miss Anna, I'm a coloured. What policeman would listen to my story? He'll just arrest me."

She thought about it. "All right. Tell him I sent you. Say I'm sorry I missed his *moerkoffie*, that I have the case of the century for him, that it's even bigger now." She insisted he repeat the address of his office.

Then she put her mouth to the crack in the doorframe. "Hey, PJ," she shouted.

No response.

"PJ. PJ. Here." She started thumping her fists against the door. "Hey! Wake up."

There was a groan and a shuffle and a body blocked out the light about the door.

"What do you want, girl?" PJ was up close; she could hear him breathing.

"I need to go to the bathroom."

"Sorry, ma'am. I'm under strict instructions."

"Listen: it's urgent."

"I don't care. Piss in the bucket."

"It's more than that. Come on, surely you don't expect me to do my business in front of a man? *Sies*. No upstanding Afrikaner would expect that of a woman. It's not right."

A silence. "That bugger wasn't supposed to arrive."

"Don't speak like that. He's here now. And I'm telling you, I need to go."

A sigh. "This is going to get me in big shit." He chuckled. "Good one, hey? But all right. Listen here, when I open, you walk out. Slowly. Just you. And close the door behind you. Understand?"

After the jingle of the lock the door swung half open. She stood in the frame, making as if to rub her eyes. She'd been right. Beyond the steps was fifteen feet of gravel and then low bush. Beyond that was the thicket of proteas and higher up the slope, the pines. PJ stood clear of the door's swing with a revolver in his hand. She stepped off the stair towards him. "Thank you," she smiled. "You're doing the right thing. Now, where do I go?"

As he indicated left with his head his beard followed in whiplash. "The outhouse. Slow, remember. I'm watching you."

She tousled her hair so that it fell across her shoulders. "Do me a favour, will you?" She said and moved closer. Then she turned her back and reached up behind herself as if trying to undo a button. "This thing got stuck last night."

"I shouldn't be doing this." He shifted on his feet.

"Please."

There was the tinkle of the key settling in his pocket. He moved towards her and next thing he was upon her, his fingers fumbling at the button. The garlic on his breath was worse than the night before and this time it was laced with brandy. Suddenly she was shaking.

"Thank you," she said, turning. She moved closer to him, her leg brushing up against him. PJ was clearly trying to stay calm but his eyes couldn't help but focus on her cleavage. She allowed the hint of a smile to tease her lips.

There was a shuffle of footsteps behind her. Must be Kleinjan. She needed to speak to cover the sounds. "It must be lonely up here, hey?"

"Ag, it's not so bad," he said. "I haven't been posted here long. Less than a month."

"Still." She bent a fraction further forward, watching his pupils widen.

"Hey," he called, head jerking up. "What's that?" His hand was at his revolver.

"What's the matter?" Anna shifted to block his view.

He shoved her out the way. "Can you believe the little bastard …?" he muttered. "Hey! Stop!" He was taking aim as he shouted. She stepped in the way again. This time he threw her towards the door. "I said stop, *onnosel*!"

Anna recovered her footing in time to see Kleinjan dive for the proteas. The shot was so loud it deafened her momentarily but then she heard the scream. It subsided to a whimper. "No," she cried as the giant took aim at the bush. Then she stooped to pick up a rock at her feet. Without thinking she hurled it at the giant. It hit him in the gut, pulling his next shot right.

"*Fok*!" He grabbed her by the hand and swung her arm into a vice grip behind her back. Then he frog-marched her back to the bunker and chucked her onto the bed. "Bitch. You think you're clever? *Fok*, I knew it. That's what comes from trusting a half-breed Englishwoman. Now you can stay where you belong."

She twisted herself from the bed. "But what about Kleinjan? We can't just leave him there!" She tried to quell her rising panic. Kleinjan was hurt, possibly dying. He didn't deserve this. Oh, Lord above. And all because she'd been so reckless as to fall in love with a German.

"Don't worry," said PJ, "He won't be going anywhere." His bulk in the doorway darkened the room. Then the door thudded closed and his breathing was the only sound.

"Right." He was by the bed. "Where were we just now?"

"Don't you dare! If Fanus hears you so much as touched me …"

"Shut up. You started this." His belt buckle clanked.

She shifted towards the wall, crouching in a foetal position.

"Don't worry," he said, taking another step. "I'm big, but I can be gentle."

Anna was screaming in rage and fear and disbelief. She heard his pants drop to the ground and then his hand was over her mouth and she was hoping not to be conscious to feel the end.

Suddenly he relaxed his grip. Far behind her there was the sound of a car engine. "Lucky bitch." PJ's voice was retreating. "Here comes your lover boy." His hand was under her and flipped her over. Then he was fastening his buckle and he said. "Now, listen here. If you say anything of this I'll kill you. You and your boyfriend."

"What's going on here," Fanus said from behind PJ.

"What isn't going on is the question," PJ said. "Your friend here let that little bastard get away. Gave me some bullshit story about choking. And hey, what took you so long? There's *fokol* time left."

Fanus pulled a fob watch from his suit pants. "Relax," he said. "There's time. You know how bad the traffic can get in the mornings." He panned the room. "What's all this about?"

PJ explained how he'd caught Kleinjan and gave his version of the escape.

Fanus swung about to survey the veld. "Better go find him," he said. "I'll keep an eye on things here."

PJ eyed him, glanced at Anna and back. "I'm sure you will."

"What's that supposed to mean?"

"Nothing." There was a pounding on gravel, growing softer.

"What happened to you?" Fanus said, pointing at her dress.

She blushed. "That horrible man didn't let me go to the bathroom."

Fanus's cheeks reddened. "I'm sorry, *my lief.* I shouldn't have left you with him. But everything has to be just right. There's no room for a mistake."

She stepped out of the shadows to the light of the doorway, eyes locked on his. "There's still time to call it off."

"We've been through this, Anna. I'm committed."

"You're not like that Nazi. I won't believe it."

"You're right on that score. I'm no Nazi. But I'm a Boer in bone and marrow, and proud of it."

She moved into his space, trying not to think of the state of her dress. "I know you are," she said, inches from his face now. "And there's no shame in that. But this sort of extremism has never helped the Afrikaner. Slagtersnek, Jopie Fourie … Where did their sacrifice get us?"

"This time it's different." He tried to pull his face back; it caught the low sun and turned golden. "Right now, thousands of people around the country, all armed and trained—even a new government—are all waiting for our signal. I told you, we must just get through the next few hours, then everything will change."

Did Fanus really believe she'd come around to his side? He was deluded.

"Come, *my lief*. We'll have a great future together."

She felt like spitting on the floor between them. Instead she let her chin drop to her chest, watched the heave and fall of her chest. "I'm sorry," she said. "If I've made this harder for you than it already is." She managed to quiver her lip when she looked up at him again. Her breasts were touching his chest and she could feel his leg on hers. "This must be a stressful time."

There was a thump on the cement outside. "The *bliksem* has disappeared," PJ said. "Can you believe it? There's a trail of blood on the sand, like it's a *bokskiet*, but no sign of the little bugger."

Fanus's voice hit a higher pitch than usual. "What do you mean, I thought you said you had him? If he's injured and on foot, how could he get away? It's impossible."

"I'm telling you. I followed the trail to the tar. Next thing it was gone. No blood, nothing. I looked everywhere—there's nothing, I swear."

"So, what are you going to do about it?"

"Ag, I wouldn't worry. He probably crawled under a bush to die."

Fanus gazed out over the veld. The morning had heated up quickly and there was a haze over the ocean beyond. "You better be right."

They stood in silence as a cloud glided past overhead and then dissipated. Then there was a bumping over the ridge, growing louder until it materialised into the shape of a motor-car, front-on, beneath a shimmer of air. It rolled and thumped across the grass and stone and drew up close by. The door opened but no one got out.

"It is time," Kurt's voice was clear and crisp. "Lock her up. We go."

Fanus walked up to the window, bent. "I'm not leaving her here."

"Soldiers only. Our orders are clear."

"I agree," PJ said. "She's trouble."

"She's coming. I'll take responsibility."

"*Nein. Einsteigen. Sofort.* You only."

"I told you. No Anna, no Fanus. And we all know what will happen—or not—without me."

Kurt inhaled. Looked like he was about to shout but then he stopped. "*Scheiße*," he spat. "Okay. Get in. Girl in the middle. Remember, you are responsible."

The tyres spun on the gravel as they pulled away up the hill. Behind them, a dust cloud hovered in the stillness. A handful of cars were parked in the lot overlooking the sea, windows rolled down. A pair of lovers sat arm-over-arm on a bench, a picnic basket at their feet.

"If you plan to scream," Kurt said, "don't. If you want your father to live."

"What do you mean?"

"You escape, your father dies."

"You're lying."

"And why is this?"

The air in the car was close and hot and Anna battled for breath. "Because he's in custody."

Kurt glanced back. They were rounding the rump of the lion and the road was a tight curve with no shoulder. He had one hand on the steering wheel, the other, sleeves rolled, rested on the window frame.

"Really?"

"Yes. He's with the police." Anna swallowed. "I arranged it myself."

He chuckled. "We tapped your phone, remember. And organised a small … distraction. I haven't heard but I'm sure your detective friend was pretty pissed off when he found your father's flat empty. Confirmed his worst fears about your reliability."

Margriet, Anna thought. They'd used her as a lure. Now, unless De Villiers figured it all out, Papa would be at Parliament. She felt despondent. Her scheme was a failure.

The car straightened at the back of the Lion's rump. Two stone pillars appeared ahead and to the left, marking the gravel service road that plunged down to the Bo-Kaap. Was it possible Kleinjan had survived? Even if just long enough to call De Villiers? It was a slender thread of hope to hang on. No. She could not rely on anything. The car was accelerating, pine trees flying past left and right. Driving like this, they'd be at Parliament in ten minutes. Every second she delayed could mean it was too late.

She lunged forward, ramming her forehead into Kurt's neck.

"*Scheiße.*" The car lurched right, missing the ditch by inches. Kurt overcorrected, only straightening as they sped past the spire of the Kramat. "Fanus!" His left hand was in the glove compartment and came out holding a pistol, muzzle resting on the steering wheel. "Control your girl or I will. Is this understood?"

"Hey, put that back," Fanus shouted. He reached about, clamped her at the wrists and wrestled her back into her seat. The car careened between the pines along the side of Lion's Head, the city sprawled below, the road rising and dropping in turns.

Satisfied, Kurt placed the revolver on the seat next to him and focused on the road. They eased onto the Kloof Nek roundabout and then dropped down the bends of Kloof Nek Road towards the city bowl in an uneasy silence.

As they approached the intersection with Orange Street Anna was overcome with regrets. Why hadn't she told De Villiers on the phone. Why the wait? People were about to die—important people, not in ones or twos but en masse, a slaughter of innocents, and she'd schemed just to protect her father. She leaned forward, calculating the odds of reaching the pistol. Even if she didn't get it, the tussle should cause a delay.

As if reading her mind, Kurt straightened, and shifted the revolver to between his legs.

Anna slumped into her seat. Hopeless, hopeless, nothing was going right. She sat back and stared out of the window at the university campus opposite. Ah, her world of comfort and innocence that could never be again. She felt like crying but held herself together as the landscape changed and soon the commercial buildings on Hatfield Street were sliding by. Then, as they descended, the harbour in the distance before them, she noticed out of the corner of her eye, that Fanus's one hand was rummaging under his seat. He withdrew what looked like an oversized pencil case on his lap, fiddled with it for a while until he managed to slide its wooden cover off. Inside, Anna could make out a box of safety matches and a miniature paraffin lamp. What on earth were they for? Could it be what she was thinking? It was horrifying, but there was no other explanation. It must be to set off the bomb. But how?

As they slowed behind a taxi, Fanus struck a match, lit the lamp's wick, and cupped the flame between his hands. Once the flame had established itself, he clutched it to his lap with both hands and stared ahead. The road soon widened, and they were bumping over Stalplein, the red and white brick walls of Parliament diagonally opposite. Anna pictured her father in the back benches, perhaps at this very moment standing to argue a point. Oblivious, all the while, to the fact that an almighty explosion was about to engulf them. She began to struggle for breath. The space inside the car, also, seemed to be shrinking.

What about the gun? She leaned forward as much as she dared. Kurt clutched it in his far hand. There was no chance to make a lunge. She looked from PJ to Fanus. Two trained killers. It seemed hopeless. She'd already tried to convince PJ to switch his allegiance. Fanus too. Together, they seemed like an impregnable fortress.

What to do when you faced an enemy of vastly superior numbers and munitions? She remembered her father, quoting some military theorist. Or was it a statesman? The answer, heard so many times in her childhood, came to her. She felt a pang of excitement. It was simple: you divide and conquer.

She nudged Fanus, then pointed at the contraption on his lap. "So that's what they hired you for?" she said, loudly enough for the others to hear. "Your expertise and local knowledge. How much are they paying you? Will it be worth it, Judas, when you sift your silver from the rubble? A life or two for each pound?"

"Listen," he spat. "Nobody hires me."

The front tyres hit a manhole cover and the flame on his lap waned and flared.

"What did they promise, then?" Anna said. "Fame, glory? I thought you were a better man, Fanus Prinsloo. What does your father think? Will it make him proud?"

"It's nothing to do with the old man. I answer to the Council. They make the rules."

"Ha," Kurt sniggered. "The Great Council! You think Pétain makes the rules in France?"

It was working. Anna felt her first stirring of hope. The car had slowed for traffic at Church Square, and she could see the unlit neon of the Sailor's Eye on the far side. She had an image of her father slurping coffee in the booth as she'd tried to dissuade him from attending Parliament. Why hadn't she told him everything, there and then? Why play games with the truth? Was it her pride? Or worse, lust? How could she live with herself if he died? Oh, Heavenly Father, she prayed, take me now or show me a way.

"What did you just say about Pétain?" Fanus said.

Silence. Fanus shifted in his seat. "You told me South Africa is to be a republic, Kraut. Those were your exact words. Don't come with this bullshit now …"

Anna allowed herself a smile. Had her prayer been answered?

"*Achtung*," Kurt shouted. "I told you. We must remain focused." He tapped the brakes as they approached Parliament Street. "There will be time for arguing later."

Fanus blew out the flame. "I'm not lifting a finger until you explain yourself."

Kurt brought the car to a standstill and swore under his breath as a soldier with an orange flash on his shoulder stepped off the pavement to cross in front of them. Then he turned, and with him, the barrel of the pistol, which was pointed at Fanus. "Light it again. You heard me correctly."

"Do it, Fanus," PJ said. "Can't you see, the bitch is trying to divide us?"

"Don't," Anna urged. "Do the right thing, for your country and for me. You're a patriot, Fanus, a true Afrikaner. You don't have to join in this … this devil's scheme!"

"Shut up, bitch." PJ snapped. Next thing she knew his palm slapped across her mouth and her head hit the seat back. His hand smelled of engine oil. She struggled to free herself, but his grip only tightened. She started to panic as her breath ran out. Convinced now, that she was going to die. That they were all going to die.

"Hey!" Fanus grabbed his wrist. "You can't do that. She'd die. I'll …"

"*Fok jou*!" PJ shoved him off.

"He's right," Kurt said. "Let her go. She will be more useful alive."

Just as Anna was about to lose consciousness, PJ's hand slackened, and then she was gasping desperately for air. They were moving again, their tyres squelching over the cobbles as they approached the gates of Parliament. The guard Anna had flirted with was on duty again but there was also a car parked in front of the entrance. Wasn't that prohibited? The vehicle's windscreen was tinted so it was impossible to make out if anyone was inside but as they got closer the figures of two uniformed men appeared, standing in the shade of the oaks. Surely they couldn't be De Villiers' men? That would mean Kleinjan had somehow survived and made contact.

PJ too, must have seen the policemen. His arm clamped across Anna's front, shoved her backward and pinned her to the seat. She struggled but his arm dug into her stomach with such force she had no choice but to stop. For a few maddening seconds she sat there, feeling helpless and useless. After everything, had it come to this? She had an image of the storeroom somewhere below them, in the tunnels. Maybe Thomas got lost. Had she given him the right instructions? How could she be sure, anyway, with all that sloshing about in the dark? Not that it mattered. He'd most likely come to his senses and fled. By now he could be as far as Skulpiestrand, if not in the bowels of his U-boat. How could she be so naïve as to trust a stranger?

Next to her, Fanus had the lamp again and the matchbox was shaking in his hand.

"*Ge,*" PJ scoffed. "Don't tell me you're scared?" He rolled down his window and leaned out. "Further forward, Kraut. Slowly. There it is. I marked the manhole cover with an O." PJ yanked the handle and let the door swing open. "That's it!" The manhole drew level with the back door and they stopped. He reached under the seat and pulled out a crowbar. "*Goed, manne.* Let's go. One minute, remember." He released his grip on Anna. "You move, girl, and I'll strangle you with my own hands." He slid out of the car and wedged his crowbar under the manhole cover.

Fanus hopped out, ran around the back of the car and crouched beside PJ. He struck a match which went out, then another.

Meantime, the guard started sauntering toward them. Come on, Anna urged under her breath, why so slowly? Her back and shoulders were knotted with stress. She glanced anxiously at the red and white grandeur of the Parliament buildings, imagining the blast going off and shaking the columns to pieces and the building tumbling down. About her father of course, but also the Prime Minister. She could see his goatee and sharp eyes narrowing. What would he be thinking in those last moments? Probably, he'd be calm. He'd seen enough action in the Anglo-Boer War. Not that any of that would help against the blast. No, she was the only person with a chance of stopping the madness. If only PJ would relent.

"Quick," PJ urged. "Do it. Thirty seconds tops."

"Now." Kurt was out the car, his revolver trained on Fanus. "I will count to three. One ..."

Fanus's hands were shaking so badly the flame was threatening to go out. He seemed to be frozen in position, turned back toward them with his face red and sweating.

"Coward," Kurt sneered. "I knew we couldn't trust an Afrikaner."

"*Fok!*" PJ grabbed at the lamp. "Let me do it."

By now the guard was close, twenty feet perhaps. "Hey," he called, "What's going on there?" He was about to march over and investigate but then he noticed Anna. "Miss van der Vliet. Where've you been? I'm so sorry, I didn't see you."

Anna was screaming but words wouldn't follow.

"You all right, ma'am?"

She was shaking her head wildly, but he didn't seem to notice. "What happened to *Meneer* van der Vliet this morning? It's not like him to be so late for a session as important as ..."

Anna tried not to panic. So, Papa was inside. Her plan had failed spectacularly. Around her, everything seemed to slow, like in a silent movie or a slideshow.

"Hey, what's that chap doing?" the guard said, his attention drawn to the manhole again.

Fanus was slumped on the cobbles, in the foetus position. Next to him, Kurt held a match, ready to strike. The end of a pipe was visible at the manhole and protruding from it, the tousled end of a rope.

"Stop them!" At last, Anna had found her voice. "It's a bomb."

For an agonising moment, the guard hesitated. He looked from Anna to the manhole. "Drop what you're doing," he shouted. PJ ignored him. He'd managed to light the flame and was shifting it toward the hole. The guard shot into the air. Almost simultaneously, the doors of the police car burst open and a thick-set figure charged toward them.

They were reacting too slowly, Anna knew, it was up to her to do something. She closed her eyes, took a deep breath and prayed. Then she screamed at the top of her lungs and at the same instant threw herself from the car. As her knee hit the cobbles she felt a flash of pain and crumpled to the ground on her back. PJ was a little more than an arm's length away, on hands and knees at the edge of the manhole. He'd managed to position the lamp just over the edge and was reaching for the pipe and its wick. Anna felt behind her and found the wheel. She steadied herself on it with both her hands, drew her legs back, bicycle-style, and took aim at PJ's backside and ...

"*Fok!*" The lamp flew from PJ's hands, brushed past the pipe and bounced off the far edge of the hole.

Had the wick been lit? It was impossible to be sure. Anna continued staring at the hole. So, she thought, the moment of reckoning. When the world as she knew it was about to be obliterated. Strangely though, she felt at peace. Perhaps it was knowing that she'd done everything she could to prevent it. Or that what would be, would be.

What happened next astonished her. Instead of a fireball coming out of the hole, a pistol appeared, barrel first, and then the top of a ladder. Anna clutched her knee, disbelieving. A man drenched and muddy, loomed. It was Thomas.

"Stay down!" His pistol was trained on Fanus, who was still lying, foetus-style, on the cobble and he hadn't seen PJ, who'd run off across the plain

"Watch out!" She cried, as she saw the glint of sunlight from the car. Then a gunshot rang out and there was a sickening thud. Thomas staggered this way and that, and then seemed to compose himself, pistol at his waist.

Just then a hand clamped over Anna's mouth from behind. She could smell perfume and gun oil. Then cold metal jammed against her temple. It had to be Kurt. "Retreat or she dies," he shouted. His arm had her neck in a vice grip.

Thomas didn't budge. Meanwhile, the third policeman had arrived, puffing. It was De Villiers. He seemed to be evaluating the situation.

It was now or never, Anna thought. She closed her eyes and sank her teeth into Kurt's forearm. He recoiled, his gun clanging to the stone. And in the moment another gunshot went off and Kurt stumbled and fell and there was silence and a fog of smoke.

Thomas was stumbling toward the car, pistol in one hand with a wisp of smoke leaking from its barrel. There, he heaved himself into the driver's seat. "Get away, Anna," he shouted. "It's me they want."

She ignored him and got into the passenger seat beside him. "You're hurt," she said, reaching for the wet patch that was spreading from his shoulder. It was warm and sticky. "I can't leave you."

"Go, Anna! Now! While you can."

There was shouting on all sides as De Villiers ordered the others to back off.

"Oh, my love," she said, stroking his arm. "Give yourself up. It's our only chance."

"Forget it. They'll hang me."

"Never. Do you know how many lives you saved?"

"You deserve the medal, not me. Leave me," he pleaded. "Please. I must travel alone."

"No. I'm not leaving."

He trained his pistol on her. His face was deadpan, drained. "I'm sorry," he said. He gave a wet cough. "I have a duty to fight to the end. Please Anna …" His pistol was shaking. "I don't want to do this."

"Listen to him," De Villiers said. "And get out. Slowly. You've done more than enough already."

She hesitated. Felt torn. How could she leave him? Yet, joining a German fugitive was a death sentence.

"Come here Anna. Here's my hand."

"N-no."

"All right then. Think about your father. You know you'll break his heart if you go and something happens to you. Not to mention what it will do to his career. Come. I know you want to do the right thing."

De Villiers stepped forward and reached out and took her hand. She hesitated one last time and then relented. The moment she stepped out of the car a shot rang out, then another with the sound of a shattering windscreen. Thomas must have ducked but still be in the driver's seat, because the car revved and then it's tyres were squealing as it tore across Stalplein, veering left and right and then it was gone.

34

ANNA LAY RUBBING HER knee as the confused shouting continued between the policemen and guards. One of De Villiers' men charged back to their car and took off with a screeching of tyres across Stalplein in pursuit of Thomas. Oh, my dear, she lamented, how are you, bleeding and in pain? How could I abandon you? She figured he had at most a two-minute head start. Probably, he'd have headed straight for De Waal Drive, the closest motorway and straight across the Cape Flats. He had perhaps twenty minutes before the roadblocks went up on all major arteries to the city: enough time to get to the coast road or the winelands. It would be madness to try Sir Lowry's Pass. But would he know all this? And how far would he get in his state? She knew she was crying but didn't care to wipe her face.

Just then a parliamentary guard came charging out of Parliament and down the steps, waving and issuing instructions. Anna suddenly remembered. Papa, was he still inside? She felt numb. Seconds after the guard, the Prime Minister emerged, slow but proud, helped on either side by younger men. The entourage spilled down the stairs and onto the paving, where they stopped to huddle under an oak. The trickle became a stream as one MP after another came out, interspersed with workers. But no sign of her father.

Anna raised herself to a seated position, scouring the crowd. Earlier, the guard had said her father hadn't been himself and arrived late for the session. But where was he? Had the guard been mistaken? But then she saw him. He stood under a column, scanning the crowd. He looked anxious, his back slightly hunched. Shrunken, even. She struggled to her feet. Her knee was tender but it held as she shuffled toward the stairs. When, finally, he saw her his face lit up in a smile.

In her joy at seeing him safe, all her anger melted. "Oh Papa, Papa," she cried, throwing her arms about him. "Are you all right? I've been so worried."

"I'm in rude health, Engel. But what about you?" He withdrew from her embrace. Held her at arm's length, his hands on her shoulders. "What's this? He dabbed at her dress. "You're bleeding!"

Anna looked down. Her floral dress had splatters of red. "Don't worry. It's the Nazi's."

"Nazi?" He looked vulnerable, confused even.

"Don't pretend you don't know." She shuddered, glanced at the stone face of the mountain shimmering grey in the heat. "Where's Kleinjan? Tell me he made it."

"How would I know? He's probably with his friends in District Six. Why?"

"Oh Papa, you don't know anything, do you?"

"Only what the guard just told us. That we need to evacuate. Something about an Axis attempt to blow up Parliament. What the hell's going on?" He was staring at the clump of people around the manhole. A paramedic had arrived with a stretcher and they'd lifted Kurt's body onto it but had made no attempt to take it away. A policeman had erected a make-shift barrier and was trying to keep a gathering crowd of onlookers at bay. "Those were gunshots I heard?"

She nodded. "Kurt's dead."

His brow furrowed. "Thomas' colleague?"

"Come on, Papa. Don't pretend you don't know anything. You're the one that's been helping them. Food and water: none of this would have been possible if you hadn't—"

"Slow down," he said. "So, I gave them shelter and sustenance. We've been through this already. Greta, the blackmail. You know the reasons. But nobody talked about Nazis or a plot."

She stared at him. Hard as it was to believe, he really was ignorant of it all. "Fanus too, he's a ringleader."

He looked bewildered. "No man. What are you talking about?"

"I told you he was a fanatic, Papa. And you thought I was just looking for an excuse not to marry him. But even I never guessed he was in the OB's high command. Did you know they've got a government in waiting? Sympathetic to the Nazi war effort, of course. Fanus was going to be Minister of Justice or something when they were done with the coup."

He shook his head slowly, lips clamped. "I guess they never fully trusted me … It's because I married an Englishwoman. And *jislaaik*: Fanus you say, plotting treason? Such a well brought-up boy." The last of the parliamentarians had exited the building and the rest of the workers were gathered on the side of the grounds. Above, a squirrel corkscrewed along a branch and then jumped to another. The wail of a fire engine started up. "What about Thomas? You say he's also a Nazi? I thought …"

"You mean Commander Thomas von Eisenheim?" came a gravelly voice from behind them.

Anna smelled his cigarette smoke before she turned. De Villiers' shirt-tails were hanging over his belt and he was breathing heavily.

"Don't think I'm fooled by your pleas of ignorance, Van der Vliet." De Villiers stepped into the space between Anna and her father. His fists were balled. "We'll get the truth from you. Just give my boys the chance."

"Leave him alone," Anna said, arm around her father. "He doesn't know. I promise."

De Villiers shuddered. "The hell he doesn't."

Anna decided to change the subject. She'd just remembered her mentor. "Where's Kleinjan?" she said. "Did he …?"

He nodded. "Pitched up on my office doorstep this morning. You should have seen them. *Jislaaik*, he was covered in blood, and with an imam in full robes, beard down to here … my men nearly kicked them out just like that. Luckily I heard the *gedoente* outside and checked it out." The wail of a fire engine made its way up Government Avenue to the edge of the safe zone now cordoned off between the fencing and the Parliament buildings. A Jeep drew up beside the manhole and four uniformed soldiers hopped out and clambered into the drain. "He's one lucky bastard, ma'am. The bullet was this close to an artery. We could dress it ourselves. He was in shock, of course, but we gave him some pills. He's a clever bugger, hey? Knows what's going on. Gave me perfect directions to the bunker on Signal Hill. Even though by the time my men got there you were on your way down. Shame, he was sick with worry. He's clearly very fond of you, ma'am, like a father. Sorry, Van der Vliet."

A shout echoed from inside the manhole and they turned to look. Next thing a crate appeared, heaved up by a pair of firemen. Then several more. De Villiers strode over to them with Anna and her father in tow.

De Villiers pointed at it with his cigarette. "It squares with what your foreman told us. Hell, it's enough to take down the House of Assembly, maybe also the library and some of the other rooms." He turned to Anna, touched the rim of his hat. "You've got guts. To crawl down there, *stoksielalleen* in the dark. Some of my men would have thought three times about it."

"What's he talking about, Engel. Crawling where?"

"Ja, ja. Pretend all you like," De Villiers scoffed. "We'll see how clever you are when we're done with questioning you."

"Enough!" she said. "It wasn't me who stopped it in the end, you know." She looked across Stalplein, the mountain and then at De Villiers. "That flame might have lit the fuse. If it wasn't for Thomas risking his life to cut it … Promise you won't kill him." Her voice was trembling. "Please."

"It's out of my hands at this point, ma'am. The roadblocks will be going up already. But you mustn't worry. Our people know it is best to capture foreign operatives alive. Especially a U-boat officer. Imagine the intelligence we'll get. Come, let me take you to the medics to check out that leg." He raised a hand to beckon for one of his men. "Boys. Stay here and watch this traitor."

She swung to face De Villiers. "You … bastard. You promised to arrest Papa, keep him away from here. You lied to me. All along you'd prejudged. You had no intention of honouring our agreement, did you?"

De Villiers' face softened. He lowered his voice. "We tried. Ask any of my men. Hell, they camped outside his door till two in the morning. No sign. We thought you'd been giving us a bull story. We had no idea he'd …"

"You could have looked a bit further. But I guess that's asking a bit much from a bureaucrat."

"Ouch. Give us a break, ma'am. What were we supposed to think? You ask us to take your father into custody and there's no sign of him, and then you don't show up for our meeting without a word. Next thing a scruffy farmworker shows up with a Mohammedan …"

The policemen were now shepherding parliamentarians into cars lining up to whisk them away. "Don't talk about Kleinjan like that," Anna said. "Anyway, God be praised it worked out." She looked out over the Cape Flats. "For us, anyway."

De Villiers ignored her comment, took her hand and led her through knots of stragglers waiting for directions. The fire engine was quiet, but the firemen bustled about looking for something to do. They got to the car at the entrance, and De Villiers opened the rear door and bent his head to see inside. "A lady has come to pay her respects," he said. "It's fine, stay where you are."

Anna peered into the dark. His face was indistinct in the gloom, but the bandages slung about his neck reflected enough light for her to recognise him. "Kleinjan!" He was sitting in the far corner. She climbed into the back and ran her hand gently over his bandages. "I'm so, so sorry," she said. "Look at you. This is all my fault."

"*Haai*, it's nothing. Just thank the Lord we're all safe." He stroked a bandage. "No need even for hospital. The detective tells me that when they've taken my statement and finished the questions I'll be free to go."

"Quite the hero, hey," said De Villiers. "And to think we almost dismissed him. Probably would have if it hadn't been the second warning on the day. You know, my men went down there. Didn't find any sign of explosives. I suppose we didn't look hard enough. Luckily I posted the guard, just in case."

"You said something about it being the second warning?"

He hesitated, then felt in his jacket and pulled out an envelope.

The handwriting was beautiful cursive and looked familiar.

"This was slipped under the office door this morning. No

name. Just a clipping from a South African Communist Party pamphlet and a note saying you'd gone missing. And that we should be on heightened alert. I dismissed it at first—we get lots of crank letters—but when your foreman arrived …"

The last of the Members of Parliament were being escorted to their cars. Only the party leaders remained to confer, outnumbered by policeman and soldiers. The drone of an airplane approached from the Cape Flats.

"Come. There will be lots of time to talk," De Villiers said, helping Anna out of the car. He took her arm and steered her back toward her father.

"Wait," she said, resisting. "First promise me you won't harm Thomas. That you'll give him medical treatment."

"Don't you worry, ma'am. We'll have him before nightfall. If he tells us what he knows, no one's going to hurt him. And he'll get the best care we have."

"And if he doesn't?"

De Villiers didn't respond. They'd got to where her father stood with the two policemen. Reporters were on the scene now, flashbulbs going poof while a policeman tried to shoo them away. "Normally an enemy agent is shown no mercy. The punishment is death. But there're extenuating circumstances in this case. And Smuts isn't stupid. He knows how deep German sympathies run in the *volk*. He'll pardon him."

"Detective," Anna said. "Please. Just give my father and me a minute in private."

De Villiers hesitated. "All right. But make it quick." He stepped out of earshot and lit a cigarette.

Anna lowered her voice. "We have to find a way to help Thomas. But how? I feel helpless. It's too awful."

He looked at her with searching eyes. There was no anger in his expression or his voice, only sadness. "You really are in love with him, aren't you?"

She nodded.

They fell silent. She stared toward the foreshore. She remembered the pier. Those special times with her mother. Without warning, tears started to stream down her cheeks.

"You're thinking of Mama, aren't you?" He took her hand. "They say time dulls the pain …" When he looked at her there was tears in his eyes. He smiled, his dimples like trenches. He tucked a strand of her hair behind her ear. "You get more and more like her every day." Then his face grew sadder still and he looked at the mountain. The dot of a cable car crawled on its upward trajectory. "And just as strong-willed."

"No—I get that from you. Anyway … At least you've still got me." Then her back stiffened. "And Margriet, I suppose."

He looked at her. "No. That's over."

"Oh?"

"Yes, and none too soon. I'm sorry, Engel, I should have listened to you. It's just, you've always objected to any woman I've shown any interest in."

"Sorry. I suppose I'm jealous. But it's not that I don't want you to find love. There's nothing I'd rather see than you happy again and laughing, like when …"

"Ja, ja. It's just so hard to commit."

"I know, but you must promise me you'll try. You need another woman in your life, Papa. I know you. Especially now that I'm at university. Although …" She looked away.

"Ag, I'm sorry, Engel. It was wrong of me to threaten like that. Of course, I would never have followed through. I know I haven't told you before, but I'm incredibly proud that you're doing a degree. You'll be the first in the family. At least on my side."

She looked away. "I'm sorry it's not law or medicine."

"Ja. You've always had your own mind. You'll visit me in the holidays, won't you?"

"As long as you don't let in any more foreign agents."

He laughed without smiling. The emergency workers were continuing their clean up. A set of stretcher bearers had just emerged from the huddle on the street, their loads covered by tarpaulins, faces grim. They made towards a Bedford parked at the edge of the square.

De Villiers let his cigarette butt drop to the paving and ground it out with his heel. "Okay," he called. "That's enough. My boys here will escort you two down to the station."

"What? You're taking us in?" her father said "Me I can understand. But Anna?" He stuck his arm out to shield her from De Villiers. "She's a national hero now."

"With respect, sir. You'll need to ..." He motioned to the police car. "Let me do my job."

"She saved your backside, dammit. Now you want to treat her like a common criminal. *Jou nat agter die ore ...*"

"Now, sir ... it's standard procedure. Everyone on the scene of a crime like this must be questioned. Anyway ..." His eyes strayed to Anna and back. "She's hardly been an angel in all of this. That German ... lover boy of hers. Right now, he's the most wanted man in South Africa."

"You ..." Her father spun about. One of the policemen grabbed his arm. The other, stepped between him and Anna.

"Stop, Papa. We don't want any more trouble."

His head shook. "Idiots."

"Don't worry," De Villiers said, pointing downtown. "We have a private cell for you to share. Two mattresses. You'll see—it's as good as a bed and breakfast."

Anna followed his finger and beyond, to the harbour. A shaft of steam was rising almost vertically from a ship moored alongside the grain silo building. So, after all that had happened, they were being detained. What would Thomas do? Would he make it to the rendezvous with his men, injured as badly as he was, and with the army and police in hot pursuit? Damn. If only she'd stayed with him she could have shown him the back roads and helped him avoid capture. It was frustrating and depressing in equal measure. For the second time in twenty-four hours, she would have to sit idly by while events took their course.

35

THE ROOM WAS A good deal cooler than the air outside, but stuffy, and the only light was a fluorescent strip in a cage on the ceiling. A far cry from the bed and breakfast De Villiers had promised, but clean. It was scant comfort though. After pacing the cell countless times, Anna had slumped on the bed next to her father. The exhilaration and relief she'd felt earlier had been replaced by despair. Sure, she'd helped her country but where had that got her? In jail with her father who was facing the death penalty for treason. And Thomas, injured and on the run. The next time she'd see him would probably be in a news photograph of his body. But, she reasoned, feeling sorry for herself was pointless. Always better to think of others. Even her crotchety, stubborn father.

"What is it, Papa?" she said. "You keep sighing."

"Ag. How can I say it?" He lifted his head and turned to face her. "I'm sorry, Engel. *Wragtag*, I am."

"Stop. Please. We've been through it already. Your hands were tied."

"Ja, but I should never have put you at risk. Greta in far off Germany shouldn't matter—you're my closest flesh and blood. Now look what I've got you into. It's not fair. I've had a full life. But you … The world's your oyster."

"It's all right. They'll have to release me sooner or later. How was I to know he'd turn out to be a U-boat officer? Falling in love isn't a crime."

"Ja, I suppose. But it must have been hell for you this past week."

"It's not all your fault," she said. "How were you to know I'd be stupid enough to take the forbidden path and stumble on all of this? No. It's one of those things. Like a hundred-year flood."

"Ja, but it's better you discovered it. Imagine if you hadn't … *Jinne*, the whole stream of history might have turned the wrong way."

Anna shivered, remembering the line of foam they'd seen from the top of the mountain, stretching south as if toward the farm. She imagined Thomas standing in a U-boat scanning the shore, a conning tower silhouetted against the sun's bulge beyond the entrance to the cove.

"What is it? You're suddenly tense again."

Anna rose, walked to the door and peered through the keyhole. Satisfied, she returned to sit beside him. "Thomas is leaving tomorrow," she whispered. "At sunset."

"Thought so." He leaned in to her, also whispering. "That's if he gets that far. Our police aren't all idiots like De Villiers. Remember what happened to Leibbrandt: he had the *volk* behind him and knew the Transvaal like the back of his hand—and they still caught him in a roadblock. All our coastal defences will be on high alert. Where's he headed?"

Anna felt a tenderness toward her father and a desperate need to unburden herself. But could she trust him? After all that had transpired the past few days, she doubted she could trust anyone again. Then again, he was her father. But if he was tortured? She shuddered. "I … I can't be sure. Somewhere familiar, he said … He never … actually said where."

"*Foeitog*, Anna. You never were a good liar. But I understand you're low on trust right now. You shouldn't worry though. There's no way I'm going to help that *doos* out there—especially after how he's treated you. But tell me, hypothetically: why would he escape from the same place he landed?"

"Who said anything about Skulpiestrand?" She shifted away. "I've said enough already. They're still going to question you. It wouldn't be fair. Besides, Thomas was probably lying. Again."

Footsteps grew louder from outside the door. Then a scraping of a key and the door opened. De Villiers entered, clutching a folder. Behind him was a man in a suit with a briefcase in hand. The man was slender with black hair, silvered where it covered his ears.

Anna's heart was beating in her throat. Had they been listening?

At first no one said anything. The light above flickered, dimmed and then steadied. Voices came from the corridor, and doors opened and closed.

De Villiers started the proceedings. "This is Gazinsky. He's here to help you, ma'am."

Gazinsky nodded at Anna's father and then offered her his hand. His skin was warm and clammy and his grip weak.

She dropped his hand but kept eye contact. "Yes? How can I help?"

He coughed, straightened his tie. "Let's just say I work for Mannie February."

Anna waited.

"He said you'd understand. 'No flies on that girl', I believe his words were."

She eyed him. Too slick to be trustworthy. "What do you want?"

"I'm a lawyer, ma'am."

"Ja. And. What do you want?"

"I'm here to get you out."

De Villiers coughed. "Not so fast, boy. I only said you could speak with her."

"Man," Gazinsky said, "Not a boy." He touched his temple. "I've got at least a decade on you." Then his briefcase was on the bed and he waved a *Cape Times* at De Villiers. The headline was something about the debate in Parliament with a photograph of Smuts. "Any guess what it's going to read tomorrow?"

De Villiers sucked in his cheeks.

"She'll be a national hero, you idiot." Gazinsky tossed the paper on the bed. "My client's people will make sure of it. Can you imagine what it will look like for our Prime Minister and his government if Miss van der Vliet has to spend her first night after saving their backsides in prison?"

From outside the cell came the sound of a short-wave radio crackling, and a muffled exchange.

"Maybe, but we're not done with her," De Villiers said.

"You have everything there, Inspector." She pointed at his folder. "My statement's five pages."

"It's not what you *said*, Miss van der Vliet. It's what you *didn't say*."

Anna swallowed.

"Are you still trying to tell me you have no idea where he's heading?" De Villiers continued. "You two got to know each other pretty well in the past few days, not so? Dancing, picnics: surely he let something slip."

"Ag, come on," her father interjected. "Von Eisenheim is an officer in the *Kriegsmarine*. His country entrusts him with command of a vessel and the lives of several dozen men. You think he's going to tell a farm girl what his plan of escape is?"

De Villiers clamped his jaw.

"Right, Inspector," Gazinsky said, gathering his briefcase. "You have no grounds to keep my client. She's co-operated in full." Besides ..." He smiled. "You and I both know you've already been ordered to release her. Come, Miss van der Vliet." He turned and took a step toward the door. "Let them stop us."

"All right," De Villiers said. "But first ..."

Gazinsky slowed. "Yes?"

"Miss van der Vliet will inform us immediately if Von Eisenheim makes any contact." He glared at Anna. "You so much as see his ghost, you call me. Understood?"

Anna nodded but in her mind she was already over Sir Lowry's Pass and hurtling southeast toward the Agulhas Plains. Kleinjan would be well enough to drive her, she was certain. She would just have to stow away in the back of the truck to prevent getting caught at a roadblock. Perhaps they could start out this evening already, spend the night somewhere along the way. She was about to follow Gazinsky until she caught sight of her father's face and stopped. After everything that had happened, how could she leave him alone?

"Go, Engel, I'll be fine. Just knowing you're staying so close by will be comfort enough." His wink was slight but unmistakable. "And you can visit me every day if you have the time. Not so detective?"

"It's not allowed—"

"Now, now," Gazinsky picked up the newspaper. "A hero, remember."

"You bugger. All right. But she must report to my office at noon tomorrow, and every day until this business is finished."

"Fine." A smile threatened at the corner of Gazinsky's lips. "And not to worry, *Meneer* van der Vliet. We'll get you out soon enough. It burns *Meneer* February's arse to help a racist capitalist. But lucky for you ..." He glanced at Anna. "He's a man of his word."

36

THE NEXT DAY THE sun had started its climb up the eastern sky as Anna and Kleinjan rumbled along the bluegum-lined drive leading from the Houw Hoek Inn to the national road. Anna had decided to break the journey with an overnight stay so that they could get through the roadblocks as soon as possible and get a good night's rest. The idea was to stretch out the journey to only get to Skulpiestrand a couple of hours before Thomas' sunset rendezvous. But that was where her plan ended. She still had no idea what she'd do when she found him. Only that she wanted to hold him, hold him close one last time and say how much she loved him.

The tops of the hotel's gables were barely visible above the mist that still hung in the valley. A cow appeared, head buried in a meadow. Anna envied its peace. Though relieved at having evaded the roadblock the other side of Grabouw the previous night, she was already fretting about the way ahead. Though she'd not mentioned Perlemoen Punt specifically as the meeting point in as many words, she was sure her father would figure it out. What if he was tortured? And besides, he'd probably be worried about her eloping and volunteer the information to make sure they could find and stop her.

She pushed these thoughts from her mind. It was important to be positive. Within minutes they were on the first uphill of the Houw Hoek Pass. Kleinjan shoved the gear lever into fourth.

"We're not just going back to the farm to rest, are we?" he said.

"What makes you say that?"

"Don't pretend," he said, shaking his head. "I have to pick you up at the back entrance of your residence; you hide under a tarpaulin to avoid the police; do I need more evidence? *Yoh*, I was sweating back there at the roadblock; you know how I hate to lie."

Anna stared at the solid white line as it snaked upward to the top of the pass.

"You still hope to find him, not so?" he said.

"Ag, Kleinjan ..."

As they crested the neck the vista widened to a patchwork of brown and golden wheat fields on undulating hills ringed by mountains. The truck's engine whined as they dropped curve by curve down the pass.

"Do you think he got out of Cape Town with all those roadblocks?"

"If they were up in time. And they didn't stop us from getting here, did they? No, someone as resourceful as Thomas would find a way out of a big city. The police must know it too. They're mainly just to show they're doing something."

Their ears popped as they descended the pass into the Bot River valley, and soon they were rising and falling through the wheat hills. The stalks were waist high, and here and there patches had already been harvested and gathered into bales. A clutch of guinea fowl emerged from the stubble, scuttled around in confusion on the side of the road and then disappeared back into the field.

"I'm your driver," Kleinjan said. "You may as well tell me now where we're going. Not to Rietvlei, surely. They'll be there, the police I mean."

"Relax. I'll tell you soon enough."

They settled into a gentle rollercoaster through the hills. Outside, the wind sent waves reverberating through the fields of wheat. At last Kleinjan said. "I thought you'd be in more of a hurry to get there. You haven't once told me to speed up since Grabouw."

"Nothing's going to happen until the sun goes down."

"Do you really think he'll be where he told you?"

"I can only pray and hope. Oh, Kleinjan, I worry so. He was shot, in the shoulder I think."

"He's a soldier. He'll know what to do."

"Ja, but I can't bear to think of him suffering alone."

They were in a dale, passing through wisps of mist still floating above a stream. A farmstead appeared by the side of the road. Abandoned implements littered its *werf*.

"And if you find him?" he said. "What then?"

"I don't know," she said. "I don't even know if I should be trying. It will put him in such a predicament. Making him choose between me and his men. He deserves better. But I just can't help myself. I have to see him. Just one last time. What am I to do?"

"*Toe maar*," he said. "You'll know. The Spirit will guide you. He has up till now, hasn't he?"

"I don't know. Who's to say I'm not just being led astray by my lust?"

"Only time will tell the truth for sure. But what lust would make you sacrifice so much? It sounds more like love to me, Miss Anna. I had the same thoughts with Hannah in the beginning. All right, it wasn't as serious as this. But you won't believe how I punished myself. Day and night, I knew no peace for weeks."

"But when did you know? And how?"

"For me it wasn't one specific moment. But looking back later, it was obvious that deep down, I'd been right all along. You know, this is what I think: for the big decisions you just have to follow your heart. No matter how much it costs."

The car started to descend in degrees, winding towards the hamlet of Napier. A sheaf of bark dropped on the windscreen and a fragment settled on the bonnet. There was a smell of resin in the dry air. Then the church steeple appeared through the forest of bluegums.

"The Akkedisberg to Elim, or the Bredasdorp road?" Kleinjan asked.

"Elim," she said, "But no stopping to chat with your people, you hear me."

He laughed. They peeled off the tar and onto a gravel road towards a gap in the mountain. Just over the rise Anna asked Kleinjan to pull over in a clearing by the side of the road. She retrieved a picnic basket from the back of the truck and offered him a sandwich. Below, the plains extended to the start of the downs and smudged into the haze above the distant sea. Was she fooling herself he'd be there? She ate to keep her strength rather than from appetite. Even if Thomas had been telling the truth about the place and time, any number of things could have gone wrong since then. Caught by the police; incapacitated by his wounds; betrayed by the U-boat crew. But she was committed now. It was past noon already and De Villiers would be mad as hell for her failing to report. He'd probably launch a search, could even be following her already. It didn't matter though: even the faintest chance of seeing Thomas was worth it.

The streets of Elim were deserted. The first sign of life was the shopkeeper, standing with his elbows resting on the stable door of his café. They exchanged waves and soon they were passing the bolted door of the church and veering out of town. But as they descended to the river, Anna tensed. A police van was parked just beyond the bridge.

"Just look ahead," Kleinjan said. "It's nothing."

Anna fixed her eyes on the road, not able to breathe properly until they were well past the meadows and the van had disappeared from the rear-view mirror. "What do you think they were doing there?"

"Fishing, probably."

"I hope you're right." Anna kept glancing in the mirror. Thankfully nothing appeared, and soon they were entering the downs and the *fynbos*. There were impromptu vleis and pools of water beside the road from the recent unseasonal rain. At the Rietvlei turnoff Anna tensed again, expecting at any moment to see a policeman or hear a plane overhead. Instead the land was empty and it was quiet as only the plains can be when the wind is soft. A buzzard flapped its wings from its perch on the telephone line and rose, fighting the breeze towards the coast where the ocean was still a shimmer above the veld.

"We're going to Perlemoen Punt?" Kleinjan said. "Are you serious? It must be years since I took you and Baas Stefan there. The road is probably bad. What's wrong? You're pale suddenly."

"Ag. I don't know. I have a bad feeling suddenly. Like it can't be this easy. I mean, no roadblocks, police on the road. It's almost as if it could be a trap."

They rumbled along the gravel, dust billowing up behind before being dispersed by the wind.

"Did Thomas say what time exactly?" Kleinjan said.

"Just that they'll wait for the sun to set."

They continued in silence. The vibration made her sleepy, and she had to fight to keep her eyelids open.

"You know, Miss Anna, I've been thinking. Is there any way Thomas could have communicated with his crew if he needed to change the plan? Not that I'm saying he did."

"Of all people, you should know the answer to that."

"You mean the missionary at Elim?"

"Exactly. Maybe he went there first. They could have kept him hidden and dressed his wounds."

"But won't the police be watching all Germans around here?"

"Eventually, yes. But they're probably stretched too thin at this stage. At least I hope so. Anyway, it's too late to turn back now and find out."

The road narrowed to a single track with proteas on either side. They veered left and sharp right in a drift of sand and the truck wiggled back to level ground. The sun was starting to drop in the sky and now there was no longer a dust cloud, so they rolled down the windows for air.

"That's it, isn't it?" Anna pointed to a track that peeled off towards the ocean.

"Ja."

The truck idled to a standstill and Kleinjan got out. He walked to the front of the car and stooped over a track. "Come," he called. "Look here." He had a stick in his hand and held its end over the mark of a tyre. "This was made after the rains. Today or yesterday."

Anna felt a void opening in her stomach. As much from hope as from fear. But she wasn't going to involve Kleinjan in another confrontation. "It's Thomas," she said. Not feeling the confidence in her voice. "I know it. Go on to the house. That way if anyone's tracking us it will buy us some time. I'm going on foot."

"*Haai*, I can't leave you like this."

"You can if I tell you to."

"With respect, Miss Anna. I'm not letting you go alone until I'm sure it's Thomas."

She was about to say something but waited. He was just feet from her, one eye looking at her, the other squinted shut to the sun. He held up a hand as a shield. "All right," she said at last. "But you must promise to give us some time alone."

He smiled. "I have no problem making myself invisible."

Anna collected two water bottles and a hat from the truck, and they set off. The track was a mile at least and straight as far as the bush that marked the edge of the sea. The sign board on the rise toward the end of the road was a pinprick and the curve of Perlemoen Punt's beach barely discernible. Beyond that, the ocean was a wide swathe, grey-blue like steel. Soon the shape of the truck had dipped below the horizon behind them, and they were alone at the end of the world.

The sand was thick in places, and Anna had to shift to the firm ground of the *middelmannetjie* to keep pace with Kleinjan. How did he have so much stamina, at more than twice her age and the trauma of the day before? They were closing in on the bush at the spring tide mark now, and the song of cicadas was audible. To the left of the track something rustled in the grass and was gone. The silent sun beat down on them until they heard the approaching rumble of breakers.

After twenty more minutes, the smell of kelp became overpowering and the crashing of the waves and fine sea spray meant they were close. Over the next half-rise their track merged with another and the bushes thinned. Then the sand changed to pebbles and dry kelp crackled underfoot.

Anna's heart raced. A car stood in the clearing before the beach, both back doors open. It was the same model that Thomas had fled in.

She stepped forward.

"Wait," Kleinjan said, grabbing her wrist. "First, we watch."

Nothing happened for a long time as the sun beat silently on the land and sea. A seagull circled over the bay and swooped to land on a rock. There was a whisper of wind from time to time. Where was he? Soon Anna's excitement gave way to disappointment and then to worry. Too sad to weep, she just stood and watched.

"It looks like we're too late," he said. "I'm sorry."

"I won't believe it," Anna said. "I simply won't. What time is it?"

Kleinjan squinted at the sun, his lips moving. "I would say about four."

They edged closer to the car. From their angle of approach it was impossible to see inside. Anna reached it first, not wanting to hope. She craned her neck towards the open door. There was a stench of sweat mingled with antiseptic lotion.

The voice from inside startled her.

"What took you so long?" It was Thomas, faint.

She moved closer to get a full view. He was lying on the back seat, feet dangling over the edge, his head propped on a coat that had been folded against the other door.

"My dear, oh, my dear," she cried. "Are you alright?" She put a hand on his shoulder. Even through the bandage it was hotter than the air. He was shirtless and glistening to the waist.

"Do you have water?" he grimaced. "I finished what I got in Elim."

"Kleinjan?" She retracted her head, straightened, and turned.

The beach was deserted. She swore and looked around frantically. A bird alighted from the bushes, otherwise all was still. Then she saw the water bottle on the ground, next to an arrow scrawled in the sand. And the word "Rietvlei". She couldn't help smiling.

Thomas held the bottle to his lips with both hands, trembling so hard that water spilled down his neck and pooled in the hollow of his chest. She was shocked at how pallid he had become.

"It's too hot in there," she said. "Come, I'll help you move to the shade."

"It's not as bad as it seems." He shifted upright. Soon some colour had returned to his cheeks but there was still pain under his smile. "The bullet didn't hit any bone or an artery, thankfully. Clean in and out."

She prodded at his shoulder. Blood had clearly seeped through the bandage and some was still fresh. "It doesn't look clean to me."

"It's better than it looks. I wouldn't be here if an artery was punctured. There is some nerve damage—it's difficult to move. But no need to write me off just yet."

"But couldn't you at least bring forward the meeting time?"

He ignored her question, peered at the dashboard clock, then to the sun, which was a handbreadth from the horizon. "It won't be long now."

"Don't tell me you were hoping I would show up," she said. "That's it, isn't it?"

He chuckled. "Maybe, maybe not. No, the missionary wasn't there, in Elim I mean. Something must have happened. Probably news has reached him of what happened at Parliament, and he's got scared. But it's no problem. At least I managed to get some antiseptic and these bandages from the minister's wife. She did promise: but I can only hope she keeps her silence." A fly landed on his bandage, then another. He brushed them aside but they rose and dropped back into a splatter of blood. "Come," he said. "There's something I'd like to show you."

Anna helped him out of the car. They struggled up the rocky outcrop. Every few steps he stopped to catch his breath. At last they arrived at a ledge where Thomas slumped, panting. They positioned themselves to face the ocean. Then he pointed to a dark shape in the sea, one third across the offing. It could have been a shark's fin or a whale, had it been closer.

"What is it?"

"The conning tower. Isn't it beautiful?"

A seagull quivered up above, holding its place in the breeze, then dropped in a flash into the water, only to appear empty-beaked a moment later.

"They'll be lowering the dinghy soon," he said.

She tried to focus on the whale-like shape in the water. It was black and, except for the rectangular chimney of the conning tower, a flat bulge just a fraction above the surface. By instinct she looked up to the sky, horizon to horizon. "What about the patrols?"

"No need to worry. They only fly every two hours."

She stared at him. "You mean, last week on the dunes, you were timing them?"

"You must know by now. I measure everything."

She put her hand through the crook of his arm; their sides were pressed against one another. She elbowed him gently. "Even your women?"

He laughed, drew her closer. "Only the most beautiful." Then he turned, caught her eyes. "Tell me, have you reconsidered my proposal?"

A wave rolled in and shucked on the pebbles on the beach below and to the left. The sea before the rocks was uneasy and breaking out of turn. Everywhere, was just rock and sea and sky. Nothing distinct, as if it was a dream.

"My darling … I can call you that, can't I?" She rested her head on his shoulder.

"Of course."

"I want nothing more than to spend forever with you." From behind them the seagull swooped overhead again, dived into a rock pool and rose with a mussel in its beak. She watched it settle on a rock shelf. "But it can't work. Not now. You know that."

He put his arm around her, hugged her tight.

"Doesn't that hurt your wound?" she said.

"Of course not," he said. "I'm a soldier, remember." He ran his finger through her hair, sweeping it back. His mouth was at her ear. "A German soldier. We don't have feelings."

She turned to him, examined his body. His shoulders were sinew and muscle and his chest smooth and glistening in the near horizontal sun. "My Nordic God."

"Don't get carried away."

She laughed. "Indulge me. Just this once." She snuggled closer.

"And you," he said. "You'd be my angel. If an angel could be a woman." His finger was at the shoulder of her dress. She felt the skin on her collarbone tingle in the wind.

"My darling. Oh. Oh, why must this end?"

"Don't think about it. Not now." He ran his lips from her chin to the base of her neck and stopped. His hands had moved to her back, slowly unzipping her dress, unhooking her bra. Then the air was warm on her breasts and it felt wonderful. Her eyes rested on the ripples of the sea.

"When the war is over," he said. "I'll be back. On my life,

we'll be together." He pulled her towards him and they were kissing and their bodies became one with the stone and the sky and nothing else mattered.

Afterwards, an oystercatcher hopped onto the rock close by them, its beak red and eyes angry. A wave whooshed and sucked on the stones. Thomas was staring at the mouth of the cove. The dingy was close to entering.

From beyond his shoulder Anna's eye caught a needle of dust rising beyond the mountain, bent in the gentle breeze. She quivered. Kleinjan wouldn't be so far off or coming from that direction. "It must be the police," she mumbled. "Papa must have told them. Or they were following all along. Oh, darling. I'm sorry: I should have been more careful."

He turned to look. They could make out a car at the head of the dust, speeding along the gravel road towards the base of the mountain. Perhaps six miles away.

"Come." He winced as he rose. "We'll say goodbye at the bottom."

Anna watched the dingy put-put through the water towards the beach. Then she glanced back towards the track. The dust column was larger now.

The boat slowed to a halt with the motor still running, and the two seamen hopped off and ploughed through the shallows. They ran up the beach towards the car, calling in German. When they got there they cast about in confusion.

"*Hier.*" Thomas called out to them from the last rock ledge before the beach. "*Hilfe. Macht schnell.*"

They helped him down and propped him up between them. He twisted round to face Anna. "There's something I forgot to tell you," he said.

"Don't," she said. "I know." She held the tip of her forefinger to her lips. "I love you too."

Thomas did likewise and for a moment time was suspended. Then he turned and they were down the beach and in the dinghy.

Inland, the sound of tyres on gravel grew above the sea. The dust was almost upon them.

"They're here," she called. "I'll try and slow them. Just go." She watched the dinghy chug through the mouth of the cove.

Behind her the police van skidded to a halt at the spring tide shelf. Two sets of boots got out and crunched on the shells. The back door opened and someone climbed out.

The boat was just beyond the cove. Anna could still make out the three figures, Thomas seated on the bow. Later, she would remember what looked like a hand lifted in a salute, held there and dropped. The dinghy rose and fell over a swell, surged forward and was in open sea.

She turned to the steps, looked up at the three figures approaching. The one in the middle was slightly ahead and towered over the others.

"Papa?" she gasped.

"*Fok*," De Villiers said, shoving her father. "You lied, Van der Vliet. You knew they'd be gone by now. Bastard."

"Think what you like," her father said. He was smiling and confident, as though he'd recaptured some of the essence of himself, without the arrogance.

Ignoring the policemen, Anna ran up to her father and threw her arms about him. After hugging him tightly she drew away.

De Villiers spat on the ground. "Whatever," he said. "Talk. Where your father's going after this he's going to be a long time. Come ..." He took the other policeman's arm and they walked back to the car.

Anna waited, staring at the ocean. The sun was a watery orange disc bulging on the horizon. It was impossible to make out the U-boat in the fading light. Satisfied that the policeman couldn't hear, she said, "You held out on telling them, didn't you?"

He nodded.

"But why, Papa? Why didn't you try to stop me? I could have run off with Thomas. You must have known."

The seagull was there again, circling over the beach, and its caw sounded like a plea. There was only the grumble of waves now. Her father lifted his chin, his nostrils widening as he inhaled. "It's hard for a father, you know. To see his little girl as a woman."

"But I'm going on twenty."

"Ja. Your mother was engaged to me by then. It's just ..."

"What is it?"

He glanced at the sky, held his eyes closed for a moment. When he looked at her his lips were compressed, thin. "I promised her I'd look after you. No matter what."

She took his hand. Was it trembling? "And you've kept your promise. You've provided magnificently for me. Oh, Papa ..." They embraced. It was first time in her memory that he didn't immediately withdraw. The worsted wool of his jersey tickled her cheek and smelled of pipe smoke and the lands.

"What's wrong, Engel? Why are you crying?"

"I don't know. It's just ... How could you do ... say the things you did all these years? It's almost as though you've been been blaming me for her death."

"Ag, *my lief.* That's not true." He sighed in sadness. "I know I can be a bear. And I struggle to show what I really feel. But I love you ... in my own way."

The orange on the horizon was a blur in her tears. "I know," she whispered. "I know. But what kind of love is it, without respect?"

Epilogue

AFTER BOARDING HIS SUBMARINE (U851) without incident, *Korvettenkapitän* Thomas von Eisenheim dispatched an enigma-encoded communique to naval headquarters in Berlin to confirm that since the delivery of Obersturmführer Kurt Streicher to Afrikaner partisans on an unmarked landfall at latitude 34°46'S, despite repeated attempts by the undersigned, the officer had failed to reconnoitre at the agreed place and time, and was therefore presumed killed or captured. With enemy agents closing in, the note ended, it was therefore decided to leave South African territorial waters without delay.

A subsequent investigation by the *Sicherheitsdienst* into the failure of the fascist revolution in the Union of South Africa cleared Thomas von Eisenheim of any culpability. He continued to captain his U-boat but was reassigned to the Pacific and, after participating in manoeuvres with a squadron of Japanese submarines in the South China Sea, was deployed to a wolf pack in the North Atlantic. With a tally of 24 Allied merchant ships sunk for a total of 165,231 tons, Von Eisenheim went on to become one of the *Kriegsmarine*'s most successful U-boat commanders in the Second World War. His bravery under sustained depth charging by American destroyers in an attack on a Cuban naval base led to his being awarded the Iron Cross 2nd Class in February 1943.

However, Thomas's military career was interrupted when, along with Claus von Staufenberg and 7,000 others, he was arrested by the Gestapo on suspicion of involvement in the failed July plot to assassinate Adolf Hitler. Thanks to the intervention of an uncle in the *Reichskanzlei*, he was one of 2,020 alleged conspirators who were spared the death sentence. He spent the rest of the war in Spandau Prison in Berlin. After a three-month debriefing by Allied intelligence agencies, the young officer was released. He took the first available passage to Cape Town.

For the duration of his campaigns, Thomas had sent Anna a letter from every neutral port he entered, always under a different pseudonym. Though necessarily vague, the messages confirmed his unwavering devotion, and the certainty of their ultimate union.

Anna, for her part, obtained her Bachelor's degree in Fine Art from the University of Cape Town in December 1943. At the urging of Professor Pickford-Dunn, she volunteered for the Special Signal Corp, and after a one-month training course on Robben Island, spent the remainder of the war as a radar cadet, working and sleeping in the Castle of Good Hope.

At every opportunity, Anna returned to Rietvlei, whether or not her father was in residence, where she loved to paint landscapes. The first of these, an oil painting of Skulpiestrand at sunset, still hangs in the farm's *voorkamer* alongside a portrait of her late mother.

On a Sunday morning in September 1945, Anna opened the front door of her apartment to find Thomas on the patio, weighed down by a bunch of king proteas wrapped in *fynbos* greens. Her first response was to smile, and then chide him for taking so long. By the end of the summer they were married by Dominee de Wet in the Dutch Reformed Church in Bredasdorp. Though the bride's father kept his head high as he walked her down the aisle, it was impossible for a bystander not to notice his tears. The reception was a highlight on the Overberg social calendar and was held in a marquee on the beach. Festivities continued throughout the night, long after the sun had risen over the dunes.

With what remained of Thomas's European inheritance, the couple bought a wild flower farm in the Elim Downs, ten miles as the fish eagle flies from Rietvlei. From there they pioneered the export of Cape wild flowers to European capitals. They had four children in six years, all of them boys. In time, the youngsters became fluent in English, German and Afrikaans.

Stefan van der Vliet was held in custody for three months following the failed coup d'etat. The state's charges of treason for aiding the enemy were, however, dropped before the end of the year. Rumours that General Jan Smuts had personally intervened were never confirmed. Van der Vliet's foster sister was released by the *Sicherheidstdienst* soon after the failed plot and lived out her days in obscurity in Düsseldorf. Van der Vliet retired from politics shortly after his release from prison to devote himself to farming. After experimenting with a herd of cattle for two years, drought, loss and Kleinjan's urging convinced him to revert to the predictability of sheep. Throughout it all, he never failed to take his breakfast at nine o'clock sharp, always with three poached eggs on toast and sausage.

Fanus Prinsloo was convicted of treason in the Cape High Court for his involvement in the plot to overthrow the government and was sentenced to death by hanging. After a high-profile media campaign by conservative politicians and right-wing organisations, including the *Ossewabrandwag*, the Prime Minister commuted his sentence to life imprisonment. After the National Party came to power in the 1948 general elections, he was released, along with other political detainees, and entered service in the Attorney General's office in Pretoria. Following the death of his father, he retired from public life to run the family business and farming interests. From time to time he ran into Thomas and Anna at agricultural shows and similar community events, but the conversation seldom ventured beyond the weather.

Kleinjan soon retired from his role as foreman at Rietvlei. He and Hannah returned to Elim, where they lived in a north-facing cottage on the Main Road. There, he remained a teetotaler and never failed to attend church on Sunday mornings. Their son Willem returned from his transport duties in Egypt in 1945, and after his meagre war allowance was depleted, found a job as a truck driver in Bredasdorp. He sometimes stopped by the Von Eisenheim homestead between transports to enjoy a cup of rooibos with Anna, his childhood friend. As strange as the sight was in those parts, they remained the greatest of friends.

Acknowledgements

I used to think that writing was a solitary occupation. I was wrong: it's a team sport.

None of this would have been possible without the support of my parents, specifically my mother, Charmian, for keeping my first cops and robbers stories and her unfailing love and encouragement. Late grandparents Eric and Iris for igniting my love of words, Ruth for teaching me that life isn't fair and Margaret Touborg for showing me the power of a single word and its placing. Family and friends here and abroad, the men of the bible study and coach Jeremy who've shared this journey.

Subversion (formerly *Featherstream*) was the dissertation for my MA in Creative Writing degree at UCT and I'm grateful for the input of my classmates and faculty, specifically my supervisor Professor Etienne van Heerden. Likewise, thanks to my editor Gwen Hewett, original typesetter and designer Andy Thesen, Monique Cleghorn for the cover design, Robin Stuart-Clark for advice on the manuscript and Alan Roux and Levine Holle for being advance readers.

Inspiration for this novel grew from the time I've spent in the Strandveld over the past 25 years, for which I wish to thank the late Diana Durrant and the extended family. I'm grateful to Peter Albertyn for sharing his love of the *vlaktes* and knowledge of sheep farming, Royal Navy officer (retired) Robert Maydon for helping me understand the life of a submariner and the late Kay Hennessy for her first-hand accounts of life at the Castle of Good Hope during World War 2. Also, to the staff of the Shipwreck, Elim, Maritime, and District Six museums, the libraries of UCT and Parliament and the National Archives.

A huge thank you to my children Angus and Isla, for so gracefully accepting the sacrifices my writing has demanded and for the joy they bring me.

And, finally, Melissa: my first reader-editor-publisher, wife of twenty-four years, soul mate and best friend: words can't describe how much I appreciate her endless love and encouragement and so much more.

Glossary of Afrikaans and German terms

Abwehr	The German military intelligence
Achtung	Attention
Adel	German nobility
Akademische viertel	Literally "academic quarter". In German culture it is polite to arrive fifteen minutes late for an appointment.
Alles ist in ordnung	Everything is in order/okay
Anderskleuriges	Literally "other-coloured people"
Asseblief	Please
Baas	Boss (male)
Bakkie	Pickup truck
Bliksem	Mild expletive, literally "lightening"
Bobotjie	Traditional Cape Malay dish of spiced mincemeat baked with an egg-based topping
Boereseun	Farmer's boy (Boer: farmer. Seun: son)
Bokskiet	Literally "buck shoot"
Braai	Barbeque
Bredie	Traditional Cape stew
Broedertwis	Disagreement between fellow Afrikaners
Bundu	Thick bush
Dassie	Rock rabbit
DF Malan	Dr Daniel Malan grew up on a farm in Riebeek West in the Western Cape, a few miles from his future political adversory Jan Smuts. Malan studied theology at Stellenbosch University and in Europe. An arch-conservative and narrow Afrikaner Nationalist, he opposed any unity between Afrikaners and English speakers and was strongly opposed to South Africa declaring war on Germany (he advocated neutrality instead). Believing in the need to keep racial groups apart, he later became an architect of the apartheid policies of the future Nationalist government in South Africa.
Die Huisgenoot	A woman's magazine
Dikbek	Literally "thick mouth", a sullen facial expression
Doek	Cloth head covering
Dominee	A minister of the Dutch Reformed Church
Duikers	Unremarkable antelope native to South Africa, the word meaning "divers" in Afrikaans.
Eina	Ouch

Einsteigen	Get in
Ein bißchen	A little bit
Foeitog	Literally "oh shame". An expression of pity
Frikadelle	Fried meat balls
Fynbos	Meaning fine bush, a small belt of natural shrub or heathland vegetation located on the Western Cape of South Africa, which constitutes the tiniest Floral Kingdom in the world.
Gatvol	Fed up (sick and tired)
Gekys	When a boy and a girl start dating
Genade	Grace
Gracht	Canal
Handlanger	Assistant
Hemel	Heaven (used as an expletive)
Hensopper	Literally a "hands upper", a Boer soldier who surrendered to the British during the Second Anglo-Boer War (1899–1902).
Hübsches mädchen	Pretty girl
Ja, bestimmt	Yes, definitely
Jan Christian Smuts	A Boer (Afrikaner) general who, after leading a division in the Second Anglo-Boer War, played a leading role in reuniting English- and Afrikaans-speaking South Afrikaans and forming the Union of South Africa in 1910. He served in the Imperial War Cabinet in both world wars, achieving the rank of Field Marshal, and became a trusted adviser to Sir Winston Churchill. He was Prime Minister of South Africa before, during and after World War 2, until losing the 1948 general election to Daniel Malan's Purified Nationalist Party.
Ja nee	Literally "yes no", an expression
Jawohl	Yes, definitely
Jinne	A mildly blasphemous explitive
Jong	Literally "young", a mildly condescending address
Kaggel	Fireplace
Kappies	Headscarves worn by Afrikaner women in the 19th century
Kettie	Slingshot
Kloof	Canyon
Kom nou	Come now
Kopje	Small, rocky hill on the African veld
Kriegsmarine	German navy

Kweekskool	Seminary
Lief	Love
Luister hier	Listen here
Macht nichts	It doesn't matter
Magtig	Literally "mighty", a mild blasphemy
Mampara	A slang term for a stupid person
Mein Gott	My God
Melkboom	Milkwood tree
Middelmannetjie	Literally "middle man", the raised ground between the parallel furrows of a jeep track
Moerkoffie	Coffee brewed on the stove, a method used by farmers
Nagmaal	Holy Communion in the Dutch Reformed Church
Nat agter die ore	"Wet behind the ears", green/inexperienced
Nee wat	An expression translated "no, don't tell me that"
Nun gut	Alright then
Oder nicht	Or nothing
Oke	Bloke/chap
Onnosel	Idiot
Oom	Uncle
Opregte Afrikaner	Upstanding Afrikaner
Ossewabrandwag (OB)	Literally "ox wagon sentinel". A paramilitary right-wing organisation formed by Afrikaners in 1938 after the centenary of the Great Trek. Although formed for "cultural purposes", it was heavily influenced by fascist/Nazi ideology and campaigned against South Africa's support of Britain in World War 2. Its members committed a string of terrorist attacks against government and military infrastructure.
Pass auf	Watch out/be careful
Perlemoen	Abalone, a seafood delicacy found on the rocks along the Southern Coast of Africa
Pieletjie	A colloquial term for a penis
Plaasmeisie	Farm girl
Predikant	Literally "preacher", a Dutch Reformed minister
Renosterbos	A hardy scrub bush found close to the ocean and named after the Afrikaans word for a rhinoceros
Reunited National Party	A very conservative, right wing political party, headed by DF Malan, which was formed in 1940 by the reunion of Malan's Purified National Party and JBM Hertzog's nationalist breakaway from the United Party.

Riempie	Leather thong
Robey Leibbrandt	An Afrikaans policeman and former Olympic boxer enamoured with Adolf Hitler, who stayed in Germany after the 1936 Berlin Olympics. He trained with the German Special Forces and returned on a secret mission in 1941 to foment a violent Nazi revolt to overthrow the South African government. After a police manhunt, he was caught and tried for treason.
Rooinekke	Literally "rednecks", a disparaging term used by Afrikaners to refer to English-speaking South Africans.
Schloss	Castle
Sicherheitsdienst	The German secret service
Sies	Term of disgust
Sitkamer	Lounge or sitting-room
Skelm	Devious
Skinnerbek	A gossip
Skulpiestrand	Literally "beach of shells"
Slim	Clever/wily
Snotklap	Literally "snot slap", a hard slap across the face.
Speurder	Detective
Sofort	Immediately
Soutie	Literally the diminutive of "salt". A derogatory term used by the Afrikaners for an English-speaking South African—referring to their divided loyalty between England and the Union of South Africa.
Stoep	Porch/patio
Stoksielalleen	All alone
UP	The United Party, the governing political party in South Africa during the war, which was formed from a union of Hertzog's Nationalist Party and General Jan Smut's South African Party in the 1930s.
Up North	A term referring to North Africa, where South African troops served with Allied forces in the desert war against General Rommel's Afrika Korps.
Vaderland	Fatherland
Vastrap	Traditional Cape dance
Veldskoen	Leather shoe
Verboten	Forbidden

Vieslik	Dreadful
Vlaktes	Flat lands
Vlei	A shallow, naturally occurring lake, often surrounded by reed
VOC	Vereenigde Oost-Indische Compagnie or, in English, Dutch East India Company. An extensive Dutch trading company which established a victualling station in Cape Town in 1652. The Company administered the Cape until the region was formally colonised by Britain.
Volk	A people
Volksverraaier	A national traitor
Voorkamer	Literally "front room", a hallway
Vreiheidsoorlog	War of freedom, the Afrikaner term for the Anglo-Boer War. The struggle of 1899–1902 was known as the Second Anglo-Boer War or Tweede Vreiheidsoorlog.
Vygies	Wild figs
Wahnsinn	Crazy
Werf	A "yard" or area about a farmhouse
Widerstand	The internal resistance movement in Germany
Wirklich	Really, as in truthful
Wragtag	Literally "really". An exclamation of anger or surprise
Zum Wohl	A toast, literally "to your health"

IAN SUTHERLAND graduated with an MA in Creative Writing from UCT in 2016. *Subversion* (previously titled *Featherstream*) was his debut novel, and he has subsequently published another historical thriller *Catastrophe*, set in Ukraine. Ian was shortlisted for the 2018 Short Sharp Stories Award and previously placed second and fourth in the annual SA Writers College short story competition. His work has appeared in publications as diverse as the *Anthology of South African Short Stories* and *Engineering News*. Ian has an MBA from Columbia University and has worked in strategy consulting and finance in New York, Sydney and Cape Town, where he currently resides. Passionate about history and travel, Ian enjoys intense, immersive research including language studies.